THE FUN HOUSE

Books by William Brinkley

Quicksand

Don't Go Near the Water

The Fun House

THE FUN HOUSE

a novel by

WILLIAM BRINKLEY

RANDOM HOUSE
NEW YORK

to my father
the Reverend Dan S. Brinkley

So passeth, in the passing of a day,

Of mortall life the leafe, the bud, the flowre,

Ne more doth flourish after first decay,

That earst was sought to decke both bed and bowre,

Of many a Ladie, and many a Paramowre:

Gather therefore the Rose, whilest yet is prime,

For soone comes age, that will her pride deflowre:

Gather the Rose of love, whilest yet is time,

Whilest loving thou mayst loved be with equall crime.

Edmund Spenser, THE FAERIE QUEENE

CONTENTS

THE FUN HOUSE

A Word to the Discerning Reader

If the historian of a thousand years hence wants to know what The American Civilization of the Twentieth Century was like—and he will, believe me he will! for the very fact of whether historian will be at that time depends, all depends, on what that civilization in that century does —he could do no better than read the files of *Vital* magazine. For *Vital* touches American life and, for that matter, modern life in general at many points indeed. Many? All, actually. Absolutely all!

Vital magazine is assuredly one of the most important elements in The American Civilization. I think I will hear no opposing voice—and I am very sensitive to noises of all kinds—if I say *the* most important journalistic element in that civilization. Which is saying a great deal in a day when the great battle of the age—for men's minds—is being fought out with words as well as rice, they say and say well. A statement in a crisp brochure once put out by the magazine proudly lighted up this fact:

"*Vital* is the country's really big magazine. In addition: No magazine has such Power. May we repeat that word? *Power.* Nothing has the impact of an article in *Vital.* An article in *Vital* can change overnight an entire nation's habits—its smoking habits, for ready example. An article in *Vital* has prompted battles in the streets in nations as far apart as Pakistan and Paraguay, blood to flow, men to die. Many a tale could be told of how *Vital* has affected the course of an advertising sales campaign, the prosperity of a business, the affairs of state of great nations . . ."

There is more but that is enough to give the discerning reader the idea. No publication in America exerts a tinker's fraction of *Vital*'s influence on American opinions and attitudes. No publication so shapes out of the raw raw clay, the raw unknowing clay, what the people of America buy, eat, drive, wear from their skin out, what movies they see, and—not least important, we fancy—what they think.

The owners of *Vital* magazine had a saying about the Vital Building. It read in full:

"This building houses the greatest collection of brains and talent of any building in the world. It is in this true sense that it is the most unusual building in the world."

The people who worked on *Vital* magazine were indeed a remarkable lot. And the magazine itself an institution, in a word—and one I use most awarely—truly: Unique. It was a truly wonderful magazine. There was nothing like it. I should like to add a superlative of my own

3

about this place: In no office in the world did people have more fun than at *Vital* magazine. That is my belief. There was a deity the people at *Vital* magazine worshiped, and its name was the Goddess of Fun. Life was much too serious, people should have fun, and indeed the having of fun was what life was all about: that was their philosophy. This point of view permeated and saturated from managing editor to office girl. We are speaking here of course not of content—*Vital* was a very serious magazine—but of the office life of the people who worked there, and even the after-hours life: For probably nowhere did the employees of an office spend so much time together, partying and the like, as the people of *Vital*. This was because after knowing each other they found the people anywhere else as dull as unseasoned cottage cheese, and the camaraderie flowed all over the place and throughout the hours of the day and the night.

But in addition, lest all be lost in the idea of fun, we wish to make this lucid point: There surely was hardly a better vantage point in the land for seeing what was happening in the world than working on *Vital*, since the raw material of the magazine and its staff was the goings and the comings, the doing good and the doing bad, the cataclysms and the fateful doings that make up this astonishing, unparalleled world we now inhabit.

One could not conceive of an America without *Vital*. And yet, oh Reader! and yet: Here is a profound fact. While *Vital* is an exceedingly important American institution and not merely claims to be but in all fact is America's most powerful editorial force; while *Vital* knows—or if it doesn't, makes it a point as the occasion rises to find out, and has developed all the facilities in the world for doing so—everything about everybody, yet: Nobody knows anything about *Vital*. And this can only be a pity, that the remarkable and wonderful life within the magazine has not been shared with the admiring millions who read the magazine itself. But I hardly have as an object the sharing of it. I would hardly waste my time, or the reader's, if it were merely to tell about life and the arresting doings, endearing, absorbing, fascinating, amusing, amatory, or what not, and always gleaming in virtuosity, on the inside of a magazine, even one so great as *Vital* magazine. But I had this thought which I believe it proper and fitting, not to mention critical, to set down here: Would it not be of a slight help to that historian of a thousand years hence, sitting in some chair or whatever they may sit in at that time—maybe an air-conditioned womb—trying to reconstruct our fateful times, if in addition to the rich and teeming source materials of the files of *Vital* magazine itself, he should have before him a modest book displaying a bit of that dazzling, wonderful magazine and the people on it, committed by a writer who along the way takes the afforded opportunity to make a comment here and there on our American society, by way of narrative, parable, or even now and then just the barest disciplined touch—no more!—of the expository, all solely for the utilitarian benefit of that historian, material which for one good reason or another could never get into the pages of *Vital* itself? . . . the magazine, touching American life at all points, being an almost providential vehicle for a writer with my intentions.

CYCLE ONE

THE MOST UNUSUAL BUILDING IN THE WORLD

1
The Gypsy Writer

Though a picture magazine, *Vital* had writers. They were an odd lot of men. In the matter of caste, the writers stood above the researchers but emphatically below the photographers. There is nothing strange in this, since *Vital* was a magazine of pictures. But the result was that whereas the photographers were as a group glamorous and self-assured, not to say in some cases swaggering—but only in a way that befits the true creative artist, who must above all else have great confidence in himself even if nobody else does—the writers were by comparison meekly, outwardly nondescript and in some cases even hangdog. They were the soul of anonymity. On a story of any size the photographer was given a bold black by-line to foster his ego. The *Vital* writer never got a by-line for anything, his name appeared nowhere except on the masthead, and there in agate type, which is the smallest type manufactured, and as regards ego, the mystique was the direct opposite of that held toward the photographers: in short, if the writer had any to start with, to wipe it out as rapidly as possible. The *Vital* photographer was expected to be temperamental, and he was accorded strong and special rights. If he felt like it he could ring up the office, merely say he didn't feel in quite the exact mood to do anything at the moment, don't you know, and take a week off. Had a *Vital* writer done this, Alvin Creech, the copy editor, who was ringmaster to the writers, would have dropped dead of Omaha heart. The *Vital* writer was expected at his desk daily whether there was anything for him to do or not, and sometimes for days on end there was literally nothing for him to do. The magazine would go to considerable lengths to placate and assuage any *Vital* photographer who was out of sorts. The *Vital* writer understood that being completely expendable he was not supposed to have sorts, in or out of.

The *Vital* writer's job was to write the captions, heads and "text-blocks"—the small islands of words—that accompanied the picture story. Considering the comparatively meager space that words occupied in the magazine, it was astonishing the care which *Vital* editors lavished on them. Never in the history of journalism was so much energy and attention given to such small chunks of prose. The editors of *Vital* were perfectionists, in a way that Toscanini would have understood and admired. It was not unusual for a textblock of two hundred words to be handed back to a writer a half dozen times for rewriting, and a head composed of forty characters, or six words, to be handed back to him a virtually unlimited number of times. *Vital* writers had been known to spend as much as eight hours and to write a hundred candidates before coming up with a head that appeased the editors. It could be quite a strain on the central nervous system; but then the magazine had plenty of central nervous systems to spare.

The *Vital* system of writing had a number of other characteristics peculiar to it. One was the sharp dichotomy between the reporting and writing functions. This existed no place in the journalistic world save on *Vital*. On a newspaper the reporter goes out and gathers the facts, covers the story, then sits down to his typewriter and writes the story. On *Vital* the writer never got near the story, never left the building on any journalistic enterprise. The story was covered, the facts gathered, by the correspondent out in the bureaus, or by a stringer, who then filed prodigally to the New York office. He might file 5,000 words on a story that would end up as 300 words in the magazine, 300 words put together, shaped, molded and refined to that perfection described above by the writer in the New York office.

This method had the virtue of giving a sense of detachment to the writer, who was thereby freed of the emotional involvements with which the actual coverage of the story might have burdened him. Alvin Creech, the headmaster of the *Vital* system of prose, had often given the classic summing up of this philosophy of journalism.

"The conception," Creech told his writers. "That is the sesame to the way we do it, now don't forget it. Don't get led down the hind alleys by one part or the other of the story—and since you weren't there the chances are less you will. Back away, stand up above, be a ruddy helicopter, forget the parts, don't get involved. In short: get the story's *conception.*"

Following this sound advice, *Vital* writers every week told thirty million people what the world was doing and what's what. But they saw less of what was going on in the world than did a subway motorman in his little cage—he at least had tracks to watch. They were the monks of the profession of journalism. Eunuchs, some said.

Henry Gaskin, a writer in the Manners and Morals Department, was somewhat an exception to most *Vital* writers, in a number of ways. One of these ways was that nobody had ever been able to tamper successfully with his ego. Another was that he did a considerable amount of traveling. Not, however, of a professional nature. His was a most curious form of travel.

Before going into that, however, it may be of some interest to the serious-minded reader to acquire some knowledge of the workaday world of *Vital* writers, first stating this briefly:

Hank Gaskin was in nearly all respects quite a man. In the first place he was really massive in a physical way. He was six feet three inches tall and weighed two hundred and five pounds. He had a squarish face, handsome to the right kind of woman but not pretty, enhanced even by a half-inch-wide, four-inch-long, duel-like white scar across one cheek, a souvenir of Saipan, where Gaskin had been a Marine platoon commander. He was enormously strong, something the more remarkable in that he loathed exercise in all guises and engaged in the minimum amount that life would tolerate. And yet his health, energy, stamina and metabolism all seemed more than average, as evidenced by such facts (among many others) that he never wore either hat or overcoat even in the coldest New York weather—though on really bitter wind-lashed days he did wear a heavy sweater—and that he could drink almost any number of martinis one might care to name and still come back to the office and work with complete competence.

He was also a man of gentleness and of code. "What I really believe is: If you can't stand the heat get out of the kitchen."

Being translated: He believed in coping with life. As opposed to either whimpering about it or giving in to it or whining about how the world was not set up precisely to his specifications. He did not descend into self-pity because he was born into an age he never made. Who ever made an age into which he was born?

Perhaps the most unusual characteristic of the professional life led by the *Vital* writer was its alternating frenzy and nothing-to-do cycle. It was like a stock-market chart with nothing but vertical lines. The writer's working week at *Vital* began on Tuesday and ended on Saturday. Stories "closed" on each day of the week and more on Saturday than any other day, this being the final day for closing stories for the current issue. Tuesday would generally be a fairly busy day. Wednesday, Thursday and Friday would vary considerably, and oftentimes a writer had absolutely nothing to do on those days. Saturday was a cadenza in frenzy. The writer reporting into the Vital Building at 10:00 A.M. would sometimes not leave it until the Sunday sunrise broke over Manhattan outside his window.

This cycle of periods of intense activity and fat periods of utter idleness supplied the writer's life with some curious features and not a few problems. The chief problem of all was that there was a good deal of pure sheer time to be filled up by *Vital* writers. One way they did *not* fill it was by discussion of national and international affairs some of them wrote about every week for thirty million people. They filled it in various ways. One traditional way was the fashioning of airplanes out of copy paper, then the sailing of these planes down on Fifth Avenue, on which the Vital Building sided for a block. *Vital* copy paper was of an extra-heavy, high-grade white, measuring nine by twelve inches, and it made superb airplanes. This game could go on for hours. Sometimes it consisted merely of sailing planes out the window at random, and sometimes, in the heat of imagination and/or desperation, it took on various refinements. One of these was to try to hit one of the tiny specks walking thirty-four stories below. This could require surpassing skill, allowing for the winds that sometimes raged around such heights. Some *Vital* writers, however, became very adept at landing on target. Many a dowager from Atlanta or Boston, down or up for a few days of shopping on the world's greatest fashion street, has found herself tapped lightly on the nose or the back of the neck by a sheet of *Vital* copy paper in the form of an airplane and has looked up in bafflement to see whence it came. There was a continuing argument as to the exact scientific method of folding the paper, the angle of the nose folds, and so on.

Hank Gaskin was perhaps the office champion at this sport. He never tired of it and after a while went so far as to purchase a pair of second-hand Japanese binoculars, the better to follow the plane's descent and especially its eventual landing field. Whenever Gaskin hit someone he yelled out ecstatically, "On target!" Another variation of this game was to type short messages in the center of the big piece of copy paper before converting it into an airplane and launching it. Gaskin invented this variation and was very fond of it. His messages could be almost anything. "Your slip's showing," and, "No holding hands in front of St. Patrick's please." Sometimes it was a piece of poetry, such as "Let's love, this life of ours/Can make no truce with time that all devours" or

> *Aloof with hermit eye I scan*
> *The present work of present man—*
> *A wild and dream-like trade of blood and guile,*
> *Too foolish for a tear, too wicked for a smile . . .*

something which might conceivably strike a spot of wonder or even terror if suddenly floated into one's hand from on high.

Once it was simply "This sheet of paper may be exchanged for a fifty-dollar bill at the Guaranty Trust Co., 40 Rockefeller Plaza." The time Gaskin sent down one hundred airplanes bearing this message there was a vicious protest from the decorous Rockefeller Plaza branch of the Guaranty, where that morning there was a scene the likes of which the New York banking world had not witnessed since the great run of 1929.

"It's unbelievable how stuffy they are over there," Gaskin remarked of this reaction. "Think of all the free advertising they got."

The writers did many things to amuse themselves when they were not writing. As Gaskin once said, "You don't do something and you'll end up in that special ward for people from here they got down at Bellevue."

Of course there was no such special ward for people from *Vital* at Bellevue or for that matter any other New York hospital. This was just one of those many rumors, jestful, ugly, or malicious, depending on your point of view or at least on your sense of humor, that were spread around New York and actually believed by some people who took things too literally. However, Gaskin's essential point was well taken. The writers did have to do something. As he also remarked, "Nothing gets at man like idleness. We must arouse ourselves so as not to be got at."

One thing the writers did on days when they had nothing to do was to take long lunches, frequently three hours or more, with a spacious amount of martini drinking. Gaskin liked to say that the martinis at lunch were the dope you took to stand it. Once Gaskin and a writer in National Affairs, Anthony Pinckney, organized a program of seeing New York during the lunch hour. The only part of New York that most people who worked in the Vital Building had seen, though they may have been coming there ten years or more, lay between their apartment or commuting station and the office. Over a period of six weeks Gaskin and Pinckney eyewitnessed the Statue of Liberty, Wall Street, the top of the Empire State Building, the Lower East Side, the Washington Market, the Cloisters, the Bowery, Grant's Tomb, Chinatown, took the Circle boat trip around Manhattan Island, and even took the tour that included their own Vital Building among neighboring ones and even on this tour saw many new and interesting things. They brought back to the office many reports of all there was to see in New York. Then when April began to come upon the city, when crocuses peeked out where there was soil for them to peek out from and the ailanthus tree gave green, there was the lunchtime rowing in Central Park.

In a conscientious rebellion against the great martini consumption, one or two of the writers started playing squash during their lunch hour, but the little popularity this pastime had was decimated when a writer by the name of Malcolm Standish, a man in his forties who for ten years had committed no more exercise than walking from the bus that stopped in front of the Vital Building the fifty steps to the elevator, got one of those sudden passions for exercise that come like an attack on people these days—in his case from writing the captions and text-blocks for a story which dealt with the salutary effects of exercise on the circulatory system and hence on the avoidance of coronaries—went down one day to the Harvard Club, took the elevator to the sixth floor and saw there a whole new world, of squash courts, sweat and steam, got into some shorts and a sweatshirt, and had reached fifty-five minutes of the one hour he had so conscientiously assigned himself to play, when, as his staggering, almost paralyzed arm was about to drive the hard little black ball against the wall, he fell entirely inert in the center of the court. A physician who was summoned from the dining room had no difficulty before returning, churlish at the interruption to his crab-meat salad, in pronouncing the man dead from a heart attack. After that the small vogue lunchtime sports had for a while at the *Vital* office evaporated with the speed of water dropped on a sizzling Franklin stove.

Following the incident on the squash court, Hank Gaskin bought out of his own pocket and nailed up in his office an English dart board. Above the dart board he pasted a picture of the writer who had had the distressing experience on the Harvard Club's Number 3 squash court. And whenever anyone at *Vital* suggested they all should get out and get more exercise, Gaskin took the suggester aside to his office and had an earnest talk with him.

"Remember the Standish," he said. "No *Vital* writer should ever permit himself more than a dart game for exercise. That good man up there"—and Gaskin would point solemnly to Standish's picture—"would be with us today had he had a martini instead of squash for lunch."

Gaskin's talk of the perils of exercise usually resulted in the frightened man's having four martinis for lunch that day, and it certainly quashed any incipient exercise program.

"There is no real danger," Gaskin would say, "in using any of the many fine facilities of the Harvard Club—with the lone exception of the sixth floor. Otherwise the Harvard Club is a perfectly harmless place."

Gaskin had not himself attended Harvard College. He had, however, attended Harvard University, for a rather curious purpose. He went there on a year's leave of absence from *Vital,* which he had obtained after gaining a Nieman Fellowship, which is granted every year to a dozen or so newspaper or magazine men to enlarge themselves at the Cambridge institution. Gaskin had applied for a fellowship after going a few times to the Harvard Club in New York as the guest of one member or another and deciding that it would be fine to be a member himself and enjoy its many privileges, such as the double-sized coffee cups, the club being so handy to the office. Unfortunately neither money nor merit will gain one membership in this fine club, so there was nothing for it but to attend the damn place. This reason was a bit at variance with the one Gaskin had given on the application form and articulated to the board which interviews the many candidates, that reason dealing in the space of a couple thousand words or so with how the study of American history would be a tidy background for a man who told the American people what's what every week via the medium of the Republic's greatest and most influential magazine. Gaskin did, however, actually study American history with considerable fascination at what is certainly one of our finer up-and-coming centers of the fairly higher learning.

Gaskin was a considerate man. Over the period of six years he had been a *Vital* writer—after two years as a researcher in the New York office and two years as a correspondent in the Washington bureau, having originally come to the magazine from a newspaper in his home state of Massachusetts—he had fixed his office up, with both himself and his colleagues in mind, for comfort and for the maximum alleviation of the periods of intense idleness that attended the job. Besides the dart board, he had installed a high-fidelity system and a fine collection of records. The hi-fi system was nearly always going, even when Gaskin was writing a story, in fact particularly then. He matched the composer to what he was doing: Mozart often when he was just sitting around; Tchaikovsky when he was beginning to write a story; Berlioz when the story had been thrown back to him by the copy editor for rewriting. The fifteen-inch Tannoy speaker was in the far corner of the room and the control panel directly by Gaskin's typewriter, so he could operate it without exercise. The machine would play, if asked to do so, four hours of music without human intervention. He also had an enormous leather couch along one wall. Gaskin did not have sufficient rank for the office to buy him a leather couch—only for heads of departments was the leather couch on the official allowance list—so he had gone out and bought one second-hand with his own money. The couch was battered and frayed, scratched and stained, and had as many ups and downs as the Shenandoah Valley. But both its size and softness suggested a history of opulence. It looked as if it had been in J. Pierpont Morgan's office in 1895 and it may well have, and it looked also as if it had been used for divers purposes. It was an almost unbelievably comfortable piece of furniture. Gaskin had a great affection for it and sometimes after a five-martini lunch used to close the door and take a nap on it. When he lay there asleep, smiling beatifically and holding on to the luscious thing, he looked as if he were in the arms of some fabled mistress of odalisquian charms. If he wasn't using it for a nap it was free for anyone to use, and it was almost always in use by someone wanting to sleep or simply to lie down and rest, rest from either work or idleness. The demand for Gaskin's couch grew so great, the traffic so heavy, that finally he was compelled to devise a system for signing up for the couch, as for a tennis court. Above the couch Gaskin had pasted a line from Ecclesiastes:

The sleep of a labouring man is sweet.

In many other ways Gaskin's office was somewhat different from the usual run of business offices in midtown Manhattan. Visitors to *Vital* were often startled, and not a few shocked, when, sauntering down the corridor, they happened to glance in. Gaskin had his reasons, however, for fixing it up that way.

"I calculate to spend one third of my life in this cell," he said. "I figure I might as well make it a cell away from home."

The window of Gaskin's office was bedecked with chintz curtains, white with red and blue polka dots the size of silver dollars; they tastefully matched two pillows on the big leather couch ensconced in the same material. There was a rug on the floor. The official allowance list contained no rugs for the writer rank, these also being reserved for department heads. Even in civilian life there must of course be some symbols of rank. Otherwise what would man have to strive for? What would be the point of it all if he could not show by such symbols that he was better, cleverer, sharper, more cunning, more unfettered by standards and codes in improving his position than the other, common mortals around him? The world would stop tomorrow if such symbols were abolished. At *Vital* the symbols included such items as couches and rugs. Many a man had devoted fifteen years of his life to getting a couch and a rug. The unhappy thing was that so oftentimes only a year or two after getting them he ended up on that page of the *Times,* "died suddenly" division, that lies so somberly opposite the editorial page.

Gaskin—since devoid of the necessary rank and as a matter of fact pretty happily so—had bought his own rug along with the room's other extra furnishings, and one nice thing about working for *Vital* was that the magazine did not in any way interfere with such inclinations of its staff. The rug was not the usual solid gray or brown rug of the offices but a large Navajo Indian rug Gaskin had ordered via a Western-goods catalog. There was an armchair which Gaskin had found at some second-hand store and covered with the same polka-dotted chintz as the curtains. Three of the walls were painted the color the company used, a flat, non-attention-drawing hue known popularly as "graveyard gray." But Gaskin himself had painted the fourth wall, the one behind the couch, a flamboyant red. He had discarded the fluorescent, swing-arm desk lamp furnished by the office, which was said to be the newest thing in ease on the eyes, and replaced it with an ordinary old-fashioned lamp with a lampshade painted the same color as the fourth wall. When the room was lighted, with the lamp casting its red glow, with its huge sagging leather couch and its great Navajo rug, the place looked like the waiting room of a Singapore bordello.

There were numerous pictures on the walls, stuck there without any particular intent for design, as if they were there because that space happened to be left over—which was precisely the case. One was a portrait of some 1880 man with mutton-chop whiskers that Gaskin had seen in the window of a shop on Sixth Avenue on the way back to the office after a martini lunch and impulsively walked in and purchased. Another was a picture of a lovely lagoon on a South Seas island. Another, of the screaming mob on Times Square on New Year's Eve. Another showed some Buddhists at meditation in Japan, another a crowded Hollywood party. Another, a line-up of cows staring placidly into the camera. The pictures apparently, both singly and taken together, had a private meaning for Gaskin. There were dozens of them, covering nearly every inch of wall space, and occasionally when he found a new one he liked somewhere, Gaskin took an old one down to make room for it. There was one other picture on the wall directly next to Gaskin's desk. It was an artist's concept of New York City as it would appear fifteen minutes after a hydrogen bomb had hit it. Occasionally Gaskin's eyes would swing in a rhythmic arc from the towers of mid-town Manhattan, which just outside his window rose in mighty shouts to the sky, to this same highly altered setting in the drawing.

Other than the pictures, there were two rather competing injunctions on the walls.

On the red wall was a declaration Gaskin had typed in the center of a sheet of copy paper and stuck there with Scotch tape. It read:

Of all sexual aberrations chastity is the strangest.—Anatole France

On the wall opposite was another declaration, also typed in the center of a sheet of copy paper and standing there like a bristling and opposing regiment to the one across the room. This one read:

The carnal pleasures of life have never made minds great.—Morarji Desai

Because of its comforts, its music and its cozy informality, Gaskin's room was a favorite gathering place for *Vital* writers during their substantial periods of idleness. Frequently a dart game would be going on, the high-fidelity system playing a Beethoven sonata, and someone napping and even snoring somewhat on the couch, while Gaskin was writing a story. He claimed that far from disturbing his composition these activities actually assisted it.

"They keep me from getting too close to the facts," Gaskin explained, "by overconcentration."

Now we must speak of that other exception in which Henry Gaskin was so different from all other *Vital* writers, his travels.

Hank Gaskin was very strong, as we have recorded, and he liked the frequent office parties a great deal. Everybody did, of course, and the frequent and gay office parties were one of the biggest attractions of working for *Vital*. They brought out various things in various people, and in no one more so than Hank Gaskin. At one office party Gaskin started kicking the water fountain in tune to a song he was singing. He liked to sing at parties, usually hymns. Each time in the beat of "Shall We Gather at the River" he kicked the fountain harder, until finally the thing flew off its hinges and landed on the far side of the room. That time only the plumber had to be called. Some of the parties did not get off so easily. There was the party held by the Religion Department in honor of the completion of a special series on the world's great religions. Things got very joyous, almost evangelistically so, and along about ten o'clock Gaskin waxed so ecstatic that he walked out into the corridor, singing "Onward, Christian Soldiers" at the top of his lungs, spotted a large fire extinguisher against the wall, and in his jubilation jerked it free of its moorings. This act sent a veritable tide of floor-eating foam flooding down the corridor and into various offices. It also tripped a bell four blocks away in the quarters of Hook and Ladder Company Number 46 of the New York Fire Department. This in turn brought thirty-seven Fire Department vehicles screaming down on the building, which was situated in the heart of the world's most expensive real estate. This example is rather extreme, however, and it had its drastic repercussions. Next day there was a memorandum from the managing editor banning all parties for a full week.

Gaskin's habit was that at the end of a party, if it was a good party, he would oftimes get on some kind of transportation—train, bus, or, most often, plane—and go somewhere. Once after a party he went down to Grand Central Station, boarded the first train leaving, and woke up next afternoon in the shuttling yards in Chicago. Another time he got on a plane and ended up in Miami. He would have to be very drunk to do any of this. But no matter how drunk he was he seemed able to find his way about any of these centers of departures and arrivals: train station, bus terminal, air terminal. All he had to do was tell the taxi driver to take him to one of them. Once inside the building, some sixth sense of his took command, and really he could have found his way to any ticket counter, said the necessary words and got on the available transportation—he had no problem due to the flight to some city being fully booked, he would simply take a flight for another city—could have done all this blindfolded. Transportation terminals brought out something deep and instinctive in him, and once inside one of them he never had any trouble. It was as if the excitement of the place and what it represented—the getaway—brought on a second, secret, almost spiritual wind in him. His company International Air Travel Card also helped, and the Business Department was regularly making deductions from his pay.

Having set off from Grand Central or Pennsylvania Station, or from La Guardia, Newark or Idlewild airport, Gaskin would wake up next morning in a hotel not knowing where he was, but being very cagey. He had an infallible system for finding out where he was without asking anybody. He mustn't, for obvious reasons, ask anybody what city he was in. First he would look out the hotel window. Sometimes he would recognize a familiar landmark identifying the city, such as the Capitol in Washington, D. C. If this didn't work—if he saw nothing familiar—he would walk over to the telephone, call Room Service and order his breakfast, then very casually, very cagily mention that he would like the morning papers sent up along with his bacon and eggs. He watched his words very carefully for fear that something he would say would indicate to the switchboard girl that he didn't know what city he was in. He didn't know why he should be so cagey about this, and he was certain it was not out of fear they would call the police, or commit him or something. Maybe it was just a shyness. If the girl, as sometimes happened, asked, "What paper would you prefer, sir?" he was very much on his guard and answered grandly, "Oh, send them all up."

When the waiter arrived with his breakfast tray he was very careful not to look at the papers on the tray for fear something in his expression would give him away. Very carefully he waited until the waiter had left. Even then he didn't look immediately. It is a very remarkable feeling, he discovered, not to know where you are. It was extremely exhilarating, almost emancipatory, so much so that he liked to hold onto it as long as possible. There was strong suspense in it. He could feel the tingling building up in him against the moment when his hand would reach over . . . Very deliberately he sipped his orange juice. Then, as casually as if there were no meaning in it and he was just about to look at the morning headlines, he would reach over, pick up the paper, unfold it, and glance at the name at the top. Then he would exclaim in triumph: "By God, Gaskin. You're in Milwaukee!"

Or Boston, St. Louis, Birmingham, Cincinnati, Charlotte, North Carolina, or Richmond, which were a few of the cities where he had been able to utter the joyful exclamation of discovery of where he was.

He would finish his breakfast, dress, check out of the hotel, and take the first available transportation back to New York.

"Sometime," Gaskin used to think, "I'm going to wake up in a city and decide not to come back from it. Provided it's far enough away and is a very nice city. Say the capital of Samoa."

2

The Nine-To-One School of Journalism

Jason Hightower was born in Virginia of a family so old and blooded it would have looked on the oldest Boston families as rather vulgarly *nouveaux,* and given to a childish, ridiculous and really embarrassing monomania about their ancestry as only people have who are unsure of possessing any intrinsic value of their own. He had attended St. John's in Maryland, the place where you read the Great Books. Thereupon he plunged with no particular splash into that fragmented, disturbed and self-searching society that the United States of America had become after the twin events of history's greatest war and the divulgence, in that war's latter days, of a cosmic force that was to leave no man safe, that was to shake and shape everything that that society, or any society in the world for that matter, had been, and nothing was ever to be the same again. And so he knew, without particularly thinking about it except for those disturbing, opening moments when it would come upon him unwarned and unawares, that he was stepping out into the most fateful age so far assigned to man—and to what fate that man, that world, nobody knew. Meantime he hoped to have a little fun out of life. In the interim, rather loosely probing year since leaving school, he had been horsing around on one of the literary magazines foaled in New York.

Jason had, or rather inhabited, an apartment in the East Sixties. This is a fashionable area of New York City and Jason had an unusually fashionable, large and attractive apartment in an unusually fashionable block, that is, one with trees on it. To be explicit, the rent on it was a good deal more than any salary he made. That is, it would have been if Jason had had to pay it. In actual practice he got the apartment for nothing. It belonged to a maternal uncle who for five years now had not returned from a villa he also owned a short piece east toward Nice from that fine lubricious hamlet named St. Tropez.

Jason's uncle's apartment consisted of a large living room, two bedrooms both large, two oversized baths, one of the biggest kitchens in New York and a terrace the size of a squash court. Despite such distances Jason was never lonely there, for its spare sleeping spaces, including if necessary the terrace, which Jason had equipped with sleeping bags for use when there was an overflow and it was snowing, were always available to any of his friends, such as those from school who very frequently popped into New York on weekends, and did so more frequently than they might otherwise from the surety of free room at Jason's. Not free board. Jason wouldn't cook for anyone. He scarcely ever kept anything in the kitchen's 15.2-foot Frigidaire or 21-foot deep-freeze—except for Crosse and Blackwell tomato juice, of which there were always at least a couple of dozen cans on ice, Jason believing very much in tomato juice—but if anyone wanted to go around the corner to Gristede's and buy some bacon and eggs and fix them, he was perfectly free to do so. If he did, he was expected to cook some for his host too.

It was in the living room of this apartment that, on this night, he and Henry Gaskin were slowly killing off most of a bottle of J and B, when Jason mentioned a casual thought off the top of the central brain mechanism, where it had perched pleasantly if uncertainly, that he was considering giving up what little work he did at the literary magazine and seeking broader pastures.

"Something, Ace," he said, "which would fly me out of that incestuous hothouse and bring me up against the great red-armed, white-bellied masses more—selling bonds or mutual funds or non-mutual funds is what I've thought of. Everybody seems to be buying these things today in our fresh new summits of money-madness."

The thought of working for *Vital* magazine never remotely entered Jason's mind. Gaskin, however, decided that the magazine was just the thing for him.

"*Vital* is less like a hothouse, incestuous or non-incestuous, and has the broadest pasture of anything I know," he said. "Don't ask me to explain that statement."

Spinning the ice cube in his Scotch with his forefinger, Jason demurred mildly that he had had no real journalistic experience or training that might qualify him to work for such a mighty organ as *Vital*.

"Oh, don't let that bother you." Gaskin dismissed it with an airy wave of his hand, as if this deficiency were the most trifling detail imaginable. "Experience is a handicap, if anything, in that place. Don't ask me to explain that statement."

Gaskin did explain carefully to Jason that he must on no account apply for a job at *Vital*. This, he said, would probably queer forever his chances of gaining employment at the magazine.

"I doubt if anyone ever got a job at *Vital* who applied for one there," Gaskin explained. "*Vital's* attitude is that there has to be something wrong about anyone who has to apply for a job. When it wants someone *it* goes after *them*."

Jason's ears perked up and he felt a touch of interest in working at a place that held such an arresting philosophy. Gaskin told him he would sow the discreet seed in one or two places, under no circumstances to make a move, but to wait to hear.

"I shall speak subtly to Harrison Duckworth, the big panjandrum in these hiring matters," Gaskin said rather avuncularly. "I shall carefully impregnate him with the fact, or non-fact, that you are a first-rate catch. Harrison Duckworth," Gaskin mused. "It will be quite an experience for you to get to know him. His motto is the Golden Rule, in a slightly abbreviated version: 'Do Unto Others.'"

That settled, they dismissed the subject and continued with their J and B. It is the one incomparable Scotch.

About a month later Jason received a phone call from a very bright-speaking young voice which identified itself as the secretary to the vice managing editor of *Vital* magazine. Jason, having been warned by Gaskin, showed the proper bafflement at the call.

"Could you have the wrong number?" he said. "This is Mr. Jason Hightower."

"I know. I wonder," the secretary said, "if it would be at all convenient for you to stop by the vice managing editor's office at ten-thirty on Thursday. Mr. Duckworth would like to have a chat with you."

"Why, let me just see here a moment," Jason said, turning over in bed and bringing the phone down on his chest. It was not yet noon. "The chat would be at ten-thirty, you say?"

"Yes, Mr. Hightower. Ten-thirty. If that would be convenient for you."

"I think I can arrange that quite all right without excessive inconvenience," Jason said as if he were looking down a desk calendar where in bloody array appointments fought each other for houseroom. The fact of the matter was that virtually the entire twenty-four hours of the day, any day, were his. But he remembered the words of Gaskin: "Above all: *don't be too eager. Vital* has a deep-abiding suspicion of anyone who is too eager. Don't ask me to explain this."

This statement had further aroused Jason's interest. Two days after the telephone call he showed himself at the vice managing editor's office at precisely 10:29 A.M. He had considered being a half-hour late but decided this would be carrying the un-eagerness too far. He was kept waiting only six minutes and at exactly ten-thirty-five the buzzer on the secretary's desk erupted mildly and she stepped to the door of the vice managing editor's office. This door had been open all the time—something else that interested Jason and still further whetted his growing appetite to work at a place where the doors of the very top brass stood so democratically ajar—and while waiting, Jason could see through the doorway a figure at the desk, but he avoided looking and instead gazed languidly out the window next to the secretary's desk, which showed the big buildings of the mid-city, and thought, "All those people. I hope the distant alert system is functioning properly today."

The secretary, standing at the door, turned to him. "Won't you come in?" she said sweetly. Her smile seemed the real article.

The vice managing editor stood up as Jason entered, and shook hands with him across his desk, which looked as if it would sleep two comfortably.

"Harrison Duckworth," he said with a smile.

"Jason Hightower," Jason said with one.

They sat down and talked. It was the most astonishing employment interview Jason had ever heard about. No reference whatsoever was made to a job. No reference, indeed, was made to Jason's journalistic experience, if any. Jason did not know if *Vital* had ways of obtaining such routine information by means of private eyes or something, or if they just didn't care about previous experience but wanted to fashion their own people from the raw, untainted clay. In any event, the vice managing editor talked, very genially, about everything else under the sun—the news from Washington, the Yankee baseball club, the Broadway theater or lack of it, some excavations that were then being undertaken around the Dead Sea, and so on. Jason tried to figure out if the subjects were supposed to reflect the catholicity, or lack of it, of his interests. They certainly covered the field and it was a most pleasant sort of talk, relaxed and uncompulsive, suggestive a bit of a good salon of the old days when conversation was a means of communication instead of the shrill, hysterical, jabbering-ape, competitive point-accumulation monologues into which conversation, so-called, has degenerated today. Jason became more and more fascinated with the idea of working at a place that did things this way. There was such grace in it.

Only shortly before he left was there the slightest intimation that this was an employment interview. At that point the vice managing editor turned back from regarding the East River side of the two New York landscapes his office offered—a calm, studious, assessing regarding, as if it were part of his property and he were debating with himself whether to let it flow on its present course or divert it across town and into Times Square—and asked, in the most utterly casual and uncompulsive tones, his first and only question.

"Oh, by the way, Mr. Hightower. Before you go. Do you have any particular interest in pictures?"

Hank Gaskin, fortunately, had coached Jason very carefully in regard to this question. Most important of all, he had told him, was not to gush. A half-dozen words of gushing at that question about how they thought photography was the greatest invention since fire had cost more than one uncoached prospective employee a job at *Vital*. Neither, however, he had told him, must he be callously disinterested. After all, this was a picture magazine. From that perilous point on Gaskin had left it to Jason as a young man of intelligence, perception, and timing, to make his own way.

"I can bring you to the gateway to the sea of the old chateau-bottled wines and of the living high off the journalistic hog, which is a bigger hog than you would imagine, provided you get in at the right trough," Gaskin had said in a thoroughly mixed metaphor. "But yourself will have to determine how to get through to them and it between dear old Scylla and Charybdis. You may not realize it at the time, but believe me, my boy, it will be the rock and the whirlpool. Steer with both hands. A decimal point of navigational error at that point will do you in forever with the great magazine."

Jason Hightower did a very wise thing right then. He did not plunge into an answer to the question. He had his answer all ready, even rehearsed, one might say if one wanted to be entirely truthful, but he did not give it immediately. Instead he reflected briefly—and showed that he was reflecting. He even gazed for a minute out one of the windows—

the towers-of-midtown-Manhattan one, as if they were a part of *his* property and he was considering moving them to . . .

"I should like to say this, Mr. Duckworth," he said then. "I know next to nothing about pictures. I suppose I know what I like and what I don't like in photographs. But these are the opinions of an utter amateur. I have not the slightest professional knowledge about photography. But I should like to say this, sir. I remember very clearly at St. John's in Annapolis—that's the school that has the Great Books course, and well"—and now Jason gave a laugh that managed simultaneously to be winning and to suggest a person who was both considerate of other people's opinions and clear about his own—"though it's a pretty controversial curriculum, I liked it"—suggesting loyalty and God knows what all—"I remember, I started to say, when we came to Da Vinci, who I suppose most people would agree is one of the three authentic geniuses we've ever had—I remember very clearly thinking," Jason said solemnly, "that if Leonardo Da Vinci were alive today he would be a photographer."

Jason Hightower was hired.

It was in the first week that Jason came to work for *Vital* that Crystal Bidwell asked him to have lunch with her.

To *Vital* researchers Crystal Bidwell was a mother, a teacher and something very akin to God all rolled into one extraordinary package. As mother she heard all their problems and not infrequently helpfully suggested to them problems they didn't even know they had. As teacher she took a new researcher in hand and accomplished the often trying task of indoctrinating him and bringing him along in the distinctive *Vital* method of journalism, making, as the phrase went, a "*Vital* type" of him or her. As God She held in those two small, slightly chubby hands the researchers' entire fates, their future with *Vital*. More than anyone else, in this role She decided how a researcher was coming along, and either, where necessary, reluctantly but dutifully eased him out of the company and into oblivion, or started him toward the first goal of all *Vital* researchers—gestation to the role of "correspondent" in a bureau. Researchers were very nice to Crystal and always went for a drink with her when invited, and listened keenly as she taught them the principles of journalism.

As director of researcher development, Crystal Bidwell was one of the two highest-ranking persons on the magazine of her sex, which was female. In more ways than one she was an exceptional woman. To have achieved her high position at the age of thirty itself bespoke an unusual talent. But along with talent she had something at least as important to her job. Understanding. How many more important things are there in this world than understanding? Researchers—coming to work in such a highly charged place, a rarer atmosphere, different as it really was from working in any other office in the world, though of course with some of the attributes common to all offices in that world of aggression which is the world of business—researchers had a lot of problems, professional and personal, until they got the hang of the *Vital* way of life, and even after they got the hang of it.

She was a woman of great vitality. The important word about her would probably be "capacity." In almost any direction one could name it was surpassing. Her capacity for work. She was untiring, of boundless energy; an eighteen-hour Saturday left her seemingly as fresh and ready for anything as when she started it. Her capacity for decision: rapid and seldom wrong. Her capacity for handling a dozen different problems at once and never being overwhelmed by them. She was an extremely cool-headed, self-controlled woman, impossible to ruffle. Her voice was even and cool, and even in the most panicky situations, which occur chronically in the practice of journalism, concerned as the profession is with recording man in his unusual manifestations, she never lost her head. And never never her temper. Her drink was the martini, which nobody can deny is the strongest drink thus far devised by man. No matter how many she drank she never got tight. In all respects her self-control was as ironlike as a Metropolitan Police horse in the after-theater rush.

Like all the top brass at *Vital* without exception, Crystal had come up through the ranks. *Vital* was thoroughly democratic and did not believe in any other way. This made for an exhilarating morale very possibly unsurpassed in American business, if *Vital* could properly be called a business. In many ways it could more accurately be described as a kind of priesthood. Thus anyone down below always knew there was nothing except his own shortage of talent, vitality and capacity, to keep him from reaching the exalted heights himself. In point of fact the magazine had to bring people up through the ranks. The *Vital* system of journalism was so absolutely unique, so totally different from the journalism practiced on newspapers or anywhere else in the country or for that matter the civilized world, that a man coming directly into one of the higher positions from the outside would have been as lost as an Episcopal bishop suddenly appointed chief of staff of the Chinese Army. *Vital* had to get its brass from the ranks. The only difference in Crystal's case was that her rise had been so spectacular. She had begun her *Vital* career as a researcher, and from then on she was off, like something out of Canaveral flaming toward the heavens with a shout to all lesser bodies, "Stand aside, jerks! Here comes something really hot." In swift succession, as these things go, she had been correspondent in the Paris bureau for a couple of years; chief of *Vital*'s Los Angeles bureau— the only female ever to head a major *Vital* bureau; then back to New York as director of researcher development. It was a remarkable achievement for her youth and very especially for her sex in a world which, never mind all pious male pretense to the contrary, still discriminates outrageously against women—of all the world's discriminations this is the greatest, affecting as it does half the human race. But it was an earned achievement, no one ever questioned that. Crystal Bidwell, on this all were agreed, brought superlative equipment to her job.

Crystal Bidwell was a strong-minded woman. She was, as noted: Decisive. Perhaps the single greatest discovery she had ever made (or, almost, that anyone can make) was the discovery of the tremendous advantage the decisive person has over the indecisive one in a world where 999 people out of 1,000 are really basically indecisive and hate and fear nothing so much as having to make up their minds or even use their minds as machines for decision. This advantage was something she had learned early in life, just from looking around at other people and observing how uncertain and hesitating about so many things they were, taking hours to decide simple things which should have been decided by reflex if they had only trained their minds to do so, and weeks to decide important things which should have taken no more than an hour, and the decision better, too, for not taking so long to make it: If anything, the rightness of a decision tends to be in direct ratio to the quickness in making it. She learned that it is far, far better to be wrong sometimes than to be indecisive, and that if you are intelligent the more you practice decision the fewer times wrong you will be. That it is the decisive rather than the wise who, by their very rarity and their ability to take action, bestride this mortal world of indecisive men and run it, though Crystal Bidwell happened to be intelligent along with decisive.

But perhaps the most significant thing about Crystal Bidwell was that she constituted proof incarnate that it is entirely possible for woman to solve her chief problem in this age of flux and crisis for women. At the risk of a bit of philosophy here, the writer would like to divert a moment to explain. The philosophy is important in order to understand the essential triumph of a woman like Crystal Bidwell and therefore forgivable, even though it is a well-known fact that American readers don't like philosophy in their books. Therefore perhaps a bit of philosophy may be excused. At least it will be by the writer. This is an age certainly in which woman is undergoing one of the profound transitions of history: She is attempting to break through to a real equality with man. The battle is even yet far from decided, and indeed now rages at its very height, and the crisis is at hand. Intellectually the writer believes in the concept of complete equality for women. Unfortunately the concept has not, in the writer's view, worked out too well in practice. Or perhaps it is a matter of defining what constitutes "equality." Many women, it is true, have gained "equality" so-called—they hold down the same jobs that men hold, they eat at the same table, they have as much right to speak as the man and indeed they exercise this right fairly often. They have also, many of them, become like men in another way. Tough, hard, masculine. Today, in reality, we have three sexes in this country and the writer is not speaking of homosexuals. We have the traditional male and female and we have a third sex, of the woman in the business world who is neither woman nor man but—well, a third sex. She has lost the chief attribute of a woman, that attribute which alone distinguishes her from all other creatures. To gain her revered goal of "equality," she has surrendered something for which nothing— in the writer's view—is worth a woman's surrendering, no, not all the treasures of the earth, nor all its ranks, titles, money, and position: femininity.

Femininity. For ourselves we feel that the woman with femininity has far more "equality" with and perhaps even superiority to anything and anybody than the woman who has lost it. But the real tragedy is even greater: The belief women hold that in order to compete with men they must become like men—and thus wittingly or unwittingly shed their femininity like a plucked chicken its feathers and with about the same results—is a monstrous and tragic delusion. They only *think* they have to. The exception we see to this now and then of the most feminine woman in the world efficiently or even brilliantly holding down a high business position is proof enough that they don't actually have to. Crystal Bidwell was such a proof, in superb degree. She had triumphed in the business world without surrendering a gram's-weight of her femininity—and triumphed on her ability alone, not using the fact of her femaleness to gain a millimeter. Her voice was not hard, her gestures were not male, there was always a slight and beguiling perfumed air about her—one was always aware, knew, she was a woman. And yet one could deal with her forthrightly, and with sex not present, as a thoroughgoingly able person at her job. This was really Crystal Bidwell's greatest triumph.

Now there is no one in this world who ever does anything but who has enemies. The only way to avoid having enemies is to become a hermit on a Pacific island and know nobody but crabs and booby birds. George Washington had enemies, Abraham Lincoln had enemies, and Jesus Christ had plenty of enemies. Crystal Bidwell had a few enemies, which meant simply in her case that she was a decisive woman, strong-minded and not flabby, nor ever bending to the passing wind in order to gain that grimiest of all goals, that cheap mob emotion which we call "popularity." She did not hesitate to "goose," the hearty phrase she used, a researcher who, as she said, was "dragging his duff." She was absolutely fearless in carrying out her duty and had told more than one big, strapping male chief of bureau, who may in the war have commanded a battalion of Marines, to get the lead out and start turning in more story ideas. She had a quickly acid tongue if acid were the medicine indicated. "Arthur. This magazine can't exist," she would re-mind him, "without a continuous transfusion of story ideas. Without that transfusion we die. Your last weekly story list, if you can call it that, contained *one* suggestion. Well, how about it?" The bureau chief invariably popped to and next week's list was likely to contain ten story suggestions.

Crystal was in reality the terror of the bureaus, their chiefs and their correspondents, but only in a way that kept them popping and thus made for a bright and effective magazine week in and week out. Be their work good or bad she reacted swiftly. She was equally ready with praise for a good job. "Well done, Commander!" would go off a wire to a bureau chief when his bureau turned in an exceptional shooting and reporting job. Or: "Twenty-one guns for the Chicago bureau!" Or: "The farm essay was a brilliant, highly imaginative job on a very difficult and ordinarily unpicturable story. Break out the Piper-Heidsieck!" a wire which would authorize the bureau concerned to have a big drunken company-paid office party. The only people who had ever applied the word "ruthless" to Crystal were a few former employees who largely or partly due to her decision that they were not proper *Vital* material had been eased out of the company. These opinions can be dismissed without further consideration. If there is any one-hundred-per-cent-worthless evidence, it is the opinions of a disgruntled former employee. The fact that virtually all former employees of *Vital* were disgruntled does not modify this fact in the slightest, the case always being that if they left, it meant they didn't have what it takes to be a *Vital* man. And the morality of easing them out was impeccable: If the magazine were to open its staff to the mediocre, instead of maintaining the highest standards of employment and tenure in American journalism . . . well, such a course would perhaps be the one thing which could ever topple the magazine from its position as the Everest of journalism.

And Crystal Bidwell's interest in the welfare of the researchers in her charge was truly without limit. For instance. Despite being one of the busiest people, probably *the* busiest, on the entire *Vital* staff (she came to work every morning one hour earlier than anybody else), Crystal was never too busy to listen to a researcher's problems, even such personal problems as current love affairs, particularly if they were with someone in the office. Indeed she actually became rather hurt if a researcher went a very long period without bringing one to her for discussion and help.

"You haven't been having any problems lately," Crystal would helpfully accuse such a researcher. "Now, John, I want you to understand that I'm here to help you and, using whatever meager experience I have—I ain't very bright, as Lord Tennyson said, but I'se a hard worker"—Crystal's smile flashed on and off—"guide you in any problems that might arise in your work—or in your life, for are they not interrelated? After all, your life affects your work, doesn't it, John, or have you thought of that? They interrelate horribly at a place like *Vital*, there's no denying that, with its intensity and its vivid interpersonal relationships along with its undeniable excitement of working here. You *must* feel that you can tell me anything, John. You understand? *Anything*."

"That's very kind of you, Crystal."

"Bullsugar. It's what I'm here for. And you wouldn't want me to be out of a job would you, John?" Crystal smiled to accent the facetiousness. *"C'est la guerre*. Now, John, no one in these times and more especially in this office can go as long without problems as you have without telling me. So! How is your emotional temperature? *Jouer cartes sur table!* French for 'Let's put our cards on the table.' Just sit back and let it roll forth, boy!"

Some critics—to give the case for the opposition here while we are about it—felt that Crystal used a little too often the phrase, "I got a better idea." But the fact of the matter was, she usually did. And in truth she said it in such a friendly manner that any intelligent and appreciative person could never really resent it but only admire someone who so often had so many better ideas. Other than that, if one only knew the code, which anyone often around Crystal learned very quickly, it was no problem. "I don't want to scare you but" meant simply "I want to scare hell out of you" and was used by Crystal in such instances as a discussion with some researcher about how he was getting along in his work (not getting along well, that is), or in relation to some assignment perilous either physically or in a job sense if one should not deliver the goods. That one expression alone did wonders in keeping people popped-to. "I am just trying to make it easy on you" was translated "I am trying to make it as hard on you as possible." "I've got the greatest assignment for you, boy!" meant "This is an assignment in which you could get your throat slit for falling down, and the chances are anyone getting this assignment will fall down." The key to the code was really the word "opposite." She meant precisely opposite of what she said. This known, communication was very clear and even challenging. It was just like learning a foreign language. It was even more challenging in that the code had sudden variations. Thus "I'll fix his wagon" was translated "I'll fix his wagon."

There was one other habit Crystal had that kept the researchers on their toes, to use a phrase we believe we've heard somewhere. This was to come up behind you while you were working or not working, but anyhow seated at your desk, and look over your shoulder. She was as soft-footed as a Marine in the boondocks, and she could be standing there five minutes before you looked up and saw her. It could be pretty startling and make various parts of you twitch or jump uncontrollably until you got used to it. But when you looked up she always smiled and had a friendly or at any rate interesting word about your work and whatever you may have been doing or not doing.

Just one other point here. We are trying in this book to give, with all our characters, the whites, the blacks and the grays. We all have some of each and we are trying to avoid the practice in the average fraudulent novel of "stacking" things, of "weighting the dice," of putting our "heroes" and "heroines" on pedestals and our "villains" and "villainesses" in the gutter. People are not that way. They just are not. We are going to tell all sides of our characters, we may as well let the reader know. We say this so that the reader will not be too quick to judge simply because the characters are not like the usual fraudulent ones in the aforementioned fraudulent novels but are the way people are. Now we feel it safe to mention a little mean and vindictive characteristic of Crystal Bidwell's: She had a habit of lifting fifths of whiskey from the desk drawers of people who had displeased her.

One of the most appealing qualities about Crystal was her informality. She did not, as the military saying has it, "stand on rank." When she wanted to have a talk with a researcher she seldom did it in her office, where the intervening desk would give an air of stiffness and rank. She almost always took the researcher out for either drinks or drinks and lunch, where people could meet as equals and the researcher be more at ease. Who can deny that anyone is more at ease with a martini inside him than otherwise? If it was for lunch it was always to a little French restaurant in the East Fifties, where the maître d' knew Crystal very and profitably well and where she could also keep a hand in on the French which she had picked up during her tour in the Paris bureau. She was always given the same table, a corner table away from the main traffic of the restaurant. Part of Crystal's job, as previously revealed, was the indoctrination of new researchers in the *Vital* method of journalism, and more journalism had surely been taught across that corner table at the small, svelte French restaurant in the Fifties than in any school of journalism in the United States.

Jason Hightower and Crystal Bidwell left the Vital Building a little after twelve-thirty and made their way up through the heavy lunch-hour traffic of Fifth Avenue, crossed over, and soon were established at the corner table by the grinning, bowing maître d', who used the phrase "Mademoiselle Bidwell" about eight times. Grinning and simpering, he asked her if it would be the usual.

"Un martini, très très sec, avec un zeste de citron, Mademoiselle Beedwell?"

"Mais toujours, Rah-ool," Crystal answered. *"Mais toujours."*

"Neuf-à-un?" said the maître d', grinning more.

"Mais natoorelmahntuh," Crystal answered. *"Toujours nuhoof-ah-unnnnh, Rah-ool."*

"*Entendu,*" the maître d' said, grinning, simpering and scribbling. "*Entendu, parfaitement entendu, Mademoiselle. Eh bien! Merci mille fois!*"

"*Pas du tout, Rah-ool.*"

Whereupon both the grinning maître d' and Crystal turned their eyes upon Jason, and he realized he was confronted with the first decision of his career with *Vital*. He was confronted with the decision in the form of two words from the maître d'.

"And Monsieur?"

Then, for Jason's benefit, the maître d' translated Mademoiselle's complicated order into English.

"Mademoiselle," he said, sniffing, "has ordered a very dry martini with lemon twist."

Just to make certain Jason understood this exotic drink, along with the translation, the maître d' brought the thumb and forefinger of his left hand together and upward and made a quick little twisting motion. And he said once more: "And Monsieur?"

Somehow it seemed to Jason that his decision here was important. If someone else, and particularly a woman, orders a martini at lunch and you then order anything else, say a vermouth cassis, a Dubonnet, or even a Scotch on the rocks, you are made to look chicken, taking refuge in comparative sobriety and too cowardly to meet your companion on the same handicapped terms, that is, with the world's strongest drink sloshing at your stomach walls like a high tide gnawing erosively away at a beach. On the other hand Jason didn't really like martinis at lunch. He knew he would be a weakling whichever he did here. To himself, if he gave in and ordered one just because Crystal had. To her, for the reasons cited above, if he ordered anything else. He choose to be a weakling to himself.

"That'll be okay here, too, Mac," he said. The maître d' winced spastically at the appellative, and Jason imagined Crystal winced some inwardly but had too much self-control to show it. But Jason had to recapture that portion of his self-respect lost with the order. Jason spoke absolutely fluent and colloquial French, but it gave him such duck bumps to see people showing off their French, almost always horrible, with New York maître d's, that when face to face with one of these dinner-coated creatures, whom he happened to loathe anyhow as a class, he took great precautions to conceal the fact of his ability in the language.

At his decision in favor of the martini, Crystal turned a smile upon him. "Well! That's a good start," she said as the maître d' pranced away bawling "Two martinis" at the barkeep in the distance. "I always feel we're on the right track when we hire another martini man."

Jason realized what a close call he'd had.

Over the first martini they talked about nothing in particular and everything in general. The ordering of the second martini provided, ritualistically, an opportunity for a change in the conversation from the general to the specific, that is, to the new future upon which Jason, in a sense with this luncheon, was embarking. Crystal, her eyes upon him, embarked him rather suddenly with a question.

"Are you scared?"

At that moment Jason had his extremely full martini glass halfway to his mouth. As is well known, even people who are not particularly nervous at all will often spill a drop or two or more from a cocktail glass if someone is watching them raise it for the first sip. This is an interesting phenomenon, which we don't have the space to explore here. Jason had always prided himself on never losing a drop, but this was an incredibly full glass. A whole sheet of the sheeny fluid seemed almost to overlap the top of the long-stemmed glass and hang in mid-air like a conjurer's trick. And now this woman had shot him a pretty direct question as he was in the act of raising the glass. He never thought the timing of the question was coincidental.

The glass came on, on course. Jason did not stop its route from table to lips. He brought it on, steadily, steadily. He could feel her eyes upon him. He took a moderate sip.

He set the glass back down.

Not a drop had been spilled.

"No," he said.

Crystal Bidwell smiled at the receipt of her second important information about the new researcher. He didn't, under rigid test, scare easy. She smiled very broadly and gleamingly.

"Well! You certainly passed that one," she said. Jason was astonished at her frankness. He began to feel slightly like one of those people in a room with the kind of windows which oneself cannot see through but through which, from the other side, a number of eyes are watching one's reactions to various probing stimuli, like a frog whose tiny thighs are being activated with electric shocks. He remained prepared for what next.

"It's a refreshing thing to come across," Crystal said, very friendly. "And a rare one. What is there to be scared of in this world? What can anyone do to you? I can't help having contempt for a scared person. I hope you read me—now and always—loud and clear."

The window, he decided, need not be completely one-way, and as she talked he took her in. So easy to take a person in when talking, since no one is so unaware of the other person as when listening to the sound of his own voice, that sweetest music in the world to us all. She was a beautifully groomed woman. She would have been almost arresting physically if she had lost fifteen pounds, and yet her slight chubbiness was not unattractive. All of her had a decidedly rounded appearance, her body, face, arms, hands, a bit like a doll. Her hair was very black save for a small premature plot of gray at left center immediately above her forehead. It was about the size and shape of a silver dollar and it gave a pleasing effect. Her movements were relaxed and easy, yet efficient, unwasted, her voice always modulated, never raised; she seemed very self-contained and unexcitable, yet always alert; her eyes—which were of a very light gray, giving a strange contrast with her black hair—cognizant and interpreting. She had an engaging, white-toothed smile, which was a controlled expression, controlled like all the rest of her, coming on, going off, like, Jason thought, a ship's blinker light. And yet, even realizing this, one did not find it displeasing. It seemed more like a brilliantly honed tool to make things pleasant and informal. She had the fine, flawless complexion which chubby people often have, God's compensation for their chubbiness. Jason could see it on her face, on her arms in the three-quarter-length sleeves, in the V the dress made.

The waiter, bringing another round of martinis, knocked Crystal's orange-colored box of du Mauriers onto the floor. The maître d' came rushing across the room screaming epithets at the waiter for his clumsiness, including certain French colloquial expressions which Jason recognized and which the man would never have used if Crystal could have. The maître d', the waiter and Jason all leaned down in a rousing competition to retrieve the du Mauriers. There was some confusion and commotion, but Jason, swift, got them. To capture the cigarettes he had to lean slightly across Crystal. As he did he most inadvertently could not help noticing, in fact his nose was almost up against, a pair that were highly un-American, in fact almost Italian, and far from needing stuffing needed if anything the ablest restraining barriers, or cages, that were available to man, that is, woman.

The bringing of the third martini presented the opportunity for a toast. Crystal lofted her glass.

"Well! Here's to a brilliant future with *Vital,* boy!"

She set her glass back down. "You know, we don't have any statistics on it but I would imagine it to be a fact that more bright young people want to work at *Vital* per job available than any other company in America. I hope that doesn't sound stuffy and I'm sure it does. I mention it only to point out that you have a right to be proud, yes, I will go so far as to say honored, that you were chosen."

Crystal sipped her martini.

"Yum-yum. I simply try to be a sort of *accoucheuse* to the researcher trying to learn the *Vital* ways. French for midwife. *Vital* magazine," she continued, "—now let us take a long hard look at things—is, I think you will find, an unusual organization. It is demanding in many ways and in a way intolerant: we will tolerate only the best. We demand a complete *fait de foi* in the magazine. French for 'act of faith.' A *Vital* person is expected to put the story first, above everything. *Everything.* With a capital E. That is to say, three o'clock on many a morning, or New Year's Eve, may find you out on a story. News is no respecter of the clock. The most astonishing things happen to peo-

ple at all hours. But we assume that anyone coming to work for *Vital*
not only understands this basic condition but appreciates and is attracted by the exhilaration of it, otherwise he would seek his career at
one of the many gray and dreary nine-to-four-thirty strongholds such
as Wall Street or International Business Machines. In any case, these
sudden rugged assignments build character." She laughed. "They
must, since no one ever quits *Vital* because of the hours. *C'est la vie ici.*
French for 'It's the nature of this rather compulsive and compressed
profession'—though there's none other I or I'm sure you would trade it
for, think how dull being a farmer or one of those galley-slave Wall
Street brokers doing nothing but bending over a mean little desk adding
up figures all day and going home to the same wife every night would
be after this, we may all die early from heart attack or lung cancer
brought on by oversmoking due to the tense nature of our work, but at
least we can say that while we lived we *lived*—we practice. *Joie de
vivre!* I have always said that I would rather *live* thirty years than *exist*
ninety. I would rather be a red camellia for one April than a cabbage
leaf all year." Crystal's smile blinkered on, off. *"Écoutez!* I want to say:
The compensations, to the right person, are manifold. To the right
person," Crystal emphasized, looking with the most calm penetration
at Jason. "Association with unusually alive people, a touchstone to the
events that make history, the exacting uncertainty of not knowing where
one may be at this time tomorrow—Washington, the Canadian bush
country, or even possibly," and here Crystal's smile blinkered on, "an
island in the Caribbean. Things do happen on islands in the Caribbean,
and naturally at the office we always hope they happen on a cold day
in January. So have your jockstrap always packed!"

Jason was startled but Crystal had said it mildly and without batting
an eye.

"As the *boys* say. Yes, I think you will discover that the other side
of the demanding coin at *Vital* is the having of fun. We believe in fun,
with a capital F. I don't think any organization—hardly the word for
us—in the country believes more in fun than we do at *Vital.* I can't
hope to get what I mean across to you but you will understand as you
go along. I hope. We aren't fussy. We *are* demanding. With a capital
D. Don't try now to reconcile this apparent contradiction. It isn't. In
fact, don't strain too much at all right now about things that may baffle
you. All will come clear in due time with you. We hope." Crystal blinkered. "What do we try to do?" Crystal tasted her martini. "All we try
to do is to put out America's best magazine each week. I should say not
a soul questions but that we do just that. This undoubtedly is what attracted you to *Vital.*"

It wasn't precisely. But Jason saw no point in splitting hairs at this
juncture. Instead he worked on his martini—it was real work keeping
up with this woman—and kept his ears open.

"I don't know why I'm going into these things here. Habit, I guess. You have to learn them really. As Destouches said, *La critique est aisée et l'art est difficile.* French for 'Criticism is easy and art is difficult.' "

She had at her martini again, the long-stemmed glass smoothly, deftly up, then down.

"What is *Vital* journalism? How does it differ from all other forms of journalism? I can't really answer that," she said as if it were he who had asked the question. Her smile blinkered on, off. "Well, let me try. *Comme il faut.* I'll have to goose that waiter. Rah-ool!"

"Oui, Mademoiselle! Oui, oui!"

The maître d' came cantering over. Jason swallowed in one gulp the half of his martini that was left—another rule in drinking martinis is that you have to keep up, particularly if it is with a woman—and soon the fourth round was sitting in front of them. He was beginning to feel definitely heady, but Crystal seemed as steady as if she had been drinking Moroccan mineral water.

"Where was I? Oh, yes." She slid the martini glass sleekly to her lips, sampled, put it down. "Yum. How does *Vital* journalism differ from all other forms of journalism? That was it, wasn't it?" She looked thoughtful for a moment. "I'll tell you later," she said briskly. "First, about you. *Attendez!* As a researcher you will have a challenging job and one of great diversity. Sometimes you will be in the office. There you will prepare queries to the bureaus concerning stories we are thinking of doing. You will also read the newspapers for ideas for stories. Read them carefully, thoroughly. Many a ten-page *Vital* essay has been pollenized in a one-paragraph story buried on page thirty-six that a bright and diligent researcher spotted and had the imagination and guts to see something bigger in. Read the newspapers for story ideas—and use your mind to think up story ideas. We don't like people who drag their duffs. We do like what I call 'self-starting researchers.' Researchers, that is to say, who don't sit around on theirs all day waiting for the Angel Gabriel Grabass," and it, like everything else, was said so calmly and unemphasizedly that hardly a ripple broke the pond of martinis in Jason's stomach, "to drop an assignment in their laps but use their minds to think up story ideas. We all have minds I'm told. Use yours! *Alors.* Sometimes you will be in the office. There you will also be assigned to check stories for accuracy. Before any piece of *Vital* copy is allowed to go to press, the researcher must put a penciled dot over every word as notary to its accuracy. Doesn't that sound interesting? It builds character beautifully, I understand." Her smile blinkered on quickly, off. "If the researcher makes more than three mistakes in a year we generally communicate to him in one way or another that he is probably better qualified to work somewhere else. I'm not trying to scare you but. You'll learn"—Crystal's smile blinkered on—"or we hope you'll learn"—off—"by practice. My, don't I sound professorial!"

Jason was bearing down hard on what she was saying. Suddenly he leapt a good three inches out of his chair. The ejector mechanism had been a touch on his left wrist by the live end of Crystal's cigarette.

"Oh, *excusez moi,*" she said, blinkering her smile. "You must have put it out. Will you give me another light?" He did so. "I'm just trying, in my own feeble way, to give you a long hard look at things. Where was I? Oh yes. *Faites attention!* At other times you will be sent out with a photographer on an assignment. The basic *Vital* field unit in action is the photographer-researcher team. Perhaps the greatest thing about working for *Vital* is the opportunity, yes, I will say honor, with a capital H, it affords you to associate with the world's greatest photographers— and naturally, I say it with no false modesty—something I rather detest anyhow—with the world's greatest picture editors, and I will say also— I honestly think this will become so obvious to you—with the most alive and intriguing people in the world. If you're really interested in learning the picture business—which I take to be a fact for anyone who comes to work for *Vital,* so speak now, or forever keep your yap shap—you have the world's greatest faculty in the form of *Vital* photographers. Learn from them! An important word here. Our photographers are definite-minded people with points of view, what some people call idio-syncrasies and what we call the running lights of genius. If you under-stand the great and rare privilege that is yours in being around these remarkable men, you will learn profound things. As with all things you must learn this first-hand to learn it truly. Precisely as in learning how to screw properly." However, Jason wondered if he heard that. But even to imagine it suggested to him, a bit distantly through the martini haze, the pace of things going on here." Rah-ool! *Ici maintenant!"*

Jason gulped and presently they got under way on their fifth martini.

"You know," Crystal said, "what lies ahead of you. A ladder with rungs. That's what the masthead is. A ladder with rungs, and one moves up it or"—Crystal blinkered—"one moves. *C'est la guerre.* Generally a researcher stays two years in the New York office. Then, if he comes along as we always hope so very passionately he comes along, we farm him out to one of the large bureaus. After that, chances are, we test him out further running his own show in one of the small one-man bureaus. After that, if he masters these rungs, and shows he has balls"—Jason thought he hadn't imagined that one—"anything can happen—over-seas to a bureau, back to New York as a writer. After that maybe chief of a large bureau. After that . . ."

Holding up one chubby but well-tended little forefinger Crystal aimed it at the restaurant ceiling.

"After that, who knows, boy!" he heard her say. "For the right sort of person—what we call, and it's an important phrase, 'the *Vital* type'—the sky up there's the limit!"

Jason thought groggily that he didn't honestly believe he would ever make it. However, he was happy to go along for the ride. Right now his ambition was more limited. It was confined to getting out of the restaurant under his own power. He looked across at Crystal. He was dimly aware of her lips lightly lipsticked and parting slightly to emit "Rahool!" and of a sixth martini being placed in front of them. Through the mist Crystal seemed to be smiling gaily. Then she was grasping her glass in a toast.

"May you—as the French say—*prendre la lune avec les dents.* Seize the moon with your teeth. May your rise be swift and glorious!"

"Swift and glorious!" Jason echoed.

"May you enjoy every minute—well, almost every minute—of your new work!"

"Every minute!" Jason echoed, picking up his glass.

"To your being the right sort of person!"

"Person!" Jason echoed.

Crystal raised her glass. "Up the ladder for Jason Hightower!"

Jason grasped his glass firmly and brought it up to join in the toast.

"Up yours!" he joined in gaily.

Somehow, after a seventh martini, Jason got through lunch. He didn't have the faintest idea in the world what he was eating, whether it was beef, pork, lamb, fish, venison, C ration, frog's legs or sheep's eyes. He only vaguely remembered leaving the restaurant but he felt a tentative triumph when he discovered himself upright on the sidewalk. However, there was still the building to be got to. And when he got to the building and in it, there was still the afternoon somehow to be got through. When they came to Fifth Avenue he could not even see across it, and it is not such a wide street. At his side he was aware of Crystal Bidwell cruising along as steadily and talking as brightly as if she had had nothing deadlier than seven soda-pops. He tried to hear what she was saying. It required the most enormous effort. Once he thought he heard her say, "Well, boy! This has been very interesting mental ping pong glurp glurp." Her voice came from afar, and as though through murky water where a couple or so mako sharks darkly slithered.

"Oh, yes," he thought he heard her say as they turned the corner and headed down the final stretch toward the Vital Building. "I promised to tell you, didn't I, how *Vital* journalism differs from all other forms of journalism."

The building was above them and they headed for the revolving doors, the mouth of the beast of the Book of Revelation.

"Well, it's this. We're hep. That's the difference, boy! Hep. There are no squares in this building. Not for long. They don't fit at *Vital.* They get unsquared quite quickly or they leave. Hep. With a capital H. Now, from there on in," Crystal said just before the revolving doors gulped her up and he thought he saw her ship's-blinker-light smile go on and off twice, "you'll have to figure it out for yourself. You can proffer a baby the tit but you can't make him drink. As the *girls* say."

As he weaved across the lobby of the Vital Building and into the elevator and shot up, up, as to an entirely new heaven and new earth, to begin an afternoon of work, Jason wasn't sure he could even sit up in a chair. But he was on his way to being that *crème de la crème* of American journalism—a *Vital* man.

3
Benevolence and Paternalism

There was perhaps no company in the country that treated its employees quite so well as did *Vital* magazine. Besides being a spiritedly democratic place—no one stood on rank around *Vital,* the lowliest researcher calling the managing editor by his first name to his face—it was a model of Benevolence and Paternalism and made the welfare state seem by comparison like a soup line. It paid, of course, the highest wages in journalism. It gave perhaps the longest paid vacations of any company in America. In addition to the regular vacation of one month, everybody got a "winter week," during which the sun-lovers went to Haiti or the Virgin Islands and the ski-lovers to Vermont, New Hampshire or Austria. The working week consisted of thirty-five hours but this in actual practice was as flexible as there are hours in the day. While in theory the working day started at 9:45 A.M., employees wandered in at all hours from then until eleven and sometimes later, and nothing was ever said. And while officially the working day ended at 5:45 P.M., employees started wandering out and off from five o'clock on. There was a time clock, but it was common practice for a group of four girl-researchers to band together in the common interest, that is, theirs, by forming what was known as a "time-clock pool." On a rotation basis each would have "the duty" for a week, that is to say, would punch the cards of all members of the pool including her own. This meant that only one week in four was a girl participating in the pool obliged to arrive and depart on time. The company could hardly have been blind to this practice. It did nothing to stop it. For overtime beyond thirty-five hours the company paid double wages. The nature of covering a story being what it is, which is a thing of the most erratic time-variants, especially if the story is out-of-town, where one must be one's own judge of the hours one needs to work or at least put in on the story, and where there are no time clocks to be dealt with even on a group basis: well, the hours of a *Vital* researcher-reporter sometimes very nearly equaled the hours there are in a week and resulted, considering that double overtime, in a pay check for that month that would have excited the envy of a number of executives in America.

The lunch period was officially one hour. Few staff members ever got back in less than two, and the three-hour lunch was not at all uncommon. The company furnished free liquor for the frequent office parties, as well as every Saturday night, on which night also it fed employees the elaborate, seven-course, six-dollar-a-head buffet dinner from the exclusive Le Porc Blanc restaurant français, dished out in the corridors from steaming gleaming silver trays by creatures in dinner coats. The company carried on every employee a life insurance policy equivalent to twice the employee's annual salary—the beneficiary, not the company but anyone designated by the employee. The company had a spectacularly generous profit-sharing plan. It had an even more elaborate and almost unbelievably generous age-sixty retirement plan, and if no one had yet stayed in *Vital* magazine's employ long enough to reap its staggering benefits the company could hardly be blamed for that, since it almost never fired anybody. The company had a hospital-and-illness plan, carried on all employees entirely at the company's expense, that was so generous as to make one feel defrauded if more than a year passed without a nice session in some pleasant, air-conditioned private room of one of New York's better hospitals, that is, those which coddle and almost cuddle the patient, as a sick person should be, right down to backrubs and airy cheese soufflés, both on order, instead of the insulted hauteur on the part of the nurse fresh from taking her Marquis de Sade oath and the swill troughed out at mealtimes at the usual meat-wagon hospitals, the former (for the guidance of the reader who may one day find himself fallen ill in the great city) being quickly identifiable from the latter by the invariable presence out front of a doorman uniformed in a manner befitting one of the city's tonier night clubs.

For a while the medical plan even included psychiatric treatment, and *Vital* was the first company in America to have a medical plan covering this elastic area of human ailments. It was also the last. *Vital* worked out an arrangement with its medical insurance company for a one-year trial of this feature, under which seventy-five percent of any employee's psychiatric treatment was paid for, the same as his other medical bills. When the plan was announced a great many persons at *Vital*, even those who apparently had no pressing need for any such treatment, decided to benefit by it. After all it made the twenty-five-dollar-hour cost the employee only six dollars and twenty-five cents, and it was a pretty cheap price to pay for a full hour of lying on a couch and talk-

ing your head off about anything and everything to some quack who
had to listen, even if you decided some days to spend the full hour in
a pleasant barrage of fulminations directed at your superiors on the
magazine which had arranged for the plan and was paying for three-
quarters of it. At those rates one could hardly afford not to take the
treatment. It was a wonderful way to let off steam, and ludi-
crously cheap. It also provided another ironclad excuse for leaving the
office for an hour during the day. *Vital* would not have dreamed of
being so cruel as to deny an employee the right and/or privilege, as
you choose, of disappearing for an hour for medical treatment. The
insurance company felt no such humanitarian compunctions, however.
In that one year of trial it came very close to going bankrupt from the
psychiatric clause in its contract with *Vital* magazine, and at midnight
on the day ending the year the clause was conclusively not renewed.

In addition *Vital* maintained on the twenty-third floor of the Vital
Building a free dispensary, with a graduate M.D., two registered nurses
and an x-ray technician in attendance the day long. Any employee
could drop down there at any time of day (on company time) to get
his sore throat sprayed, his congested nose cleared with a one-percent
solution of Neo-synephrine, his possibly tubercular or cancerous chest
x-rayed, his blood pressure taken after a particularly trying session with
one of the editors, his headache treated with aspirin, his nerves with a
tranquilizing tablet—or for something that there was a lot of on any
windy day in the soot-cursed melting pot of New York, a foreign body
removed from his eye. The dispensary even had four darkened twin-
bedded bedrooms, two for each of the usual sexes, where one could
sack out for an hour or two (company time) if one felt a little under the
weather from any cause, such as a hangover from the night before or
from one of the martini lunches which were so popular at the magazine.
The company had a free educational plan which paid the tuition of any
course, including Berlitz languages, fencing, and body-building, in any
of the many higher or lower institutions of learning in the City of New
York which any employee might care to take by night or on his two
days a week off or even during his lunch hour, as three or four persons
in a short burst of self-recrimination, will power and self-improve-
ment gave up their martini lunches for two weeks to do when this
feature was first put into effect.

But great as its benevolence was, despite the many benefits with which
at any current time it was drenching its employees, the company was
never in this area content, to use the journalistic phrase, to "rest on its
laurels." In fact *Vital* had an eleven-member committee, five full-time
employees and six ex-officio members—senior personnel of the magazine—whose sole task was to seek out fresh new benefits to thrust at
Vital employees. It was called the Committee on Employee Morale,
Benefits, Health and Well-Being: known more handily as the Com-

mittee on More for Us. It was unceasing in its far-ranging search for new
and exotic benevolences to impose upon the help.

It is interesting, and would be amusing if it did not speak so
pathetically of their character, how churlish some people can be. There
are some people who the more one attempts to please them and embrace them with good and benevolent things, the more churlish they
are. There is a legend for this, dealing with "biting the hand that feeds
you." It was in this spirit that *Vital*, unbelievable as it may sound, had
some employees who took a cynical and sour attitude toward the company's mighty array of benevolences. "It just means the company has a
guilt complex toward its employees which it is trying to assuage by
giving us all these things," so the matter was neatly put by Price "Sorehead" Steadman, a researcher in the Science Department, who had
never fully recovered from reading Thorstein Veblen in college, and
a volunteer spokesman for this cynical group (no member of which,
however, failed to accept a single one of the benevolences). If he had
arrived in heaven and the Lord God had presented him with a pair of
brand-new custom-built hydromatic angel wings, Sorehead Steadman
would have searched voraciously for an evil motive in the gift. Steadman was so rabidly anti-company and anti-capitalist as to have made the
most progressive, left-wing businessman long for the good old days of
sixteen-hour-six-day-twelve-dollar-a-week, fire-the-bastards-if-they-
don't-pop-to-and-tip-their-hats *laissez faire.*

No, no company in America was better to its employees than was
Vital magazine. Besides all of the above, the company even permitted
thievery among its employees. Perhaps it was not so unusual that its
employees stole the company blind. This happens with a fair number of companies. What was unusual about *Vital* was that the company
tacitly approved its employees stealing it blind.

The opportunities were endless, and detection, even if the company
had been so minded, difficult to impossible. The stealing opportunities
at *Vital* were of pencils of every conceivable kind, Number 1 through
Number 4AAA, and of colors red, blue and green in addition to the
traditional black; typewriter ribbons, portable and standard; spiral
notebooks of two sizes; looseleaf binders of three sizes; letterhead stationery of several sizes (very good to steal, since it impressed people to
receive a letter on a *Vital* letterhead and brought much swifter attention
if it were something such as a complaint to the gas company about the
service at one's home); envelopes to match all the sizes of stationery;
manila envelopes of three sizes; plain high-grade-bond paper; copy
paper; fine steel rulers; desk pen sets; American College Dictionaries;
typewriter erasers; typewriter cleaning fluid; paper clips of three sizes;
rubber bands of five sizes; carbon paper; desk appointment calendars;
clipboards of two sizes, regular and long—to mention a few of the available items from which an employee could choose and most did.

These items left the building in small packages and monumental quantities. A large manila envelope, itself stolen, could transport several typewriter ribbons, a dozen or two pencils, a half hundred sheets of bond paper and a couple of dozen business-size envelopes. The thievery varied seasonably. Around the beginning of school in September, for instance, the pencil pilferage was enormous and the business office always forethoughtfully laid in large extra supplies in August. For the pencils to have been used on legitimate *Vital* labor, someone on the business side who had nothing else to do at the moment once figured out, each employee on the magazine would have had to consume nine full pencils a day. The big double-circumference Chinese-red pencils inscribed in gold "*Vital*—The Nation's Picture Magazine" were, as befitted something singled out to carry this proud escutcheon, the finest pencils made and the children of *Vital* employees loved them.

When the owners of *Vital* decided to bring in a management consultant it was not remotely with any notion of halting or even in the slightest curtailing the magazine's mighty pageantry of employee benevolences, including the unofficial one of permitted pilferage. It was certainly not because the magazine was not doing well and hoped the management consultant would unearth a formula of success. *Vital* was selling more copies, carrying more advertising, printing fatter and fatter issues and making more money, great huge gobs of money, than at any moment since its founding. A management consultant was brought in for the simple reason that all the better names in American business were doing it. The management consultant, sometimes called in the cruder vernacular an "efficiency expert," was in point of fact a very useful profession that had grown up to expose inefficiencies in the operation of a given business and to devise healthier procedures for that business. The management consultant did not necessarily know anything about the given business itself. What he did know, inside and out, was Efficiency, which is a quality unto itself applicable to any business from the manufacture of paper clips to the manufacture of threshing machines, and, supposedly, to the manufacture of magazines. The fact that *Vital* was making money hand over fist was no argument against bringing in a management consultant, and the philosophy "If it works don't tinker with it" is hardly defensible in the higher metaphysics of business. Efficiency, in the Twentieth Century age, is a goal quite worthy of being pursued puristically for itself, without any crass calculations of possible financial benefits.

Though, of course, hardly any business would object if these also should ensue.

The management consultant firm retained by *Vital* went simply and discreetly under the name of Advisory, Inc. It was, as to be expected

of any such organization called in by *Vital* magazine, the most distinguished in its field. Similarly, the man Advisory, Inc. assigned to the
Vital job was its star performer. His fee was five hundred dollars a day
and he was worth every dollar of it. He was a brilliant man in his early
forties by the name of Tompkins Armbruster, who had previously done
really notable management consultant jobs on the New York head-
quarters offices of some of the most renowned names in American business. His recommendations after several weeks' intensive study of each
company had led to sweeping reorganizations in these great firms,
enormously improved the efficiency of their operations and saved each
untold hundreds of thousands of dollars annually.

Besides being a man of an extraordinarily brilliant and fast-working
mind, Armbruster was a very nice guy, as T. S. Eliot would say, and
Hank Gaskin came to like him a good deal. Ordinarily a person of Gaskin's rank would not have had much, if anything, to do with a man on
the level of Tompkins Armbruster, who as a professional exterminator
of the termites of inefficiency would be dealing with some of the very
top brass of the magazine. However, it was deemed desirable to get the
management consultant as close to the daily operations as possible. The
Vital management considered, for this purpose, having him impersonate
a researcher, but this was vetoed on dual grounds: one, that the bona-
fide researchers, especially types like Sorehead Steadman, might seize
upon and twist it as company espionage if Armbruster's real identity got
out; and, two, that Armbruster, due to age and other considerations,
looked anything but a *Vital* researcher, of which more very presently.
It was decided therefore not to cloak his identity but as an alternative
to park him in an office in the heart of the magazine's editorial operation. The Manners and Morals office seemed a good place. A spare desk
was put temporarily in Gaskin's office and Tompkins Armbruster established there for his dissection of the mechanics of *Vital*.

Gaskin had heard of the profession of management consultant but he
had never before met a live one. He was immediately taken with Tompkins Armbruster from the time he walked in one afternoon and introduced himself. From appearance and manner he could have been an
assistant professor at a good small college of the order of Oberlin,
Kenyon, or Swarthmore. He was thoroughly mild of speech and bearing
and wore rimless glasses. He was a man of the most extreme courtesy,
to a point of graciousness, that lost art. Only a few thin and lonely
wisps of reddish hair remained on the top of his head, where
they roamed feebly about with any faint breeze or even movement.
He was of the medium height and decidedly on the thin side. His flesh
was pale and he had a slight stoop. His clothes suggested the assistant
professor who paid not much attention to things so ephemeral and
unimportant. He wore a conservative gray suit slightly frayed, black not
fully shined shoes, a clean white shirt with a collar scalloped a bit by

wear, and a dark tie with modest, non-regimental stripes, pin stripes in fact, of a shade hardly discernible against the tie. He was altogether unobtrusive, of thoroughly discreet air, and in fact there was something just faintly ascetic about him. One felt he ate salads for lunch.

It did not seem at all strange that he smoked a pipe. The fact that he did just brought to Gaskin's awareness for the first time that, apart from Harrison Duckworth, the vice managing editor, he had never seen anyone smoke a pipe at *Vital*. Gaskin supposed the air was a little too vibrating at *Vital* to permit of proper pipe smoking. Armbruster smoked a fine-smelling aromatic tobacco, and it was pleasing and soothing, Gaskin soon discovered, to have its aroma engorging the room. He learned later that the mixture was something expensive called Dunhill A9160.

Gaskin always remembered the disarming and enigmatic way Tompkins Armbruster walked in and introduced himself.

"I'm Tompkins Armbruster from Advisory, Incorporated," he said in a quiet, unassaulting voice. "I'm here to see what's wrong with this magazine."

"Oh, is something wrong with it?" Gaskin said.

"There's always something wrong with any business when we go to work on it."

"That's interesting," Gaskin said. "It's the most successful magazine in America. In the world, for that matter."

" 'Most' is but a comparative word," Tompkins Armbruster said in tones of mildness and graciousness. "It can always be more."

"I see," Gaskin said.

"Not to mention that it may be the most successful and still not be efficient."

"I see," Gaskin said. "I had always thought the two attributes had a rough synonymity."

"It can still need a little tidying up, a little piano tuning as it were, here and there."

"I see," Gaskin said.

"I'm joking of course," Armbruster said. "More or less."

At that moment there was a deafening crash of drums in the corridor.

"What's that?" Tompkins Armbruster exclaimed, startled.

The management consultant stepped to the door, Gaskin behind him. Down the long length of the corridor Tompkins Armbruster saw a sight that made his eyes distend. Coming toward him was a procession. The procession was led by a jacketless-tieless young man carrying a quite enormous flag. The flag, which hung from a pole, was of a dirty white cloth, tattered from much use, and bore on its folds a huge, tilted martini glass in which floated gallantly, like the yellow ribbon of the cavalry, a twist of lemon peel. Behind the flag-bearer came another young man, also unencumbered by either jacket or tie, tooting a fife. Behind him

came the source of the noise that had drawn Tompkins Armbruster to
the door of his new office and others to theirs, since from all the offices
down the corridor heads now stuck out: Three young ladies carrying
slung from their pretty necks dime-store toy drums on which they were
beating out a swift and crashing rhythm. They wore perfectly sober expressions and they were very pretty as they parade-stepped down the
corridor, flinging their winsome, lithesome, make-you-want-to-reach-
out-and-give-a-friendly-stroke-or-two-to little rumps hither and yon,
behind the young man with the fife, and now they began to sing the tune
which this worthy was tooting on his instrument. Armbruster recognized the stirring strains of "The British Grenadiers" and he heard the
young ladies, marching down the corridor with much smartness, raise
their voices in crisp, clear song:

> *"Some talk of Alexander and some of Hercules,*
> *Of Hector and Lysander and such brave men as these,*
> *But of all the world's great 'eroes there's none that can compare*
> *With a tow-row-row-row-row-row-row for the British Grenadiers . . ."*

Their voices came clear and sweet and rose in swelling strains as they
drew nearer to him:

> *"Then let us fill a bumper, and drink a health to those*
> *Who carry caps and pouches, and wear the lopèd clothes;*
> *May they and their commander live happy all their years*
> *With a tow-row-row-row-row-row-row for the British Grenadiers . . ."*

Now, on the crest of the martial music, the fife shrilled, the drums
beat and the young sweet voices sounded down the corridor, triumphant
and defiant, and now all of it rushed into the management consultant's
ear with a force nearly adequate to pierce an eardrum, for they were
now just opposite him and no more than eight inches away, as they
modulated into a stirring, spine-tingling climax:

> *"Rule! Britannia,*
> *Britannia, rule the waves!*
> *For Eng-lish-men never, nev-er*
> *Shall-l-l-l be-e-e-e sl-uh-aves!"*

With a roll of drums the procession swept past Tompkins Armbruster and, striking up the "Grenadiers" again, on toward the National Affairs bullpen, whose members stood and cheered wildly, like the
Navy side of the field violently applauding the West Point brigade to
exhibit its sportsmanship. Reaching the bullpen the procession turned a
smart military right—the management consultant stood transfixed by
the way the pert trio of little behinds snapped apocalyptically out in a

fashion almost double-jointed—then swung down the corridor at the end of the building.

"What is it?" Tompkins Armbruster asked Gaskin.

"A party," Gaskin said. "A parade led by the martini flag is the traditional manner of announcing the commencement of a party around here."

"Oh? And who were those worthies?"

"Those? Why, they're researchers in the Foreign News Department."

"Well," Tompkins Armbruster said uncertainly.

"The Foreign News Department," Gaskin explained, "is having the party to celebrate British Empire Day—observed, of course, throughout the Empire, including in the distant possessions."

"How interesting," Tompkins Armbruster said graciously. "Is this one of them?"

"In a way," Gaskin said. "Foreign News, you know. The British Empire is located overseas from the United States."

It was a moment before the management consultant spoke again. "May I ask," he said courteously. "Who pays for the party?"

"Pays for the party?" Gaskin echoed surprise at the question. "Why, the company of course. Who else would pay for it?"

"How," Tompkins Armbruster said, "generous of them."

"They're the generous sort," Gaskin said.

Tompkins Armbruster was thoughtfully silent a moment. "Very interesting," he said pleasantly. "May I ask. Is the head of the Foreign News Department by chance either British or a steaming Anglophile?"

"He's from Mississippi," Gaskin said. "I don't know how he feels personally about the British."

"Then why . . ."

Tompkins Armbruster's voice faded off but Gaskin imagined he understood the question that at the moment filled his new roommate's mental corridors. "British Empire Day is celebrated," he explained, "because it happens to be today."

Tompkins Armbruster said nothing for a good many moments. "May I ask," he said then with great courtesy. "Are any other anniversaries similarly observed?"

"A few," Gaskin said. He inhaled deeply to get a lot of breath for the purpose of answering the question. "There's Pearl Harbor Day . . . Columbus Day . . . Halloween . . . Mother's Day . . . Guy Fawkes Day . . . Gandhi's birthday . . . Shakespeare's birthday . . . Armistice Day of course . . . Bunker Hill Day . . . Valentine's Day . . . the Battle of Hastings . . . the birthday of Florence Nightingale . . . the founding of the Girl Scouts . . . the Pope's birthday, which is observed by the Religion Department . . . Christmas, it goes without saying . . . Hanukkah, that's to keep it even with the goys, if you do one you

have to do the other . . . Martin Luther's birthday, that's to balance the
Pope's birthday . . . Perry's victory on Lake Erie . . . the discovery of
the planet Pluto . . . the discovery of America . . . Babe Ruth's birthday, which is observed by the Sports Department . . . the Battle of Tra-
falgar . . . D-Day in Normandy . . . Garibaldi's birthday . . . the birthday of Audubon, that one is celebrated by the Nature Department . . .
the birthday of Ulysses S. Grant, observed by the Military Affairs Department . . . the birthday of Robert E. Lee, that's to bal . . ."

"May I ask," Tompkins Armbruster interposed graciously. "When
one department holds a party, is the party attended only by members
of that department?"

". . . ance the Yankees. Indonesian Independence Day. And the
landing of Bonnie Prince Charlie. Oh no," Gaskin said. "The department holding the party is just the location of it. They act only as the
hosts. Everyone on the magazine who so wishes—and many generally
do—attends all parties held by all departments. When, for example, the
Science Department holds a party in honor of the birthday of Louis
Pasteur, the great Frenchman—and recently," Gaskin said parenthet-
ically, "the Science Department has added to its list of party observances
one to honor that American whose discovery has already saved so many
thousands of lives from that crippling disease, I speak of polio and Jonas
Salk . . ."

"May I ask," Tompkins Armbruster interjected to forestall a fresh
onslaught of anniversaries observed at the magazine—he had heard
enough to get the point. "Does overlapping not occur?"

". . . the observance being held on October 28, which is Doctor
Jonas Salk's birthday. Well," Gaskin said genially in answer to the question, "there is seldom a day when some department is not observing
some noteworthy or at least observable anniversary by way of a party.
But it does happen sometimes that there are two or more—I remember
one time there were five—parties scheduled the same day. In that event
a more or less progressive party is held by some of us from department
to department and from floor to floor. This happens unavoidably when
two or more anniversaries calling for an observance fall on the same
day. In addition . . ."

"Most progressive, the entire practice," Tompkins Armbruster interjected briefly.

". . . In addition," Gaskin continued as if he had not been interrupted—he hated for anyone to interrupt anyone in conversation, and
his own defense against this loathsome and growing practice was to continue just as if he had not been interrupted, not to recognize the interruption and if it persisted to talk on, even if he had to yell: this usually
got the point over and stopped all interruptions thereafter, and his new
roommate might as well learn now how he felt about this matter . . .

"In addition to the birthdays of the great personages and the anniversaries of the great climacterics of history, we also observe such local events as the departure of a staff member for a bureau, foreign or domestic, the arrival of a staff member back in New York after a tour of duty in a bureau—there is, fortunately, a lot of movement in and out of here—and other such important local personal events. It is very great for morale."

"I can heartily imagine," Tompkins Armbruster said pleasantly. "And the company, you say, pays for all of these observances?"

"Well, of course," Gaskin said—the question showed how little the man knew of the workings of *Vital*. "It certainly wouldn't help anyone's morale if we had to pay for them ourselves, and the whole point of them is morale."

"The morale of the personnel of *Vital* magazine," Tompkins Armbruster said cordially, "must reach fresh new summits for American workers."

"I doubt," Gaskin said proudly, "if it's higher anywhere. We don't call this place The Fun House for nothing," he added.

Tompkins Armbruster was thoughtfully silent for a few moments. He seemed to have something on his mind but to be a little shy at mentioning it. He seemed to Gaskin to be a definitely shy person, and Gaskin found this an attractive quality. Finally he spoke, very politely and very tentatively.

"Can I go to the party?"

"Not to," Gaskin said immediately, putting much hospitality and warmth into it in order to make the new man feel at home, "would be almost an affront. To Anglo-American unity if not to the Foreign News Department."

"I think," said Tompkins Armbruster shyly, and in a faraway tone, "I would just like to see the morale in action."

"In addition to which," Gaskin said, putting a sly tone into it, "a drink might, as the Limeys say, taste a bit of all right. Heh, heh."

Tompkins Armbruster laughed feebly, and it seemed to Gaskin, a little forcedly.

"It's British Empire Day, you know, old chop," Gaskin said. "Heh, heh."

And Gaskin gave his new roommate a friendly, hearty slap on the shoulder. Armbruster, who was about two-thirds Gaskin's size, jerked forward coughing.

"It just might at that," the management consultant, when he had recovered his voice, said weakly but very graciously.

"Don't forget, the British gave us Milton, Shakespeare and Agatha Christie, not to mention Magna Carta and Beefeater gin. Ah yes! Not to attend the party would be unbearably rude to both England and the magazine. For . . ." And now Gaskin declaimed the soaring lines:

> "*This royal throne of kings, this scept'red isle,*
> *This earth of majesty, this seat of Mars,*
> *This other Eden, demi-paradise,*
> *This fortress built by Nature for herself*
> *Against infection and the hand of war,*
> *This happy breed of men, this little world,*
> *This precious stone set in the silver sea,*
> *Which serves it in the office of a wall,*
> *Or as a moat defensive to a house,*
> *Against the envy of less happier lands;*
> *This blessed plot . . . this earth . . . this realm . . .*
>   *this England!"*

"Come along, old friend," Gaskin said, propelling his astonished roommate by his elbow out of the office and into the corridor on the cadences of *King Richard II,* "and see the happy breed."

Armbruster and Gaskin went on down to the party in the Foreign News Department. It was jammed beyond belief and made a terrifying assault on the unaccustomed ear. Such noise! Tompkins Armbruster thought. More than any other single thing in the world Tompkins Armbruster hated unnecessary noise. Even a door not closed quietly disturbed him. In fact the distinguished management consultant had very nearly an actual allergy to noise. It accelerated his pulse rate and made him break out in duck bumps. The two men were soon separated in the push and surge but not before Gaskin noticed that Armbruster, almost from the moment of his entrance to the party, had been steadily watching one girl who stood a little beyond them. He knew the girl worked in the National Affairs Department and that was about all he knew about her. She was probably the unprettiest girl in the room, so that Gaskin wondered mildly why his new roommate was keeping such a fix on her. Every man to his taste! he figured, leaving Armbruster to his own devices.

That was the last Gaskin saw of Tompkins Armbruster that evening. Four hours later the consultant followed the girl out of the party. He saw her go into the ladies' room. Then, lingering in the corridor, he saw her get her coat and hat. Then, just before she stepped out to the elevator bank, he saw her go to the time clock and punch it. The girl was decidedly tight but she was not too tight, the management consultant reflected, to punch that clock *after* the party. He watched her leave. Then he went back to his office and got out a big black loose-leaf notebook from his desk. He opened the notebook, wet his pencil with the tip of his tongue and made his first entry in respect to the operation and procedures of *Vital* magazine:

   1. For drinking company-paid pink gins—the drink prevalent in alleged tribute to British Empire Day—the company paid a researcher

$16.25. I.e., she drank four repeat four hours on company time. $16.25—besides the undeterminable, but substantial, cost of the pink gins.

Tompkins Armbruster, from the boning up he had done at Advisory, Inc., on information furnished by *Vital* before coming over to begin the job on the premises, was able to arrive quickly at this figure from his acquired knowledge of the average salary of a researcher who had been with the magazine a couple of years. From the way she knew so many people at the party and from her general line of overheard talk, Armbruster, who in addition to being an ace management consultant was a pretty fair detective, figured the girl must have been with the company at least that long.

He read the brief item he had written in the big notebook. Then he wet his pencil and added after it:

Comment: An almost unbelievable business practice. Certainly an outrageously flagrant one.

He closed the notebook, put it in the desk, locked the desk with a key he found in the center drawer and went on home to his apartment on the unfashionable West Side. Going down in the elevator—where he felt he would lose both eardrums from the hyenalike, shrilling, braying, howling, screaming, neighing, spastic-laughter sounds engendered by its full load of drunken employees departing from the British Empire Day party, all of whom, he was sure, had punched the time clock the very last thing before they left, making sure even that they went to the head and got their wraps before doing so, in order to mulct the company of the last possible minute—the management consultant said to himself: "Tompkins, this is not going to be like the job at Union Carbide —or at Simmons mattress."

4

The Common Good

Tompkins Armbruster, as he came to know him in the next few days, was the most relaxed man Gaskin had ever encountered. He seemed also the most thoroughly organized. His movements were easy, never jerky; his voice even and unemotional, never compulsive, never bursting out in unaware, nervous and uncontrolled torrents; his speech an exemplar of coherency, communicative but with none of the appalling, psychotic wastage of words in a day when speech has become widely a nervous mannerism rather than a means of communication; his whole manner restrained, moderate, logical. He was a paragon of Orderliness and Method. It was not strange that Gaskin, when first seeing him, had thought he looked like an assistant professor. He *was*, it turned out, an assistant professor, that is, had been one, and a good one, until two years ago, when he made a rather contrasting change of professions. Such was his genius, and such the abject salaries in America of those to whom we entrust the formation of our children's minds, as compared with the salaries of those to whom we entrust our economic and business aggrandizement, that in no time at all Tompkins Armbruster was making in salary with Advisory, Inc., precisely seven times what he had made as an assistant professor. He had gone from an annual salary of $5,000 to one of $35,000, though he had probably been assisting society and mankind far more in the $5,000-a-year job than he ever could in the $35,000 one. However, it is the very foundation stone of our hierarchy of caste and values that jobs where one is really being useful never pay much.

Whatever the truth generally in the saying that the ivory tower of academic life pulverizes in a man any and all ability to function well in the world of practical affairs—a proposition the writer keenly questions—it certainly did not prove true in the case of the assistant professor of English (for that was Tompkins Armbruster's field). He had turned out to be a wizard in the very elite of business callings, that of management consultant. The assistant professor had stormed and conquered the business world's innermost sanctum. And so also in the field of personal finance. In the past year he had tripled his investments, into which went most of his salary, since he was accustomed to living on little and found it hard to break the habit. And Armbruster had done it without trying particularly hard. In whatever he did Tompkins Armbruster was a craftsman, which used to be a great and noble word.

In the days following the British Empire Day party Tompkins Armbruster began to discover in *Vital* magazine an entire new world. He observed phenomena he had not before seen in his experience as a management consultant and he recorded them all exhaustively in the big loose-leaf notebook which he had brought to the job. Gaskin could not see what his roommate was composing in the pages of that black notebook, and Armbruster carefully and almost ceremoniously, as if it were the Book of Life, locked it in his desk whenever he left for the day. However, there was something Gaskin did see.

Tompkins Armbruster commenced to prepare a series of what Gaskin presently discovered were called, in the language of Armbruster's profession, "flow charts." These were so large and so grandly obvious, spread out of necessity on Armbruster's desk abutting Gaskin's at right angles, that Armbruster felt it best to explain them to Gaskin. A "flow chart" showed the course of any given operation of the magazine "from origin to terminus," as Armbruster put it in consultantese. Thus, in the case of pictures, it showed the pictures arriving in the building and exactly what happened to them, step by step—who handled them and how much time each step consumed—until that point at which they either ended up in printed form in the magazine for the millions to see or faded forever into the ignominious oblivion of the "Unused" file. Armbruster constructed another flow chart for written material which entered the building by teletype or otherwise. The point of these charts, he explained to Gaskin, was to get all the steps of all the operations out in front of you with the aim of seeing if there were any steps which could be shortened or even eliminated, for example, that a set of pictures might possibly leapfrog from 3 to 5, eliminating Step 4 altogether.

To some people this sort of thing may have been as dry as a man's throat the morning after a martini drunk, but to Gaskin it was fascinating. He saw in Tompkins Armbruster the highest manifestation of the business world. He also found Armbruster about as civilized a man, and as comfortable company, as he had run into.

Day after day Armbruster kept at his flow charts, pursuing his gargantuan task of documenting every movement made in the building whether by human or of thing. Now and then, after a good steady session of methodically charting a "flow," he would lift his head, lean back in his chair and perform the slow and easy ritual of filling his pipe and lighting up. This became the signal for himself and Gaskin to talk a little before Armbruster went back to his charts and Gaskin went back to whatever he was doing or not doing.

"How did you happen to renounce the noble profession of teaching, Armbruster?" Gaskin asked after they had been rooming together for several days. "Forgive me and ignore the question if I'm being too personal."

"Money."

"Well, that's a fine, explicit reason. In the grand old American tradition. 'By their income shall ye know them.' "

Wetting his pencil, Tompkins Armbruster went back to his flow charts.

A couple days later Armbruster paused and leaned back in his chair to stoke his pipe.

"Armbruster," Gaskin said, "yours is a rather freak profession and I've been sitting here these past few days trying to make up my mind whether or not it has any validity. I am still considering and I want to know more before reaching a final decision. I say this to make plain what an open mind I have. Now, you're out to make everything and everybody efficient. I see all that, most clearly. But this is what I've been sitting here wondering, turning over and over and over in my mind. What is efficiency?"

"What is efficiency?" The words were a little garbled coming out on the sucking of the pipe. "Hm, hm. Efficiency is, what would I say. Doing things better."

"Well, I'll pass over for the time being what you mean by 'better,' Armbruster. Obviously the definition would be arguable. Right now, however, in order to get on with it, I'll ask you: What is the purpose of doing things better? Tersely, isn't it to make more money for the management? And is that a valid end? Something for a grown man to be doing?"

"Hm, hm. That's certainly a part of it," Armbruster answered the first part of this series of questions. "A part, I say."

"Part? Don't infiltrate me with that capitalistic talk, Armbruster. It's all of it. You're with friends here, you know. You don't have to pretend with old Hank Gaskin."

"Well, it isn't. But even if it were," the consultant continued mildly, "I don't think it has yet been declared unconstitutional for a company to make money. Do you have some kind of religious opposition to the profit motive? If I'm not being too personal."

"The best practice is to answer a question with a question," Gaskin said. "So: Can you just offhand think of a lower motive?"

"Hm, hm . . ." pipe-sucking. It occurred to Gaskin that that was another good reason for smoking a pipe. You could just ruminate and suck on it like a cow its cud—*it was something to do*—while contemplating, and stall off answering questions much more handily. He made a mental note to consider taking up the dirty, noisy practice himself.

"It places the highest premium on greed, doesn't it now," Gaskin said. "In fact, if you run it out to its logical end, it exalts greed to a religion."

"Hm, hm . . ." pipe-sucking.

"Actually I'm as certain as that we sit here, that when man grows up morally the profit motive will be gerfloot forever, replaced by something. I raise these thoughts since your profession is so dedicated to the profit motive. You may want to start looking around for other work."

"I'm not panicking," Armbruster said.

"Well, something else is coming, comrade."

"You're not speaking of Communism?"

"Oh, Christ no. That places an even greater premium on greed than does Capitalism. Actually Communism is the ultimate and worst form of Capitalism—the whole bloody Soviet Union in fact is one big monopoly, very special privileges, including for the leaders free and unlimited decapitation privileges for citizens who irritate one. But I was saying: for the profit motive we live by, there will, *must*, some day be a replacement."

"Hm. What sort of replacement would you have in mind there?"

"I don't know. Goodness maybe."

"It'll never happen," the consultant said promptly. "Man will never grow up to it."

"Who are we to say? There are one or two around even now. Maybe they're the forerunners of a great new race." Gaskin was silent a moment. Then he said, almost to himself: "And maybe one day I'll walk out of here and join them."

Then, coming back quickly, he said: "But to the immediate. Armbruster, let me tell you something. Let me give you a friendly tip which I hope you'll take in the spirit in which it's offered. You'll never prevail here. I say that as a friend. Efficiency would ruin this company, sir. I know what I'm talking about. Believe me. Stop now before it's too late. Believe me, sir."

"I can't believe you."

"Naturally. Not to be inquisitive," Gaskin said inquisitively, "are you finding fecund soil for your studies here, Armbruster?"

Tompkins Armbruster drew in long and slowly on his pipe. Then he said quietly: "I never knew what inefficiency was until the day I walked into this building. *Vital* magazine is the management consultant's dream —or nightmare, I hardly know which."

Tompkins Armbruster went back to his flow charts—and to making entries in his big black loose-leaf notebook.

Over the following few days Gaskin began to detect in the management consultant the very dimmest portendings, like a hand of cloud in the distant blue sky, of a nervousness he was certain had not been there on his commencement of the job, at which point he remembered thinking he had never known such a relaxed man. One day when Gaskin was actually doing some work, writing the textblock and captions for a little story about a new craze of seeing how many people could be got into a telephone booth, he was surprised to hear Armbruster speak to him. He was surprised because the consultant had never interrupted him those few times when he had been working.

"Gaskin, old man. Doesn't that noise bother you?"

Gaskin looked up. "What noise?"

From the corridor just outside their office came a torrent of babbling, of shrill, laughing, screaming, neighing, braying, hysterical whinnying *talk* from people gathered around the coffee machine.

"Why, *that* noise," Armbruster said in stupefaction.

Gaskin focused and finally heard it. "Oh, *that*," he said. "You get to where you don't notice it at all. I suppose in the same way the electrical engineer doesn't notice the 150,000-kilowatt generator next to him in a power plant—I've been told."

"It would drive me"—Tompkins Armbruster hesitated, but he realized he was committed, it was the first time he could remember when speech had slipped out of him unaware—"crazy," he finished limply. "It *must* affect people's concentration," he said with an emotion unusual for him.

A fresh fusillade came from around the coffee machine, smashing into the room.

"Just listen to it!" the management consultant said.

With a rather abrupt movement he got up from his desk to go out and get a drink of water from the fountain down the corridor. He was almost hit in the head by a softball. Two writers were playing catch in the corridor; neither of them could throw very straight. Hugging the wall for protection he reached the water fountain. It was by a window. Standing there three grown men were making airplanes and sailing them out the window. He came back and sat down at his desk. Renewed bombardments of words from the corridor assaulted him unmercifully.

Tompkins Armbruster felt his pulse rate climb dangerously and his body break out in a harvest of duck bumps. The coffee machine! he thought. There was the whole trouble with this place: the coffee machine! Leaning abruptly over his desk he began to construct a flow chart on the object which *caused* the chief movement on the magazine.

The coffee machine made unchallengeably the world's worst coffee. However, mechanically it was quite a contrivance. By inserting a dime —it was one thing not paid for by the company—and pressing the correct button you could get coffee as you liked it, or at least the color and sweetness you liked it: black, black with sugar, with cream alone, with sugar and cream. The inserted dime set off a series of tremors and violent, ominous sounds in the machine, which shook and choked as if it were in its death rattle, a medley which could be heard three departments away and made one certain the machine was going to fly apart at any moment. This was succeeded by a fresh paroxysm, a medley of gurgling, rumbling, belching noises inside the machine, before, presently, there was utter silence, then: a paper cup dropped with a smart *click* down into a lipped holder and there was only the gurgle-gurgle sound of the awful stuff spewing out. It had an incredibly foul and moldy flavor, heightened by the waxy lining of the cup, which one also tasted strongly and a little sickeningly. It was hot, that was all one could say for it. However, the machine was one of the modern mechanical marvels—when it worked. It was constantly going out of order, so that when one put in a dime one got only the noises and an empty waxen cup. This, when it happened, outraged all *Vital* staff members, on principle.

A man who made $15,000 a year would then storm back in rage to his office, get out a sheet of expensive letterhead, ram it into his type-writer and in righteous fury beat out

This machine owes me ten cents—Anthony Pinckney

get his hands on some Scotch tape and march back and angrily plaster the sheet of paper on the machine with the sense of outraged righteous-ness and protest to tyranny of Martin Luther posting his theses on the church door at Wittenburg. Often the machine was literally blanketed in such documents and became nothing but a bulletin board of out-raged complaints.

The coffee machine was the most popular gathering place on the entire premises of *Vital* magazine. It was strategically located in the corridor exactly on the equator between the two poles of the magazine's largest departments, the National Affairs and Foreign News Depart-ments, which meant directly outside the Manners and Morals office. The location was also hard by the elevator bank, so that people—staff and visitors—poured out and by and oftentimes stopped there for a spell. It was a highly congested area. It was the traditional meeting place for exchanging chitchat and gossip of all kinds, or merely talking, a sport of which *Vital* employees were extremely fond and a practice encour-aged by the fact that the coffee machine was flanked on either side by some large vacant tables upon which one could heist oneself and relax and swing his legs or her legs while having one's coffee. Nobody knew the official reason the tables were there, for they had no other apparent purpose. All in all it was a fine place to kill time of ten minutes to an hour or more, and one could always count on finding similarly-minded people there to pass the time of day with. The company's time of day. It was a most pleasant place.

The fact that the coffee machine was located immediately outside the door of the office he was using, so that the cacophony of noise which poured incessantly from there into the office made his post something like occupying a parterre box in the Tower of Babel, perhaps ac-celerated Armbruster's fastening upon the coffee machine like the hawk upon the chicken. He saw unbelievable numbers of people congre-gated there, he saw a coming and going like a busy commuter station, but worst of all he heard the talk. The talk! He had never heard any-thing like it. He heard the most insane, shrill, spastic, useless jabber-ings, often going off into hysterical, bloodcurdling neighings of laughter that surely must be audible in the next building—talk no syllable of which had anything to do with the work of the magazine, and nothing to do with anything as a matter of fact. It was an outrage to Tompkins Armbruster and his profession. He began foxily to watch the faces and one day he saw one researcher make six trips to the coffee machine and spend a total of 124 minutes standing there or sitting, dangling legs moving contentedly, on one of those tables, as clocked on the stopwatch which Tompkins Armbruster professionally was never without and which, when the occasion called for it, he could start and stop in his pocket with no one being aware that some action of his was being timed to the second. Those tables! Armbruster thought. They had absolutely no functional use, no use pertinent to the legitimate business of the company, which was to publish a magazine; they did not hold dictionaries or reference books, they held nothing but arses. Little arses, big arses, and medium-sized arses: all conking out on the company's time.

Tompkins Armbruster, the ace management consultant from the distinguished firm of Advisory, Inc., seized upon the coffee machine as the heart and the core, the symbol and the seat, of everything that was wrong with *Vital* magazine.

Which was, he came slowly to the conviction, just about everything.

He began to get decidedly nervous on the job. So he speeded up his work, putting in longer hours, to get it over. He had never been so restless on a job. Above all, the infernal noise from that machine and the court which was always in progress around it was driving him mad. He felt his pulse rate climb dangerously and his skin convert itself more or less permanently into a canvas of duck bumps. If he didn't finish soon or if the noise didn't stop—and it never, never stopped—he felt he would go out of his mind or contract a coronary. Or both. Pushing himself viciously, Tompkins Armbruster finally finished—or finished, he told himself with a deep and melancholy sigh, as much as he would ever finish here. He put in twelve-hour days for a week on his recommendations.

Which he then presented to the management.

A committee of the management presided over by Harrison Duckworth, the vice managing editor, met to consider these recommendations, which Armbruster had entitled crisply, "Faulty Practices Among *Vital* Employees," and after a discussion on each which varied in intensity and length with the item reached the following decisions:

1. The two- and three-hour lunches. Decided it was impossible to halt these: There was no way to *force* anyone to return earlier from lunch. Checked off as "Unenforceable."

2. Staff members sitting around doing nothing. This recommendation revealed a lack of understanding of the essential nature of the magazine business, namely, that news events follow a sharply varying graph: nothing happening today, and war or other disaster breaking out tomorrow. It was the nature of the business of putting out a magazine, which was not the same as manufacturing Beautyrest mattresses on eight-hour shifts. In the event of the graph hitting high, all employees

would be needed, as reflected in the fact that on occasion every employee on the staff had worked eighteen-hour days. Obviously nothing could be done about it.

3. Airplane sailing and baseball catch in the corridors. These didn't hurt anybody. Even from thirty-four stories a paper airplane is incapable of injuring anyone walking on Fifth Avenue. No action.

4. Pilferage. Tabled like a hot brick. All the members of the committee silently remembered the time years ago when one unfortunate and overzealous vice managing editor made the mistake of sending around a sharp memo concerning the "wholesale vanishment of pencils." Unhappily the memo came to the attention of the editor-in-chief owner, who promptly demoted the vice managing editor and flashed down from his Olympian heights a thunderous and since-famous rescinding memo: "To All Staff Members: The day *Vital* magazine has to start worrying about pencil consumption, that day *Vital* magazine will close shop. Steal all you please." Remembering individually in silence —the subject was never mentioned aloud around *Vital*—the unhappy fate of the vice managing editor, the committee fled from this recommendation as a United States Army major general from a recommendation to set up official whorehouses for the troops.

5. The parties. No. The parties were one of the great attractions of working for *Vital,* and possibly the staunchest backbone of its remarkable *esprit.* Besides, they were tax-deductible, which meant the United States Government was paying a good share of the cost of each and every party.

6. Employees departing before 5:45. No action. Keeping idle people forcibly sitting around would only arouse the keenest resentment.

7. Employees arriving late for work and yet the time clock not showing the fact. There was no way to control this without hiring the entire corps of the Pinkerton's detective agency, a step which would be terrifyingly resented and resisted by the staff to the last man and girl. Checked off as "Unenforceable."

8. Noise. Impossible. No one could shut *Vital* employees up. If one could they wouldn't be good *Vital* types.

9. The coffee machine. Of all the recommendations the management committee considered this one the longest and in fact had several special meetings on it alone, having disposed of all others in a single meeting. The committee finally decided to act on the recommendation. It felt, perhaps, that it had to act on something the consultant had recommended to justify having retained him in the first place. It acted by removing the machine to the new and remote location recommended by Armbruster: a charwoman's closet not presently in use, and without facilities, such as empty tables, for sitting around and talking. And by installing a new machine which worked. It was the sole action taken on the management consultant's sheaf of recommendations.

The company paid the consultant his $15,000 fee. With vast relief Tompkins Armbruster fled; first to a much-needed vacation on the loneliest, most unpeopled and above all quietest island he could find, a tiny speck of almost uninhabited land in the Lesser Antilles—Gaskin got an ecstatic and exotic picture postcard from him there; then, after a long rest out of the range of human voices, with further relief into the arms of his next management consultant job, which was with a fine normal old firm named International Harvester.

One day after the removal of the old coffee machine and the situating of the new one in the new place, the greatest howl of protest in *Vital*'s history went up from its employees. One would have thought the management had tripled the hours, halved the pay and ordered all employees to say "sir" when speaking to a superior.

Acting with the speed of summer lightning the employees took their own action, as follows:

1. Presented to the management a petition-ultimatum composed by Sorehead Steadman, in a genre reminiscent of "The Song of the Shirt," and signed without exception by every employee. The petition began: "Whereas, we the undersigned employees of *Vital* magazine unanimously regard the removal of the employees' coffee machine from its traditional and convenient location as a high-handed, arbitrary, unilateral, brutal action reminiscent of the worst aspects of the robber-baron employees-be-damned Capitalism of the nineteenth century and of the scornful Bourbon spirit of the eighteenth, 'Let them eat cake . . .' " and ended with: "Unless this action be immediately revoked we, the employees of *Vital* magazine, will not be responsible for any inefficiency that may occur in the form of lost pictures, embarrassing errors getting into the magazine, and the like."

2. One morning in a protest demonstration walked en masse out of the building at 10:15 A.M., into the counters surrounding the building, where they all sat drinking cup after cup of coffee for one full hour and then went back to work at 11:15 A.M. Informed the management that pending such time as the action in regard to the coffee machine should be revoked, the demonstration would be repeated in the morning and afternoon of each day, with a ten-minute increase daily in the absent periods until the "coffee break" exactly equaled the full working day.

The management was thunderstruck by the employees' reaction. The employees furthermore let it be known that they not only violently preferred the old location for the coffee machine but actually preferred the old coffee machine itself to the new one. This stupefied the management, which was unaware of a curious truth:

The employees of *Vital* actually took a delight in the coffee machine's vagaries and even in the horrible liquid it gave forth and, yes, even in the fact it often gave forth nothing, so that they had to scream at it and plaster it with their outraged protests. This was not a general state of masochism so much as a tradition, like a fondness for some flea-bitten, mangy, hair-shedding, bleary-eyed, coughing, scratching, slobbery, smelly, good-for-nothing old dog in whose behalf nothing can be said except that he has been around a long time. *Vital* employees loved it and lavished fondly upon it their own special brand of Paternalism.

The management instantly capitulated. To everything. It threw out the new machine. It brought the old machine back. It brought it back to its previous location, where *Vital* employees could resume their favorite pastime and, indeed, urgent need—which was to *talk*—deprived of which they were as querulous and irritable as a baby deprived of its bottle. This meant the management got nothing for its $15,000 management consultant fee. However, everybody, including the management, agreed it had been an interesting, and certainly illuminating, experience. And the management could take solace in one abiding thing. The chairman of the committee, Harrison Duckworth, who had played a leading role in bringing the consultant in in the first place, expressed it best.

"After all," said Duckworth, "why should any company change when it is putting out the best product of its kind in the country. Correction: the world. After all we *are* the world's greatest magazine. Our watchword, Gentlemen, should be something I have said over and over again and will repeat now: 'If it works don't tinker with it.' "

The management agreed most of all that in future everyone must be very careful before tampering with the slightest *Vital* employee benevolence, and to show its heart, if not its head, was in the right place added two new benevolences which it announced by general memo:

1. In future it would pay one-half of the round-trip fare for any staff member who cared to take his month's annual paid vacation in Europe.

2. Commencing immediately *Vital* would add to its medical facilities on the twenty-third floor three full-time dentists to fill free all *Vital* cavities.

So in a way Tompkins Armbruster's job on *Vital* magazine did do something for the good—for the common, not the management, good. But that, Gaskin told himself—in a rather fondly nostalgic mood for old Armbruster, to whom these fresh benevolences were in a way due— was what was important: The common good.

5

The American Royalty

The only persons in America who can order the President of the United States around with impunity are the photographers. When a photographer in a no-nonsense tone barks instructively, "Raise your hand and give us a wave now, Mr. President!" the hand is dutifully raised, the wave executed. When a photographer yells sharply, "Give us a smile, Mr. President!" the smile is forthcoming. Usually the order is this wheedling "Give us . . ." something or the other, in the manner in which one deals with a not overly bright child. There is no more revealing index of the relationship in which the photographer stands to the President than that implied in the "Give us" phrase. One or two of our Presidents tried to fight against this servitude but finally surrendered and from then on did as they were told. They discovered that it is absolutely impossible to escape domination by the photographers. To the credit of these Presidents, and their ability to rise to great events, it may be said that they recognized when they were licked and thereafter devoted their attention to matters where they had a fighting chance, such as getting bills through Congress, keeping us out of war and trying to figure out what the Communists were up to next.

All of the Presidents since the onset of the camera have commented on this domination of the President by the photographers. The phrase "One more" as a peremptory command, never disobeyed or disobeyable, from the photographers to the President has become so hackneyed that one President of the United States, in a rather melancholy gesture, founded the "One More Club," consisting of photographers and one civilian member, himself. This same President was once obliged to make a rapid explanation to the Shah of Iran when he met this visiting monarch at the airport in Washington. The Shah was somewhat taken aback, not to say thunderstruck, to see and hear the photographers, hurling themselves around like a pack of jabbering apes shouting, now brusque and snarling, now wheedling, and always remarkably loud and insistent orders at the Republic's leader, not to mention his royal self— the latter such commands as "Hey, Shaw, give us a wave!" and "Hey, Shaw, smile, we said smile. *Smile!*" "The photographers, they are to be obeyed, Your Majesty," gently explained the President; "they are the only royalty we have in America," the President apparently feeling that this identification was the only possible way to get the salient point across to a king and tendering the explanation in a laconic and resigned but helpful, orienting and fatherly manner to the young, flabbergasted and perplexed Shah.

No truer definition of the photographer's unique status in our society has ever been projected. Any attempt or even suggestion of rebellion from these limpid truths and what photographers consider virtually their constitutional, not to say divine, right is without exception unhesitatingly dealt with by the photographers, that is to say, ruthlessly crushed. Their dominion is by now unchallenged on American soil, and any American public figure who may be foolishly led to think otherwise and seek a bit of privacy is quickly educated by the photographers themselves. Even on foreign soil and with foreign statesmen, who with their own photographers have managed to remain in a posture of comparative equality, the American photographer is almost impossible to outflank, being the only American left who still looks upon himself as having extraterritorial rights anywhere. No one in the world is a match for the American photographer. Once, one of them, approaching aftwise, placed his hand on the arm of Sir Winston Churchill on the island of Bermuda, which is Empire soil, where the well-known British statesman had gone for a rendezvous of state with the President of the United States. The Prime Minister was walking from his plane to his automobile, and all the photographer had in mind was to turn him crisply around for a picture. The look on the face of the Briton, as his great leonine head slowly rotated in disbelieving astonishment at this impertinence, and his rumbling, menacing roar, "Young man, unhand me," were of a genre which had previously made the Empire's most powerful enemies tremble. It did not, however, for a moment faze the American photographer. On the contrary. At that instant he leapt back and shot the picture which is one of the greatest and justly most famous ever taken of the eminent statesman: the look of determination and rumbling anger on his face, the mouth-gripped cigar and the slightly raised cane are the very quintessence of the British Empire at defiant bay.

But within any aristocracy there are degrees and degrees of nobility. And *Vital* photographers were a breed apart, the noblest of the noble.

Vital photographers were a breed apart. In the first place, as the world's greatest picture magazine, *Vital* had assembled on its masthead by far the greatest array of photographic talent in the history of the camera. More than any other single influence, more indeed than all other influences combined, *Vital* made photography what it is today. To give just one example, *Vital* photographers created what one of them, Wolfgang Breuber von und zu Strassburg, first called "the unguarded moment." Even today most newspaper photographs are of the posed variety that came in with the invention of the camera. For instance, the eternal dreary "gimmick" picture typified by the classic month-of-August one of a pretty girl in a bathing suit sitting legs crossed on a 500-pound cake of ice and holding an outsized thermometer showing the temperature to be 98° Fahrenheit and lending itself to some outrageously Kute caption such as "Kool Kitten." There are hundreds of such hoary classics in the run-of-the-muck photographer's book and all carry the label of 100-proof corn. In a picture of four people it is having three look at one who presumably is saying something weighty, making some point with the traditional raised forefinger, maybe holding up a red apple, and the whole quartet as stiff and self-conscious as only such photographers can make them. In politics it is the candidate holding a slice of watermelon from which, for a half-dozen pictures or so, his mouth transfixedly open, indeed almost paralyzed open from holding the position so long, and his molars gold and glittering, he is about to take an ear-to-ear bite. After the picture ordeal is over he can get a fork or, for all the photographers care, throw the damn thing away. In sports the man who pitches a no-run no-hitter is told to describe two "O's" with his two thumbs and two forefingers and to grin into the camera like an idiot child. And so on. And so on. How seldom one sees a real, communicative photograph in an American newspaper! A *Vital* photographer was as far above either setting up or shooting such pictures as Cézanne was above painting the pathetic trash that is exhibited twice annually in the Washington Square outdoor "art" exhibits.

Indeed, on news stories *Vital* photographers never even bothered to shoot when other photographers were shooting. They waited until the subject thought the photographic ordeal was over and was doing someting natural, such as scratching the back of his ear, blowing his nose, telling his assistant what for, or holding his hand against his brow, to start shooting. "The unguarded moment" philosophy of photography therefore produced pictures that were far more accurate, infinitely more communicating, not to say devastating, of the subject than the dull, calculatingly smiling or calculatingly stern pictures that commonly disfigure the nation's newspapers. The remarkable thing is that after all these years newspapers still haven't caught on to this, leaving *Vital* an easy supremacy in the field. An interesting study could be made by someone working on his doctor's dissertation at some place like, say, the Columbia School of Journalism, of the pictures carried by newspapers and by *Vital* on the same story. The study would reveal a startling difference in the quality of the two and explain why *Vital*, though coming out several days after newspaper coverage of an event, in effect gives the reader his first real photographic reportage of it.

One technical reason for *Vital*'s ability to get "the unguarded moment," such as the blowing of his presidential nose by someone like the Chief Executive of the United States, was that its photographers operated almost exclusively with the 120-millimeter and especially the 35-millimeter camera. The customary camera used by newspaper photographers is the shoebox-like Speed Graphic. It is so large, conspicuous and clumsy an instrument that a myopic elephant would know if he were being photographed with it. The greatest photographer in the world could not get unguarded moments with a Speed Graphic. Its very presence is a warning for the subject to be on his guard, and, in any event, by the time the photographer gets it into place the subject can be thoroughly posed, composed and properly artificial. By comparison the 35-millimeter camera is so unobtrusive as to be almost invisible and can be flicked to the eye-shooting position and have several frames taken before the subject has the remotest idea that some pretty private motions of his have been recorded for all time on cellulose acetate emulsion.

But his professional tools were but a minor facet of the *Vital* photographer's enormous superiority over his brethren in the field. His real Brahminism lay in the great philosophical gap that stretched like a Grand Canyon between him and the run-of-the-muck journalistic photographers. As the great von und zu Strassburg once classically put it, "Da truly great photographer does not geeve two fooks for da equipment he is using. Da truly great photographer can get da greatest fooking picture in da world with a fooking Brownie. Vat counts," Wolfgang added in words that became memorable and very nearly scriptural at *Vital,* especially to the photographers, "is da *peersonality* of da photographer."

Now von und zu Strassburg meant a good deal by that statement, a good deal more than a cursory reading of the word "personality" would suggest. He meant that the personality of the truly great photographer was such as to reduce his subject to an almost Pavlovian submission. But—and this is the great secret of it—a *natural* submission, to where the subject was and remained always natural, at least while the story was being shot, to where he became literally oblivious of the photographer's presence and did everything he would naturally do if no photographer and indeed nobody at all were present. This is the entire philosophy and secret of *Vital* photography, the philosophy and secret that have made it by far the world's greatest photography: *The subject must literally become unaware that the photographer and his camera are even there.* It was a form of hypnosis.

A case in point which Wolfgang liked to cite as an example of what he was talking about was his assignment to do a photographic essay on a woman who had America's largest television following, for a daily show she did called "Love and Iron Are How to Bring Up a Family." The show dealt with the problems and vicissitudes of the mother-wife of the house in rearing and bossing a family and consisted largely of inspirational talks from the creature in a manner that combined the more emotional aspects of Pola Negri, Louisa May Alcott and Dorothy Dix with the attitudinal aspect of Bismarck the Iron Chancellor, with heavy instructional emphasis on keeping the husband-father in his place as a kind of tolerated lackey and regrettably necessary part of having a family, living in eternal terror that what few crumb-sized privileges he has will be instantly withdrawn by the queen bee if he steps out of place for a moment. Thus the American man. When Wolfgang arrived at her home to have an introductory chat before starting on the month-long assignment, the woman made only one request, which she considered mild enough: that he not photograph her while she was drinking.

"You know how those goddamn people are," she told Wolfgang, taking a cozy, you-and-me-artists-against-the-ignorant-masses tone. "I'm Miss Inspiration to thirty-five million American women who are too stupid to think for themselves, and I don't think my sponsor, the pious son of a bitch, would like it if a picture of me drinking a beaker of Beefeater came out. You and I know these people," she added with a comradely familiarity—the two artists against the crass Philistine businessman—that could not have been more misplaced.

Without a word Wolfgang instantly got to his feet and picked up his hat.

"Madam," he said, in tones so frozen they sent a chill of distilled fear coursing through the Messiahess of thirty-five million American women, "it eez eempossible for me to conteenue. Dat request of yours vould mean I vould haf to ration myself in vat eez an effort to do a photographic and *troo* exploration een depth on you. I vould haf to constantly tell myself, 'Von und zu Strassburg, dere arc certain times you cannot shoot.' Madam: dis eez eentolerable. Abso-ootly eentolerable!" Von und zu Strassburg waved his hand across his face. "You vould be self-conscious and I know *I* vould be. Madam"—and Wolfgang gave a St. James bow which managed to be royally dismissing, even though he was the one about to depart—"it has been somevat pleasant—in any ee-vent een-formative—to meet you. I vill not vaste any more of your time—nor certainly any more of mine dan has already been vasted. I bit you gut day."

And he turned for the door. The poor woman was so taken aback by this commanding manner, seeing every performer's golden dream —a story in *Vital* magazine—fleeing before her frantic face, that she immediately was on her feet, instantly withdrawing her objection, and begging Wolfgang to reconsider. After a little thought he agreed to stay on, provided she not so forget herself again.

"I cannot possibly ooperate vitout an abso-ootly free hand," Wolfgang explained, waving his hand across his face. "I must be troo to vat da camera brings out, *vatever* it is. Ven I am behind da camera I cannot ration my fooking self."

The woman humbly agreed to everything and Wolfgang then proceeded to shoot the story, which explored in such depth and truth that eight weeks later a ten-page *Vital* story was on the newsstands all over America showing the woman not only drinking gin all over the layout but giving rather decadent parties, playing her favorite game of dollar-a-chip poker, and other unguarded-moment photography. In nearly every picture she had a drink in her hand, so obsessed—and not inaccurately so, as a matter of fact—had Wolfgang become by the concept that Beefeater gin was the whole key to her. It would have appeared from the pictures that he rationed himself only when she was not drinking. She more or less staggered through the layout, and some readers who did not bother to read the text actually thought it was a picture story on alcoholism.

The sponsor immediately canceled Miss Inspiration's contract, but the woman could console herself that she had made *Vital*. In this connection it might be added that professional people would do almost anything to make *Vital,* even if it meant they might not be professional people much longer. This astonishing fact, with its unexplored masochistic overtones, could be the subject of another doctor's dissertation, by, say, someone at the Missouri School of Journalism, for it did much to make possible *Vital*'s existence.

"Never accept da lie," Wolfgang said in relating this incident and holding up his terms on this story as the model of the photographic code. "Never take part in da lie. And never take da back talk or da eensolence from a subject. Da subject must *alvays* be made to know who is da master and who is merely da canvas for his mastery: dat is, da fooking subject."

The *Vital* photographer's relation vis-à-vis his subject brings up a fascinating matter basic to the magazine's entire rationale. This is a matter of principle. If there was one principle *Vital* magazine was based on it was the Principle of Selectivity. May we repeat that word please: Selectivity. This principle operated on a number of levels. In the first place a *Vital* photographer "shot" prodigiously. On a five-day story he might easily shoot two thousand pictures. Out of these, only a dozen might make the magazine. *If* the story ran at all. For not only were far more pictures shot on a given story than were used. In addition—the wondrous Principle of Selectivity working up a full head of steam now —a good many more stories were shot than were ever used at all, even to the extent of a single picture. Selectivity. To achieve this principle *Vital* naturally had to upset a lot of people's lives for nothing. There was no helping it and the magazine never flinched in making any request for a picture or for a picture story, whatever its inconvenience or difficulty to the subject or its unmentioned mortality chances.

There were cases of people almost having a nervous breakdown after a week of a *Vital* photographer's shooting them. Once he was assigned to do a picture story on somebody a *Vital* photographer really took

over that person's life. He demanded that he be a subject very nearly in
the classic sense of that word when kings of divine right sat upon
thrones. The *Vital* photographer carried about him like a very nearly
visible aura the lofty, art-true concept that there was nothing, including
a pretty full debasement, the subject should not be willing and even
anxious to do for his, that is, the photographer's, Art. He assumed the
unquestioned and unquestionable right to be anywhere any time with
anybody doing anything. A *Vital* subject often had to turn some pretty
astonishing handsprings, emotional and physical, and hurl his normal
life out of joint most thoroughly, besides undergoing a nerve-racking and
in some cases downright traumatic experience, and no *Vital* photographer had a moment's hesitation in asking him to do so: indeed, with the
proper hauteur of the true Artist, considered it only natural that he do
so, certainly not a matter involving thanks. If there was any thanking
or calming to be done, that was the researcher's concern, not the Artist-
Photographer's, who had loftier thoughts to occupy his mind than the
piddling pettishnesses of subjects. Some of these subjects were decidedly
important and extremely busy people in both their own and the general world's eyes, but that hardly impressed *Vital* and certainly did not
affect in the slightest either the request or the operation of the Principle. Many a *Vital* photographer had monopolized the important and
busy life of a household name for an entire week or even an entire
month and nothing in the form of a printed story had ever come from
it. Selectivity.

The magazine's position in this matter was the unassailable, certainly
unquenchable, and even moral one that nothing should ever be allowed
to stand in the way of principle, however inconvenient or upsetting to
somebody—else. And that furthermore, without the Principle of Selectivity the magazine's high standards could never be maintained. Having
infinitely more pictures and many more stories to choose from than
were ever run, and only those that were photographically best being
chosen: This lay at the very heart of *Vital* magazine's enormous success. That was the magazine's position, and there is no problem understanding it. But from the point of view of the subject, having violently
disarranged his life for a hearty hunk of time in the hearty expectation
of getting in the great magazine; having all but debased himself for
some brassy, superior photographer who took it as only his due; and
then for nothing to come from it except a few prints for his scrapbook
from the *Vital* Complimentary Picture Department: well, sir, the wrath
of such persons was seldom receptive to the reasonable explanation of
principle of any kind. Nevertheless, and here is another curious fact,
even people such as politicians and performers, among whom this fact
was very well known by reputation—having had friends or colleagues
who had undergone the ordeal for a *Vital* story that never ran—would
still without exception agree to do so themselves if asked. And even,

and this is most curious of all, those who had personally suffered the
disordering and the ordeal on a previous story attempt without visible
results, would always readily overcome their previous memorable wrath
and say yes to a fresh disordering of their lives, a fresh ordeal, when
Vital got another idea. This is a mystery. It was a case surely of either
or both: masochism; or hope springing eternal in the human breast that
this time they would actually make *Vital*.

The subject's subsequent wrath at the non-appearance of the story
could not have been of less interest to the *Vital* photographer, who
never saw the creature again once the shooting was over and by the
time the wrath developed was long since into another story and working
on fresh meat of a subject. And in any event the photographer took the
position expressed once more by the great von und zu Strassburg.

"Dey should be honored to be shot by us vedder it runs or not," von
und zu Strassburg luminously put the *Vital* photographer's position.
"Vat concern is dat of da subject's vedder it runs in da magazine or not?
Vunce he is finished as a subject, vat business is eet of his vat happens
to da artist's vork? Vould a painter consult a model on vat to do vit his
picture? And in any case it is no sveat off our fine ahsses."

Thus, personality. Without exception every single *Vital* photographer had personality. It was as necessary a piece of equipment for a
Vital photographer as the knowledge of how to operate a light meter.
They may each and all have been highly narcissistic, egocentric and all
the other handbook words that the psychiatric quacks like to toss
around, but these qualities are an absolute *sine qua non,* in the Tuscan
phrase, for a great photographer or for that matter for any creative soul.
Leastwise we've never known one who wasn't. If the world expects
great works of creation out of these people, let it learn to put up with
the fact that no Rotarian has ever yet won the Nobel Prize for Literature,
no Kiwanian has ever been a great artist, no Lion has ever been conductor of the New York Philharmonic, and no Optimist has ever been
named Photographer of the Year.

Within the above general characterization the individual personalities of *Vital* photographers varied enormously. Aside from all being
absolutely first-rate photographers, among them were some of the most
interesting men on earth; often, indeed, far more interesting than the
subjects they shot. Above all they were creative, using that word in its
classic conceptual sense of the soaring flights of the imagination. As
the clods of the world should know by now, the creative personality
must not be fettered lest it stifle. A code that would be a thing of honor
for most men might be a literal evil for the creative personality, steel
handcuffs binding the imagination. Rules that apply to the ordinary
mortal do not, and must not, apply to the creative one. The awareness of this special code of the creative artist was felt keenly by all *Vital*
photographers, they saw to it that it was felt by others who associated

with them either as co-workers or subjects, and all this made them very interesting men, as well as creative artists, indeed.

Montgomery Shanks was one of these.

There were only two things in life that interested Montgomery Shanks: photography and fornication. He never (unless it was on professional assignment) went to a play, never read a book, never played tennis, never saw the ballet, never heard a concert, never went to an art museum, although, with the exception of tennis, some of the world's great manifestations of these sundry arts were all within five minutes' walking distance of his apartment. Of his two interests it would have been impossible to say which was paramount, for the simple reason that both were. It would be like a man given a choice between giving up either eating or breathing.

It has been often said that some men are ruined in their careers by women. This is probably a piece of fraudulent trash. In any event, with Shanks, far from being competitive or destructive, the two interests were thoroughly complementary one to the other, as will be shown. Each helped each most prodigally. Montgomery Shanks was a superb craftsman in both. He was a very good photographer. And he was very good at women. He was really a specialist and like any good specialist he had become highly expert in his field—his two fields, in Shanks' case. Expert—and dedicated, truly dedicated, to both fields, and to nothing in the world else. Any evening not spent with a woman was to Shanks an evening insanely lost for all time—unless, of course, it was an evening spent shooting a story. There were almost no evenings in the 365 of them possessed by the average year not spent in one or the other of these two enterprises. His reputation with women was well known, as such a reputation always is, and it had the geometric effect it always has, which was to attract ever more women to him. In the same manner of that expression "Money makes money." It would have been impossible for him to itemize or even remember all the women he had slept with. Sometimes it would have been very difficult for him to remember a woman, or at least her name, he had slept with as little as a month ago.

Merely to be with Shanks was exhilarating. Could the reason have been that all men who are interesting and alive, all who do anything in this world (we except the religious), have this abiding and vibrating dedication to *woman,* and want, *want,* women and go after them and get them? We deduce: this and accomplishment in his work usually go together in a man. If you were with Shanks the chances were that you were either in his vermilion Cadillac convertible, by special arrangement with the people at General Motors the only one in the world painted that particular color, or in his Central Park South apartment, for Shanks spent nearly all the time when he wasn't actually shooting a story in one or the other of these two locations. The Cadillac was new every year, but he had had the apartment for several years. The apartment was numerically small, consisting of only two rooms, a living room and a bedroom, both with breathtaking views of Central Park through the glass that was the complete wall on that side. What the apartment lacked in number of rooms it made up eagerly in their size. Outside of one or two commercial places like the Starlight Roof, the Commodore grand ballroom, and Roseland, Shanks must have had two of the largest rooms on all of Manhattan Island. They were panoramic in their acreage. Part of this was professional need. One end of the living room, into which a squash court would have fitted like a closet, was used by Shanks as a studio on the occasions he shot a posed picture, such as a cover. The bedroom, speaking with regard to a creative artist and his needs, was quasi-professional. Its central piece was a bed that was almost unbelievable in its dimensions. It could probably have slept a dozen people racked alongside, and when one looked at it one's first reaction was, "A bed just can't be that large," and one's second was to wonder where in the world anyone could even buy a bed like that and if so how could it possibly be got into the bedroom. The answer to the first part of this second reaction was that one could not buy that size bed. Shanks had had it specially made. The answer to the second part was that such a bed could not be got into the apartment. The carpenters had constructed it on the spot. Once Hank Gaskin asked Shanks why in the world he had wanted a bed of that size.

"How should I know?" the photographer said querulously. He didn't like to be asked questions. "It would take someone else to figure out why. All I know is that ever since I was a kid I wanted a bed you could turn around in."

"I think the ambition has been gratified," Gaskin said. "You could turn the Caddy around in this one. You know how the magazine loves to use superlatives. I imagine if we were doing a story on you we could safely red-check this as the largest bed in the world."

"I never gave a crap for *why* things are, only *what* they are," Shanks said tartly, and pretty profoundly when you stop to think about it. "Probably some stupid brain-quack would say it was because I had to sleep on a cot when I was a kid. Matter of fact I did have to sleep on a cot. I never give a crap for reasons like that or even going into them. It's all phony as a three-dollar bill, all of that crap."

At the foot of the bed, screen aimed inward and with bedside controls, was a twenty-four-inch television set. That is as big as they come and Shanks had probably found out you couldn't even have one made to order any larger. Monty had big tastes—in cars, beds, television sets. He was a high liver, both on his own money and the magazine's. His expense accounts were legendary but they were never padded. Monty just believed in living.

"What else is money for?" he said once in the simple but eloquent philosophy that so characterized him. "I can't sleep with money, I can't eat money—what else is money for?"

Shanks had an air of great swagger and spectacular insolence. It was a quality enormously appealing to women, since he also had the looks and the physique to go with it. He was of only medium height but his shoulders were broad, his belly flat, his hair black and thick, his face very manly in a manliness enhanced by a broken nose he had incurred professionally when he went up on a Ferris wheel, which he had hired for the afternoon to photograph the crowd below at a state fair, and while leaning far over to get the angle he wanted fell off. He did everything in the grand manner. Wherever he went he took hotel suites, never rooms. He ate only in the very best restaurants. He tipped only with money that folded. It always pleased him if a story seemed to require his hiring a private plane or helicopter. He loved to put that $50-an-hour down on his expense account. As for women, he had them in both quantities and quality that would have made an Arab oil potentate go into a trembling black rage of jealousy.

One other word needs saying about the supernal manner in which women were attracted to Montgomery Shanks. It is true that everything about him—his looks, his swagger, his air of assumption that any woman would find it a pretty considerable undertaking to resist him: all were the most powerful weapons in his arsenal of love. But as if these were not enough, Shanks had another weapon of inestimable power and, what was more, one possessed by not over three dozen men in the entire Republic. A word about this power.

To understand this power the following background, please: The accessory advantages that attend upon being a journalistic photographer and especially a New York photographer and most, most especially a *Vital* photographer are multifold. There is much ignorance as to these advantages and for the benefit of any of our younger readers as yet unsettled on a profession we wish briefly to point out one or two of them. The power of being the only human beings alive who can issue commands to the President of the United States, not to mention to such lesser lights as Cabinet officers, senators and movie stars, is one of the rewarding things about being a photographer. What this does for the ego may be easily imagined. The profession of photographer may be the only one where the inferiority complex never exists. But besides the power there are many many other advantages attendant upon the profession. And one chief of all.

And here we have a thing to say.

What we want to say had best be said in forthright English. To wrap it up in language would take several pages to say what can be said more communicatively in a single sentence. The sentence is this: If Don

Juan were alive today he would unhesitatingly choose as profession that of photographer.

Consider: Only the photographer, of all men living, can instruct a woman, a complete stranger, to hoist her dress halfway up her thighs for the picture. Only the photographer—for instance on a story *Vital* may be doing on the career of a model who hopes the pictures he is taking will if and when published transform her into a million-dollar-a-year movie actress and a household name more famous in the run-of-the-muck American household than that of the President, or certainly the most distinguished novelist we have around live or dead—can eyewitness a woman-stranger dressing and undressing, for purposes of photographing her amid these sometimes private operations. A *Vital* photographer can readily inform a movie starlet, and with more arrogance than apology, that he desires a picture of her taking a bath: the first one in the history of the motion-picture industry has yet to refuse. In addition *Vital* did innumerable stories involving very appealing nonprofessional-beauty girls: a secretary coming to New York to live and have the big adventure, whatever that is; a picture of a young handsome widow of a dead handsome-pilot-hero husband; a story on the new rage in oriental, choke-collar, slit-skirt dresses, the most feminine and alluring in the world. The opportunities of a photographer, especially a *Vital* photographer, for meeting women were literally endless, and especially under circumstances where the possibility lurking in them of rapid after-hours deepening of the acquaintanceship—what look was in her eyes when she started undressing for his picture, et cetera—is so readily evident. In fact, smashes you in the face.

In short: No one whose real interest in life is women (and besides the arts and the fully, truly spiritual life it is the only really worthwhile one, the only other productive of real joy) should ever even consider going into any profession other than photographer. That is our advice to all young men.

But even over other photographers the *Vital* photographer possesses many advantages in this area as in all others. One of these is what might be called the "cover syndrome."

Occasionally a *Vital* cover was something esoteric like the President of the United States or a Kansas wheat field. But on at least nine issues out of ten the cover would be some beautiful young female. The cover was meant for one purpose only—to sell the magazine—and the differential in sales between an issue with a wheat field for a cover and one with a beautiful wheat-haired, wheat-bosomed, wheat-thighed young female for a cover, a differential proved by actual tests, was of dimensions sufficient to put the fear of God in anyone on the business side. As for its worth to a subject, the figure of a million dollars was the round one generally used by the advertising and public relations crowd when attempting to place a value on a *Vital* cover; by which these dollar-sign scorpions meant it was worth that in publicity to, for example, a hopeful but unestablished young starlet.

One other general comment: It was absolutely and incorruptibly impossible, directly or indirectly, to buy a *Vital* cover. Not for fifty million dollars.

To proceed: Over the years a number of women had capitulated, if that is the word, to Montgomery Shanks at least partly and in some cases solely because of the conviction that he was going to get them on the cover of *Vital* magazine and that this capitulation would expedite the achievement if not actually be the differential between gaining the achievement and not gaining it. Lest this statement prompt the reader to an unfavorable assessment of the code of honor held by our photographer, we hasten to make explicit that Shanks in point of fact had an extremely clear-cut and unvarying code of honor in this matter. Not so much as once in a brilliant and even distinguished photographic career had Montgomery Shanks in the slightest, directly or indirectly, promised a woman she would make *Vital*'s cover if she would confer upon him that gift on the conferment of which women place such a curiously exalted value, as if they had only one of it to give and having given it once would have no more left, when the fact is, of course, precisely the opposite, that the more it is given the more there is of it to give, and the more exquisite it is, much like the hibiscus bush which needs regularly to be plucked in order to put forth more, and more elegant, blooms.

Shanks had never promised one of them a blessed thing. But women are creatures of great imagination, particularly if the matter at point concerns a dear ambition of theirs, and placing such a ridiculously high and twisted value on this possession—as if it were the only one of its kind anywhere, some unique jewel existent only in the number of one, when as a matter of common knowledge the exact same possession is held by one out of every two people on earth—they can easily conclude in a delusion entirely self-fertilizing that the conferment of this possession can obtain for them anything in the world they may happen to desire. There are few women in America who would not be honored to be a *Vital* cover, and there are some, a not insignificant number, who are thrilled beyond belief at the prospect and would do just about anything to be one, so that Shanks had had many a free gift given to him willingly by women, many of whom did not give it at all readily to other men despite the irrefutable philosophy expressed in the lines above, which philosophy might be called the "hibiscus syndrome." No. Shanks had never promised one of them a thing. It was not Montgomery Shanks' fault if women gave it to him because they thought this would get them on *Vital*'s cover. Many a time he had asked himself this rhetorical question: Am I responsible for what women *think*?

In addition to their false assumption that the conferment of this gift on our photographer implied the guarantee of an equally major return gift from him in the form of their gorgeous likeness on the cover of the nation's greatest magazine, these women made a second and even more profoundly false assumption. This was that Shanks had the *power* to put them on the cover of *Vital* in the first place. In point of fact no such power resided in one iota in Shanks or in any other of *Vital*'s photographers. The situation in regard to *Vital* covers was this: The magazine had on its staff some three dozen photographers. In the course of a given week perhaps ten of these photographers would be assigned to shoot a specific subject selected by the picture editors as a "candidate" for a cover. From the ten or twelve subjects, Cy Tadlock, the managing editor, would then, upon the arrival of all the pictures in New York, select one to be the following week's cover. Thus, in the first place, a cover was almost never used unless it had been assigned specifically for cover shooting. And in the second place, the selection of the cover was done in New York by a man—the managing editor—who never even saw in the flesh the actual cover candidates but only their pictures and selected solely on the incorruptible basis of the pictures themselves. The notion that Montgomery Shanks could march in to the managing editor and say, "Here is a picture of Agnes Youngblood. I would appreciate it as a personal favor if you would put her on the cover in view of the fact she conferred upon me the other evening an interesting gift," was as preposterous as the idea that someone who had contributed ten dollars to the Republican Campaign Fund could march in to the President of the United States and brace him, "See here, I gave ten dollars to elect you President, and in pursuance of the time-honored political philosophy of *quid pro quo* I expect you to get me a million-dollar contract to make uniforms for the Army. You hear?" Shanks had absolutely nothing whatsoever to do with who appeared on the cover of *Vital* magazine. But to indoctrinate every Mary, Jane and Betty he ran across who had ambitions to be a *Vital* cover and for the sake of this ambition hurled her gift at him—to indoctrinate her, we say, in the profound complications and intricacies of getting out a large magazine week after week would have been a hopeless undertaking, so Shanks was forced not even to try.

Naturally the "cover syndrome" in Shanks' operations with women could hardly be activated with those who happened to work for the magazine and knew damn well just how a cover became a cover. However, no greater proof could be offered of the fact that Shanks' possession of the aura of the "cover syndrome" was only another weapon in his arsenal of love, and that, having so many other weapons, he could get along very well without it, than his success with *Vital* researchers.

On a story the *Vital* photographer worked with what was listed on the masthead as a "reporter," and around the office was called a "researcher." The official function of the "reporter" was to get captions and otherwise gather material that would be shaped like loose putty by *Vital* "writers" into the textblocks which appeared under or alongside the photographer's pictures. This was the official function. In theory the reporter was the photographer's equal, and that was also a theory. The actual relationship of the *Vital* reporter to the *Vital* photographer in the field was much like that of the sixteenth-century English lackey-valet to his titled master, and quite a bit more. The reporter carried the photographer's bags and extra cameras, took care of hotel arrangements, and especially and above all kept him soothed and happy, since a creative artist must be in the proper frame of mind to shoot the story properly and creatively, and *Vital* photographers were temperamental and not at all infrequently lordly in a way that would make a La Scala diva look like a shy and thumb-sucking ribbon-haired girl intoning her first catechism. The reporter did all these things whether it happened to be a man or a girl reporter, with the one exception of bag-carrying. If a girl reporter was assigned she carried some of the photographer's camera gear, within the strength limitations of her sex, but not all of it. A man reporter was considered to have no limitations as to strength—or damn well better not have. Hernia was a not uncommon disease among *Vital* male researchers.

We wish to take this occasion to correct a vile slander. The story has sometimes been aired and sniggered around that most *Vital* girl researchers compensated for the strength limitations of their sex by carrying their helpfulness to the photographer a step or so further than the above-mentioned researcher functions. This is an absolute lie. On many, many stories nothing of the kind ever happened, especially if the photographer's wife went along with him on the story. What is more, some of *Vital*'s photographers were fairly venerable men who used and indeed needed all their strength on a story to do the story itself. They had no time, or at least strength, for frills once the day's work was over. A *Vital* photographer put a lot of emotional energy into a story and sometimes all he had. If it is a fact that temporary, even fleeting, relationships on occasion flowered between a *Vital* photographer and researcher out on a story, provided their sexes were different—well, let places like Wall Street and Madison Avenue be very chary about being too pious right here. If a *Vital* photographer and researcher sometimes saw something of each other after hours, under Suetonius! what else could be expected where a man and a girl with common interests, such as both working for *Vital*, were thrown into close contact for an extended period in a city where they knew no one else. Such as Columbus, Ohio? Have you ever been in Columbus with an evening on your hands? The researcher could hardly tell the photographer to eat by himself in Columbus, Ohio, where they both found themselves for the first time in their lives.

Some photographers, it is true, from being younger, unmarried, or married longer, or just from their metabolism, had more left at the end of the workday than did others. Montgomery Shanks was very, very high on metabolism. Also he had a way that brought out the metabolism of the other sex. Not to put too fine a point on it, Shanks hadn't had to rape anybody yet.

He had a horror of involvement. Or not a horror so much as a *refusal* to involvement. He would *not* get involved. It was himself who would set the terms and the frequencies. If a girl came to like it on that bed and if Shanks for some reason or another—probably that he had got interested in another woman and wanted a diet of subtle imported caviar for a while instead of unseasoned U.S. prime red meat rare all the time—did not summon her as time passed and she pestered him in the slightest such as phoning him too much or coming even close to demanding that he see her Shanks hung up the phone and that was that for that girl.

"You're bothering me," Shanks said simply and hung up.

This almost always did it. The woman may have then gone away unreasonably hating Shanks—like a child grown accustomed to a daily ration of chocolate sundae and then to have it cut off with no warning, which Shanks never gave, never discussed anything about their relationship with the woman, never permitted the slightest emotional content ("Look, are we going to bed or are we going to psychoanalyze each other?" he would say sharply whenever it started; "take your choice.") The woman may have been bitter when Shanks abruptly cut off the rations, for it is very easy to get used to chocolate sundaes. But there was something about Shanks, something rather ominous and vaguely threatening, that made her leave it at that, however bitterly, and "bother" him no more when he gave the word. This "bothering" is one area in which women, whose instincts in so many basic things are so much righter than man's, have no intelligence whatsoever, as they would know if they but asked themselves a few simple questions, e.g.: "Why does his doing with me what, after all, is exactly what I did with him give me any rights over him?" (Shanks had nothing to do with "rights," much in the manner that D. H. Lawrence shot back so definitively, when someone mentioned he ought to do such-and-such thing, he really should, "With *ought* and with *should* I have nothing to do.")

If it was a girl researcher assigned to him on a story, it depended on how Shanks felt whether or not he conferred upon her what was supposed to be akin to receiving the Dame Commander Order of the British Empire. Shanks almost always felt like conferring it. He didn't feel right unless he had it. The correlation between getting this and the creative output of the creative artist is well known, for it is crucial above all else to keep him soothed and happy—and what soothes a man more?

6

Jason

Jason Hightower found himself liking the people at the magazine a good deal. Except for the inevitable main-chancer here and there (if there were no bad, what would we have to compare the good against?) they formed as honest an association of people as he believed existed in the high plateaus of the business world, honest and interesting, good and rewarding people indeed to have communication with. If they didn't know where they were headed, most of them, they seemed determined to have a lot of fun getting there. It was a very rare person indeed who had the old knife out for anybody. And there was brought together there quite a variety indeed of the human race, and everybody was not really like everybody else. It was a pleasant circumstance to come upon in the business world, which supposedly stamped everyone into more or less the same repetitive mold. He enjoyed the life, the constant state of expectancy of what news would happen today, or tomorrow, or the next hour, what cataclysms in Washington or the world, and they were right in the middle of it all in that these cataclysms and the workings of the world in general were their raw material, instead of something like steel, carbide and carbon, or the fluctuations of the stock market.

Jason had now been working at *Vital* for some six months, as a researcher in the National Affairs Department. Mostly this meant staying in the office, checking stories, and occasionally going out with a photographer to cover a story in New York or nearby. Sometimes when he was out on an assignment, say in Connecticut, Jason liked to send telegrams to people in the office. He sent them to people he liked, very often to Hank Gaskin. The wires would usually be in either an historical or hortatory vein. Gaskin enjoyed receiving them. "Lest we become misologists: no worse thing can happen to a man than this," one might read. "For as there are misanthropists, or haters of men, there are also misologists, or haters of ideas, and both spring from the same cause, which is ignorance of the world Stop Phaedo."

Another went: "Am planning self-glorifying public works project to relieve critical unemployment this area—a stately castle on present Xanadu slum site Stop Kubla." Jason possessed one of the cards the magazine issued authorizing telegraph companies to accept collect messages from the holder. Since he addressed the wires only to his friends, it was a form of expenditure the magazine would probably never catch up with. Jason certainly would never have addressed one to Harrison Duckworth, the vice managing editor, though once when he was down in Pennsylvania on a story he had a hard-to-conquer impulse to do so. This one said lugubriously: "Bitter cold water here off Rapallo Third and last time up Stop Will the world ever stop killing its poets Stop Farewell Shelley." He mastered the impulse out of the knowledge that that would mean an end to his collect wires and sent it to Gaskin instead.

He wouldn't want to give up his telegrams. They gave him something to do when he was out on a story in some strange town. And the collect card enabled him to pamper two other impulses which abided in Jason. One was a general reluctance to spend his own money; the other, a distinct pleasure in mild embezzlement of the magazine's.

Sometimes the telegraph operator would read the message, then look up questioningly at the prospective sender of it. In the few cases where this functionary raised the objection that he and the signature— which might, say, be Harry Truman, St. Francis of Assisi, Toussaint L'Ouverture, or Pierre Gustave Toutant de Beauregard—did not appear exactly to correspond and that Western Union had some pretty rigid rules about these matters, Jason had a way of making that the last question the telegraph operator asked. He would look back at the questioner with just the proper lifting of the head that made the man appear to be attempting to interfere with the constitutional guarantees of freedom of the press.

"My good man," he would say, "I suppose you've heard of *Vital* magazine. If not, you may well have the shady distinction of being the only man in America who hasn't. Well, I'm on the staff of *Vital*," and Jason would pull out his billfold and treat the telegraph operator to a glimpse of the identification card featuring his picture. "We're doing a secret story on your town here, and that which you have just taken it so gratuitously upon yourself to question is the code we use in such matters on a magazine like *Vital*. It's a very secret story concerning a few things I'm not free to speak about going on in your town here. Now that's all I have to say about it. I've already said too much. Any further questions and are you going to send that telegram or aren't you?"

"No, sir, yes, sir," the man usually said in a tone that was one-third apology, one-third fright, and one-third greedy curiosity. "I hadn't realized you were with *Vital*. Oh, yes indeed," said the telegraph operator of the town which might have 2,500 population if the surrounding farmers were thrown in, "we all read *Vital*. Yes, *sir*. So you're going to do a story on us, you say? Uh, and it's a secret?" the man said greedily. "You couldn't give us a hint now?"

Jason would give the telegraph operator another look which suggested that he was now undertaking to interfere with still another hallowed press liberty: secrecy about itself if not about anybody else.

"You keep your eye on the next eighteen or twenty issues," Jason said easily. There was no point, after all, in telling the man that the story concerned something such as an apple blossom festival.

Back in New York, Jason found it pleasant that in a business establishment he could, of a morning, play a couple of games of darts in Hank Gaskin's office while listening to music from an excellent high-fidelity system, could take a quite long and pleasant lunch with fellow staff members and then, if he felt so moved, take a nap on that large and wonderfully comfortable couch, also in Gaskin's office. He found Gaskin in particular both an educational and a pleasantly communicative man to know, and he spent many an hour, all of them paid for by this most benevolent of companies, stretched out on the leather couch and gabbing hither and yon with him about all sorts of matters.

"Gaskin, is this where you'll be when the great ding dong bell of judgment sounds, the clocks stop, the clouds part with a fearful thunderclap, and de Lawd steps down the sky to pronounce sentence on us all?"

"Depends on how soon it happens, my lad. I've got plans, like everybody else, for shaking loose. But I'm not too unhappy here. Fine working conditions, as we say in the union, and somewhat of a sabbatical for the mind. You're not holding heaven in your hand exactly, but if it's the pursuit of happiness we're all after—well, there's quite a bit of it futzing around here, me lad."

"Pursuit of happiness? Is that what we're after, old man?"

"I guess so. I gu-ess so. I haven't exactly figured out anything else."

"What is happiness to you, old man? By gad, I like your collection of Mozart here. You've fixed this shack up for living all right, Gaskin. I like this couch very much."

"I ought to start charging you rent. You get by with very little work around here, Hightower."

"They always know where they can find me if they need—or want —me."

"Well, sir, I think happiness is women, really. I don't think there's any other real happiness for a man but that. All the rest of it is just basically to fill the time. Oh, I like spaghetti *aglio e olio* and a bottle of Soave. And I like having a couple of martinis in me. And sleep now, I really like to sleep. And, hell, I like to read, of course. And I like my music here. But hell, boy, when you come down to it: Isn't it a fact that a man lives pretty much between good swatches of that iridescent jewel only woman has to offer? All the rest is really just to fill in the time between. I think women, *women,* is what we all really live for. Getting our ashes hauled, as Robert Browning said: that's what it's all about. From a good woman I mean, a *real* woman. And I think if we could all do it more, and without all the complications, I mean if you could just go out and *do* it, well I think three-fourths of the world's troubles would be over, and we'd all stop screaming at each other so much and getting irritated at each other, or worse. Yes, my boy! A more ready accessibility to the fruit of the loom would keep us from having to have our frustrations out by all this gnawing at each other. By the dog! sometimes I think of the world as one big daisy chain where everybody is snarling and gnawing away at everybody else and being snarled at and gnawed on. All that comes out of frustration, my boy. Nobody ever got up from a good bout of fornication to eat out his neighbors. I like it here. At least it's easier here. And better. Not that you still don't have to go through a lot of the old twiddle-twaddle, I mean the involvements, and all."

"I get you, Ace. I get you, all right. Still and all: well, I keep thinking this. I think this, Gaskin, let me say this one thing. I think you and I happen to be living in the most fateful period of history with which man has ever been blessed or cursed, in which he's ever been set down. What I mean, old man, is: It's all going to be decided in this century. Probably quite before the end of the century. And while I'd like to get my share of the old roger I also feel, well, I feel about like this: A man can't stay out of the other. Or *shouldn't.* A man can't be born in this time and stay out of doing whatever he can to help decide it."

"You got any ideas, Prometheus?"

"No, as a matter of fact I haven't." Jason stretched long and yawning on the couch, then drew his knees up and cupped his hands behind his head, pulling down on it. "I ain't got any ideas, quite frankly, but I'm thinking. I'm thinking about it, I want you to know that."

"Well, let me know if you get any hot flashes there. Hellsfire, I'm willing to do my part. Yassuh! But I tell you frankly I just can't think of a goddamn thing to do."

"You think there's nothing to do?"

"No-o," Gaskin said, his lips rounded. "I don't think there's a thing to do. I don't think there's anything a damn one of us can do will avoid whatever's going to happen. Not a blessed thing."

"And what does that leave, O sage. O wise one!"

"It leaves just one thing: forgetting about this fe-rigged-up world and trying to get yourself the best personal life possible. All I hope is that when I get fried to a crisp in my bed by all that radiation I have something there with me. Caught *in flagrante* by the H-bomb! All I want is to go down screwing to the last. It's the only thing left for us, young one! The *only* thing."

"Well, naturally," Jason said, "I would be the last, or at least one of the last—you, we'll all have to admit, would be *the* last person in the world—to deny its importance. But there has to be something else we can do about things. I'm not ready quite yet to believe that we all have to sit here and be destroyed like so many helpless imbeciles. The good personal life versus *that* commitment: That, in case you're interested, is the great moral conflict that rages unceasingly within me."

"You'll doubtless get over it."

"I don't think there's going to be time. I truly don't. Unless we do something, there ain't going to be any personal life around that's very available. To sit still and *see* it happen," Jason mused, looking into space. "The voyeur of history: Who is so culpable as he?"

"Well, I suppose you've got a point in the higher metaphysics, don't you know. You've got a point of sorts there. But what can I do about it?" Gaskin held his palms up in mock despair. "What can I do about the idiots? There are so many of them. Since I obviously can't— well, I like it pretty well in The Fun House here. The Fun House," Gaskin repeated and laughed shortly and rubbed his head, then smiled in a wry amusement. He reached for a piece of copy paper and started making a paper airplane. "It is a fact, sometimes I think that elegant term applies to the whole blessed blooming country. Yes, sir! Just one big Fun House, living it up and fiddling away like a bunch of de- mented and deaf idiots, and jabbering like half-witted banshees, fid- dling away while the world, she burns . . . and burns . . . and burns. So! I don't mind admitting with all due charity, if that's what you're saying, old horse, that on present dead reckoning we're headed straight for hell in a basket, I believe they call it. Unless we pop to."

"Yes—unless we pop to," Jason said.

"And hell, boy, I think it's too late really for that. I truly do. And anyhow did you ever try to get an idiot to give up ten bucks, or endure ten minutes of sacrifice, if it was going to affect *his* fun one damn whit? So goddamn it to hell, if that's the way it's going to be, let's have a little fun is what I say!" Gaskin said in mock declamation. Swiveling in his chair—Jason could see the long, duel-like scar across his cheek, and suddenly thought, irrelevantly, of that line in Bunyan, *My marks and scars I carry with me, to be a witness for me that I have fought his battles*—he sailed the paper airplane out the window. "Yes, sir, I truly think it's too late, old chum, for the other—or almost."

"Almost . . ." Jason said.

And another time, over a game of darts, they talked of:

"But tell me, O sage, what is love?"

"Well, my boy, I can tell you what love is *not*," Gaskin said in that avuncular tone he took with anyone as much as six months younger than himself. "What love is not is game playing." He threw a dart. "From knowing almost no married couples who are truly happy, I deduce," Gaskin said, a bit oracularly, "that human love is the world's most difficult summit to conquer. Since man wants it so much, and gets it so seldom, something obviously is wrong somewhere."

"Any fool," said Jason, "can point out that something is wrong. Where is the sage to tell us what it is and what to do about it?"

Gaskin threw a vicious dart, which came very near to going out the window. "I was coming to that, before you interrupted me. My observation has been reasonably limited, but what there has been suggests to me that monogamy is a questionable state and that perhaps the trouble lies there. I have not permitted myself to determine this by experience, however, so it remains a doubtful conclusion."

"It's very difficult to tell without the experience."

"It *is,* however, obvious," Gaskin continued, tossing another dart—this one hit the wall, but at least stayed safely in the room, "that variety and novelty are extremely strong drives in man . . ."

"They certainly are with you, no question about that."

". . . and not at all necessarily evil ones," Gaskin continued as if uninterrupted. "Perhaps, who knows, if they were accepted and satisfied, the alarming and immoral divorce rate would drop along with the unspeakable misery progenated by Puritanism, and so the sanctity of marriage increase."

"I know how strongly you feel about the sanctity of marriage," Jason said piously.

"Part of the trouble at least—and *this* certainly should be obvious even to one so inexperienced as yourself—lies in this terrible, festering synonymizing of Marriage and Proprietorship. Obviously marriage *per se* couldn't be wrong. Very handy institution, I would think. It's the identity of it with Ownership. The way things are set up, a wife *has* to destroy one's personality. There's no helping it."

"And you have such a beautiful personality," Jason said.

"Monogamy," Gaskin continued declamatorily. "It is our leading evil, the author of half our miseries and three-fourths of our frustrations. And this is the reason why, this is the heart of it all: It is the one thing above all that stifles everything man is."

Jason threw a very accurate dart—he customarily beat Gaskin easily, though his elder never stopped trying and wanted very much to master Hightower in the game. He threw a gentle, arcing dart which hit true and neatly in the zero circle, and as it did, said, musingly, almost as if to himself: "What is love?"

"Love is a gentle thing," Henry Gaskin said quietly.

And another time, while Gaskin sat all but buried in his Do-More chair, with his huge legs up on the desk, heels digging into an enormous pile of research on the excruciation of being a suburban wife, and Jason lay stretched out on the couch, from which vantage point he could see the two competing legends on Gaskin's walls—"Of all sexual aberrations chastity is the strangest" and "The carnal pleasures of life have never made minds great":

"Gaskin, there's something I've been meaning to ask you. I wanted to ask you in particular because your uncanny virility is so well known, as I imagine you would be the first to admit. My question is: Is there a correlation between sex and energy, particularly between sex and creative energy? Or are they the mortal enemies of each other?"

"It's a very important question, my lad," Gaskin said avuncularly. "I recall that Victor Hugo thought so much of the importance of fornication that his diary recorded faithfully, if that is the word, the frequency of it, for instance, when he was eighty-three years old, that he enjoyed it eight times in three months."

"He was a fair writer."

"It's nice of you to say so. Dickens, Lord Byron and Algernon Charles Swinburne, to mention three who were mighty fruitful with the pen, got plenty of their share, if not more, of the sweet jewel. Puccini—to cross over the hard line between the arts—when reproached by his wife that he was undertaking to sleep with every soprano in the world, replied loftily, 'I am guilty. It is my destiny.' Dozens of other examples of the concupiscence of great men could be given but I believe I make my point. Yes, my boy. One cannot help conclude, at a very minimum of conclusion, that there is a high correlation between fornication and energy, particularly between fornication and creative energy. Yes," Gaskin said judiciously, "I'm just afraid that one must conclude that sex is the very fuel of the creative arts; in short, that the artist who fornicates tonight, provided only it is good, will create better on the morrow."

Jason cupped his hands under his head. "Perhaps. It is interesting, however, that Baudelaire—who was so right in so much—held that the exact opposite was true, that fornication was the enemy of the creative arts and chastity their correlative and spur. In other words, that the energy went either into a woman or into a book."

"It is equally interesting," said Gaskin, "that, believing that, his own production was so small—wonderful but small—and his place remains a bright star of the second magnitude. Had he believed otherwise, would he have reached the first magnitude?"

"We'll never know," Jason said.

And another time: Jason cruised into Gaskin's office and stopped short. His friend was looking steadily at the picture on the wall. It was a woodcut, actually, and it was quite graphic, what with the great towers sheared off, the ghost of smoke rising from the heaving mass of rubble, bodies or what was left of them piled about, and from the ruins a hand here and there struggling out imploring extrication. One could almost hear the moaning and terrible cries of the people, who, minutes before, had gone about their tasks and sought out their enjoyments in the great city. Beyond Gaskin's shoulder Jason could see out the window the untouched towers themselves. Together, picture and reality formed a most graphic set of before-and-after pictures.

"Do you think it will happen, Gaskin?"

Gaskin turned easily and looked at his friend for a moment before speaking. "I don't know what I think. But we'll surely know before long, won't we? And perhaps that means," he added thoughtfully, "that we had better do our living while living's still around to do."

"It will be interesting," Jason said, "to see how it all comes out. Anyhow, I believe man will find a way out of it. He's *got* to."

"Do you believe that much in man?"

"Is there anything else to believe in?"

And the picture seemed always to hover over them; either from afar, or very close, very close indeed.

And so it went.

Gaskin enjoyed the company of the chief user of his office facilities. There was one central fact about Jason Hightower: He considered it all nonsense. By "it all" I mean just about everything in this world, *as the world is.* He rejected virtually everything around him: values, way of life, man's choice of things on which to expend his energy and his mind. The only trouble with this philosophy is that, carried to the point of purism, it can bring one to the brink of total inertia. After all, as Pindar said, the only world there is is the world that happens to be. Jason Hightower was fully aware of this defect in this philosophy and he had worked out a system that was satisfying at least to himself of retaining the philosophy and making it work, which was to modify it only to the most minimal degree necessary to function in the world of the great mirage. He realized that if you don't modify such a philosophy at all you simply cease to function. He modified it enough in the one instance to get a job he felt he would like to have, and since he was intelligent he could modify it enough to do this job competently. He was not modifying it more than that. It was almost as if he were saving himself for something.

At age twenty-three, as this book opens, Jason Hightower had had very little "experience." What is called "first-hand" experience, that is. However, he believed in the quest, believed in it very much, out of this reasoning: Satisfaction with one's life to date or as of now, or assessment of what one considers the best, is measurable only against that to which one has been exposed. But how does one know but what there is something better beyond that which one has so far known? One cannot, and therefore one must constantly "expose" one's life to fresh experience. The only correct life, he thus believed, is that life which is constantly striving to break through to unknown worlds, which may be far better than anything one has thus far known, may be a life so exquisitely wonderful, yea, rapturous, that one cannot even imagine it or what it would be like, since it may have elements so beyond anything one has ever experienced, one being now without any touchstones whatsoever to it. For this reason, he believed, one must continually strive for new breakthroughs, to reach new plateaus of knowledge and penetration, and seek new worlds. That, to Jason, was what life was all about.

Thus, assuming that man represents an entity of one hundred percent, he believed that most persons during the course of their years upon this earth lived no more than five or six percent of the potential that is in them, and a great many only about one percent. Of all the great sins and errors of which man is capable, this—save only for cruelty to another—is the greatest and constitutes the greatest denial of God and/or nature possible to man, since rejecting His or its supreme creation, namely oneself. He was determined to avoid this sin, to live as close to one hundred percent as is humanly possible. And in this connection he believed the purpose of life was that expressed by the Greek peasant poet Hesiod: Excellence through sweat.

It was beginning to impinge on his consciousness that some terrible and frenetic and nameless force had come into being, and was growing yearly, to destroy communication between men: A swelling tide of throwing one's personality around, of the striving for petty, worthless, mean little conversational triumphs, and of suspicion and calculation, in the presence of which no real communication between two individuals was even possible. Man, strange man! It was enough to make one laugh, in a rather eerie laughter. More than anything else, man wanted communication with another individual. And yet this very surge of calculation and suspicion was making it impossible for him to achieve that which he wanted most of all and without which life was as a dry husk. The devils squatting happily on their red coals in hell must really be chuckling quite throatily these days. Goodness between men! Without this there was no communication. It could disturb a man if he started to think about it: the increasing personal calculation, the smugness upon the land. And by a thing that perhaps went with it: the increasing joylessness of the people.

Thanks to his uncle's apartment, and such accompanying possessions of his uncle's which went with it as a membership in the Eastside Club, certain phases of Jason's life were out of all proportion to his income. But Jason did not take the easy way out and attempt to win popularity by throwing around money which he didn't have. Quite the reverse was true. Indeed it could be fairly expensive having a friendship with Jason Hightower. Jason's parsimony combined with his expansive usage of his uncle's possessions made for a certain interesting dichotomy in his life.

The Eastside Club is miles ahead New York's most exclusive club and makes places like the Racquet Club, the Union League, and the like, seem by comparison like Y.M.C.A.'s open to the general public. It has the only good indoor tennis court in New York, *en-tout-cas* and beautifully lighted, and one entered it to play after dressing in a locker room the elegance of which was otherwise unknown even in New York and made the locker rooms of places like the University Club and the Harvard Club appear by comparison like smelly, fungicidal high-school gym locker rooms. The locker room of the Eastside Club was sprayed every two hours with a Flit gun containing a mixture of Cuir de Russie eau de cologne and Clorox. The room was decked with lockers of the finest West Indies mahogany, each large enough for two people to stand in were there any occasion to do so, a glittering bar of matching mahogany from which the most gracious and discreetly understanding barkeep in Manhattan held quiet and comforting salon, and attendants who, kneeling, as is proper or at least necessary for the lower classes engaged in such intimate attendance upon their betters, helped you on and off with your gym sox and tennis shoes.

Once a week or so Jason took three fellow researchers who were tennis buffs there to play a game of lunchtime doubles and satisfy that almost emotional need he had for exercise. Entering the Eastside's lavish premises, the *Vital* researchers—at least the other three, Jason himself was not for a moment in the least awed by the Eastside's air of unostentatious grandeur—looked like the Dead End kids who used to inhabit this precise situs where the Eastside Club now stood, as if the grimy ghosts had come back to claim their grounds from the swells who had pre-empted it. Gaskin often came along, not to play but to sit on the side of the tennis court with a martini in hand, to watch and occasionally to cheer a bad shot or boo a good one. On the way back to the office in the taxi Jason collected from each of his three friends a dollar bill toward the four-dollar service fee to members for use of the court. He paid his own share. When the taxi arrived at the office he got out and let the other three fight it out for the privilege of paying the hackie. His share of the taxi ride, he felt and soundly enough, consisted in sharing his Eastside Club privileges with his friends.

Like most National Affairs researchers Jason Hightower usually worked late on Saturdays. Therefore he was a fairly regular customer of the six-dollar-a-plate buffet which Le Porc Blanc brought in and served the working people. Jason was a great admirer of this feed and oftentimes went back for seconds. As the weeks went on, a certain potential correlation between two facts began to engage Jason's attention. One of these facts was that there always seemed so much food on the buffet, more than enough to spare, since it would have been embarrassing both for Le Porc and for the magazine to run out. The other fact was that he always now had two, three or more friends from school visiting him on weekends and sharing the ample quarters of his apartment.

Jason, with an idea stirring in his mind, began carefully to observe the Saturday night dinner situation. He observed that no one kept a check of who went through the line. There were always people in the line he didn't know, from one department or another of the magazine. No one, he was sure, could know them all.

After a while the idea took firm shape and he decided to try it.

He tried it first in a very limited way. He told one of his friends who was in town from school for the weekend to drop by the office about eight on Saturday and not to eat beforehand. Jason well knew that all college youth, no matter what money their families have and even especially if they do, take great satisfaction in freeloading. The friend dropped by, went through the line with no difficulty, ate sumptuously, and then left for a party. The friend was overjoyed at what a wonderful free dinner it was. This made Jason happy. He liked to do things for his friends, especially if someone else paid for it. Also it gave him pleasure for a company of wealth to be led into unwitting philanthropy.

The following week Jason brought two friends to the dinner. They went through the bountiful *Vital* chow line without the slightest difficulty.

After that the word must have spread to the campus, for Jason found himself the recipient of more and more letters from school friends saying they were coming up for the weekend. Sometimes they brought with them one or more schoolmates Jason didn't even know. The word of the great free dinner must have spread even to other schools, because occasionally young men from Harvard, Princeton, Yale, Williams, Amherst, and the like, turned up at Jason's apartment, mentioning some vague connection. Jason turned none of them away. Soon his friends and his friends' friends began to expect as a part of the New York facilities not only the use of Jason's apartment but also the free dinner at Jason's place of employment. They began to look upon it as only their due. Some weeks Jason would have as many as seven or eight of them enjoying his banquet hospitality at *Vital* at the company's expense. It made him feel exceptionally warm toward the magazine.

As for detection, he estimated that it was impossible. Since *Vital* got so many of its editorial employees from these colleges, Jason's friends were about the same in appearance and manner as the majority of people authentically employed there. All in all it was a beautiful arrangement. Until the Office S.O.B. took a hand.

7
The Office S.O.B.

Even the S.O.B. at *Vital* was pretty wonderful. In fact the only reason *Vital* had an S.O.B. at all had been put best by the S.O.B. himself. Speaking of the duty as if it were a regular staff position listed on the masthead he explained cheerfully:

"Every modern office has to have an S.O.B. and I guess I'm it."

The S.O.B., who had the official title of vice managing editor, was the magazine's administrative officer for the editorial side. His undisputed realm embraced such matters as hiring, expense accounts and, where it became absolutely and unavoidably necessary, firing. There was nothing *Vital* hated more than to fire someone. It would go to fantastic lengths to avoid it, such as putting the person at The Thinking Desk on the twenty-fifth floor, which was a kind of solitary confinement, where, bracketed by the Maintenance Department on the one side and Central Purchasing on the other, the person was told to think up projects for the magazine to do. None of these was ever done. Another thing the magazine would do to avoid firing a person was to give him nothing to do for weeks on end until he went out of his mind. In either case after a few weeks he would usually quit. Now and then it became absolutely necessary to fire someone, when everything else had been tried and failed. A case in point was Wadsworth Oakes, who was an assistant editor in the Foreign News Department and fell from favor with its chief for some reason that is not important to the story. Oakes was assigned to The Thinking Desk. He must have been rather on edge to start with because at the end of a week there he sent up this memorandum:

> *To:* Vice Managing Editor
> *From:* Wadsworth Oakes
> Suggest we do a photographic essay on the lesser islands of the Caribbean. Wadsworth Oakes is available to cover it.

It was hardly the sort of story suggestion you made at *Vital*—it was too bald, not spelled out, and the second and last sentence was scarcely in the accepted selfless approach. The vice managing editor sent no reply down from the thirty-fourth to the twenty-fifth floor. At the end of Oakes' second week on The Thinking Desk he sent up another suggestion. The magazine had been doing a series of picture essays on such subjects as the world's outstanding restaurants, the great churches of the world, and so on. Oakes' memorandum went:

> *To:* Vice Editor
> *Fm:* Oakes
> Suggest we do an essay on the world's outstanding brothels. The able Wadsworth Oakes is available to cover this one.

Oakes had been at The Thinking Desk three weeks when he sent up another memorandum, this one in the shocking-pink interoffice envelope which was labeled in large black letters URGENT for matters of that character.

> *To:* V.M.E.
> *From:* Thinking Desk
> Carrying out motto used in our house advertising that *"Vital* is full of surprises every week," suggest we do an issue of entirely blank pages. Nothing (n.b. the *double entendre*) would surprise readers more than such an issue. All pages would be blank, including cover, which would be blank except for one word VITAL in usual corner space. Ideally, carrying out blankness theme, cover should be entirely blank too but suppose word VITAL, although violating theme, is reluctantly necessary, otherwise readers would be unaware of who is doing this unusual issue and *Vital* would not be credited with enormous impact and uninhibited reader response such an issue is certain to make on newsstands and in mailboxes.
> Wadsworth Oakes is available to be issue editor for this issue.

The vice managing editor did not answer this memorandum. Then, suddenly, Wadsworth Oakes began to fire off whole volleys of memoranda. Not just once a week, but every day, and oftentimes several memoranda a day, all addressed to the vice managing editor. Some of them were pretty esoteric. None of them got an answer. Then one day Wadsworth Oakes arose from The Thinking Desk, went out to the elevator, rode it to the thirty-fourth floor, got out and walked down the corridor to the vice managing editor's office. He stood in the doorway. The vice managing editor looked up from his desk.

"Oh, Wadsworth," he said cheerfully. "Well, how have you been? What can I do for you?"

Wadsworth Oakes let out a scream to show how he had been. To show what the vice managing editor could do for him he followed the scream with a torrent of abuse impossible to reproduce in such a book as this, intended, like *Vital* itself, for family reading. It is enough to say that the vice managing editor, who was a man not easily provoked, fired Oakes on the spot.

Some people around the office held that Oakes' dramatic action was

deliberate, calculated to goad the vice managing editor into firing him.
If you were fired you got "severance pay." Its amount was gauged on
your longevity with the magazine, and in the case of Oakes, who had
been with the magazine eleven years, would have been a very tidy
sum. If you just quit all you got was a farewell party. I never believed
Oakes' action was deliberate, for the reason that the vice managing
editor was an extremely shrewd man, knowledgeable of human character in all its chromatic manifestations. Had getting fired been Oakes'
motive he would have known it and never have let himself be provoked. I think he just figured that despite *Vital*'s great reluctance to
fire anyone, this was a case where it was urgent the man go before
something extreme, such as homicide of somebody or other in the
office, happened. Oakes was obviously dangerous. In fact something
Wadsworth Oakes himself told Henry Gaskin a couple of years later
supported this view. At that time Wadsworth was still recuperating on
his severance pay in a house at Sag Harbor, a summer resort at the end
of Long Island and very gray and depressing in winter, where he was
now living year round, doing nothing and looking, said Gaskin, who
had gone out to visit him as one goes to visit a sick friend in a hospital,
"like someone who had been castrated." Wadsworth told Gaskin: "I
went stir-crazy at The Thinking Desk. That place down there was
like the water torture. I was John on Patmos but there was no manner
of the poet in me to create the great Revelation." And then Oakes, so
Gaskin related, let out a bombardment of obscenity on the magazine
beyond anything Gaskin, who was not unversed in this field of seman-
tics, had ever heard or even knew existed. The language was unbelievable—and of course cannot be reproduced here. It was like something
out of a cesspool. It was as if Oakes were spending all his time, day in
and day out there where he lived all alone at Sag Harbor—his wife
had left him, and one can see why—thinking up impossible obscenities and combinations of obscenities to heap on the organization which
for eleven years had given him everything he had in life. No, the vice
managing editor was a man who on the rare occasions he got provoked
did so with full awareness and intent. Not the least of his catalogue of
high abilities was his superb emotional control, along with his abiding
sense of humor.

"Someone has to be the office S.O.B. and I guess I'm nominated,
even though no one appreciates it," the vice managing editor would
say. "Laughter in the wings."

The *Vital* S.O.B. was a man by the name of Harrison Duckworth.
He was one of the most good-natured men it would be possible to
know. Considering what he had to do, his duties being both myriad
and frequently the kind of work no man likes to do, it was difficult to
understand how he could retain his enormous, unfailing good nature.
But he did. His good-naturedness was often weighed in the balance;

it was never found wanting. He was really a wonderful S.O.B. However, anyone would have made a dreadful mistake—and a few had, to their immortal regret—to equate this good nature with naïveté in any form. Harrison Duckworth was an exceedingly shrewd, clever, knowledgeable man and he had his own way of being tough, some might say ruthless, and some might say, and these we believe most accurate of all, Machiavellian, if the situation demanded. This feature of Harrison Duckworth was accompanied by that ability which usually accompanies it: an almost kinetic sense of being able quickly to identify anyone's particular weakness and, and few things are more important in character assessment than this, quickly distinguish the weak from the strong, the strong from the weak. He was a man in his early fifties and nearly half of his life, after several years in the newspaper business, had been spent with *Vital*. This alone testified to his great staying powers. His march up The Ladder had been steady if not spectacular. He had served in almost every *Vital* capacity and this almost boundless experience was an immeasurable asset in the position he now held, in which he dealt with all editorial personnel. Having been at one time or another in the job of almost anyone with whom he dealt, he understood that person's problems and there was no fooling him. Save for Crystal Bidwell, he more than anyone else had to do with molding raw material which came to work for the magazine into the personality that made a good *Vital* type. His understanding and insight were of an extreme order. For instance, there was the time the future of one of the researchers, a young man by the name of Avery Bush, was being jeopardized.

Bush was an unusually bright and pleasant young man who had come to *Vital* straight from a newspaper and might seem to have an excellent future with the magazine. But he had one subtle fault. It was Duckworth who straightened him out. One day when Bush had been working at *Vital* about six months Duckworth ran across him in the corridor.

"Oh, by the way, Avery," he said. "Could you spare a minute?"

The vice managing editor never summoned anyone into his office through his secretary. If he had something to talk over with someone he waited until he ran across the person in the corridor. There was something more democratic and less formal about doing it this way, and democracy and informality were stressed a great deal at *Vital*. Bush followed the vice managing editor into his office.

The vice managing editor had the huge corner office and the huge double-size executive desk which befitted his rank as Number 2 man on the nation's Number 1 magazine. It was a pleasant office and at the same time a striking one, a triumph in interior decoration. If one were to give it a name that name would immediately be The Brown Room.

In fact many people around *Vital* did give it this name. Virtually every-thing in it was some shade or another of brown: the warm tan leather couch and chairs, the desk, the carpeting, even the walls. Even the desk-side safe labeled "Duckworth Personal" was brown. It was some-how a rather reassuring room to see in a business establishment. On the desk sat a rack of brown pipes, seven in number and under each a tiny typed label specifying the day of the week on which it was to be smoked. Even this reassured: No pipe-smoker could be anything but a really good man. The wall facing the desk and therefore visible to the vice managing editor seated there was nothing but a gigantic map of the world. Not a map *hung* on the wall. The wall *was* the world. It was a beautiful job of map-making, capable of being lighted up from his desk, and was decorated prettily with two kinds of hatpin-size-headed pins, red ones to indicate *Vital* bureaus the world around and blue ones to indicate cities and towns containing *Vital* "stringers"— part-time correspondents. Moving clockwise, the next wall, which would be to the right of the seated vice managing editor and thirty-four stories below which Fifth Avenue spangled itself north and south, af-forded a spectacular view of the mid-East Side, including the United Nations and the East River. The wall behind the vice managing edi-tor gave another even more splendid view of the soaring towers of mid-town Manhattan.

The remaining wall contained four discreet and moderate-sized boating pictures, showing the vice managing editor's boat and the vice managing editor himself in the informal attire of boating, of which he was an enthusiast, and one of the photographs showing his wife. She was a very handsome woman and Harrison Duckworth had the repu-tation of being a very Puritan sort of man. This wall was also inter-rupted by a door which led into an oversized private closet containing one item and nothing else: an Exercycle on which the vice managing editor pedaled fifteen minutes every day the first thing on arriving at his office in the morning—he arrived a half hour before the start of the working day, giving him more than enough minutes to accomplish on his own time the exercise which did a lot to keep him in a good deal better physical shape than most *Vital* employees. Oddly enough, not a soul at *Vital* other than himself knew even of the existence of the Exercycle in the closet. The vice managing editor had had it de-livered on an empty Sunday, the closet was always kept locked, and he had the only key.

"Sit down, Avery."

Bush did so, in the indicated chair to the side of the desk, and not until he was seated did the vice managing editor seat himself behind the desk; first standing there for a few moments and looking down at the researcher. When he was seated the vice managing editor told a little story, dealing with the two admirals who asked each other what was the most embarrassing moment in his life.

Bush laughed rather overgenerously if anything, and a little nervously. The vice managing editor had a habit of telling a story to put at ease the person he asked into his office.

The vice managing editor lifted his Phi Beta Kappa key from across his vest, raised and blew on it as people do with spectacles, took out his handkerchief, polished it a bit, and restored his handkerchief after patting his eyes with it. He selected his Tuesday pipe from the tray and began filling it from a bronze tobacco humidor on his desk.

"Avery, do you mind if I ask you something?"

"Why, no, sir."

"Avery. How has your metabolism been lately?"

"Metabolism, sir?"

"Metabolism, metabolism. Is that too big a word for you? Laughter in the wings, Avery. Metabolism, emotional and otherwise, is very important around here. You've been on the premises long enough to know."

"Oh, yes, sir. Why, I think it's very good, sir—as much as a man can judge himself."

"If he can't somebody else will sooner or later, Avery. Laughter in the wings."

Over the small interchange of laughter the vice managing editor lighted up his pipe and sucked in comfortably. Then, between staccato puffings, he commenced to ask Bush how he was getting along, how by this time he enjoyed working for *Vital,* and several other questions of this general tenor. Coming from anyone else less helpful than Harrison Duckworth this easy line of foreboding questions could have struck terror into the heart of a young researcher, and Bush, to tell the truth, wished he could reach into his pocket and extract one of the tranquilizing tablets he had recently started carrying to the office and pop it in his mouth. Of course he couldn't very well do that in front of Duckworth and he had not had a chance to do it before coming into his office. The vice managing editor's habit of running across you in the corridor and taking you into his office may have had the advantage of being informal and democratic; its disadvantage was that it gave you no time to prepare. Then when they had got inside that huge office the vice managing editor did something that really terrorized Bush. He closed the door. Only someone who worked at *Vital* could realize how ominous this seemingly routine act could be. *Vital* did not believe in anyone, whatever his position, closing his door. The closed door suggested a violation of the magazine's spirit of great accessibility, that no one, however lofty of position, should shut himself off from access to anyone, however humble of position. Only if something ei-

ther extremely secret or extremely personal was involved was a door
to be closed. It is a tribute to the way Duckworth handled things that
even with the closed door and the questions he was now asking, Bush
did not faint dead away. He knew he was in there for something and
finally the vice managing editor got to it.

"Well, the reports I hear," he said, leaning back and gazing san-
guinely out over the East River vista with a suck-suck and a puff-
puff, "are that you're doing quite adequately. But, oh, by the way,
Avery. There is one thing. Before you go."

The vice managing editor swiveled slowly until he was looking not
at the East River, but straight at Avery Bush, and pretty keenly.

"Avery." Suck-suck. Puff-puff. "I know you'll understand this. I
used to be a newspaperman once myself. That was a long time ago
and sometime we'll have to have a chat about the newspaper life, and
how it's all right as far as it goes, but how newspapers are so lacking
in so many ways, mainly in this old-fashioned idea of journalism they
still creak on with, of being 'objective'—why, God himself is not objective!—and therefore a magazine like *Vital* has to step in and by
having a point of view fill a national gap which the newspapers,
which have no point of view about anything but ignorantly boast
about being objective and unbiased—an invariable synonym incidentally for 'flabbiness'—leave. But some other time for that. What I
wanted to tell you, Avery, was." The vice managing editor sucked in
on his pipe and laid down a smoke screen. When it had cleared Bush
felt himself being looked at quite meaningfully over a briar pipe, in
a way somehow to give him still further the terrors and the shakes.
"Avery: did you ever realize that you smile quite a bit?"

"What was that, sir?" Bush wasn't sure he had heard quite right. He
thought about his mouth. The question made him so self-conscious
about it that he felt it was twisting around in strange formations, to
where he had no idea what it was doing right now, smiling, biting, or
what.

"I said," the vice managing editor repeated easily, "that you seem
to smile a very great deal. Avery, I wouldn't be taking the trouble to
talk with you if I didn't think you had potential. You must realize that,
of course."

When Bush, not realizing an answer was expected, gave none, the
vice managing editor said softly but with just a slight insistency, "Don't
you?"

"Which, sir?" Bush said. "About your taking the trouble to talk
with me or about my having potential?"

"Avery," the vice managing editor said more crisply. "I don't think
the question was all that cryptic. I would hardly ask you if you
thought you had potential. You just wouldn't be unbiased on that sub-

ject, now would you? I mean, of course, that you realize why I'm bothering to talk with you."

"Oh, indeed yes, sir," Bush said quickly. He was very unhappy. He felt his mouth was making strange gyrations and he was making a passionate effort to keep anything resembling a smile off it. To bring his mouth under some measure of control he decided to light a cigarette. As he lit up, it tasted rather odd, but that was hardly a surprise. Anything, he calculated, would right now.

"Avery," the vice managing editor said.

"Yes?"

"Turn that cigarette around."

With a quick nervous jerk Bush brought the cigarette out of his mouth and realized in horror that he had lighted the filter end. Putting the thing out in a stand-ashtray alongside the chair he got another lit, with shaking hands but at least the right end. He inhaled a drag which burned a full half-inch of ash on it and engorged the last corner of his lungs.

"I would hate to see a small and correctable personality trait," the vice managing editor was continuing, "stand in the way of a future acceptable to *Vital*. Just don't smile at everything and all the time, Avery. I know it's just a mannerism that you probably picked up from working on a newspaper. Sometimes," he said reflectively, tilting back, "I don't know whether the journalistic experience of someone we hire who has worked on a newspaper is worth the effort we have to make in retraining him. Sometimes I feel it's simpler and better to get people with no journalistic experience at all, just a general zest about the world, and train them ourselves. As you may have noticed, we're hiring quite a few more of the latter nowadays than the former." This was a statement that served to raise even higher Bush's temperature of terror. "Forgive this digression about general policy, Avery. We're talking about you, I believe. I just wanted you to know that I realize one hundred and one percent this habit you seem to have of smiling all the time is probably something you picked up from working on a newspaper. I want you to know I realize that you're probably not trying to suck up or anything like that."

"Suck up, sir?" Bush said, astonished. "Why, no, sir, I don't think I would ever do that."

"One thing that makes *Vital* the great organ it is," the vice managing editor continued, "is the utter contempt we have around here for anyone who tries to suck up. Now of course you wouldn't. But oversmiling can give people the idea that you're flabby."

"Flabby, sir?" Bush said, trying hard to get the point and learn.

"Flabby," the vice managing editor repeated. He sucked in and blew out. "Smiling has nothing to do with happiness. Some of the people who smile the most are the unhappiest, not to mention the sickest. It's all right to smile sometimes, you understand. I'm not suggesting you give it up altogether. I'm not trying to change you into a sourpuss. We all believe in smiling around here." To prove it the vice managing editor now smiled himself. "It's just that it gives people the wrong impression if you do it all the time. We all try to be happier around here than anyone is anywhere. You've never worked at a happier place, have you, Avery?" And the vice managing editor gave Bush a very direct look.

"Why, sir, I hadn't thought too much about it," said Bush, who was trying to be honest and above all not to suck up. But his head was spinning. "I've never worked at a more *stimulating* place."

"I believe the word I used was *happier*, Avery," Duckworth said, and Bush felt, rightly or wrongly, that there was something faintly ominous in his voice. He was afraid if he answered too favorably he would be thought to be sucking up.

"Well, sir," he said, and he was slightly frantic now, "the Washington *Post* was a pretty happy place . . ."

"Avery."

Something in the way his name was said convinced Bush that far from being considered sucking up, a favorable answer here was almost urgently indicated.

"But, no, sir," Bush said hurriedly. "I'm sure this is the *happiest* place I ever worked . . ."

"Good," the vice managing editor said as if Bush had just passed a test. Suck-suck. Puff-puff. "I'm glad you feel that way, Avery. Myself, I have always looked upon it as an honor to work for the nation's greatest magazine and for a young man like yourself to learn under this country's most brilliant editors—I except myself. I'm sure you are one hundred and one percent conscious of that honor, Avery. I know I always was."

"I certainly am conscious of it. I've been very, very deeply *happy* here," Bush, encouraged, went on. "By comparison with *Vital,* things were perfectly miserable at the *Post.* Why, they had an assistant city editor there who was the . . ."

"Avery," the vice managing editor said quietly.

"Yes, sir?"

"Avery. Let's not go overboard. Excessive emotion can be very bad for a *Vital* man. And the *Post* is not a bad sheet as newspapers go. Flabby and soft-headed, of course. They never know what they want, but then few newspapers do. I've known worse. So I wouldn't attack it too much if I were you. It suggests disloyalty to an organization which gave you your start."

Bush, who thought the Washington *Post* was a great newspaper, had been extremely happy there, and never realized more than right now how happy he had been there, where life by comparison suddenly seemed so uncomplicated, said, "Yes, sir."

"But I'm glad you feel happy here, Avery. Just watch the smile and I wouldn't be surprised if your future got quite acceptable around here. And Avery."

"Yes, sir?"

"Keep up that metabolism!"

For a few days after that Bush was extremely baffled, not to mention terrified. He learned, however, which proves both his intelligence and Duckworth's judgment as to his potential with *Vital*. Within a year from that conversation, smiling only for very specific reasons, he was chief researcher in Foreign News. Within two years from it he was a correspondent in the Paris bureau. Within four years he was chief of the London bureau. Now people were beginning to speak of him as senior editor timber. His future at *Vital* had become highly acceptable. When he smiled now it really meant something and was not just an unwitting habit. He was going up The Ladder, and a great deal of it was due to the fact that Harrison Duckworth had taken the time and interest to set a young man on course.

The ability to understand and analyze personality and to handle detail: Not many on earth are polished in both of these. By nature they are antagonistic traits. But Harrison Duckworth, the vice managing editor and S.O.B. of *Vital* magazine, was enormously adept and shrewd in both. He had an extremely difficult job, for he dealt with personalities so surpassingly difficult and complex that the executive vice-president for personnel of even a highly progressive company like Procter and Gamble would probably, despite the Wagner Act, have kicked nearly all of them in justifiable rage out the door. Recently a problem so ticklish as to challenge even Duckworth's great competence in matters of *Vital* personnel had arisen.

The problem was in connection with the elegant buffet dinner which was served in the office to late workers on Saturday night. One Wednesday morning Duckworth sat examining the bill from the previous Saturday night which had come along from Le Porc Blanc. He had been startled to see that the bill was for eighty-four dinners. It was unbelievable. He felt absolutely certain that no more than seventy *Vital* people at the most had had to work late last Saturday night. The figure varied on different Saturday nights, the number staying over to work ranging from fifty to seventy-five. The vice managing editor sat back and rubbed his bluish chin thoughtfully, then, swinging around, looked out over the towers of midtown Manhattan. Could Le Porc Blanc, he wondered, have padded the bill? He rejected the idea at once. *Vital* had been doing business with Le Porc Blanc for years. Not only during all that time had the restaurant had the Saturday night account; it also did a vast amount of catering for *Vital* parties, and besides that, many of the highest business and editorial positions of the magazine, the only ones whose expense or personal accounts could afford such a place, gave it their custom. It would have been the height of penny-wise pound-foolishness for the restaurant to jeopardize this highly lucrative trade for the sake of sneaking in a few unconsumed dinners on the Saturday night buffet job.

The vice managing editor swung in his chair for a change of scenery. Now he contemplated the East River vista. It could mean only one thing: It meant that freeloading people from the outside who had nothing whatsoever to do with *Vital* were sneaking into the buffet line.

Harrison Duckworth sat and thought and polished his Phi Beta Kappa key. If it had been just the researchers, writers and editors the problem would have been simple. He knew all of these, and all he would have to do would be, come next Saturday night, to observe what strange faces were in the line. The problem was that people from the teletype room, the copy room, the Morgue, the photo lab and the layout room were also entitled, provided they worked late, to eat the Saturday night dinner. Duckworth did not have the time to deal directly with the employment of the functionaries in these departments. This meant that there might be people in the chow line who were perfectly entitled to the dinner and yet whom he didn't know. This made it a problem. It would be unthinkable to go up to someone in the line strange to him and ask the person who was on the point of receiving a generous slice of the succulent roast prime ribs of beef along with the Yorkshire pudding—it would be impossible, Duckworth was thinking, for him to ask such a person, "Do you work here?" If the person did turn out to work for *Vital,* it would be horrible. Even if he didn't it was a demeaning thing, hardly worthy of the stature and dignity of the position of vice managing editor.

For a few moments, swinging to change the view back to the towers of midtown Manhattan, Harrison Duckworth contemplated ways and means. His executive method had for years now been jelled. It was invariably to proceed slowly, to expose himself thoroughly to facts before he decided what action to take. The first thing to do, he decided now, was to case the buffet line this next Saturday night just for a general impression of how many faces in it were strange to him. Even this, he realized, would have to be done delicately, unobtrusively. The vice managing editor of *Vital* could not appear to be standing there visually frisking people.

It would be a ticklish problem all right. But *Vital*'s S.O.B. never doubted for a moment that he would solve it.

One Wednesday, after some two months or so of vicarious philanthropy, a mimeographed memorandum landed on Jason's desk.

To: All *Vital* Personnel
From: Vice Managing Editor

As you all know, *Vital* each Saturday night provides a dinner in for the convenience of such of its personnel as may be working late. All of you equally know that *Vital* is more than happy to provide this dinner for its working personnel and we hope you all find the dinner satisfactory. At least we have not so far had any raging complaints.

Quite the contrary. The dinner seems to be so good that the number of people devouring it each Saturday night is reflected in a steady graph upward—a graph for which there seems no logical explanation.

In an effort to penetrate the mystery of the increasing number of people enjoying the dinner, we would like to try an experiment which we are sure all *Vital* personnel will understand.

Commencing next Saturday night a clipboard will be placed at the head of the buffet line. Would you each please sign your name just before you pass through the line?

Happy eating!—to *Vital* personnel.
(Signed) H. D.

Jason Hightower, reading the memorandum, did not consider for a moment solving the problem simply by telling his friends the gravy train had been derailed, and that they would have to seek nourishment elsewhere. He didn't like to ask his friends to give up a hospitality to which so many of them had, at his instance, become accustomed. Furthermore, the memorandum presented itself to Jason as a challenge. He knew already that at least three self-invited guests were coming up from college this weekend, and since all three had long since become steady patrons of the Saturday night meal he knew they would be seriously disappointed if they had to buy their own dinners. Besides that, having come to expect the dinner, they might not even have enough money set aside to buy their own and Jason had no intention of feeding the lot of them himself.

Therefore he now began quietly to think the problem through. It was no more than five minutes before an idea hit him.

The mind, he paused to think for a moment, is a wonderful mechanism if people would only use it, and distinguishes us from the bears.

He then went on to assemble a plan which appeared to him so beautiful as to be almost classic in its lines. The way to handle the situation was obvious: He would find out who on the staff would *not* be working late on the given Saturday night. Then, from that considerable choice, he would assign two or three of their names for use to his friends.

It was never possible to know for sure until during the day Saturday who would and who would not be there late, but this would leave him plenty of time to phone his friends at his apartment. That Friday night, when his three friends arrived, Jason explained to them the minor problem which had arisen and told them to stand by in his apartment

at six on Saturday, at which time he would phone and tell them which
staff members they would be for dinner. The friends were as delighted
as Jason with the plan. They liked very much the idea of becoming
other persons, and *Vital* persons at that, for purpose of rations.

On Saturday Jason had more than enough names far before six
o'clock. He simply found out which stories left over from Friday would
be closed by Saturday noon or so and jotted down the names of the
researchers and writers working on them. At fifteen minutes after six
—as a matter of principle Jason never did anything on time—he
phoned his apartment and supplied the friend who answered with
three staff names.

"You can each choose your own name," Jason said. "Be whichever
of those three respectively pleases you. See you up here at eight."

That evening three young men entered the *Vital* dinner line as Robert Jefferson, John Mitchell and James Stuart, affixed their signatures
to the clipboard, and emerged respectively as Anthony Pinckney,
James Bernstein and Avery Bush. They ate their dinner with the
voracious appetite of college youth eating for free, and left.

The thing was uneventful in entirety.

The system having worked so perfectly, Jason continued to use it.
Whatever number of friends came up on the weekend he always had
names, and to spare, to metamorphose them into other persons. Actually the only problem was one of selection—of names. It was so ridiculously easy that once Jason gave a friend from college by the name
of Emory Slade III a name to use which caused Slade a brief surprise.

"See here, Slade," Jason said over the phone to his apartment one
Saturday night, "tonight you will be Charity Cabot."

"But that's a girl's name!" Slade protested.

"Your incisive grasp of things has always profoundly impressed me,
Slade. I have long felt that it would lead you far."

"But what am I using a girl's name for?"

"To jazz it up, dumbness. Nobody looks when you sign in."

"Oh," Slade said. "I get it."

"You're very quick, Slade."

Weeks went on, the freeloading continued, and nothing happened.
On Saturday nights Jason would see Duckworth pacing the corridors
as dinner was being served, peering curiously at the people who passed
through the chow line. He looked very frustrated. He did his pacing
and his peering so adroitly, however, that probably only Jason noticed, he being the only one really interested, that Duckworth seemed
to find a lot of excuses to go up and down the corridor during serving
time before he went into the line himself. The fact of having so much
in common made Jason feel very close to the vice managing editor,
in the well-known manner of the police officer and the criminal he is
hunting.

One Saturday a very rare thing happened: No friends of Jason's were coming to New York. They always gave him at least a couple of days' notice, to make sure of bed space. Often the notice was much further in advance, almost like the February bookings at Round Hill in Montego Bay. The reason for this foresight was that Jason took on guests in order of application. It was a principle with him not to show favoritism and he numbered letters requesting space in the order in which they were received. Late applications often had to use the outdoor terrace, which slept eight in bags. For this weekend, however, Jason had received no applications whatsoever. It was the first time in memory this had happened, and he was puzzled. Then he remembered why: It was finals week at school.

At about a quarter after six Jason went on down with Gaskin and another writer named John Marshall Reasoner for a pre-dinner drink at the Eagle's Nest. This establishment was a small restaurant-bar located in a basement directly across from the office. Its name was a mystery, since no self-respecting eagle would have even considered going, much less making his nest, there. It was steamy, dark and none too clean. It had a vague species of unpleasant smell. Its food was so bad that even the owner of the place, a friendly man from the township of Licata, Sicily, advised against eating it, and even though it was a restaurant, too, with some vague kind of kitchen in the back, no one had ever been actually seen eating there. The waiter—there was only one, the only help beside the bartender-owner—would have been seriously shocked if anyone had asked for a menu. However, the Eagle's Nest did a prodigious business in drinking whiskey. Its clientele was almost exclusively the personnel of *Vital*. There were always some there every evening after work, but on Saturday night the place was jam-crammed with *Vital* people who were stuck at the office closing the issue. Everyone tried to get over there for two, three or four drinks before dinner to tide them over until the management broke out whiskey in the office at 10.00 P.M.

Jason staked out a few inches of space in the pungent, rustling posse of those who stand to drink and in a few minutes had received, relayed from the bartender's sweating hands through the hands of two *Vital* staffers, one of those incredibly dark drinks—dark for strength —which the Eagle's Nest gave out and which served no little to make it such a favorite of the *Vital* crowd. Then before too long he got another of them via the same relay system. He had just dug into this second drink when the waiter somehow found his way over to him, or at least near him, to tell him, in Sicilian tones, that he was wanted at the telephone. Jason, toting his drink—there was no place to set it down— made his way out through the solidity and got into the phone booth in the hallway. He set his drink down on the ledge, picked up the instrument and spoke into it.

"Old Mahse Hightower heah."

"Jason," a voice with those clipped tones of New England that so grated on Jason's ear said. "Guess who?"

"I don't know," Jason said, "but unless you tell me in the next two words you speak you will find this connection cut off."

"Emory Slade the Third," the voice said immediately.

"Oh, Slade," Jason said. "Well, what is it?"

"You don't sound very hospitable, Jason."

"Hospitable? Hell, Conrad Hilton is about to sue me for unfair competition. What services can I render you, Slade? I assume you've called for services."

"Good old Jason," Slade said.

"Listen, Slade," Jason said. "Come off it. What the hell you want?"

"Jason," Slade said quickly, "I just got up from school. Finished my last final this afternoon. No time to write sorry."

Jason didn't wonder how Slade knew he was at the Eagle's Nest. All of Jason's clients from school knew the habits of *Vital* people so well by now they were almost like *Vital* people.

"I was wondering if you could put me up, Jason," Slade was saying.

"Help yourself. You know where the key is."

"Got you, Jason," Slade said. "And oh, Jason."

"Yes, Emory," Jason said wearily.

"Could I eat too?" He sounded very wistful, like a child anticipating Sunday dinner.

"Sure," Jason said. "Come on up."

"Jason," Slade said hurriedly. "There's just one other thing. Who am I tonight?"

Maybe it was the drinks. In any event Jason had momentarily forgotten Slade would need a name to eat.

"Just a moment, Emory."

It was a small predicament. Not knowing anyone was coming Jason had not bothered to check which staff personnel would be working late tonight, or rather which would not. Now two or three names, then four or five, occurred to him that he was almost certain would not be there. But not having checked he didn't want to assign their names. It was foolish to run any kind of risk on a deal that was so sure as long as you didn't get careless. The surest things in the world, Jason told himself cannily, had jumped the tracks for slight and unnecessary carelessness. He thought some more. Then a name shot up at him out of all the staff members of *Vital* of someone he knew was never there on Saturday nights. As a matter of fact, even if he was working late he always ate out, at some place like Hamburg Heaven, where you eat at a school desk, or Nedick's, those omnipresent palaces which drench New York in orange drink and clobber it with hot dogs and where you eat standing up. Eat standing up! Jason thought in quick parenthesis: The ultimate horror and how symbolic of the times! Then this man (Jason returning rigidly to the problem) came back to the office. This idiosyncrasy had become a minor legend at *Vital* and its reason was lost in antiquity, at least right now it was lost in Jason's antiquity. Anyhow, the reason the particular staff member never ate the dinner in was beside the point, and very much to the point was the fact that his name was the safest of all to use. Also to the point was the fact that the connection would be cut off in a moment on this pay phone, he could not be sure Slade had another nickel and he certainly wasn't going to spend a dime of his own to call him back wherever he was.

"Here's who you are for tonight, Slade," Jason said into the telephone. "It's a rather peculiar spelling for a provincial person like yourself, so write it down. You got a pencil and paper?"

"Just a moment. Okay."

"The name," Jason said into the mouthpiece, "is Antora Ganlivov."

"What's that?" his friend said into the phone. "What kind of name is that?"

"Emory," Jason said, "I don't have time to give you an education in the science of names and nationality, particularly over the phone. All that need concern what mind you have is getting the spelling right. You don't even have to pronounce it. Now here it is. Now spell it back to me."

Slade started to do that . . .

"No, no, no!" Jason shouted into the phone. "My God, Slade! A little mistake like that could cut off the dinners of a hundred people for the next year."

"I'm terribly sorry, Jason," Slade said humbly. "It's an unusual name . . ."

"Listen urgently, Slade," Jason said. "That's a *v* after the *o*, not an *f*. No true native of that land ever uses an *f* following a vowel but I can't go into that now. I'll spell it once more."

He did. Slade spelled it back correctly.

"Fine." Jason sighed. "Just sign Antora Gan . . ."

"Deposit another nickel for the next five min . . ."

Jason hung up, picked up his drink, swallowed the rest of it there in the booth and went back for another. Waiting for it he suddenly began to feel very happy at having thought of such a sure name on such lack of notice. He wondered why it hadn't occurred to him before to use Ganlivov's name. Probably, he thought, because the interesting mechanics of figuring out on Saturday morning which names would not be staying in for dinner had so absorbed him that he did not think to use a name where no figuring at all was required. He felt happy at the name's coming to him when he really needed it. He would have hated to disappoint old Slade. Slade wasn't very bright but Jason

rather liked him in the way one might like a beagle pup which wasn't
as intelligent as a man but had a good-hearted way of wagging its tail.

He finished his third drink. They certainly made them virile at the
Eagle's Nest, he thought, it was the one bar in New York where they
just splashed the whiskey in, and pretty reckless splashing, instead of
measuring it out almost like an eyedropper into one of those thimble-
sized jiggers. He felt very good. He noticed it was almost eight and
went on out with Gaskin and Reasoner, across the street and up the
elevator, ready to eat, his digestive muscles being now in good, happy,
relaxed working order.

As he stepped out of the elevator on the thirty-fourth floor a thought
occurred to him. For one fraction of a second he felt something in the
pit of his stomach. Then it was gone. The thought that prompted the
feeling was that perhaps the vice managing editor was familiar with
Ganlivov's custom of never eating in on Saturday nights, even if working. Whereupon, seeing his name on the clipboard list, he would wonder . . . Then the feeling had evaporated in a quickly conceived
way to make sure about this. After dinner he would just ring Ganlivov
up and explain what he had done. Ganlivov, he was confident, would
be delighted his name had been used for the philanthropic purpose of
gypping the company, especially where it concerned the Saturday night
dinner he had such a complex about anyway.

For another fraction of a second Jason was bothered by the fact he
hadn't thought of this detail when he gave Slade the name. Not that
it mattered. But on principle Jason didn't like the idea that his mind
could overlook any pertinent detail. He attributed the oversight to the
darkness of the drinks at the Eagle's Nest. Then he forgot it and went
on down the corridor looking for Slade.

Jason saw him up ahead, shuffling around in the corridor. He was
a blond-haired, simple-faced youth with very American features,
someone who could never, never be mistaken for anything but an
American. Jason smiled, amused at the idea of Slade's passing off as
Antora Ganlivov. They greeted each other warmly and got into the
chow line, Slade immediately in front of Jason. When they reached the
clipboard, Slade spent a rather long time with the pencil. Jason could
feel the people behind him beginning to rustle impatiently. He gave
Slade a sharp jab in the ribs to hurry him up. Slade stifled a cry of
pain and finished signing. Coming right after him and signing his own
name, Jason was glad to see Slade had spelled Antora Ganlivov with
a thorough correctness. The last *v* went off a little crazy, probably
because he had jabbed Slade right then, but it just looked like a flourish and if anything gave the forgery more authenticity.

Jason, continuing down the line, had never felt such a delicious-
ness in enabling his friends to eat as guests of *Vital* as this evening. It
was *noblesse oblige,* it was the feeling known to the lords of the manor

in the olden time dispensing largesse to the grateful peasants. It was doubtless, he decided, because it had come up so unexpectedly and he had been able to think of a name so quickly. The true pleasures of life, he thought expansively, are those which come upon us without warning. The other way, of knowing ahead of time and being able to get up such a fat list of names to assign from, had become dull with the dullness that goes with easiness. He felt a new and met challenge to his skill for the problem to have arisen so suddenly tonight and yet to have been solved so quickly, so adroitly.

Following his friend he went on down the line. Jason and Emory Slade Ganlivov joined Joy Morehouse and Paisley Fairlamb—a couple of fellow researchers who were sitting at their desks in the National Affairs bullpen eating. Then both he and his friend had generous seconds of everything, turkey and dressing through mince pie with a healthy hunk of good cured cheddar on it. At about nine-thirty Slade, thanking Jason warmly, left for a party he was going to.

"I will see you later, Antora," Jason said.

They both, Jason and Slade, laughed appreciatively at this jest, their full stomachs shaking a little.

Jason decided to have a piece of the pumpkin pie, which he had not tried, and another cup of coffee. He was feeling very happy and this emotion always enlarged his appetite. Finishing these, he sat back and patted his tummy comfortably. For quite a while his hand rested in relaxed delight on his very full stomach. He felt almost beatifically content. He decided, before getting back to work on the Oklahoma tornado, that he would give Ganlivov that phone call. He looked up his number in the home telephone list and dialed it. While waiting he hummed some little song to himself, a little French song:

> *"Au clair de la lune,*
> *Mon ami Pierrot,*
> *Prête-moi ta plume*
> *Pour écrire un mot . . ."*

Jason often hummed French songs when he was happy.

A woman's voice answered. It had a fairly heavy accent. He had a vague feeling of having met Mrs. Ganlivov at a party somewhere. But he wasn't sure. The thing to do, he knew at once, was to call her Madame.

"Madame Ganlivov?" he said cheerfully. "Hightower at the office. Jason Hightower, Madame Ganlivov. I don't know if you remember me."

"Who's that? Oh, of coh-urse," the voice said. Jason was pretty sure she didn't remember him, probably because she had never met or seen him, but he knew that the thing for her to say about anyone at the office was of course. "How ahr you?"

"Tolerably well, Madame Ganlivov. And yourself?"

"Oh, soh-soh," Mrs. Ganlivov said. "Of coh-urse I mees Antora."

Jason Hightower straightened up ever so imperceptibly in his Do-More chair.

"What do you mean, Madame Ganlivov, you miss Antora?"

The compassionate thought moved into his mind that perhaps Antora and Mrs. Ganlivov were divorced, separated or had some other arrangement. The Lord knew there were more different arrangements at *Vital* than Kinsey had ever heard about, much less interviewed and recorded on those eternal code cards of his. Jason prepared to be sympathetic—he could be checking his story while being sympathetic over the phone—then when she had run on with it awhile to get Antora's number at whatever hotel he might be inhabiting during the dissolution of his household. Reaching for his copy of the Oklahoma tornado story to start checking it he heard Mrs. Ganlivov's voice going on. Her voice seemed surprised about something . . .

"Why, don't you know, Meester Hightower," Mrs. Ganlivov was saying. "Antora is out doing a story. For *Vee-tal*'s Great Adventure series. He's been goh-ne two months. Tonight I think he's in Katmandu . . ."

Jason Hightower never remembered saying good-bye. He assumed he must have said something civil, he was too much of a gentleman and had too much presence of mind to hang up on a lady without a thanks and a good-bye. At least a good-bye.

He jumped to his feet and ran down the hall to the head of the chow line.

The clipboard was gone.

He went back to his desk. He sat down and started thinking seriously. He considered the possibilities.

However, none of them seemed very good.

The day of judgment, he estimated, would be around Wednesday or maybe Thursday. Duckworth would somehow get to the bottom of it. Jason didn't quite know how—he could have made a couple of educated guesses—but he would.

He went back to his Oklahoma tornado. He wished he were out there right now.

It was not Wednesday or Thursday. It was Friday following that Jason ran into Duckworth in the corridor, or Duckworth ran into him, he didn't know which. Jason had been avoiding the vice managing editor. If he could avoid running into him in the corridor he might never have to discuss this. Wishful thinking. Of course you could not forever avoid running into Duckworth. He seemed able almost to make you run into him if he wanted to see you.

"Oh, by the way, Jason," the vice managing editor said affably.

"There was something I wanted to speak to you about. What was it?" He bunched his lower lip between thumb and forefinger. "Oh, yes. Could you spare a minute?"

Jason thought of several possible answers to that. He chose, "Certainly."

"Good," Duckworth said, as if he had not been entirely confident of the reply.

Jason followed the vice managing editor into his office. They sat down. The vice managing editor leaned back in his chair. He looked out the window for a moment—his East River estate. Then he turned back, and twirling his Phi Beta Kappa key, looked easily at Jason.

"Well, Jason," he said. "How are you liking it here by now?"

"Why, I like it fine," Jason said. He decided not to say more. When you have nothing to say, Jason believed, don't say it.

"Good," the vice managing editor said. He plucked a pipe from his tray and started filling it. "There's nothing quite like a man being happy in his work."

He looked out the window for a moment—this time at the midtown Manhattan view—and with a medley of sucking noises lighted up his pipe. Then he looked back at Jason, with ease and casualness.

"Jason," he said, "I was talking to Mrs. Ganlivov this morning." Suck-suck, puff-puff. "I decided I would like to talk with Mrs. Ganlivov. Do you happen to know Mrs. Ganlivov, Jason?"

"Not well," Jason said. "I know her well enough to speak to her."

"A very interesting woman, Mrs. Ganlivov," the vice managing editor said. "Her husband Antora is doing very well here. I imagine she's a big help to him. One of those old-fashioned European wives, you know, that really help their husbands instead of chawing at them all the time—a type that is just about extinct in America by now and in ten years or so I imagine will be completely so. Already they're as rare as the ivory-billed woodpecker."

The vice managing editor, with a whole series of suck-sucks and puff-puffs, regarded the East River view. "One can learn a lot from talking to Mrs. Ganlivov. Don't you think, Jason?"

There was one moment of profound silence. Then the vice managing editor, leaning deep in his chair, said out of the cloudless blue: "Philanthropy is a very fine thing, isn't it, Jason? I'm sure we all believe in philanthropy. Don't we, Jason?"

"It would be pretty hard to be opposed to it," Jason said.

"Yes, indeed," the vice managing editor continued. "One thinks of the Rockefellers, the Ford Foundation, of Andrew Carnegie and all those libraries and pipe organs of his so decoratively strewing the land. Of John Simon Guggenheim, George F. Baker and Edward Stephen Harkness. Of Mellon . . . Well, the list could go on and on. In a way we are a people of philanthropists and the tradition surely must be judged by one and all a glorious one. The greatest of these is charity. The quality of substance is to share with one's fellow man. I wonder who was the first philanthropist?"

"Eve, I guess. She shared her apple with Adam."

"You do have such a fine sense of wit, Jason. That also is a most admirable quality. But let us stick with philanthropy for the moment. You know of course what Thoreau said on the subject."

"Right offhand I don't believe I do."

"Would you like for me to quote it to you?"

"I'd appreciate that very much."

" 'Philanthropy is almost the only virtue which is sufficiently appreciated by mankind.' "

"Yes, they certainly seem to appreciate it," Jason said reflectively. "What's that from, sir?"

"Never mind what it's from, Jason. If there's anything we must all believe in it's philanthropy. However." Swiveling with ominous slowness the vice managing editor fixed Jason straight in the eye. "However," he said. "There's another thing we must remember, which is: There can be too much of a good thing. Now don't ask me what that's from. Do you agree with the philosophy contained in that statement, Jason?"

"I don't believe I could find any fault with it," Jason said, getting the point.

"Good!" the vice managing editor exclaimed.

Duckworth relit his pipe. Suck-suck. Puff-puff. And then a rather unforgettable thing happened, at least it would always remain unforgettable to Jason Hightower. With absolute abruptness the vice managing editor burst into a piercing laugh, a cry of hilarity so wildly rollicking Jason thought it must surely bring the people from outside the office, and maybe even the building, rushing in to see what was the matter. Simultaneously the vice managing editor's hand shot across and gave Jason's thigh a slap that cut through the fourteen-ounce flannel trousers he was wearing as if they were the work clothes of a belly dancer and set up a stinging so intense it was all Jason could do to keep from crying out himself.

"Jason, my boy," the vice managing editor said when he was able to bring his hurricane of laughter under partial control. His eyes were wet with laughter. "Jason, I think it's one of the funniest things I ever heard of. How long have you been doing it?"

"About three months," Jason said. He felt in a blizzard of astonishment.

"A perfectly wonderful joke," the vice managing editor said. Suddenly he looked most intently at Hightower. "Jason: Do you know what we really love on *Vital* magazine?"

"Why, no, sir," Jason said, flabbergasted beyond extensive speech.

"Legends."

"What was that, sir?"

"I said legends. We love legends on *Vital* and do you know what you have done, Jason?"

"Well, in general," Jason said with authentic vagueness. "Not specifically though. Apparently."

The vice managing editor leaned deeply toward Jason. "My boy," he said, "you have created what may shape up as one of our greatest legends around here. Have you thought of it that way?"

"To tell you the truth I hadn't."

"There is nothing we love at *Vital* more than legends. The ability in a person to create a legend: Well, as an experienced *Vital* personnel man, I can tell you this: no other single thing so upbuilds a man in our estimation of him, our conclusion as to his real, untapped potential as a *Vital* man. Did you know that, Hightower?"

"No." Jason thought it best to keep his answers as short as possible.

Abruptly the vice managing editor went off into fresh new, startling peals of laughter. He got out his handkerchief and dried his eyes then blew his nose.

"Well, that's all, Jason," he said. "Keep up that metabolism."

Jason left the vice managing editor's office. He walked in rather a daze back to his desk and sat down. He felt decidedly shaken.

Even the S.O.B. at *Vital* was pretty wonderful. Also, he really merited that Phi Beta Kappa key.

8

Random Lovemaking

I find it very difficult in this book to avoid the use of superlatives. But the fact of the matter is that so many superlatives, all true, can be applied to *Vital* magazine. There is one, however, which was sometimes applied which I seriously question. This is that more random lovemaking left from this building than from any other building in the world. I profoundly question that statement. Not that this form of human endeavor was entirely absent from the place. What I would say is that possibly the very best random lovemaking in New York had its origins there. This itself was something of which the magazine could justly be proud.

I must speak yet once more in superlatives. This is in the matter of researchers. Before *Vital* there had been nothing comparable to "re-

searchers" in the journalistic world, and even today there is nothing
really to compare with *Vital*'s staff of researchers. Some three-fourths
of them were of the female persuasion and they were a highly intelligent lot. In addition, most of them were decidedly pretty, attractive,
or beguiling in one manner or another. I think it would be hard to gain-
say the statement that more charming and desirable young ladies
worked at *Vital* than at any other office in New York and that their
average IQ surpassed by a considerable margin that of any other female group in the great city. How did *Vital* get them?

One way *Vital* got researchers was by means of a tour made each
springtime of the higher girl factories of the East. A personnel team
went around to Vassar, Smith, Bryn Mawr, Wellesley, Bennington,
Sarah Lawrence and Radcliffe and discussed with the new upcoming
flock of graduates the employment opportunities at *Vital*. It was a very
interesting assignment. Hank Gaskin was always trying to get a writer,
namely, himself, sent along on the grounds that the writer worked
more closely with the researcher than anyone else and therefore could
best determine which raw material would make the best *Vital* researchers. Since Gaskin's standards of employment and proposed methods of
operations on the various campuses—including a number of very interesting tests—would have varied steeply from that of the standard
personnel team, he was never sent along. There were also girls at *Vital*
sprung from such outlands as the University of California, Southern
Methodist University and the University of Michigan, but they were in
a decided minority. Five minutes of being with them was sufficient to
identify them as not being from any of the Eastern women's collegiate
emporiums which provided most of *Vital*'s girl researchers. There are
a hundred different blessed touches which distinguish the girl from the
Eastern women's college from all other females on earth, and there are
a score which distinguish those from one Eastern women's college from
those from another. Gaskin claimed that if you gave him ten minutes
each with a girl from each of the seven colleges listed above, with no
hints being dropped in the conversation of the school she attended, he
could tell you at the end of that time which school it was. The boast
was never put to the test but I think it would have been very easy.
Each of these great schools leaves its own valued trademark on a girl,
as indelibly as the brand on the rump of a Texas steer.

It was a great attraction to a girl to work for *Vital*. It meant prestige, it meant a constant association with fascinating people, a working
place free of the stuffiness which afflicts so many business offices—free
on both the intellectual and personal levels, ideas being eagerly wel-
comed from the lowliest, and high-borne editors hobnobbing with researchers in perfect ease, in or out of the office, a democratic point of
view which allowed for the maximum closeness, no caste being permitted for an instant to stand in the way of either communication or

fraternization—and there were a lot of men at *Vital,* too. What was more, they were a different kind of men, entirely unlike the stockbroker, legal or Madison Avenue types. Any girl in the world with the slightest sense of discrimination and imagination would prefer to work for *Vital* rather than for a Wall Street investment firm or an advertising firm situated on Madison Avenue. Now as regards random lovemaking and these business enterprises, the chances would be that less of it went on at *Vital* than on Madison Avenue and more than on Wall Street. And perhaps we have also a clue as to why that which did go on at *Vital* was so far better than the New York average: It was because the girls at *Vital* were more interesting, of course, but perhaps above all because, girl for girl, they had infinitely less calculation than the girl would naturally have who worked for, say, an advertising agency, where to be lacking in calculation is as severe a handicap as for a minister of the gospel to be lacking in compassion. And to the degree that calculation enters in, just exactly to that degree good lovemaking is impossible. This is Law Number 1 about Lovemaking—or Love.

Despite the unfavorable quantitative balance at *Vital* in relation to Madison Avenue, Henry Gaskin had done very well there. But he was not typical . . .

A pertinent word here about hobbies. Every man ought to have a hobby, they say. For relaxation. What it is hardly matters. It can be cabinetmaking, stamp collecting, oil painting, golf, flapjack-cookery, bird hunting, bird watching, or raising orchids. It can be almost anything. The hobbies all have the same purpose, which is to slow down the pace of life that is killing us all off in good old America, the land of the free, the brave and the mentally desperate, the people unable to pull joy from life, making our best brains die twenty years before their time, twenty years in which all their accumulation of knowledge, intelligence, wisdom, as the case may be, could have been offered us and the world. We speak there from society's viewpoint. Not to mention their own, which is that they kick off just when life is ready to get going for them, the normal fumblings of the first forty years of any man's life behind. Reader, we sincerely hope that if you don't have a hobby you rush out and stop at nothing until you get one.

Henry Gaskin's hobby was women.

In fact it would be more nearly correct to say this was his vocation and that his employment as a *Vital* writer was only the necessary economic nuisance to support the only activity which he considered of any importance in life. In this he differed mortally from a man like the photographer Montgomery Shanks, to whom women were only of equal importance to photography.

As concerns researchers, Gaskin, to be explicit, had known eight of them on the sweet frontier. I hesitate to cite this figure lest it be considered typical by the hasty-minded. I repeat that it wasn't and I repeat that this was Gaskin's chief aim and interest in life, the one to which he devoted most of his time and literally all of his vigilance and energy. It had been Gaskin's experience, admittedly limited, that girls from colleges other than the great women's colleges of the East were infinitely better in bed, or, lest that blunt statement offend some in nonacademic circles, I will call a spade a rose and correct it to say infinitely better in matters of love. Gaskin had his own explanation of this, which was that the girl from the Eastern women's college was so tied up in psychic knots—he had no idea what they did to them there, though as a guess he would have said they learned, along with other brilliant academic tutelage, "equality" for women, which is translated as looking upon man as their natural enemy as much so as the chicken upon the hawk, and could judge only the results—that it was literally impossible for her to make good love. It is a dangerous generalization, like all generalizations, and Hank Gaskin remained perfectly willing to be convinced otherwise. In fact he was constantly broad-mindedly exposing himself to situations that might convert him. He never lost hope. In particular he would have liked to become congenial with someone from the one school he hadn't tried, Sarah Lawrence. Meantime he did recognize full well the fact, and this from real experience, that the girls from *Vital* were much better than the girls from, for example, an advertising agency, even if from the same school. This alone spoke very well for the magazine.

Perhaps one might essay a brief summary here: The fact that writers and editors (men usually) worked in close teams with researchers (girls usually), added to the nature of the hours, added furthermore to the attractive aspects of both parties to a story, did tend to make the circumstances for random lovemaking, if one should be interested in such a thing, very nearly ideal. It would certainly have been strange, unnatural, a teasing of Fate, and a cause for regret when one got to be eighty if nothing had ever happened.

But I stray from the narrative of this chapter, even if, as Socrates says, digression is the right of a philosopher, and according to Thackeray and to Stendhal (two worthy authorities), even of a novelist. So, with my apologies of a sort for this amiable and well-intentioned diversion, let us return to the immediate subject, which concerns a researcher by the name of Paisley Fairlamb.

Paisley Fairlamb was no exception to the rule that *Vital* researchers were both uncommonly intelligent and attractive, except that she was more so of both than most. She was a bright, animated girl, very quick. Physically she was on the short side by the rangy Seabiscuit standards of the Miss America contest, being only five feet one and a half inches and weighing a hundred and five pounds. But what she had, all of it was very much alive and there, keenly probing for what was best for Paisley Fairlamb. She knew how to dress. If she walked down a street this occurrence would not disrupt traffic and send cars crashing into buildings. But it would cause about every other man, having passed her, to turn around for a further view and one from a corroborative vantage point. She had fine chestnut hair, a small face, rather a college-girl face still, and quick blue eyes which suggested she did her own thinking. Her skin was very fair. She had a handsome little apartment in a good block on a good street, East 61st, she gave quite a few parties and she knew a number of quite interesting people in New York. She liked her work and did not take anything at the magazine very seriously, or scarcely anything in life for that matter. She was most content and happy—and with a controlled relaxation. She was twenty.

Paisley Fairlamb was quite a young lady. She had drawn a face card in the accident of birth, into a family whose worries in life never included the chief worry of mankind the world over, which is money to buy things with. Not that the family was in the Rockefeller–Harriman– Ford–Vanderbilt major leagues of American families, by any means, but they did know where the money to pay the light bill was coming from every month, and no one in the family ever knew what it was not to be certain he would be eating three squares a day come this time next week. This equability was made possible by Paisley's father's ownership of a medium-sized textile mill near Greensboro. The Fairlambs divided their time pleasantily between their New York apartment and their place in North Carolina. Upon her graduation from college Paisley had gone to work as a researcher for the magazine by route of catching the fancy of the *Vital* personnel team. She had majored in international affairs and was proficient at languages. Therefore they put her in the Sports Department.

After six months in the world of Saturday heroes and jockstraps she was transferred to the Science Department. Now in her second year she was working in the National Affairs Department, the world of power-crazed politicians and any-means-to-an-end achievement. Which world she found the more horror-filled and venal, she would have been hard put to it to say. Scientists were inventing things to destroy the world. The politicians were committing acts which, armed with these scientists' inventions, appeared to range the odds on that destruction at about eighty-five to one. Sports people were generally barely above the cretin plateau mentally but at least they didn't do much harm. With the handicap of a background in international affairs it was unlikely that she would ever work in *Vital*'s Foreign Affairs Department. Nevertheless her reigning ambition was to get assigned to the magazine's Paris bureau, a city where she had spent her "third year" of college, and she had little doubt that sooner or later, and probably sooner, she would manage that in some way; she always had managed to end up getting what she wanted, for Paisley Fairlamb was an exquisite little arranger. Meantime her aim was both simple and profound, which was to enjoy life while it was around, since now of all times in history, she fancied, no man could underwrite tomorrow, above all not to get serious about life, and she was doing a pretty decent job at this goal.

Paisley Fairlamb was aware that men in the office at times looked at her with something more than the professional relationship demanded and she was entirely aware of what was going through their minds at such times. However, she had no intention of following the trite pattern of having a few drinks in or out of the office, and then . . . and then. That was not the way she was going to have it happen, when it happened. And the plain fact—and one that would have startled every man in the office—was that it had never happened.

Paisley Fairlamb was virginal. She was virginal but by no means innocent. These days, indeed, the two qualities are likely not to come in pairs. The fact of the matter was that if called upon to do so, Paisley Fairlamb could have written a manual on the subject that would have made Kinsey, Havelock Ellis and Henry Miller in triple collaboration look like people who scarcely knew what the bees do or where the flowers come from. Yet she was a virgin.

Paisley Fairlamb had had the benefits of the best education the United States affords, which may not be much but she had had the best there was. Much of her learning on her favorite subject had been obtained, noncurricularly, at these schools, beginning with the National Cathedral School for girls, where she had prepped. Her higher learning on the subject had then progressed at Sarah Lawrence. It is a tribute to both of these fine schools that though she learned so much on the subject at them, she remained free of first-hand experience. It was somewhat like a student of pure science, than the study of which there is nothing higher.

Paisley Fairlamb was an exceptionally fine specimen even for these schools. I don't believe anyone could have said anything that would have seriously shocked Paisley Fairlamb. She would just have looked at him studiously. The converse, however, was by no means true. You could never be sure whether Paisley *intended* to shock people or not, though I am inclined to think not. She simply practiced the subject, as it were, and spoke of it in the even tones one of her professors might have used to discourse on the Elizabethans.

This talk of Paisley Fairlamb's had led a long string of males to believe that the wheat was ripe for the harvest and the voice of the turtle about to be heard in the land. All had been more or less shocked to learn that nothing could be further from the truth. And Paisley certainly knew how to take care of herself. Once a first-team halfback of the Washington and Lee football team made the dreadful mistake of thinking her line of talk meant what it appeared to mean. That was one night down on the rolling green lawns at the North Carolina place and he watched next Saturday's game from the bench.

When the time came it would be Paisley who did the raping, so to speak. She would decide when—as a matter of fact that she had already decided, that it would be when she reached the age of twenty-one—and she would decide whom, and it would be forthwith done. Otherwise she wouldn't be in control of the situation. If there was one thing Paisley hated it was not being in control. The man wouldn't stand a chance.

Though I never saw any reason either why he would want to stand a chance.

The job of the *Vital* researcher was twofold. One part of it was to go out with photographers to cover stories in the New York area, and sometimes beyond it. The researcher gathered material for the captions and textblocks and kept the photographer happy. The other part of the researcher's job, in the office, was to work with the writer who was writing the captions, textblocks and heads to accompany a picture story. If the story had been covered by one of the bureaus, this meant, in the first place, assembling for the writer research material which came in from the bureau, and where necessary supplementing it with newspaper clippings and material from the Morgue. Then when the writer had written the story, there came what was by far the most important and infinitely the most nerve-racking part of the researcher's job.

This was to "check" for accuracy what the writer had written. It was a sensationally meticulous process. No piece of *Vital* copy could go to press until a researcher had literally placed a penciled dot over each and every word as her sworn testimony to its veracity. It could be a terrible thing sometimes. The writers generally had a tendency to keep their prose colorful. For example, if the story concerned a man who had built a submarine in his back yard in Alabama, the writer might spin in the statement that it was "the world's first submarine built in a back yard." There might be not the slightest shred of evidence for the statement. This never kept the writer from making it in his copy. It was up to the researcher to prove or disprove the statement. The statement written so airily, and even with a soaring creative feeling on the part of the writer, could lead to a perfect nightmare for the researcher. Those nine innocent words could mean six hours of work for her and drive her almost to distraction. If it was early enough in the day she could ask the Washington bureau to try to check the statement out with someone at the Navy Department. But if it was Saturday night when the copy landed on her desk it meant that she herself had to track down a submarine historian somewhere in the

United States, at home, at a cocktail party, at his weekend in the country, or even on a submarine, surfaced or submerged. *Vital* researchers
were extremely good at tracking people down. In ferreting out checking sources they had the nose of a San Quentin bloodhound. It was
almost impossible for any American citizen to escape the *Vital* researcher at any hour of day or night if she wanted to get him. In particular the researchers had an entrancing ability to find the greatest
expert on any given subject. Even if it was four o'clock on Sunday
morning and he was at a hunting lodge in the Maine woods, the chances
were that the *Vital* researcher would find him. The only trouble was
that sometimes even the world's greatest expert on submarines might
be unwilling to go out on the limb the researcher had whittled so
neatly for him and say this was "the world's first submarine built in a
back yard."

At this point the researcher went in to see the writer. Depending
on her temperament and how fairly certain or not she was of the statement, she would either let it go or try to talk the writer out of it. Depending on his temperament and how he felt at the moment, he agreed
or did not agree. If the writer was one of those nasty, stubborn writers, there materialized a battle of nerves, to be arbitrated by the copy
editor. This struggle between researchers fighting for accuracy and
writers fighting for their prose went on, a constant factor in more or
less degree. The weapons of the researchers varied enormously, depending chiefly on whether they hated men on principle or not. Those
who did were what were called "picky." Those who didn't often
worked wonders by way of a lot of discreet flattery of the writer, such
as: "You are the greatest writer in America and are certainly being
wasted here." *Vital* writers had an extremely low temperature of cre-
dulity toward such flattery. There was almost nothing they wouldn't
believe about themselves when it came to the subject of wasted talent.

The reason the checking of a story—putting dots over words—was
so nerve-twitching and could drive you out of your mind was that it
could change the whole course of one's life to dot a statement like the
one about homemade, back-yard-built submarines. For looming always above the researcher, like a busy Reign of Terror guillotine, was
something called the Errors Report. This necessary form of human
torture—necessary if *Vital* was to preserve its marvelous record of factual accuracy—meant that if any reader wrote in, and it turned out to
be so, that a factual error had been made in a *Vital* story, fourteen
copies of the Errors Report, with the guilty researcher's name in red
capital letters, were sent to everyone of importance on the magazine,
beginning with the managing editor. There was no fixed rule on the
matter, but it was a more or less unwritten law around *Vital* that if a
researcher got as many as three Errors Reports in one year she had
struck out and probably would end up in an office where errors were

not so critical, such as a Wall Street investment firm; or even an advertising agency, where of course accuracy if anything would be a mortal handicap.

It was no wonder that the researcher oftentimes really had to hold herself in to keep from picking up an inkwell and clobbering some writer who was reluctant to change some line in his copy, as if it were the King James Version. It didn't affect *him* a sweet damn. There were no Errors Reports for writers. The writer had not the remotest responsibility for the accuracy of anything he wrote. That was one point of the system, to leave the imagination of the writer free as the March breeze on Tobago. A girl could not have stood it had it not been for such attractions in working for *Vital* as the prestige, the parties, and the remarkable people one was slung against day in and day out, and oftentimes night in and night out.

On a cold Tuesday in February Paisley Fairlamb was assigned to a story concerning a domesticated lion. The writer on the story was Henry Gaskin, who was doing it because the Nature editor was on his winter week. The lion, by the name of Wendell, which was full-grown and had a mane that would have qualified him to model for the MGM trademark, was the household pet of a family in the town of Alton, Indiana. In some Mendelian suspension of his heritage, the great beast acted around the house very much like a large, friendly, slobbering dog. The photographer, who had gone from the Chicago bureau to do the story, had shot voluminously. There were hundreds of pictures showing the lion around the house. The story was not to be very long. It was going for only a page and a half. When it came time to lay the story out, the managing editor was momentarily undecided which of two photographs to use for the full page. One photograph showed Wendell lying in an almost Miltownish docility in front of the fireplace while the family entertained guests. The family, including the children, looked thoroughly relaxed. The guests, however, appeared somewhat restive, as if in fear the lion might abruptly revert to ancestral type. The other candidate for the full page was a picture of Wendell sharing the master bed with the master of the house. Both man and lion were asleep. After a moment's hesitation Cy Tadlock, the managing editor, chose the picture of the lion in bed for the opener. Then out of the hundreds available he selected three pictures for the half page: the lion reclining in front of the fireplace, the lion being hand-fed great hunks of meat by the mother of the house in the kitchen, and the lion giving a piggyback ride to the family's five children, ages two to eight. The youngest was holding on ecstatically to the creature's mane and the eldest to his tail.

It was by now six o'clock, which was extremely late to start closing a story.

Two problems came up in checking the story. One was that Gaskin's textblock opened with the luminous statement: "Above is a photograph of the only King of the Jungle ever to cuddle up with a man." Gaskin may have thought this an amusing piece of writing. Paisley Fairlamb could even imagine his smiling, the self-satisfied smile of creative triumph, as he wrote it. It was creative, all right. When the textblock landed on her desk and she read it, the sentence instantly infuriated her. She could see at once the enormous difficulty of checking it. The other problem was that Alvin Creech, the copy editor, decided he would like some outstanding authority's explanation as to why the lion acted in such an unnatural manner. *Vital* liked for its stories to carry the tones of authority, and the lateness of the hour interfered in no way with Creech's decision. The expert decided on was the director of the National Zoölogical Park in Washington, who would be quite authoritative, this zoo being a part of the Smithsonian Institution.

The two problems were related and it was just possible the same source could solve both. Paisley Fairlamb got a copy of the Congressional Directory and ascertained the name of the zoo director. Then she got the Washington operator on the line, gave her the man's name and asked her to ring up his residence. The operator went away for about a minute. Then she came back.

"I-yuh uh-have no luh-isting for suh-ch a par-tee," the operator said in dispassionate formality.

"But he lives in Washington," Paisley Fairlamb repeated. "He is the director of the National Zoölogical Park."

"I-yuh am sorry," the operator repeated steadily, "but there-uh is no luh-isting for yuh-ohr par-tee."

Paisley Fairlamb thanked her and hung up. She sat there for a moment, thinking hard. Then she pulled open a drawer of her desk and fetched out a thick mass of stapled sheets which gave the home addresses and telephone numbers of all bureau correspondents. She got the Washington operator back on the phone and gave her the number of *Vital*'s Washington bureau chief. Presently this worthy was on the line and she told him her problem.

"I need to get in touch with the director of the National Zoölogical Park," she said in bright, bell tones. "I have his name and home address but the Washington operator says she has no phone listing for him."

The bureau chief chuckled in the manner of a man who understood all about these human frailties and constant problems and was used to handling sixty of them a day. He also chuckled in the manner of a man who has had about three eight-to-one martinis.

"It's very simple," he said huskily. "His phone is unlisted. The reason is"—and now the bureau chief employed the opportunity to show

exactly how well he knew the inner political workings of Washington
—"that if it were listed he would be getting prankster calls all night
long. You know the sort of thing. Some clown calling up and saying,
'This is Mr. Gray R. Seal. Would you please run the water in my
bath?' Or, 'This is . . .'"

Paisley Fairlamb listened patiently while the bureau chief expansively gave three or four more such examples in the customary avuncular tones of one of the experts on Washington, which is the world's
most exclusive club and whose membership understands that all out-
siders in their abysmal ignorance of the workings of that intricate city
must be dealt with in lofty and condescending patience, and if possible in parables. She listened because she had learned you must not
interrupt a bureau chief. Certainly a researcher must not. Finally, when
he had run through the Boaz P. Constrictors with their complaints of
aching backs, the Tinted G. Peacocks with their requests for
feather-tinting jobs and the Harry Polar Bears with their demands
for a cake of ice, she inserted her question.

"I wonder if you would know how to find out the director's home
number?"

"Know how to find it?" the bureau chief said in an air half of being
insulted, half of being deeply gratified at the opportunity to give this
whippersnapper researcher in New York the surprise of her life. He
emitted a condescending chuckle. "I hardly think that's necessary. I
have it right here."

"Oh, that's wonderful," Paisley Fairlamb said insincerely.

The bureau chief took this effusion as only his due. Presently he
gave her the phone number, Paisley Fairlamb thanked him reful-
gently, he hung up and went back to a fourth martini with a thought
of how stupid as always they were in the New York office, and Paisley
Fairlamb, articulating a distinct, "The jerk," gave the Washington
operator the telephone number she had just received.

The number must have rung about a dozen times, and Paisley Fairlamb's spirits were beginning to sink again, when it was answered.

"Dr. Cowley, please."

"He not heah," a voice said. "He in Flah-ada."

"Florida!" Paisley Fairlamb exclaimed. "Whereabouts in Florida?"

"Who dis?" the voice said, suddenly suspicious. "He don' lak to be
distuhbed on vay-cation."

Paisley Fairlamb then went into her most beguiling manner. She
mentioned sweetly but most clearly the fact that this was *Vital* magazine, that it was a matter of the most urgent importance, that . . .

"Aw righ den," the voice said in put-upon tones. "Ahm not suah
he lak hit but hit's Foht Lauduhdale Flah-ada phone numbah Logan
fouah three two wun wun."

Paisley Fairlamb thanked the voice very deeply and sincerely and hung up. Instantly she picked up the phone again and gave the long-distance operator Fort Lauderdale, Florida, Logan 4-3211.

"I'll talk with anyone," she said.

"The Jolly Roger good evening at your service may I be of any help to you," was the next thing she heard in a voice so fawning that it caught her up for a moment. Right now it sounded wonderful. Her impression had been that the number was a private residence. She asked for her par-tee.

"Immediately, Madam," the voice said. "I will put you through at once, and thank you very much for ringing the Jolly Roger."

The phone rang and rang. The voice, despite its almost crawling courtesy, continued to let it ring about twenty-five times. Finally Paisley Fairlamb banged the receiver button vigorously.

"This is the New Yuh-ork operator," a grating voice said, and Paisley Fairlamb knew she had returned from the South.

"I've been cut off from Fort Lauderdale, Florida, Logan 4-3211," Paisley Fairlamb said crisply.

The operator did some things.

"The Jolly Roger good evening at your service may I be of any . . ."

Patiently Paisley Fairlamb explained that this was *Vital* magazine and the matter urgent. She could hear on the other end the impression this made. The voice sounded as if its owner were visualizing already a nine-page color story in *Vital* on the Jolly Roger. Yes, he would do everything in the world to find the party and have him call her back. She hung up and looked at her watch. It was 10:00 P.M.

She decided meantime to tackle the enormous checking problem involved in Gaskin's opening sentence. She read it again: "Above is a photograph of the only King of the Jungle ever to cuddle up with a man." "The bastard," she murmured and sat thinking who might be the best authority in this field. Then it hit her: The chief lion tamer of Ringling Bros. and Barnum and Bailey Circus. She picked up the phone, called the Morgue and asked for the clippings on the circus. In twenty-five minutes a young man laden like a Sierra Nevada pack mule approached her desk and with an unburdening sigh of relief dumped on it fifteen fat folders. There were hundreds of newspaper and magazine clippings on Ringling Bros. and Barnum and Bailey extending back over a period of twenty years. Ten minutes of flapping through and she found what she was looking for—a circus brochure. It gave, as she had suspected, the name of the circus' press agent. She knew on her own that the circus wintered in Sarasota, Florida. She picked up the phone and gave the long-distance operator the name of the press agent and, though it was night, the name of the circus. She was in great luck. In five minutes the press agent was on the phone. She explained her problem and that she would like to speak with the circus' chief lion tamer. She was given his name. This gentleman, it appeared, lived on a small island off the Gulf Coast and came in by boat when he came in. She held her breath while she asked if he had a phone. He did, and she got it. It was no more than ten minutes before she had on the line the chief lion tamer of Ringling Bros. and Barnum and Bailey, to whom she identified herself and explained the story that *Vital* was planning to run.

"This story is about a very tame lion," she told the lion tamer. "We would like to be able to say that it is the only lion ever to share a bed with a man."

She was surprised at the lion tamer's reaction. He was immediately hostile. He had a Continental accent and in this accent he refused to believe the story and, furthermore, took the hostile position that the whole thing was an assault on his profession—that is to say, a malicious effort to convince the public that lions were really very gentle creatures, that what he went through, which was to expose himself to fourteen of these man-eaters in one cage twice a day in season, was in all essence a fraud.

"No, we're not implying that at all, Mr. Zablova," she was finally able to get in hurriedly. "Quite the contrary. We're saying that this is a very exceptional lion. As a matter of fact we'd like to say it was the *only* lion ever to do such a thing."

"I do not bee-leeve it," the lion tamer said.

"But Mr. Zablova," Paisley Fairlamb said firmly, "I have the picture right in front of me." She picked it up and looked at it as she talked. "It shows a full-grown lion in bed with a man. They are both asleep. I realize—and so does *Vital*—Mr. Zablova, that this is most unusual. As a matter of fact that's precisely why we're carrying the story, because it *is* so unusual for a lion to be so tame a man can sleep in the same bed with one. We're very aware that ordinarily lions are *extremely* dangerous creatures," she said placatingly. "You may be certain we will make that point, sir. We are just trying to find out if it is not only unusual but also *unique*."

The thought crossed her mind that possibly Mr. Zablova did not know the meaning of the word. Not that he wasn't intelligent. He was probably highly intelligent, at least she had that impression from seeing circuses as a child, remembering, and with a quick flash of nostalgic fondness, the Continental-type, white-jodhpured, black-booted lion tamer cracking a black whip around the cage. It was just that his English was not too good. It was good enough, however, for him to absorb very clearly the idea that they were preparing to carry a story on a tame lion, a beast he had risked his life hundreds of times defying. She decided to make one more try.

"May I ask you this question, Mr. Zablova. Did you yourself ever sleep with a lion?"

On the other end of the line, from an island off Florida, she heard a noise that certainly was not English. It was not any language she could identify and in fact it sounded less like language than the roar of a lion. Then:

"Young lady," the voice said with a hauteur beyond anything Paisley Fairlamb had ever heard, "I beed you good night."

And the phone slammed violently. She was so startled she didn't realize it for a moment. She hung up the phone. By now she hated Gaskin with a livid hate. She waited only to get her breath and rub her ear a moment and was about to call the lion tamer back—*Vital* researchers were sensationally persistent in their work—when her own phone rang. She picked it up. It was Fort Lauderdale, Florida, the Jolly Roger Hotel, and the director of the National Zoölogical Park in Washington was on the line.

"Hello, Dr. Cowley? This is Paisley Fairlamb at *Vital* magazine in New York. We're doing a story on a lion which belongs to a family in Indiana. We have a picture showing the lion in bed with a man. The man is head of the family. We would like to be able to say that"—she picked up her copy and read Gaskin's statement—" 'Above is a photograph of the only lion' "—she could not bring herself to say "King of the Jungle"—" 'ever to cuddle up with a man.' "

On the other end of the line there was a profound silence. Then she heard a voice that managed at once to be quietly scholarly and incredulous.

"Do you mean to say that you took me away from a beach party in the middle of the night to ask me that?"

"I'm sorry you had to come away from a beach party, Dr. Cowley . . ."

"It was a long walk over deep sand. And it was a very good beach party."

"I'm very sorry, Dr. Cowley," she made this one sweetly. "But we do have a lot of readers and we like to be accurate. We felt you were the best authority on the subject. Do you know if any lion ever slept with a man before?"

"How the hell should I know?" the director said irritably and in tones quite unscholarly. "And how the hell did you get my phone number? I left rigid instructions . . ."

"Dr. Cowley," Paisley Fairlamb bore in, "I know you'll help me." Now she turned on the full-blast of her false-coyness. "As a zoölogist and as the director of a zoo, what might lead a lion to act in such a manner, that is, to become domesticated . . ."

Maybe it was her voice, half its own professional sweetness and personal coquetry and half carrying the insistent authority of the mighty organ in whose name she ventured these questions, disturbed you on your vacation, pulled you off . . . In any event, the director of the National Zoölogical Park settled down and talked with her for fifteen minutes about lions and why the lion in Alton, Indiana, could be, temperamentally, a mutation. She thanked him profusely, sincerely so, and hung up the phone. She pressed her lips together and carrying her notes marched in to see Gaskin. As she came down the corridor she heard a voice singing:

> *"Through rain, hail, and snow, froze plumb to the gills*
> *They call me the orphant of the dreary Black Hills . . ."*

She looked at her watch. It was 1:00 A.M. She swung into his office, planted herself in a chair by his desk and came to the point.

"About that being the only lion ever to go to bed with a man," she said crisply, her whole small and fetching body bristling like a Siamese kitten facing off against a Great Dane, "I've talked with the chief lion tamer of Ringling Bros. and Barnum and Bailey and I've talked with the director of the National Zoölogical Park. Incidentally, one was at home and one on vacation and at a beach party and they were both hopping mad. We can't make the statement. Nobody in the world could prove it."

Maybe it was the lateness of the hour and maybe he wanted to get home too. Still she was greatly surprised that Gaskin offered not the slightest opposition. But she didn't really know Gaskin. She knew him around the office, and had heard a good deal about him, but she had never worked with him before.

"I'll tell you," he said mildly, picking up his copy of the textblock. "How would it be if between the phrase 'photograph of' and the phrase 'the only King of the Jungle ever' we insert the word 'possibly.' "

Her hatred of Gaskin evaporated at once. She quickly knew that even if *Vital* readers turned up fourteen other lions who had done the same thing the word "possibly" gave her complete protection against an Errors Report.

From her notes she was able to give Gaskin ample material for a statement from the director of the National Zoölogical Park on the whole phenomenon. The story had long since been written, edited waiting only on this statement, and ready to go. Gaskin wrote out a one-line statement and she went back to her desk and finished putting dots over the words. Only as she put the last dot, bringing the pencil down so hard the lead broke, did she suddenly realize how exhausted she was. She looked at her watch. It was 2:00 A.M.

She knew, everyone at *Vital* knew, that when you worked that long doing a story you did not go home and immediately go to sleep. The tensions built up over the hours would not release so easily, not all at once. It took them a while to release themselves and you read or you had a drink until they were gone enough for sleep to come to you, or you did something. Paisley Fairlamb always ate an apple before going to bed. Apples relaxed her.

She stood up and walked over to the coat racks. From the thirty-fourth-floor windows it looked very cold outside, the windows were trembling and a strong suggestion of impending snow hovered in the air. She felt the enormous emptiness of the building in the heart of the great city. Except for a girl in the copy room down the hall, and for her, and for Gaskin, the place was deserted. She stood in the littered researchers' bullpen, the desks strewn with newspapers, research, photographs, reference books, and put on her coat. Even at this hour and in this setting she was an attractive little bundle. She never wore a hat. She walked by to tell Gaskin good night.

As she came up to his door she saw that he was making a phone call. His back was turned to her and he did not see her. She stood just outside, waiting for him to finish, in case the call was private, which seemed likely at this hour. But she could not help overhearing the conversation.

"Chatham Hotel? . . . Do you have a single for tonight? . . . Okay, good-bye."

She could hear a quick dialing again.

"New Weston? . . . Do you have a single for tonight? . . . Okay, good-bye."

Another dialing.

"Gotham? . . . Good-bye."

When she had heard four more calls to four more hotels she went into the office. Gaskin, who was just putting down the phone, turned and looked up at her.

"Well, it's all in," she said. "Sweet dreams."

"Sweet dreams to you," Gaskin said. He waited a moment then added: "Wendell and I apologize for causing you so much trouble. Let sleeping lions lie."

"I hope this one doesn't lie," she said, and smiled. "That's a very poor pun but it's two-thirty in the morning. Well, good night."

"Good night."

She turned to go. Then she stopped. The decision was instantaneous and was: After all she couldn't let him sleep in the park.

"You miss your last train?" she said, assuming from the calls that Gaskin lived in one of the suburbs.

"Riding commuter trains is one torture I escape," Gaskin said. "My apartment's being painted. There must be fifty conventions in town. Why can't they go to Columbus, Ohio, or somewhere . . ." His finger was moving down a page in the classified directory. "I'm even going to try the Waldorf . . ."

He rang the number. "Have a single for tonight?"

Gaskin sighed and hung up the phone.

Matter-of-factly Paisley said: "There's a couch in my living room you're welcome to. I don't know how comfortable it is but at least there'll be a blanket."

Gaskin looked at her. "Why, thanks. It is a pretty cold night."

They went down the elevator and out of the building. The wind which whips so confidently around the great New York towers came roaring and rushing around this one and for a moment held them still. Then, leaning into it, they moved slowly on up the walk, eyes riding point for a cab. The first intimations of the oncoming snow appeared, no more than a slightly shaken salt cellar, and whipped around in a whirlpool. As is the case in New York those cabbies people are always telling such quaint stories about had, sensing bad weather, run for cover or were running for it now. Gaskin used a trick he had found sometimes worked to prevail upon their Good Samaritan side. He stood on a corner flapping a high-held piece of green. After fifteen minutes of this the only sentiment that can stop one of them stopped one of them. They crawled in, half frozen. As the taxi started up Fifth Avenue, Paisley Fairlamb gave the driver her address.

As they rode up Fifth Avenue Gaskin's thoughts dwelt idly along the line that, the little he had seen of her, Paisley Fairlamb was considerably too animated and agitated for his tastes, and rather *too* self-assured. He was not overly fond of Paisley Fairlamb. It had never occurred to him to practice his hobby with her, though he assumed, this idly also, that she probably practiced it a good deal herself. Aside from all this, at this particular hour he was really bushed. He had had a couple of very late and very interesting non-working nights before the present late working one and his ambitions were fixed exclusively on that couch, and exclusively in terms of slumber, sweet slumber.

Then, almost simultaneously, the thoughts of both of them were caught up in the scene which now unfolded before them. For the snow had quickened and was now coming down full. Fifth Avenue under snow at two-thirty in the morning, when the street and all the busy stores which by day boom with the chatter and rush of the commercial world are stilled, at two-thirty when the silence is so sweet that even the sound of the snow falling can be heard . . . oh! then there is something to the great avenue that reaches to the spirit. The two night laborers felt it and they sat silent in the wonder of it. The scene reached into them and laid hold of their nerves, inflamed by the strain of doing the story, and soothed them.

The taxi pulled up in front of her address. Gaskin paid the fare and gave the driver the green paper he had waved, he was not thanked, and they got out and walked through the iron gate. Now the snow was coming down very heavily. But here in the mews there were none of the great winds born of the tall buildings midtown. It was entirely soundless, except for the falling of the snow and the sounds their footsteps made on the walk through the snow. Hers, the click, snap, click of a girl's shoes. His, a flat thud, smack, thud. The ailanthus trees arched over them as they moved slowly in the enormous silence down the mews toward her apartment.

She unlocked the door and they went inside. Paisley was completely at ease. She showed him where to hang his jacket. She fixed him a drink and they sat down. They talked a little of nothing in particular, of the snow and things in the office.

"Well," she said then. "There's your couch. You must be sleepy."

"That I am," and Gaskin yawned heavily.

She went through the bathroom into the bedroom and brought him back two blankets. She laid them on the couch.

"Good night," she said. "Sweet dreams."

"Sweet dreams," he said, yawning heavily. He was really almost asleep on his feet and in three minutes was literally so on his back.

The layout of the apartment was a living room and a bedroom and a bathroom which connected the two. She went through the bathroom into the bedroom, closed the door, got ready for bed, then lay in bed about a half hour chewing idly on an apple she had got out of a bed-side stand, where she always kept several of them, and musing about a party she was giving that weekend. Suddenly a thought struck her— struck her so strongly her jaw dropped in mid-chew. She was twenty-one years old—had been for three hours. She put down the apple, got up and looked at herself in the full-length mirror, decided she had every right in the world to be excited and disturbed in a wonderful, tingling way by what she saw, gave an exquisite little feminine sigh, and articulating an even more feminine, sweet and brisk, "Well, here goes," marched through the darkened bathroom into the darkened living room. She could hear him soundly breathing. She padded over and crisply seized his shoulder and shook it.

"Gaskin," she said. "I know you're pretty old. But I want someone experienced to do it. No apes. Someone experienced. I hear you're pretty competent."

He awoke, startled out of his wits.

"I happen to know," this voice out of the darkness was going on, quite impudently, and with a matter-of-factness that chilled him to the bone, "specifically of _____, _____, _____, _____, _____, _____, _____, and _____," she pealed off all eight.

Gaskin sat bolt upright in bed as if agitated by a red-hot poker, startled and flabbergasted by the accuracy of the list, and particularly coming from Paisley Fairlamb. Thoroughly alarmed, appalled, defensive, and actually shocked and embarrassed, he started speaking like a machine gun:

"Who told you that? Where did you get that information? Who gave you those names? That list is a hundred-percent fictional! I hardly know them. My relationship with every one of them is entirely professional. Any experience of mine has been greatly exaggerated. Don't believe everything you hear . . ."

While he was talking she climbed in lithe as a cat and closed his words with her lips. As the snow came down outside like sweet white thunder, Paisley Fairlamb—exactly on schedule, and entirely to the astonishment and awe of Henry Gaskin, who had had no intention of practicing his hobby on this particular evening, no intention ever of practicing it with this creature, and was astonished how delightful it was, from one so young—put a dot over her womanhood. Paisley Fairlamb had researched her subject thoroughly.

9

Droit du Seigneur(e)

Crystal Bidwell believed, to be sure, in the *droit du seigneur(e)*. However, this was in no way unreasonable. In the first place it is very hard on a woman being single in this country. For her to come to terms with something which if she does not come to terms with her life is going to be in reality a species of hell on earth—well, by comparison, the familiar camel's canter through the needle's eye is as easy as falling downward if you plunge briskly from the Empire State Building. Some women attempt to achieve a state identified by that word which the psychiatric crowd has made so familiar and at which all decent women must recoil in horror and revulsion—we speak of "sublimation"—in the world of business or of charity. It was a credit to Crystal Bidwell and a mark of courage that, instead of giving in to life the easy and cowardly way as so many women do, selling their sweet birthright for a string of savagely superstitious words, she would not settle for that. She was very good at her job, far better than almost any man would have been at it, but it is a credit to her that she did not let the job be a substitute for the other. No, Crystal had to have hers.

Yes. The truth is that the cards are so stacked against a single

woman in this country, with a cruel and brutalizing unfairness, the
more so since it is all done in the pious sheep's-clothing name of morality, that a woman certainly has every right in the world to fight fire with
fire, to use any and all means available, subtle or otherwise, to get
what she needs and indeed has every human, natural and God-given
birthright to. Fortunately for Crystal, she held almost entirely in her
hands, like some modern goddess of the fates, the future of a good
many exceptionally attractive young men, with more always coming
up. If she but made use of the weapons and the facilities so prodigally available to her, it was no problem to appease the human-
warmth side of her life quite generously, even satiatingly. The means
of Crystal Bidwell, she being a woman of culture with scarcely a cell
of uncouthness in her whole body—one can be vivid in the mother
tongue and still not in the slightest uncouth—were highly on the side
of subtlety. So subtle was Crystal, so adroitly manipulative, that not
once was anyone able to establish any overt tieline between whether
a researcher got a good bureau assignment and whether he had occasionally assisted Crystal in appeasing that side of her life.

From the above the naïve reader might gather that the greatest trial
a man could endure would be thus to assist Crystal Bidwell. Of course
only some of our women readers will have derived this conclusion. All
of our men readers will know that there are very few women in the
world it is a trial for a man to have to sleep with, provided he does
not have to do it regularly, such as in marriage. The point is not at
all that all cats in the dark are gray. Quite the opposite. It is rather
that almost any new woman, whoever she be, is exciting to a man the
first time. What a happier place the world would be if we would all
but recognize this fact. And one never really had to do it permanently
with Crystal Bidwell. Only a few times at the most, since by then one's
reward for this warmth was on its way in the form of a tasty bureau assignment and one was speeding out of New York leaving the chores of
friendship to fresh, upcoming waves of researchers.

But, in addition, Crystal Bidwell was not in the slightest a repulsive woman. She had a very full body, and even if a man prefers, for
some odd reason, the model-type, button-breasted, toothpick-thighed,
skeletal-hipped, concave-bellied body, hers, with its refulgent white
breasts, lavish buttocks and sturdy columnar thighs, would have been
exciting at least for a change of scenery to any man with the slightest
pretense to virility, like harvesting a gloriously fecund and golden
wheat field after being accustomed to scissoring off anemic rosebuds.
In short, Crystal Bidwell was something a man could get his teeth
into, to borrow T. S. Eliot's phrase. Another wisdom of hers: to know
that the true secret of lovemaking is to be found in the word diversion
—hearty, healthy, eager, lusty and laughing diversion.

It is true that the odd man now and then could not go through with it. There is in this world a strange species, a type of man who cannot sleep with a woman, however beautiful and excitative, unless he is attracted to her mentally or to her character. Unless he is, this type of man just cannot do it, he literally, physically cannot do it. Such a man obviously operates under an appalling handicap in this world. Indeed it is difficult to see how the poor wretch functions at all, at least with women, burdened as he is with the need for a perfectionism as rare in this fine sex as tamaracks in the Sahara. Fortunately he is very rare himself and when he turned up at *Vital* and applied this excessively idealistic divining rod upon Crystal Bidwell, one could hardly waste pity on him that he had to shovel the consequences. Especially since Crystal did some very interesting things not every American woman by any means did in bed (not for nothing had she had a two-year tour in the Paris bureau, and being a woman alive instead of a cabbage she had wasted hardly a minute of it), and she gave a man a good royal time.

So it must be concluded, first, that Crystal Bidwell's *parenthetical* use of her job to satisfy this important side of any woman's life was entirely justified, fair and honorable. And, second, that it hurt nobody and operated toward the general welfare. The odd man who was so prissily idealistic as to refuse must, we must also conclude, be written down as uncharitable not to mention suspiciously feeble-minded. Besides which, he probably wouldn't make a good *Vital* type in the long haul anyhow.

Thus Crystal Bidwell's *droit du seigneur(e)*.

Crystal Bidwell, we hurry to add, was not promiscuous. In fact she could be considered decidedly selective, in that there were more researchers who had not been singled out to provide her with human warmth than there were ones who had. And even toward the latter her feelings varied quite considerably. If she had looked back over her years as director of researcher development and, equipping herself with a pencil and a sheet—two sheets—of copy paper, had listed the chosen and rated the measure of her desire toward each, the list would have shown great variation and many a latitude. We might mention as an aside here that Crystal tended to recommend overseas assignments for those near the bottom of the list and domestic assignments for those near the top. There was a very clear and present logical reason for this: her job took her on rhythmic inspection tours of the domestic bureaus and it was convenient to have deployed strategically around the Republic ones who had provided her with human warmth in the past and would be on tap to provide her with it again, if, shall we say, a need for human warmth should suddenly overtake her in Denver, or Los Angeles, or in Atlanta, Georgia, which is very likely.

Yes, Crystal's sense of selectivity was very keen indeed. By no means all were called, and few, we speak comparatively, were chosen. And

Crystal's degree of feeling toward those that were varied most enormously. For example: Very near the top of the list was a man with whom she had not, as yet, exchanged the far cadences of human warmth. His name was Anthony Pinckney. He was a man of dimensions—two hundred twenty pounds spread over six feet five inches. And he was something else: He was a discriminating man.

The important thing to say about Anthony Pinckney was that he had a sense of idealism. The Lord knows where he acquired it. He had it before attending the University of Virginia. He had it before joining the paratroops. He had it already and his dropping down in combat upon Gela, Sicily, Paestum, Italy, and Grave, Holland, during which he had been wounded twice, once almost with finality, if anything aggravated this sense. It was there, the most important thing about Anthony Pinckney by far, and marbled with that sense of stubbornness which invariably is found where idealism is found.

As for sharing sleeping quarters for a spell with another man's wife, or with some girl in the office, which meant that under the Puritan code he was "unfaithful" since he had a wife of his own, Pinckney did this readily enough. At least he had done it a few times. He felt a decided sense of guilt each time, for no one is able in America entirely to overcome his environment which sniggers loudly in his ear, however wrongly, that this is wrong, no one is able entirely to overcome it even though he knows in his heart of compassion and in his mind of logic that the environment and the Puritan "code" are one rampant fabric of superstition (even obscenity, since no one in America so sacredly values and perpetuates obscenity as does the Puritan: remove Puritanism today and that plague of salacious literature and photography—that evil substitute for human love—which festers on a million newsstands, drugstore counters and airport gift shops like suppurating sores upon the complexion of our fair land would vanish tomorrow). However, Pinckney, "victim" of the flesh, was obliged to do it now and then despite the sense of guilt.

Why did Anthony Pinckney sleep with women other than his wife? Did we hear someone in the fourth pew ask that? Deacon, the answer is simplicity incarnate. His wife was not very good in bed. Why was she not very good in bed did you ask? Was it because she was ugly, flat-chested or harelipped? No. She was by no manner of means ugly, she was endowed with a most acceptable brace of breasts, dear Deacon, she had unusually wantable lips and a remarkable and flawless skin. She was, in a word, a decidedly, even immoderately attractive woman. She was not good in bed simply because she had been brought up, like many another American girl, to believe there was essentially something dirty, nasty and wrong about that business, that nevertheless one had to submit to a certain quantity of it, but that the thing was to keep the quantity down, and even then get it over with as expeditiously as possible: Therefore it was of course a joyless thing coming from her. One might as well have done it with a salt mackerel. There was also the fact she was selfish, including in bed. No such woman, however bountifully endowed physically, is even capable of making good love, and of course will never be the recipient of any good love, so that in the end her selfishness and calculation are self-defeating and even self-annihilating. It was for this reason that Pinckney, while working hard and swiftly toward death to provide his prissy wife and four prissy children with a good living—his code required that—in Westport, Connecticut, a commuting village near New York, was obliged to satisfy the sex part of his life from women not his wife.

Aside from this, Pinckney had one immediate ambition. He wanted to get assigned to Washington as chief of the *Vital* bureau there—the premier bureau assignment in the entire magazine. For one thing his wife wanted to live in Washington because her family was there. She was one of those untransplantable people who are only happy in their home town near their mamas and papas. And Pinckney himself thought a change would be good for all of them, for him and his whole family life. Maybe if they could get out of Westport, start somewhat anew in a new place, in a nice place like Washington, perhaps some freshness of spirit would come into their lives, and of joy. For little or no joy was there now and Pinckney knew this must be as hard on his wife as on himself. She was, after all, a member of the human race. So he was aiming for the Washington job. A change in *Vital* bureau chiefs was due soon in this greatsome city and Pinckney had let it be known, in the subtle, insidious ways it was necessary to make this known at the office with the proper big-tiger panjandrums, chiefly Crystal Bidwell and Harrison Duckworth, that he would like a crack at Washington. He felt his chances were very good: He had acquitted himself well and even with metronomic flashes of brilliance on the various rungs of the *Vital* ladder leading up to being chief of the most important bureau.

His estimate, we shall say expositorily, was not wrong. The fact was, about this time Anthony Pinckney was being most actively considered for the position of chief of the Washington bureau. From the Washington bureau one went to the top rungs of the *Vital* ladder, so this meant additionally that Anthony Pinckney was considered material for the highest executive positions on the magazine.

The incidents which were to prove so fateful in Anthony Pinckney's life were very short ones as the clock goes its one-way, no-round-trip-available rounds. The first took place between the hour of 4:59 and the hour of 5:07 A.M.—repeat A.M—on a Sunday in the month of April. It took place where so many things of import and interest around

Vital had taken place, on the amazing leather couch, which we shall now introduce, with brevity we promise the Reader, before getting on with the story. Gung-ho.

Before doing this there is but one other thing we wish to say here about Anthony Pinckney. He was something of an idealist in regard to women too. That is to say, he would not sleep with a woman he did not like as a person. Did I say would not? He *could* not. Even if she were a most beautiful creature physically. He had to like her, to be comfortable with her, before he would, or even could, sleep with her. It was his one most obvious failing. We all have our failings, and this was Pinckney's.

It was a remarkable piece of furniture. There was its size. Its simple dimensions were ten feet long and three feet deep. There was its texture. It was of the finest leather, to which the years had done nothing except to make it more velvety, more pliant, more caressful. It had been washed in the spillings of thousands of martinis, of both gin and vodka, in Scotch, bourbon, Jack Daniel's sour mash, a dozen different blends, and occasionally even champagne of a fair vintage. These baptisms, far from wreaking any ill effects on the couch, had toned and textured it in the manner which a good saddle soap does for more ordinary leathers and had given it a luster which was like ripe golden wheat with a three-o'clock September sun on it.

No one had been with *Vital* longer than the great leather couch. It had started when *Vital* itself started, and when the beanstalking magazine swarmed from its old quarters into its new, monumental and institutional thirty-four-story building in midtown Manhattan, the leather couch was brought along. Everything else in the new building was new: new desks, new lamps, new typewriters, new chairs, new filing cabinets. Only the great leather couch made the transfer. No one could bear to see it go. It even had an office all its own. It resided in the recess of an anteroom, otherwise bare, that opened off the National Affairs bullpen.

In its long life at *Vital* magazine the couch had seen a great deal of history. Many a future had been decided on that couch; many a fate resolved. Many persons had spent the night on it. Many had passed out on it and revived refreshed to face the world and its chronic troubles and woes. The couch had an infinitude of uses. It was the favorite place for discussing assignments, for bull sessions and for general killing of time—it had slain hundreds of man-years of that. It made all the modern furniture of the rest of the *Vital* office, the Do-More chairs, the Eze-Eye swivel lamps, the Clean-Top gun-metal desks, seem cold, hard and forbidding. It is not too much to say that it was the most beloved member of the staff of *Vital* magazine.

Thus the great leather couch. Now, with apologies to the reader

for this dull—describing things as opposed to persons always is, essentially—but necessary interlude, on with the story. Banzai!

Being the Education editor-writer, Anthony Pinckney worked a
Monday–Friday week. Late one Friday afternoon the copy editor,
Alvin Creech, called him in to tell him the National Affairs Department would need some help tomorrow and would he be so good as
to come in? (*Vital* magazine was a great place for the rhetorical question—at times it seemed to be its chief means of communication.)

"I regret vividly that I could not have told you sooner, Pinckney,"
said the copy editor. "But is it my fault? Do I have any control over
such acts of God as floods in Kansas City?"

Thus one result of the great Kansas City flood, besides the considerable decimation of property and life it achieved out there, was one of
the fateful incidents which were to have so much bearing on Anthony
Pinckney's life. If one chooses to reason this way, one can say with
all accuracy that but for the flood in Kansas City nothing would ever
have happened. However, this is a dangerous way to reason in life,
and done enough, and it doesn't take very much to be enough, equips
one with the shortest route to raving insanity, whether walking or
incarcerable.

The undeveloped film of the flood did not arrive at Idlewild airport
until 12:35 P.M. Saturday (TWA Flight 711) and it was an hour
later before it was in the office. It had to be developed and printed and
then the story had to be laid out and it was whipping five o'clock before Pinckney got much of an idea of what he would be writing about
and of the space he would have to say it in. He went to work and kept
at it until six-thirty. Then he took the elevator down and crossed the
cross-street to the dungeon called the Eagle's Nest. From getting
started so late on the story Pinckney knew he was in for the night.
He had already called his wife to tell her he would not be home
until sometime in the hours of Sunday morning and heard that worthy
hang up in a sulk, as if Pinckney had done it from choice rather than
from the inspired necessity of feeding her and five other mouths. By
this time there was nothing to be gained by trying to rush things, the
ritual of editing, writing, reëditing and checking had to take its slow,
tortuous course, it was better not to fight it but to ride with it, and
Pinckney mentally settled back.

Lo, he found himself enjoying himself quite a bit in the cacophonous
and shrill mob from the office which engorged the Eagle's Nest. One of
the things about changing over from being a National Affairs writer,
when you worked a Tuesday–Saturday week, to a back-of-the-book
department editor was that you missed these Saturday nights. Most
of it you were glad to miss—the eighteen-hour Saturday itself, which
could be brutal, and needing most of Sunday to recover and unwind

your screaming nerves, so that it amounted to your really having only one day, Monday, off. However, the fraternization of Saturday night, beginning with the assembling for drinks in the Eagle's Nest, was a pleasant thing, and Pinckney sincerely missed those nights, at least certain aspects of them. Saturday night was like no other night at the magazine. There was something in the air that was different, a certain underground-river throb of excitement. It was the night when the magazine "closed" its final stories, when the editors committed themselves irrevocably before the great presses situated in strategic cities over the country began to roll out their millions of copies for the entertainment, education and titillation of the great American public. Liquor was broken out at ten Saturday night, everyone worked very late and violated the Fourth Commandment, and even after you had finished there were commonly parties in the apartment of one staff member or another, where you could continue the drinking and sometimes violate some of the other more interesting Commandments, for the remainder of the night all through the night if you fancied.

Now as Pinckney stood tall in the ten-deep crowd at the bar having his second fat martini he felt a pleasant glow. People were talking, laughing, drinking, everybody was wedged freely against everybody rump to rump, and glasses were passed back and forth from bar to the far perimeters of the crowd like a bucket brigade, and there was a royal and merry camaraderie. A feeling of goodness toward everybody, and especially right now toward his colleagues, suffused Anthony Pinckney. By and large they were good people. They were perhaps caught up in something—and who shall name it?—from which they would never get uncaught, but then—a certain warm attack of philosophy came flanking upon him—are not most people on the earth caught up in something they can never get out of, only, of course, from thinking they cannot get out of it, since of course man can do anything once he makes up his mind to do it instead of being passive to life and letting it decide things willy-nilly for him, but then if that thinking is the one thing that chains them, it is a very strong thing, and where is the one to rise up, call himself man, and with one Samsonian heave break his bondage? Pinckney felt all these thoughts and if he felt philosophical in this manner it was in a beneficent way and by no means depressing. Jason Hightower was on one side of him and Crystal Bidwell on the other and Hank Gaskin was on his belly side and he talked with them. He liked Hightower and Gaskin. He could have lived without Bidwell's presence amongst the living if forced to at the point of a gun but now his sense of well-being was all-encompassing enough to take in her as well, as the ritualistic humor fed away.

"I say, Pinckney old slob." It was Hightower. "Interesting to see you among the working people for a change."

"Yes, they decided they needed some of the first team in to get the magazine out tonight."

"*Écoutez! Écoutez!*"

That was the sort of thing Crystal Bidwell said, being an alive and vibrant sort of person. But far from its twinging and twanging his nerves as it usually did, Pinckney tonight found all embraced by his general air of beneficence and well-being.

"The scuttlebutt I hear, Pinckney," Gaskin said, "is that they're on the threshold of shipping part of the first team the royal hell out to one of the more favored boondocks." Gaskin was a little tight.

"I surely will be the last to know." Pinckney laughed softly. He had an astonishingly soft, quiet laugh, and a voice a little high-pitched, both of which surprised one coming out of such a big man.

"Dear Crystal would know though, wouldn't she?" Gaskin turned to Crystal Bidwell. "How about it, Crystal my pet—tigress." Gaskin said the last word *sotto voce* and with his head turned into the noisy room. He turned it back. "Who is for God and His maid? Who is for Washington with Pinckney?"

"Now, Hank," Crystal said with a patient smile.

"Oh, come, come, Crystal. We're all friends here roughly, and shall we get with it? Come, my pet—hyenaess," Gaskin said the last word *sotto voce,* head turned. He turned it back. "What about old fat-assed Pinckney here and Washington?"

"I haven't got a fat ass," Pinckney said.

"Don't apologize for it!" Gaskin said. "But as to Washington now, Crystal my pet."

Crystal Bidwell smiled mysteriously. "Pinckney may have the biggest ass, but one thing about you, Hank, *quel* big ears."

A mightily pleased smile enveloped Gaskin's face. "Did you hear what the lady said, Pinckney? My boy!" He stuck out a somewhat wavering hand of congratulations. "Crystal and me've known each other donkey's years, I know how to translate her, and if Crystal says what she just said, my advice to you, my boy, would be for you and your eclectic ass to take a weekend off and look over the real estate situation in Chevy Chase. I imagine the usual important pay raise goes with the noble transfer."

"There'll be plenty of time for looking over real estate," Crystal Bidwell said. She looked up brightly at Pinckney. "What story are you doing *ce soir,* Anthony?"

"The great Kansas City flood."

"Flood in Kansas City!" Gaskin exclaimed. "Another round of drinks here on that one, Pasquale!"

After the buffet dinner back in the office Pinckney resumed the flood story. It was midnight, what with layout changes, before he had all his copy in. Then it was always a couple of hours at the inside before editing was completed, and then there was the checking. This for sure, not to mention an unpredictable amount of rewriting. Pinckney dropped by the artists' bullpen, where the whiskey was, and got himself a drink. He had that one there and then fixed himself another, and carrying it wandered up the corridor toward the National Affairs bullpen, looking in writers' and editors' offices to see who wasn't busy, stopping and bulling a little. He swung around by the bullpen and started the circle back on the opposite side of the building. Crystal Bidwell's office was at the turn.

"Why, hello, Anthony," he heard her call.

He looked in. She was seated at her typewriter.

"Well, what keeps you so late, Crystal?" Crystal Bidwell almost never worked late on Saturday night, not this late.

"Oh, bureau administrative stuff," she said.

"Sounds thrilling."

"You've no idea. Bullsugar. *Quel* bullsugar. Well, *c'est la guerre*. It got piled up on me and I decided to reserve tonight for catching up. I'm barely started. How about yourself?"

"With luck I should be out of here by dawn."

"No rest for the wicked." Crystal laughed. "*Voilà!* I imagine I'll be fairly close to dawn myself."

"Well, I'm going to massage my nerves with some more Vat 69."

"I'll be seeing you, I would imagine."

"Doubtless. We'll probably be the last two out of here."

"Doubtless."

The following three hours were devoted by Pinckney to drinking, bulling with people in the office—a number which dwindled as the night wore on and various writers, researchers and editors finished their stories—writing headlines and rewriting four captions and one textblock. Pinckney's story would be the last to close. He kept in touch with his researcher and wandered around the office. He did not go past Crystal Bidwell's office again. He imagined she had gone home, until about four o'clock the two of them intersected going for drinks to the long artists' table where the bottles were standing. Pinckney started picking them up one by one and letting the empties fall on each other into the huge metal wastebasket with a sound like cannon fire.

"My God," he said, appalled, when he had lifted the last one, held it to the shaded artists' light and dropped it into the wastebasket. "They're all empty! The last blessed one of them! What a catastrophe!"

"Come with me, my boy," Crystal intoned slyly.

She led him down to her office, unlocked a desk drawer and got out a bottle. Bottles were stashed around in various offices, like squirrels hiding nuts, and for the same reason, for just such emergencies as this. Pinckney was grateful to Crystal for having that bottle and he thanked her as she poured generously.

"Well, I've got to go into deep conference with my researcher. A few vibrating checking points, I'm told."

Crystal sat back to her typewriter. "The bottle will be here, Anthony—and I imagine *moi aussi.*" She sighed lightly. *"C'est la guerre."*

"In that case I'll surely be seeing you both."

It was 4:30 A.M. before the last of the copy had been checked. Pinckney said good night to the researcher and went on down the long corridor. The building was utterly deserted. On that thirty-fourth story, oh, there where the corridors were strewn with old copy paper and long yellow tearings from the AP ticker full of the deeds and misdeeds of man, high up on the celestial ramparts of Manhattan and all the quietness of the city around him: nothing more alone, strangely, strangely alone, than that. He felt a shade tight. He remembered that the first morning train to Westport would not be until 5:50. An hour to kill here before leaving to walk twenty minutes to the station. Suddenly a great fatigue came upon him. It was curious: At 4:29, while you were still working on the story, there was something in you that kept the eighteen-hour exhaustion in check, as behind a dam. 4:30, and the last thing done on the story, the dam broke and it assaulted you defenceless, overran you. Pinckney felt bone-bushed going down that corridor, every step more so. The thought of living in Washington, where he would be running his own bureau and certainly living a more civilized life than this, with no late, brutal Saturday nights—for by now all the camaraderie of earlier in the evening, and how long ago down there at the Eagle's Nest it seemed, had been crushed in the emotions of exhaustion—was enormously appealing. Then another remembrance shored him up. The couch! For Pinckney was a particular lover of the great leather couch. His step quickened.

First he stopped by Bidwell's office. She was gone but there—thank God!—right in the middle of the desk sat most of a bottle of J and B. Gratefully Pinckney filled half a glass, swallowed half of that, replaced the bottle, and taking the glass with him re-entered the corridor. Thinking, that was awfully nice of her to leave that bottle, it really was, he reached corridor's end and turned into the room. Set over in the recess the couch was not immediately visible from the door. He closed the door behind him, turned, yawning heavily, took two steps toward the couch. He stopped, startled, yawn frozen in mid-cavern.

She was half-lying, half-sitting, on the couch. She held a drink and she smiled up at him.

"Hello, Anthony." She was not drunk. Crystal Bidwell was never drunk.

"Why, hello, Crystal. I thought you'd have gone home hours ago. I helped myself to your Scotch"—he raised his glass—"as you can see and I thank you. Finish your astute chores?"

"Well, no, I didn't finish. And right at this moment I'm not sure I will tonight. *À votre santé!*" She raised hers. "I was tired. So: Where else does one go around here when one is tired?"

"Two minds with but a single . . . I've got an hour till my train."

Crystal smiled quietly. "We must be the only two people left in the building, don't you imagine?"

"The elevator man," Pinckney said.

"He doesn't count. Blind like Justice. Isn't it always strange to be here at this hour, Anthony, no one but yourself in a thirty-four-story building, even the charwomen gone home, and the whole city, and all its noises and all its rush gone, all quiet around you, like you never felt the city could be that quiet. It's almost dawn, Anthony." She waited a moment then said, reflectively, almost as to herself, and with a strange, unlaughing little laugh: " '*Tous songes sont mensonges,*' the French say. 'All dreams are lies.' "

Looking out the window on the dark silence of the great midtown city, great empty shafts, haunted specters against the sky—the darkling tombs of the Twentieth Century—Anthony Pinckney suddenly felt the most enormous and profound sense of sadness. And somehow, hearing Crystal say that language which was rather honest, he felt terribly sorry for her. He felt sadness for her, for himself, and for all of mankind, for the whole human race.

"We are all lost souls," he said.

"What did you say, Anthony?"

"I said it's rather eerie all right. Well, since you got here first . . . I guess I'll embrace a table outside. Don't think I can stand upright much longer and women first, I always say. That's what I always say."

He turned around from the window. She was sitting back on the great couch, legs crossed.

"You know what I always say? I always say—this is quite a large couch, Anthony. I have always said that. It is a very large, very comfortable, an unbelievably soothing couch. Roomy."

There was something, in his present bushed state, almost hypnotizing about her voice. It took him a little while to comprehend that her hand had taken his and was exerting upon it the gentlest, almost imperceptible downward pull. A woman who wants only a release—and is that such a bad thing to want? something said within him. Wants only human warmth. Is that such an evil thing to want? And suddenly he felt terribly terribly sorry for Crystal Bidwell and he was tempted. Passing also in dim parade somewhere in the far back regions of his consciousness was the knowledge that it was dangerous to go in Crystal's face, for she was a powerful woman, and nowhere more so than in assignments to the bureaus: if Crystal really opposed it you could never get sent to a bureau you may have devoutly wished to be sent to, as Pinckney did now. And so with considerations that were a strange mixture of pathos for her, and plain common sense if not calculation, now for one moment he stood forth to her. Even now: he was yielding to her hand, his big lumbering body tilted toward the couch to where he stood directly over her, tilted while he felt all her sensual desire spread out on the couch oozing up to him.

And then he said it.

If it had not been for the consumption of a considerable amount of Scotch he would never have said it. He wouldn't have done it either way, but being full sober he would have got out of it differently. After all she had said nothing really. But Anthony Pinckney was convinced the stories about Crystal were true. And even that may have been all right if he had just said good night and left.

But he didn't.

He straightened himself and pulled his hand away. He was a tall and broad figure standing there against the window through which the first slim intimations of dawn now came. Then he said it. He looked down at her and said:

"Crystal, mine's not for trade. I'm a married man, remember."

And he turned and left. Instantly, even through the Scotch haze, he regretted saying it. It was such a crude not to mention stupid and even unkind and certainly uncompassionate way to handle it.

That was one of two incidents in the setting of the leather couch that were to prove fateful to Anthony Pinckney's life. The second occurred three weeks later short of a day.

The situation was almost identical, so we shall avoid repetition by stating only the few minor changes in it: It was Friday. Pinckney this time had been given a Washington political story to do (he felt there was significance in his being given that particular story). The great building was again almost deserted when he finished the story about 3:30 A.M. Saturday. The drinking and the long hours had the effect on him they always had—deep fatigue, a certain light-headedness, a vaguely erotic feeling. This night he had over two hours to wait for the first train to Westport. He also had a bottle in his desk. Again, taking the bottle with him, he went on down to the leather-couch room. There was one difference more. Going with him this time down to the room of the couch was his researcher for tonight, a young lady by the name of Joy Morehouse.

In addition to an S.O.B., every good office has its roundheel. A good modern office can hardly function these days without one, and certainly *Vital* magazine, as the nation's greatest and most successful magazine, was a good modern office. The position of roundheel in the *Vital* office was occupied undisputed by Joy Morehouse.

Joy Morehouse had the morals of a red snapper. She thought no more of doing it than she did of brushing her teeth. Whether anyone had ever told her how wrong this was seemed doubtful. She did not do it in any sense of rebellion. She did it for one reason only: she liked it.

Joy was not a beautiful girl but there was something about her. One always had a strong doubt that she wore anything beneath the black jersey dresses she favored. She was an unusually tiny girl, barely five feet tall and barely an even hundred pounds in weight. Her body suggested an almost supernal litheness. Perhaps the most remarkable visual thing about her was the unusual whiteness of her skin. And the perfection of it. Perhaps the most remarkable temperamental thing, the sense of well-being she gave off. Joy Morehouse gave a man a very good time and the fact was, she laughed a lot while doing it. Men, having been taught in this country that this is a solemn, guilty, sneaky business, were surprised at this and surprised even more at how much it made a general joy prevail unconfined. Joy Morehouse did it with a natural sense of fun, enjoyment, guiltlessness and, yes, laughter. Not to put too fine a point on it, she found the male body a source of astonishing enjoyment for a good healthy woman and she never needed to read any books on the subject. It just came naturally with her, as natural as a good chocolate malt. She also liked good chocolate malts.

Joy Morehouse was one of the calmest girls you could have imagined. We suppose that even American women themselves would unanimously agree that their breed, the world's most interesting, runs to shrillness. An American woman of the writer's acquaintance, the wife of a Navy doctor stationed two years in Japan, once gave this description of the Japanese woman: "She never raises her voice, even in the worst bars." By antithesis, this observation also provides an almost mathematically exact description of the American woman. With all her numerous virtues she is a rather shrill and agitated creature, for good reason we might say, all of which is gone into elsewhere in this book. Joy Morehouse was an outstanding exception to this prevailing *modus* of her species. She never raised her voice. One was always comfortable in her presence. And she was a good girl, of good heart, and meanness was not in her soul. Whether there was any correlation between these various traits and the fact she was not at all frustrated in an area where many American women (and they are creatures to be pitied rather than criticized and defamed) find themselves frustrated, we shall not undertake to say. If there is anything the writer believes, it is avoiding generalizations on matters such as these. Enough for us as a novelist to say that Joy Morehouse was a highly relaxed woman, leaving psychological deductions as to the reason to the numerous and ever-growing legions of professional practitioners in this field.

Some, curiously enough, may find fault in the fact that Joy Morehouse did not apparently wear lingerie. Some may even conclude from this tiny detail that she was a brazen woman. Nothing could be further from the truth. She wore no lingerie, not for purposes of brazenness but only because her body felt freer and more comfortable without it and she did not like fetters. She was in no respect immodest in appearance. Her dresses were not calculated to aggrandize her breasts in the twin-Bofors-gun effect sought by some women, chiefly the frigid ones; she did not spend her time in the repeated calisthenics of crossing and recrossing her legs to give a man a quick peek in the approved fashion of titillation which should cause revulsion in anyone of the slightest morality; she did not take the afforded opportunities to rub or nudge up against one when leaning over his desk or walking with him down the corridor. All of these things would have seemed decidedly juvenile to her, not to say obscene and unladylike. She was entirely modest and proper. All she did, in fact, was sleep with men.

Pinckney closed the door. He and Joy sat down on the couch. They poured themselves drinks into their uniced glasses. They talked, they laughed together. Pinckney liked Joy Morehouse. He was thoroughly comfortable with her, in a way he never was with his wife. He felt she was a good girl. He also knew, in that picturesque and cruel phrase men use, that she "slept around." He wondered mildly if this had anything to do with her goodness. There was something entirely natural and ungame-playing and giving about her. One felt she really and truly liked to give herself and did not think of that precious thing she had as something to hold back and use as trading stock. It was most refreshing, this attitude. No sense of guilt hung in the air with Joy Morehouse. With her a man vanquished Puritanism entirely.

Ah, but everything was so natural. Pinckney did one thing, which was to turn out the light in the room. They both had their shoes off, and they stood at the window looking out over the towers, great black weird shafts against the gray-black canvas, where the first tiniest reaches of oncoming dawn could be seen tickling the sky. Oh, Manhattan! Oh, New York, thou holy city amongst all upon the Twentieth-Century earth! Off and away they looked, then down, down.

"It's going to be light," she was saying. She laughed. Like soft and pleasant chimes. "Let's go to the couch before it's light."

That was like Joy Morehouse to say that, he thought. Pinckney laughed. What a joyful thing she made of it! They went back to the couch and lay down, he stretched out against the back of it and holding her tiny body, less than one half the substance of his, up against his great one, and her dress came up as easily and naturally as the thing should be itself, always, if man ever became right. And as it was now.

Light was shining in his eyes. He must have fallen asleep and they must have left the lights on after all. Then no, he became aware . . . It was God's light. Dawn! That was dawn coming slanting and slaking, dust-moted rays, dust-moted by the millions of motes, there through the window, millions of motes caught in that glittering dull-red beam. Pinckney sat up halfway on the couch. He felt his arm held by something and looking down saw that it was by the body of Joy Morehouse, sweet weight which he was still holding, and saw her now, and dear it was and made him feel toward her, rubbing her sleepy eyes and smiling sleepily, smile which he returned, how dear too on waking she was! Then he looked up. Standing in the doorway was Crystal Bidwell.

"Oh, I'm sorry. *Quel gauche* of me. Why, Joy, what brings you to work so early? Why, Anthony. What a highly idealistic creature you are, Anthony—or should I say selective? The others will be coming in in an hour. It's Saturday and a busy day you know. You've only got an hour. Carry on, my children."

She left, closing the door. Very quietly. Crystal Bidwell was not without class.

One Monday morning a month later Harrison Duckworth ran into Pinckney in the corridor and asked him into his office. Duckworth sat behind his desk, looked at the seated Pinckney over tented fingers pursed to his lips, toyed with his Phi Beta Kappa key for a moment or two, then, abruptly, sat back, beaming.

"Anthony," he said, "I have the most marvelous news for you I'm sure."

Pinckney smiled softly. "I always like marvelous news."

The vice managing editor lifted his "Monday" pipe from the labeled rack and started filling it. "It gives me I think my greatest pleasure to relay marvelous news to someone. I hate telling anyone bad news. Do you know what's wrong with me in this job, Anthony?"

"Why, I hadn't thought about that particularly," Pinckney said.

"No, I suppose not. It's that essentially I'm too soft for this job." The vice managing editor lighted up his pipe with a series of sucking noises and blew out a gust of smoke. "Too soft for the job, that's always been my trouble. This is between you and me of course—imagine the face I'd lose with the younger researchers if they knew! But you and I are equals, in a rough sense, more or less." His laughter sounded forth over the cadenced suckings. "Yes, I do *despise* telling anyone bad news. Fortunately we've got such a grand staff—do you think there's any building in the world that has more compressed talent in it, Anthony?—I seldom have to. And this morning: Well, all I can say is: You don't have a weak heart so far as I know, do you, Anthony?"

"It depends on the kind of news. When it's marvelous news I have a surprisingly strong heart."

The vice managing editor laughed appreciatively. He sucked-sucked on his pipe and emitted smoke. "Can your metabolism take it all at once or shall I break the marvelous news gently?"

"I believe I can bear it in a lump sum."

"All right, Anthony, you asked for it." Suck-suck. "But if you have a heart attack in my office don't say I didn't warn you. Anyhow there's always a doctor on duty in the dispensary downstairs—wonderful the beneficences of this company, aren't they?—do you believe there's any company in the world that has the beneficences for its employees this company does, Anthony?" Suck-suck. "Profit-sharing, five-week vacation, free educational plan . . . Well, don't get me started listing them now, Anthony, or I won't even have time to get around to this marvelous news of yours. So you have a strong heart! You have spoke, as the man said." Suck-suck. "Here it is, Anthony. On your mark, get set: Anthony, you're being sent to a bureau!"

Something nice and warm and quite wonderful and actually soothing, like a good Japanese massage, started feeling its way into Pinckney's muscles and blood, trickling, then flooding, into him, all warm and massaging and relaxing.

"Well, that *is* good news," he said, trying to keep down the rising tide of excitement. Overexcitement wasn't approved of at *Vital*, overenthusiasm, being considered "immature," which was much worse around there than being called a royal son of a bitch; the latter in some cases being considered highly flattering.

"I had something of an intimation it would be. One of my intimations, you know. Sometimes I almost feel I direct my entire office here by intimation, and there are worse ways." Suck-suck, suck-suck. "And, Anthony, I don't imagine you'd ever in the world guess where."

This was part of the drill. Equally, Pinckney knew it would not be in the drill if he said right off, "Washington."

"Anthony," the vice managing editor said. He sucked and blew out a tremendous burst of smoke. "How I envy you going out like this to a place where such great and fateful things are the order of the day! How I wish I were going out instead of sitting here handling this miserable and endless administrative detail. I've no business at all being behind a desk, or being an executive. I've no business at all really being in this job. How I wish I were in the field again! I'd give anything in the world to trade jobs with you. Well, shall we do that little thing?" The vice managing editor laughed appreciatively at this sally. "Basically I'm a reporter, one hundred and one percent, always was and always will be. Greatest title a man can have. I'm just not a desk man, not an executive at heart, do you know that, Anthony? But someone has to do this they tell me, Anthony. If you don't mind, would you step over here with me."

Duckworth got up, and taking Pinckney in somewhat avuncular fashion by the back of the arm, but with definite pressure on the elbow, more than was necessary to where Pinckney could feel it, a mere but unmistakable touch of pain, guided him across the room to where the enormous map of the world, which was the entire wall, was inset. It was a wonderful and really beautiful map, all colors, and capable of being lighted up. The day was cloudy, so Duckworth did that now, and the map and its red and white pins came to glowing life. The vice managing editor, who, Pinckney knew, liked to savor these moments, stood back and regarded the map.

"Pretty, isn't it? A pretty thing, the world. Too bad the people in it mess it up so much, isn't it, Anthony? But I don't have you in here to philosophize. A lot of pins," he mused, jabbing toward the map with his pipe. "A lot of pins, aren't there, Anthony?"

"You can hardly see the map for the pinheads."

The vice managing editor laughed appreciatively. He sucked and blew smoke. "Anthony, you do have an abiding sense of humor, I will say that for you. I have always stood up for you on that score." For the first time something in Pinckney was a little disturbed at that statement. Then he forgot it. Big things were ahead: he was going to Washington! The warm feeling reflooded him. "And I know you must be on pins and needles." The vice managing editor let out a deep laugh. "Isn't that an outrageous pun, Anthony?"

"Well, I've heard worse," Pinckney said.

"Yes, I imagine. 'Pinheads.' That's not bad either. Do you know where you're going to be the chief pinhead, Anthony?"

Lifting his pipe arm rather grandly, the vice managing editor arced it back and forth across the map of the world, almost as if he were a symphony conductor—conducting the world, and the pipe his baton.

"Anthony, my boy, you would never guess. No, lad, you would not, I'm sure, so there's no point in your even trying . . ." His pipe arm ranged the continents . . . "Never, never would you guess, my lad . . ." His arm swayed grandly . . . "I don't believe in ten guesses you would make it . . . so let's not try, eh? It's *here*."

With a movement so swift it startled Pinckney, the vice managing editor's arm, with pipestem extended, shot forward like the sudden rapier thrust of a fencer. The pipestem seemed, or so Pinckney thought, to head for Washington, then, playfully, to swerve sharply to the right, arc, sway, go upward and downward, swaying crazily, and Pinckney felt his head swimming a little, sway, arc, jab forward, parry to the right, then finally to come to rest on one of the red pinheads. Pinckney, leaning forward, eyes squinting, looked. He could see first that the pipestem had not alighted on Washington. Then that it had not alighted even on the United States of America. Then he could see that it had not alighted on the continent of North America. Something coming up in him, he could then begin to see that it had not alighted on Europe. Then, and something began to change in him decidedly, something different quite from that warm flooding floodlike floodtide feeling—was it alarm? the emotion was so swift he could hardly label it—Pinckney's eye fled across the European land mass, sped through Constantinople, swam the Bosporus, paused momentarily, then leapt the Middle Eastern states, sailed across Afghanistan, descended swiftly the great Himalayan range, following always the moving pipestem, now seeming to enlarge, to become preternaturally larger than any pipestem could possibly be, until he saw —and now a very great change, something monumentally and metabolically different from that warm flood, filled him, and he felt his entire metabolism had changed in seconds and that physical tests taken a minute ago and right now would vary enormously in cholesterol content of the blood, heart beat, sugar content, and most everything else short of the Wassermann, which he supposed remained, whatever it happened to be, relatively steady in the face of these things—where it rested.

"India!" the vice managing editor burst out. "Pinckney! Just think of it! You're going to India!"

Anthony Pinckney remained in the vice managing editor's office for a good twenty-five minutes more, but for all the information he got, much less the good it did him, he might as well have left immediately. It was sealed and Pinckney knew it. You would never in a million years find out why. He kept thinking of what his wife would say when he told her. He had attained the point of frankness of saying that, while of course he was very grateful for this bureau assignment and was sure it would be terribly exciting, he had rather expected Washington. If he had said more against India, he would have been considered chicken, a coward, unwilling to face the hardships of abroad, not a "good soldier," and therefore not a good *Vital* type: In which case you might as well fold up your tent and steal away into heaven knows what other job: public relations, advertising, one of those "foundation" jobs, or something equally horrible. He got not one scintilla of evidence as to why he was not being sent to Washington. He even, as cautiously as possible, brought up the matter of the Washington political story he had done a month ago and asked outright, though one was not supposed to do these unsubtle things, if there was something in the way he handled the story that made them decide he was not the man they wanted to head up their Washington bureau. This was as far as he could go and apparently even further than he should have gone, for Duckworth seemed surprised even at that question. Why, he said, after hesitating a pregnant moment and looking at Pinckney carefully, he had known only vaguely that Pinckney had written that story.

"Anthony," the vice managing editor said. He leaned forward against his desk a little, toward Pinckney. "Please don't misunderstand this question. But you know me well enough to know that I regard utter one-hundred-and-one-percent frankness as the foundation stone of any viable personnel policy." Pinckney could isolate in a test tube in the corner of his mind the slightest hardening in the vice managing editor's voice—slight but unmistakable. The vice managing editor sucked-sucked on his pipe, blew out smoke, then pointed the pipestem at Pinckney like a dagger. "Anthony. Perhaps it's only my imagination, surely it must be, but: Do I detect some note of reluctance in you to go to India?"

"Oh, no, sir," Pinckney said immediately. "Not the slightest. It should be wonderfully exciting. It's just that I was expecting a bigger bureau. But as to India: well, what more exciting place could there be than India?"

"Good, then. Because you know of course we'd never send anyone where he didn't want to go. Wouldn't make good sense, for him or for us, now would it? Doesn't that strike you as reasonable, as a reasonable personnel policy, even a wise one?"

"Thoroughly reasonable," Pinckney said, "and emphatically wise."

"There is one thing I won't stand for"—and that slight, and unmistakable hardening of tone was there again, and now the vice managing editor made a series of sharp little dagger-stabs toward Pinckney with his pipestem—"and that's for a man to go to any bureau against his will, no, not if he has the slightest opposition to it. I can guarantee you one hundred and one percent that I will never tolerate such a thing. You're quite sure you don't?"

"Positive."

Suck-suck. "Then that settles it." Duckworth laughed and stood up. "Tell your wife to go out and buy a selection of saris and I think what you wear is some baggy diapers called a *dhoti*. With your size I imagine the Indians will mistake you promptly for a Sikh. Some *dhotis*—and perhaps a turban or two." Suck-suck. "I imagine Brooks carries them both."

"Or if not, surely Abercrombie and Fitch," Pinckney said, prodding himself to join in the laughter.

"And of course you and your whole family should get a whole raft of shots." Suck-suck-suck, the noise of the pipe came to Pinckney. "You have four children, haven't you, Anthony."

"That's right. It's good of you to remember."

"And why shouldn't I? I have your complete personnel record right in this desk." Duckworth tapped it sharply with his pipe. "Laughter in the wings, Anthony." Suck-suck. "Yes, all of you—you and your wife and the four young ones—better get all the shots there are. From what Jackson Flowers, whom you're relieving, tells me, the diseases in India start with something very mild called chronic amoebic dysentery and go on from there to slightly stronger diseases such as"—suck-suck—"leprosy and bubonic plague—before they really get into the diseases that are tough, harder to cure. We would hate for you, your wife or those four children to return with something permanent—though, of course"—suck-suck—"everything is covered in the company medical plan."

The vice managing editor was standing up and holding out his hand.

"Keep up that metabolism, Jawaharlal. I'll see you in two years. Or no, you'll surely come in to tell me good-bye, won't you?"

"Yes, I'll do that," Pinckney said.

And he fled. Knowing that he would henceforth be counted among that considerable tribe, the living dead. *Vital* never fired anybody.

10

Rapture of the Depths

Charity Cabot was by no measurement the most beautiful researcher ever to work for *Vital*. To the discriminating eye, however, there was something about her that set her apart from the general run of researchers or even the general run of women. Her basic statistics were five feet four inches of height and one hundred one pounds of weight. Her face was not a "beautiful" face. It was a "pretty" face, however, and a "sweet" one. These are words that do not ordinarily accompany the denotation of character. However, in the case of Charity Cabot, her face had great character. This is not physically definable, since what makes character is inside a person, but the face mirrors the quality with an accuracy no one has ever been able to explain. Why should evil show on the face, or goodness? In addition she had a very remarkable complexion. It was absolutely unflawed and touched with rose. A good painter would have fallen in love with that complexion alone.

There was one other thing about Charity Cabot: she was a most religious girl; in a non-pious yet explicitly practicing way. Among other things that she did not do were smoking and drinking, unusual and very nearly unique shortcomings for anyone working at *Vital* magazine. Charity Cabot was truly sweet and friendly but she was nobody's pushover. She was not impressed by many things that impress people. On the other hand she was impressed by many things that many people miss entirely. The Cub Room of the Stork Club would not have thrilled her nearly so much as an hour's conversation with a person of honesty, perception and non-calculation. She had a mind which felt things that others missed.

As for the "physical" life, she was free of the compulsion which torments many American women to do it because, having the equipment therefor, one should do it. She kept busy doing too many other things. She was a very self-sufficient girl. She loved the plays and the museums, a ballet or an opera could scarcely leave New York without her witness, she had got an enormous amount out of New York since coming there two years ago from her home in a small town in Ohio, where she had attended Oberlin College, and she was an excellent swimmer. Life, and this was the great thing about it, was full of all these riches around one and inside one. Charity Cabot was a perfect proof that a girl really didn't have to do anything she didn't want to do even in that sinful Babylon that is New York City, against whose towered walls so many self-appointed Daniels come to judgment have brayed *mene mene tekel upharsin,* and the city still stands, defiantly its own. Its sin is somewhat exaggerated. A girl can go year after year and no one is going to force sin on her. Whatever people in the outlands may believe, there is very little rape in New York. It is true that the great city, which above all is a city of shrugs, will permit a girl to have it or not have it as she chooses. But this is no definition of rape. Charity Cabot kept happy and she kept busy, which is the greatest lid for concupiscence man has yet discovered. Her interests in life and indeed her whole attitude and vantage point upon it were about as antithetical to Montgomery Shanks' as could be imagined. What these two had "in common," in the saying, would have fitted comfortably on the top of a thin dime. It was little more than that both were members of the human race.

The suggestion for the story had come into the *Vital* office from its Miami stringer. A man by the curious name of Isaiah Virtue was going to attempt, off the coast of Florida, to go farther down than any man had ever previously gone in free diving—that is to say, using only an Aqua-Lung. The present record of 307 feet was held by a Frenchman. No one had ever descended farther than that into water: No one, that is, had ever descended farther than that and then ascended to tell about it. Despite his curious name, Isaiah Virtue, the stringer related, was no fanatic. In point of fact he was a serious-minded stockbroker in

Miami, where he had now lived for ten years. He had come to Miami solely because he had become so captivated by skin diving on a vacation in the Bahamas from his New York brokerage office that he decided he could not live without it, though he had never in his life done one second of it before that vacation, or even heard of the thing. Since Miami was a city where he could both earn his living in his profession and engage in skin diving, he sold everything he had in New York and moved there. He opened a brokerage office, where he spent just enough time to enable him to support himself while spending all the rest of the time at what had become his passion in life. The strange world beneath the changing surface of the sea had become his real, beckoning home. Over the years it had grown and grown into a supreme passion: to go deeper into that world than man had ever gone before. Now, after ten years of preparation, he was ready to make the attempt.

Charity Cabot was assigned to the story because she was a very good swimmer: This may seem an odd reason when it is considered that the story did not involve the researcher's even touching her toes in the water. All she had to do was stay on the diving boat and report what happened. However, since the story was concerned with water, there seemed *some* reason for sending her over anyone else. This sort of reasoning sometimes went on in the *Vital* office. Maybe they thought the researcher might fall overboard, in which case, the boat being in 600 feet of water, it *would* be helpful if she could swim.

The reason Montgomery Shanks was assigned as the photographer on the story had a much sounder base. In the past few years Shanks had become one of the pioneers in underwater photography, a comparatively new and rapidly developing art form. He had turned in some very fine stories shot underwater. And all underwater stories on *Vital* went to Shanks.

Shanks decided they would drive down to Florida from New York. They had time to do it and Shanks always liked to take his vermilion Cadillac convertible with him whenever possible. The reasons were two. One was that a *Vital* photographer carried a very considerable amount of photographic equipment; this was especially true if the story required special underwater cameras and submerging gear. Rather than move it all in and out of a plane, into a rental car in Miami, then twenty miles north to Fort Lauderdale, the Florida town off which Virtue was to make his attempt, it seemed a lot simpler, at least to Shanks, to take the Cadillac thirteen hundred miles—and it was only a couple days' drive to Florida, the way Shanks drove. The other reason was that Shanks felt happiest and most secure when behind either the lens of his camera or the wheel of his Cadillac. So he decided they would drive and told Charity Cabot so. He had never met her, but when he was told she was the researcher on the story he dropped by the National Affairs Department, where she worked. The chief researcher pointed her out to him where she was seated at her desk. Shanks walked over. He had a 35-millimeter camera slung around his neck: he never moved without carrying a camera, you could never tell when the greatest photograph in history might suddenly for one instant and one only be right in front of your eyes. He leaned against her desk—Shanks had a slovenly slouch that actually added to his appeal—and said something to her.

"I'm Shanks," he said.

Charity Cabot looked up and smiled. "Oh, hello," she said pleasantly. "I was just reading the research from our Miami stringer about Isaiah Virtue and . . ."

"You won't need any of that," Shanks interrupted. "This is a picture story." He grinned but the grin had something of command in it. Shanks always made a point of establishing right off the relationship between himself and a new researcher, just in case any of them might get the idea they were equals. "Forget it."

"Well, I thought it wouldn't hurt . . ."

"Where do you live?" Shanks cut her off again.

This time Charity Cabot looked surprised. She sat up a little straighter. She took another look at Shanks. It was a close look.

"I live," she said easily, "at 75 West Ninth Street."

"One of those Village clowns, eh?" Shanks grinned that grin of his. It was a very special grin. "We're driving down. I'll pick you up at nine tomorrow morning. Sharp."

And he turned and was gone. Charity Cabot sat watching him go. Her face looked very thoughtful, assessing. Then she went back to the clips.

Next morning Shanks picked her up on Ninth Street at ten o'clock. He never apologized for or even referred to the fact he was an hour late. He did, however, complain of the four flights of stairs he had to climb to get to her apartment. The complaint was accompanied by a laugh and was in friendly fashion. Shanks, when he chose, could spray charm like a DDT bomb.

"Where's your luggage?" he asked.

She started to pick up the one small bag she had packed. Shanks' muscular hand flashed out and got on the handle at the same time. It was no effort for him to flick it away from her.

"You mean this is all? No evening dresses for the summery nights of Florida with the palm trees gently waving?"

She smiled a little. "Hadn't we better go?"

They climbed down the four flights to where the vermilion Cadillac stood along the curb like a huge shiny apple on a coal pile. Shanks, catching with satisfaction her look of unprepared startlement on first viewing this monstrous beast, flung her bag in the back seat. They got in. Shanks started the monster and they shot west on Ninth like a jet-assisted take-off from the flight deck of the *Saratoga*.

Charity Cabot was neither a constrained girl nor a sulky one and they made easy conversation as they rammed through the Holland Tunnel, through the maze of those lands that lie in desolate disarray beyond the great city, and soon onto the Jersey Turnpike. It was a very cold January day, with a thin, icy rain and the eternal thick black soot fighting it out for command of the air and ending in the coagulating compromise of a wet, gritty, almost choking mush which would have gagged and maybe throttled to death in five minutes a healthy Polynesian. For both Charity Cabot and Montgomery Shanks there was a sense of exhilaration that every mile was taking them closer to the land of warm skies, blue water, white beaches and breathable air. Shanks was a very fast driver. He kept the Cadillac at a minimum of eighty and often the needle was tickling a hundred. After a while they fell into silence. Then without saying a word Shanks pulled up on the side of the turnpike, itself an illegal act.

"You drive?" he said when the car had stopped.

"Why, yes." She seemed surprised. "But I've never driven a Cadillac."

"They've got a steering wheel and four wheels like the rest of them. I need some sleep to go with that two hours I got last night."

Without waiting for an answer Shanks got out of the car, got into the back seat and started pulling over him an Abercrombie and Fitch blanket that he kept stowed there. She hesitated momentarily, then slid over behind the wheel, looked at the huge panel of gadgets briefly— the maximum car she had ever driven up to now was her family's 1949 Chevrolet—then started up, very smoothly actually. Charity Cabot was a coping sort of girl. Shanks had the ability to go to sleep anywhere when he needed sleep, and almost immediately he was very soundly asleep, and most comfortable, in the spacious leathery back seat of the Cadillac.

It was sometime between that moment and Washington that Montgomery Shanks made his decision. It was probably due to the fact that he had to get out of New York really to see what a girl like Charity Cabot had. In any event he saw her all at once, it came over him all at once, and his mind was made up. The precise moment of decision was when, after he had been asleep perhaps three hours, he raised up on his elbow in the back seat. The fact that he had got his sleep out and that she had stopped at a red light—the town was Laurel, Maryland, but he never knew that—brought him awake. He raised up slowly on his elbow. His head was pillowed on the right side of the back seat, so that he had a superb view of her profile. And a view, which as a photographer he valued, of her without her knowing she was being watched. One of her hands, in a feminine gesture, came up off the steering wheel and touched back lightly over her hair. The winter's sun was slanting in from her right and he noticed then how perfectly soft and lovely her hair was; it actually had a lot of gold in it which the light brought out. And her face, as he saw it now: He had never seen anything so innocent, so, so . . . virginal was the word. *Let there be sought for my lord the king a young virgin.* Only a photographer, he told himself, could appreciate that moment of seeing her that way. It came over him, of a sudden: of what exquisite plumage this girl was! She would probably be too thin, but the other would make up for it, as a variety. His mind, all in an instant, was made up.

"Where are we?" he said, yawning heavily. "Virginia?"

Just then the light changed and she started the car. He was impressed by how she did it smoothly, she was not startled by his voice. This told Shanks she had quality. Shanks appreciated quality.

"We're in Maryland," she said.

"Maryland!" Shanks yelled. He was astonished. "How fast have you been driving?"

"Forty miles an hour."

"Forty miles an hour!" Shanks shouted. He was incredulous. "My God, I didn't know the boat would go that slow! Jesus God Almighty it'll be Easter Sunday before we get to Florida!"

Without a word she pulled up on the side of the road. "If you don't like the way I drive suppose you just drive yourself."

And she moved crisply over to the other side of the seat. Shanks burst out laughing. He pushed the back of the driver's seat, opened the front door, got out, got back in and started the engine. He yawned, a long, deep yawn of contentment from a good nap. "You're not mad now, are you, baby?"

"I am not. But I've got something to live for if you haven't. And my name isn't baby."

"What's that?" Shanks could hardly believe his ears. He turned and looked at her. "Where they been keeping you? And what is it so priceless exactly you've got to live for?"

"Hadn't we better get going? If you're in such a hurry."

Shanks laughed and shrugged. He pressed a button on his side of the car which shot down the window on her side. She had never been in a car that did that and she was startled. Shanks laughed again. Then, jamming the accelerator to the floor, he shot the car forward to eighty miles an hour, so suddenly that she was thrown back sharply against the seat.

"Now if you'll just pay close attention," he said, "I will show you the proper way to get to Florida. Excuse me," he said, yawning, and streaking around a row of three cars which were doing a crawling seventy m.p.h.

At Shanks' rate of driving nightfall brought them into the countryside of U. S. 1 south of Richmond. He kept driving after dark for another hour, and about seven, when he saw what looked like a good motel with a sign outside that said "Vacancy," he roared into it and came to a stop with a suddenness that sent a machine-gun burst of gravel chattering against the wall of the motel office.

"Doesn't look like a bad flophouse," Shanks said, "for a one-night stand. Motels are a lot simpler than hotels, I imagine or at least hope you'll agree. Well, here we go, Comrade Cabot."

He got out, got two of his three bags and got her only one and they walked into the office. The desk clerk, who had seen that they had come up in a Cadillac—indeed had heard it—and a most astonishing-looking Cadillac at that, smiled broadly.

"Double or twin beds?" he asked pleasantly.

"Two double rooms, son," Shanks said. The desk clerk was a gray-haired man twice Shanks' age. His eyes shot wide open. Then he popped to. Shanks had a tone and manner of authority that made just about anyone in the world pop to.

Shanks registered for both of them. He wrote "Montgomery Shanks" on one card and "Charity Cabot" on the other, and deliberately left blank the various spaces that said "address," "business," "license number," and so on. The clerk picked up the cards, read them, looked at one and then at the other of the two of them and his eyes got a little wider. He looked just a fraction too long for Shanks' taste.

"Got any questions, son?" Shanks snapped. "Actually we're bank thieves and the loot is all in the car out there but I didn't think it best to put that on the card."

"Heh, heh," the clerk laughed nervously. "Heh, heh . . ."

"Come off it, junior," Shanks snapped. "Let's get moving."

The cards the clerk was holding shot down. "Yes, sir. Straight away, sir. This way if you please, sir—and you, Madam."

"She's no Madam, she's one of the working girls. Working the road, you know. I picked her up north of Richmond. Heh, heh," Shanks said, mimicking the clerk.

The clerk laughed nervously. Charity Cabot did not laugh at all. The clerk came around the counter, picked up Charity's bag and started to pick up Shanks'.

"Just take the lady's," Shanks ordered him.

The clerk led them outside. The motel was in a U-shape and the clerk took them to two rooms that formed the bottom of the U.

"Our very best rooms," he said ingratiatingly. "Farthest off the highway."

"Looks like the best is none too good," Shanks said, glancing around him. Actually the place was nicely laid out, with flower plots between the two arms of the U. Shanks yawned. "I don't suppose they have anything to eat down in this part of the country."

The clerk laughed with ingratiating heartiness. "Yes, *sir,*" he said rather proudly. "A very excellent restaurant lies one-quarter mile down the road, recommended by Dunc . . ."

"Does anything to drink lie there?" Shanks cut him off. It was almost impossible for anyone ever to finish a sentence with Shanks.

"I'm afraid not, sir," the clerk said apologetically. "One thing Virginia doesn't have is bars. Except of course beer . . ."

"No bars!" Shanks exploded, shocked. "Is this in the United States?"

The clerk laughed appreciatively. "Why, yes, sir," he began, and essayed a jest himself. "Of course Vuh-ginia did try to get out during the Civ . . ."

"Yes, we've heard all about the Civil War," Shanks cut that one off.

Shanks stood at Charity's door as the clerk showed her in. Watching her walk into the bedroom he felt something very definite. "Ten minutes okay with you or you want a bath?"

"Ten minutes will be fine. I'll take the bath later."

Shanks' forehead crinkled pleasantly. "A fine idea. A bath later." Suddenly he noticed the clerk standing there. "What the hell are *you* waiting for? Oh." He fished in his pocket, pulled out a dollar bill and tossed it to him. Actually the clerk had not been waiting for a tip— he was no bellhop but owned the place—but was just standing there in open-mouthed fascination at Shanks and possibly in wonder at whatever the relationship here was. He almost hopped away, like a frightened rabbit in flight.

When Shanks came out of his room a little later and picked up Charity, he was carrying the most beautiful attaché case she had ever seen. She didn't know it but it had a reason for being beautiful. It was of that incomparable grayish-brown leather, radiating subtle affluence, made by the firm of Gucci. She could only wonder why in the world Shanks was taking an attaché case to dinner.

The restaurant was very pleasant, even quite smart. It would not have been there but for the heavy winter traffic that now flowed over this highway between the rich cities of the East and the Florida sun. Shanks guided them inside and crisply instructed the maître d' to give them a table for four. Arrived there, he set the attaché case on the table top, covering two of the four places, and he and Charity took the other two. A man wearing black pants and a red jacket came and hovered over them. With a quick and expert movement, Shanks reached over and snapped open the two clamps of the case so suddenly that it startled Charity. She looked at the inside of it in astonishment.

The attaché case was in all fact a portable bar. It was an exquisite thing indeed. Lined like a jewel case with the choicest red velvet, it was fitted out not only with flasks for Scotch, bourbon, rye, gin, vodka and extra-dry vermouth but also with the various correct glasses—two of each—for serving drinks made from these commodities.

"I never move without this," Shanks explained briefly. "Tonight you can see why. You never know when you're going to get caught short in these primitive areas. What's yours going to be?" and his fingers riffled over the flasks in the case.

"I'll have a Seven-up."

"Up what? Bourbon, rye . . ."

"Just a Seven-up."

Shanks paused a moment, looking at her. "One Seven-up—straight," he said then with elaborate disgust to the waiter, "and one very extra-dry double vodka martini." He extracted from the Gucci two flasks, one containing Smirnoff vodka and the other Boissiere vermouth, and then reached in and unstrapped an impeccable long-stemmed Baccarat glass and handed these items up to the waiter. "You know what extra-dry means?"

"Yes, sir," the waiter said. He laughed appreciatively at his oncoming wit. "You take the vermouth cork and . . ."

"Please," Shanks said with a pained expression, holding up his hand. "No martini jokes. Just bring it."

"Yes, sir," the waiter said, hurrying away.

"You hung over?"

She smiled. "I don't drink."

Shanks' mouth was a little open. "Oh-h-h."

He was fascinated. He had never run into this before. He had two double martinis while she was having one Seven-up. He was really more fascinated all the time. He was finding her a new kind of thrill and besides that a very remarkable girl in many ways.

They went in and ate. For conversation they talked about Isaiah Virtue.

"I wonder what he's like," she said. "I'm anxious to see. I can understand a man like that. Wanting to do something no one has ever done before."

Shanks looked at her with a kind of casual studiousness. He hated words, really, and he hated people putting things into words. "Yeh," he said. "He wants to make a dive. I hope the son of a bitch makes it."

She waited a moment. "I hope he makes it, too. Well, I'm a little tired if you don't mind."

"Why should I mind?" Shanks said. "I don't mind at all!" he exclaimed in a sudden outburst of assumed enthusiasm. He laughed heartily. "Let's tool the hell out of this dump," he said. The waiter stood staring at him and he stared even more when Shanks put a forty percent tip down on the table. He leapt over and pulled back Shanks' chair. Charity Cabot got up by herself.

They drove up in front of the motel and got out. Side by side they walked down the arm of the U. It was a long walk and at the end of it they could see two bedrooms lighted where each had left a lamp on. They looked almost beckoning in the darkness, the rooms alongside being all unlighted.

"How anyone can go to bed so early," Shanks said, "beats the hell out of me."

"They're tired from traveling," she said. "They always go to bed early in motels."

"Is that a fact?"

"Yes, it is. And I'm tired too."

They passed his room first. He stopped and waited a moment. "Come in for a nightcap?" he said.

She smiled. "I don't drink," she said.

"Oh, that's right," he said. "I forgot. It's a hard fact to remember about anyone under eighty." He leaned against the wall of the building and gave her what he knew to be a sultry look. "Don't drink, I haven't seen you smoke, no vice of any size, shape or description, correct me if I'm wrong."

"One. I like a bath every day and I want one now. Good night."

Before even he could wrest himself off the wall, she was gone, inside her room, the door had closed behind her and he heard distinctly a chain bolt being put into place. He sighed, shrugged, laughed, pushed himself off the wall and went inside his own room.

He sat down on the bed and just sat there for a moment looking at the wall. He turned his head and looked at the bed. It was a large double bed. He turned back and looked again at the wall. Then he sprang off the bed, jerked open his Gucci bar and pulled out the Scotch flask. He opened it and, carrying it with him, stepped into the bathroom to get a glass. He had just poured himself a generous half-glass of the Scotch when abruptly he heard the sound of water running beyond the bathroom wall. He stood there, listening. The water ran for a while. Then it was off. Then, very distinctly, he could hear the sound of a foot being placed into a tubful of water. Jesus Christ, he thought, these walls are thin! He swallowed off half the whiskey. He started to move, then found himself just standing there. He heard, unmistakably, a body descend into the water. He finished off the Scotch and poured himself some more. He started to go back into the room but found himself not moving. He could hear her splashing around behind the wall. This went on for what must have been ten minutes. A damn clean girl, he thought. He heard splashing and he even thought he heard, though he may have imagined this for he had drunk quite a bit in a very short time, the soaping of a body. Then he did hear the sound of stepping from the tub. He thought he heard the drying with a towel.

He stepped out of the bathroom, slammed the bathroom door violently, took off his clothes and got into bed.

It was exactly one and one half hours before he could get to sleep. It was something that had never happened to him before.

"Christ in a pinch-bottle," he thought before he finally dozed restlessly off. "She doesn't even drink."

Through the paper-thin wall in her room Charity Cabot finished toweling herself. She put on a nightgown, got a beautiful calf-bound book from her suitcase—the book was the Cambridge edition—and sitting at the tiny motel table did her devotions by reading a chapter from the Psalms. Then she turned out the light and got into bed. She was asleep within three minutes.

One accessory advantage of believing in God is that those who do sleep well. People who believe in God—really believe, we mean, not as a form but as the most important thing in life: These almost never have insomnia.

He came awake with extreme grogginess. It was a while before he realized it was the knocking that had done it. He stepped to the door.

"Who's there?" he rasped.

"It's me."

"Oh."

"It's nine o'clock. Hadn't we better get going?" What a sweet voice she had!

That day they drove through the Virginia countryside, where the smoke curled up blue and thin from the weathered tobacco barns, and into the Carolinas, where the woods now of the long pine, now of blackjack fell away from the road. The sun was out and the intake of air fragrant with the smell of pine needles and wood rather than of rasping soot was a blessed pleasure, a thing that can be treasured properly only by people coming out of the Soot Capital of the world, New York, New York. It was still not warm enough, though, to put the top of a convertible down.

"You know," he said happily, "there really is something about this business of driving out of a cold climate into a hot one. Getting it in stages this way, I mean. How about that?"

She was happy, too, and for the same reason. "Yes, isn't there! Look, there's a red deer!"

"Where?" he said excitedly. He was surprised at his excitement.

"There," she pointed. He slowed down and saw it. It was just standing there at the edge of some woods. It was the color of warm clay, very young, and seemed to be looking at them with the same curiosity as theirs at him. The two people from the asphalt pavements of New York looked at and praised its beauty with an excess of admiration and excitement.

"I'm glad we came by car," he said as he started up. "Aren't you?"

"I'm enjoying this trip very much."

"I'll be glad when we can put the top down."

He began to drive more slowly. Throughout the day he felt very relaxed. He was astonished what a comfortable person she was to be with. He would have thought he would be bored to be with her long. He wasn't. They talked when they felt like it and lots of times they went quite a while without saying a word. He wasn't bored even then. It was very comfortable just to be with her.

But then night came on.

"I think we'll stay in a hotel tonight."

"I thought you liked motels. You said they were simpler."

"I didn't sleep very well last night. I'm not so sure about these motels. They let in a lot of noise. From the highway," he added.

"Odd. I didn't notice any."

They stopped in a fair-sized town and found its best hotel, which was not bad. There were no two rooms left on the same floor. They ate in the hotel dining room then went promptly upstairs. That night, to his surprise, it took him two hours to get to sleep. He had never had this kind of trouble. Tonight he missed even listening to her take a bath. With her on a different floor, it was worse even than last night.

Next day took them through Georgia, where some white-faced cattle held them up for ten minutes crossing a road—they found themselves laughing at this—and where they saw flocks of wood duck rising from the misty marshes; and into Florida, where they stopped at the first orange-juice stand and drank nearly a quart each. Then they put the top down. It was almost like a ceremony.

With the sun beating down on him in his vermilion Cadillac convertible and with his jacket and tie off, Shanks was beginning to feel very good. And suddenly he began to feel good for another reason. This thing had become a challenge. It had been ten years since he had had any serious trouble in this direction and suddenly the obstacle that confronted him began to stir a palpable exhilaration in him. It was something new and it began to give him a kick for its newness alone, and its challenge. He had no doubt of the outcome, but it was going to take a little doing. Well, there was nothing like the sun and the beach to loosen up a woman. Then he began to wonder if he was just wanting her because she was being difficult. This could cloud a man's vision, twist his sense of values about a woman. Then he remembered that moment when he had awakened in the back seat in Maryland and seen her. He had wanted her *then,* which was before he knew she was going to be difficult and right after, too, a very interesting night in New York with someone who was not difficult and because of whose interesting-ness he had just taken that nap. And, yet—well, she was certainly no glamour girl. At least he didn't think so. She wore such outrageously proper clothes it was very difficult to tell much about her that way. And yet she was undoubtedly thin. He didn't like girls that were too thin.

His emotions, he decided, were pretty mixed up about the whole thing. Anyhow he knew he was driving the Cadillac slower than he had ever driven it.

When they got into Fort Lauderdale they drove around until Shanks saw a motel with a "Vacancy" sign.

"I thought you decided you didn't like motels," she said.

"Who the hell said I didn't like motels? I didn't like *that* motel. Actually I do like *motels*. Much simpler."

All the motels down here had some sort of ridiculous "motif." This one used the pirate one, which meant the dining room was a "pirate's cave" so dark you could scarcely see your food; the bar seats were uncomfortable rum kegs; and the waitresses wore black pantaloons that hit them at mid-calf, red blouses, black sashes, and black head-kerchiefs decorated with a skull-and-bones. One would have thought one had come upon some kind of playland for seven-year-olds, but the whole thing was commercially serious. They ate and left. Their rooms were side by side on the second floor of the two-story structure, in a series of rooms that had an outside passageway overlooking the swimming pool directly below and the sea beyond it. Tonight Shanks took two one-and-a-half-grain capsules of seconal and went right off to sleep. He had decided on a strategy, which was to stay away from her for a while.

Tomorrow Isaiah Virtue was to make his attempt to go deeper than man had ever gone. He was arriving in Fort Lauderdale today to complete arrangements. That afternoon they went down to see him at the motel where he was staying. He certainly didn't look the classic hero type fresh from the palestra. He was in his mid-forties, short, had lost most of his hair and had a decided potbelly. He was a quiet man, self-assured, and they enjoyed talking with him.

"Why are you doing it?" Charity Cabot asked him at one point. She had her notebook out.

"I want to do it," Isaiah Virtue said.

"Are you married?"

"No."

"Relatives?"

"Nobody close."

Later when they were having dinner she told Shanks she liked him. "But I have a queer feeling about this whole thing."

"What do you mean queer?"

"I don't know. Just queer. He has quite a potbelly, doesn't he?"

"You see that with free divers. You get it from the breathing. Actually it's not fat. It's all muscle down there with them."

She was taking notes.

"You don't have to take so many notes, baby. This is a goddamn picture story, haven't you heard?"

"Do you have to call me 'baby'?" she said quietly. "And do you have to use goddamn every other word?" She went right on making notes.

"Well, I'll be goddamned," Shanks said. And he laughed. "I'm going to bed."

He thought she seemed surprised at that, and he felt his strategy was beginning to take hold.

Next day when they came down to breakfast there were heavy blue-black clouds overhead. They looked mean and it looked like rain or worse. From the passageway outside their rooms they had both seen heavy, charging whitecaps on the sea.

"Will he put it off?" she asked.

"Probably," Shanks said. "Unless he's a goddamned fool. Put that in your notes."

They were to pick Virtue up at his motel and drive him to the wharf where the diving boat was tied up.

"Better go call him and make sure he's canceling," Shanks instructed her. "Then we can all go back to our several beds."

She went over to the desk and made the call. She came back to the table. "He's going to do it today," she said. "He says it'll be all right when we get out there."

The photographer shrugged and stood up. "Okay, let's go."

They picked Virtue up and drove to the wharf. They walked down it to the diving boat.

"All ready?" Virtue asked the captain.

"You're not going to do it today, Isaiah?" the captain said. It was curious to hear that first name used. The captain was obviously a friend of Virtue's from taking him out on dives before.

"Why not?" Virtue said.

"Just look out there and see why not," the captain said.

"It doesn't make any difference what the water is like above," Virtue said. "I've told you that a thousand times." He said this affectionately. The captain was an older man. "I'll be through that in one minute. It's what's down below that counts." He waited a moment, then said: "It's always quiet down below."

The captain sighed. "Okay. I think you ought to wait until tomorrow. What's your hurry? But whatever you say, Isaiah."

They went out the channel and soon were starting into open sea. It was hellish rough. The boat was a well-built forty-footer but it was soon both pitching and rolling, the quick steep waves slamming against it. You could hear their *slap, slap.* Rain blown by a gathering wind began to whip across the bow. It was a solid hour before they reached the diving place. Then the boat captain tried to heave to. The boat was bouncing like hell.

"We're going to have a hard time keep from drifting, Isaiah," the captain said. He had to yell over the wind. "Even when you get back up we may have drifted half a mile. You've waited ten years for this. What's wrong with waiting one more day? Let's go back!"

"Let's go down," Virtue said. He was taking off his trousers, leaving himself in bathing trunks. His belly stuck way out, and with his bald head he was a funny-looking little man. He strapped on his Aqua-Lung. Shanks was getting set, too, with his, and his camera. The idea was that he would accompany Virtue down around fifty or sixty feet and get a picture of him headed for his record, then hang around there and get another picture of him coming up. It was dangerous for him, too, in this water, if not so much as for the deeper-going Virtue. Charity Cabot looked worried. Virtue put a weighted marked line over the side that would tell him how deep he was. Then Virtue and Shanks lowered themselves over the side. The boat was rising and falling steeply and they almost slammed against it. Then they shoved away and disappeared into the water.

She went in to watch them on the fathometer. She saw the two tiny specks going slowly down. Finally at about the sixty-foot mark she saw one speck stop. The other continued down slowly. 100 feet . . . 200 . . . 250 . . . Watching the screen it seemed an age . . . 300 . . . 305 . . . When the speck passed 310 the captain let out a mighty shout that startled her.

"By god, he made it!" the captain said. "The fool has guts."

To give himself a little space between the old and the new world's record, the speck continued going down. This was according to plan. Then, according to plan, they saw the speck stop at 350. The captain gave a great sigh. The speck stopped at 350 awhile. Virtue would be resting there by the marked line before the ascent. Charity Cabot's eyes came up and saw the other speck at sixty feet.

The crewman brought Charity Cabot and the captain some hot coffee. They smiled and touched the thick white mugs in a victory toast. Then they drank, feeling warm and happy at Virtue's achievement of his great goal.

"I used to think he was half nuts," the captain said. "Now I know what he was talking about. Don't you?"

"I think I do," Charity said. Her eyes were glowing and she looked very happy.

"Well, about time for him to come up," the captain said. They both resumed watching the fathometer. The captain seemed a little impatient. "There . . ."

Charity Cabot was taking a sip of her coffee when she saw the speck begin to move. She stopped in horror and the cup came down.

"Oh, my God," the captain said.

"What is it, what is it?" she said. "What's happened?"

"I don't know," the captain said. "Oh, my God." The "God" seemed literal, not profane.

As they watched in hypnotized horror, they saw the white speck moving, not up, but down. Down, down, down it went: 375 feet . . . 385 feet . . . 400 feet. Charity could hear the captain crying softly. She couldn't take her eyes off the fathometer. She felt something very terrible grabbing like an iron claw at the pit of her stomach. 410 feet . . . 415 . . . 425 . . . 435 feet . . . 450 feet . . . 475 feet . . .

The fathometer's depth-recording limit was 550 feet. The white speck went off the bottom of the screen and disappeared.

"What happened?" Charity said. She felt closer to fainting than ever in her life.

"I don't know," the captain said. He was not crying now. But his face was very pale. He looked at the fathometer and saw the other speck hovering at eighty feet. He had almost forgotten it was there. "Give that photographer fifteen minutes, then signal him to come up," the captain told the crewman.

He was waiting against the chance that suddenly the other pip would come up from below and appear, upward, on the bottom of the screen at 550. They both kept their eyes on the fathometer. Charity felt as if hers were going to pop from their sockets but she couldn't take her eyes off the screen.

"Okay now, Captain?" the crewman called in after a while. "It's fifteen minutes."

"Signal him up," the captain said.

Over the line they passed the signal to Shanks to come up. On the screen they saw the white pip that was Shanks start slowly up. When he was aboard they took him out of his Aqua-Lung, put a blanket around him, a cup of hot coffee in his hands, and told him about Isaiah Virtue.

Back at their motel Charity and Shanks didn't talk very much. He explained the various possibilities of what could have happened to Virtue. One was something which the Anglo-Saxon calls "nitrogen narcosis," and which the Frenchman calls "rapture of the depths." It is a feeling of great exhilaration which comes over divers at great depths, Shanks explained.

"One diver described it," Shanks said, "that he felt so happy he wanted to take off his mask and offer it to a passing fish. In which case he would be dead in ten seconds. That could have happened to Virtue. He would have been a very happy man down there.

"The second thing," he said, "is that at those depths a man can sometimes mistake down for up. Virtue, knowing he had attained his record, may have thought, very triumphantly, that he was going up when he was actually going down."

"What a horrible thing," Charity said. "Which do you think it was?"

"I hope," said Shanks, "it was rapture of the depths."

They air-expressed the film and captions and research to New York. Late that night when they sat down to dinner they were both very tired. Charity knew Shanks must be terribly tired from his dive. And they both were exhausted, gone-out, from the emotions of the day. They didn't talk about it.

"I think I'll have a drink," she said before dinner.

He looked up at her. He was too bushed to feel very surprised. "What'll it be?" he said.

"Anything."

He ordered two extra-dry vodka martinis. They sat sipping them.

"Your first?" he said.

"Second."

He didn't ask when the other was. They finished their drinks.

"Another one?"

"No, thank you," she said.

She didn't seem to show any effects from the drink. They ordered dinner from one of the pirate girls. Neither ate very much. Then they went to bed, each.

Both slept in very late next morning. Shanks slept later, as always. Also he was probably more tired. She was having breakfast out by the pool when he came down. He walked down the outside stairs and emerged by the pool before he saw her. When he did see her he came to a dead stop.

It was a dancing day. The sun was out bright and warm and the blue of the sky kept on going and going with, wherever the eye looked, not the smallest scrap of cloud and the sea was that satin surface when no whisper of wind blows. She was sitting at her table having orange juice and watching three or four people swimming in the pool. She was sitting there watching, and she was wearing a bathing suit.

The French have a phrase for what she was, a phrase for which there is no very good translation. The phrase is *fausse maigre*, meaning literally "false thin." The French value such a bodily proportion in a woman perhaps more than any other. It means just the right amount of fullness with no fat. In a dress such a body is never really revealed, particularly in the dresses that Charity Cabot wore. The dress must come off to reveal it and it is a startling thing, and one of the pleasures of the earth, to know a *fausse maigre* woman in such dresses for a while then to see her as Montgomery Shanks, standing there at the bottom of the stairs, saw Charity Cabot.

He walked over and sat down. They finished breakfast. They both felt happy. Shanks felt very, very excited. They both had decided, without saying it, not to talk about yesterday.

"Let's go for a swim," he said. "Not in this goddamn pool. In the ocean."

"Monty."

"Yes?" He turned.

"Do you always have to use those words?"

He looked at her, astonished. "You don't teach Sunday school, do you?"

"What's wrong with Sunday school?"

"You took a drink last night, didn't you? Didn't you?"

"You saw me. Why ask it? Monty," she said quietly, "do you ever think about anything serious. About God or life or ideals?"

He looked at her, his eyes widening. "Listen, don't try to change me," he said. He waited a moment. "I don't know where in the world you came from but . . ." He looked at her again, and felt everything going in him. "Forget it. I'll meet you in five minutes here."

He went upstairs and got into his bathing trunks. Coming down the stairs he looked at her again. She was standing now, by the pool. It was incredible how ravishing she looked. She would drive a Trappist monk to rape, he thought. His mind was at work on her, and it was all building up terribly in him.

They crossed the road to the beach. They sat there awhile, then she started walking slowly up and down the beach, stopping frequently to pick up shells. He couldn't take his eyes off her. And through the eyes of Shanks, who was accustomed to women flapping and flopping when he semaphored his two little fingers, she was beginning to seem history's most desirable woman. He had entirely ceased even to be able to consider whether this was because of what she had or because she was so unattainable. And actually it no longer mattered. All he knew was that this was something he had to have.

He had arranged for lunch to be served them on the beach. Across the little beach table he kept trying to look at her when she wasn't watching him. Once their bare knees touched under the table. Hers drew quickly away.

Afterward they lay down under the umbrella to take a nap. The umbrella pole was between them. She went promptly to sleep. It was impossible for him to sleep, he kept turning and twisting on the sand.

He raised on his elbow and watched her sleeping. She was lying on her back. She slept beautifully. He was eight inches away from her and watching her he thought if he didn't have her he was going to go off his rocker. What would she do if he just leaned over . . . He remembered her knee drawing away beneath the table. It would kill all his chances. He got up, ran toward the water and with a mighty leap plunged into the surf. He was a very good swimmer and he tried to work some of it off by taking a long, hard swim. He was out there an hour before he came out. He walked slowly up the beach toward her. She was sitting with her legs together, pulled up, and her hands resting on her knees. He could see the undersides of her thighs. He had seen hundreds of pairs of thighs in his life but right now he couldn't believe such thighs as hers existed. The complexion seen on her face held for all over her body. It was perfectly flawless flesh.

He had to do something.

He sat down and started drying himself. Well, he thought, here goes.

"Charity."

"Yes?"

"Charity, why don't we stop playing games. I'm no good at playing games."

She looked over at him. "What in the world are you talking about?"

He turned and looked straight at her. He had to know. He looked straight into her eyes. By God. She *didn't* know. She was certainly Miss Innocence all wrapped up in Christmas tinsel. He wanted her all the more.

"Charity, I want to sleep with you."

He was looking at her and she waited a long, long time, it seemed to him. She was not embarrassed. He was quite sure no one had ever said anything like this to her in her life, but she was not embarrassed. This was because she was able to handle anything. That was her trouble, he thought. She was too able to handle anything. There was not a grain of helplessness in her. He thought of giving her this unsolicited advice but decided against it.

Then she smiled. "Well, you're not going to."

"What's wrong with it, Charity. My God, don't you believe in sex?" he said, quite frenetically for him. "It's the most natural thing in the world. A person isn't complete without sex. It isn't right *not* to have it," he said in fluent missionary tones. "It isn't even *healthy*."

She smiled. "I feel pretty healthy."

Looking at her glowing body he knew it had been a mistake to bring health into it. "But Charity . . ."

"Monty," she interrupted him. She smiled at him as one might at a candy-craving child. "This isn't going to get either of us anywhere. I just happen to believe differently. And, Monty, I'm not going to change. Why spend a lot of time on something that time's not going to change?"

She said this very quietly and very rationally. She was too quiet and much too rational, he thought. But he could not believe the other.

"You mean you've never done it?"

"Of course not," she said, surprised at his surprise.

"How old are you?"

"Twenty-six."

He sighed heavily. "Ready to go in?"

"If you are," she said pleasantly.

They picked up the towels and made their way back across the road. They walked by the pool and upstairs along the passageway that ran outside the rooms. They walked down until they reached theirs. Hers was first. She opened the door. She walked in and started to pull the door to. He held it open.

"Charity," he said.

She waited. He just couldn't believe it.

"Charity," he said. "Oh, Jesus Christ, Charity."

His hand reached around her. She drew away.

"No, Monty, *no* . . ."

She said the "no" so sharply that his hand snapped down. His pride was stung. He had never had this happen to him, at least not for a very long time. He turned angrily away, went to his room, and slammed the door so violently the jalousies trembled. He sat down on the bed, very angry.

He got up and went to the bathroom to get a glass for some Scotch. Suddenly he could hear water running in the adjoining room, hers. Just beyond that wall. The tub fill . . . He tore out of the bathroom, out of his room, and stepped down the passageway to hers. Very gently he tried the door. She had left it unlocked! Probably because it was broad daylight, and people were only a few steps away. You could hear the voices of the swimmers below.

He stepped into the bedroom. She wasn't there. He waited a moment. He was shaking all over. Then . . . he felt something on his chest. It was his Leica, his 35-millimeter. He had had it with him even on the beach. Then something very cool and calming came over him. Feeling the camera in his fingers he felt all his sense of mastery come back. He was perfectly cool now, and quiet as a cat. He fingered the camera. He estimated the distance. Then very softly he stepped to the bathroom door and with a quick, catlike flick of his wrist flung it open and stepped back.

She was standing there ready to step into the bath. Her face in surprise turned directly toward him. Very calmly Montgomery Shanks found her through the range finder. The camera clicked. He was a fast worker, and for good measure he clicked another. He had time for two more before she moved, so by surprise had he taken her. Then he turned and left the room.

Back in his own room, Shanks wound the spool up, removed it from the camera, sealed it, walked over and put it in his suitcase. He lay down for a nap. He felt very happy and he went immediately to sleep.

It was almost dusk when he woke. He took a shower and dressed at a leisurely rate. Then he dropped by her room. He spoke through the door.

"Ready for dinner, baby?"

In a moment she was at the door. She wore a light green dress and she was beautiful, aglow with a light sunburn.

"Yes, I'm ready."

They went down and had dinner. Afterward they went back upstairs. They stopped at her room.

"Well," he said.

She looked straight up at him. There was a glint in her eyes. He tried to remember where he had seen that glint. Then he remembered: in the eyes of Isaiah Virtue.

"Monty," she said, "go ahead and do what you like with the pictures. Send them to *Vital*. Send them to a calendar company. Develop them and pass them out to your friends. And good night."

She slammed the door, leaving him standing there with his mouth open.

Why, she is just like Isaiah Virtue, he was thinking. They were the same breed. And that was the rarest breed on earth.

Next morning at breakfast two things happened. He took the roll of film out of his pocket, opened it and strung it out so that the sunlight destroyed forever her emulsified nakedness. He wasn't trying to be dramatic. He just wanted her to be sure and see him do it, so she would believe it. And across the Florida orange juice he said to her,

"Charity, I want to marry you."

She didn't say anything, and he said, "Charity will you marry me? Today."

"No."

"Soon?"

"No."

"Ever?"

"I don't know. Let's see. You mustn't rush something like that. But let's see."

"Anything you say," Shanks said humbly. "Charity. I'll do anything for you."

"I don't want you to do anything for me. But we'll have to see. I want a man to marry. Maybe you have it. I thought out on the boat you had it. But I don't know. We'll see. You're just like a child in many ways and when I marry I want a man. I don't want to marry a child or a coarse-mouthed brute."

"You're describing me, I take it."

"I'm just saying what I want and don't want. Those things may be your idea of manhood. They aren't mine. You know the kind of man I would like to marry?"

"Isaiah Virtue," Shanks said.

She looked at him in astonishment. "Why, how in the world did you know that?" she said. "You know, you may just be more intelligent than I thought."

CYCLE TWO
CAMPAIGN TRAIN

And now Jason got a remarkable assignment: on a Presidential cam-
paign train swathing across the continent and back for five weeks.
Nothing in his life had ever excited him so much. Four weeks of
seeing this wondrous manifestation and at the same time seeing over
half the states of the Republic, crossing the mighty land one route and
coming back another. For what a great and mighty thing is the Repub-
lic! What manner of thing has there ever been like the United States
of America! It was an experience which was to take on great meaning
for him.

the man in the end car

Ward Weed, the photographer on the assignment, and Jason flew
down to Washington and got aboard the Presidential Special in mid-
afternoon. They walked through the train until they found the drawing room that had been assigned them and unloaded the staggering
amount of photographic gear they, mostly Hightower, were carrying.
Theoretically the *Vital* reporter and the *Vital* photographer were
equals, but this was only theory. Actually, Jason had often thought,
the *Vital* reporter's status would be more accurately defined by dropping the first two letters of the title. There were twelve bags of the
photographic gear and they filled every available space, nook and
cranny in the drawing room and had to be wedged in some very difficult places even to leave them room to stand. What was left over
went at the foot of one of the berths—Jason's berth.

"I'll take the lower berth," Weed said.

"Naturally," Jason said.

By five o'clock, as the train thrust westward at seventy miles an
hour, Jason and Weed were sitting in their drawing room across the
folding table. They were working on a bottle of Scotch which sat on
the table and were looking out the window at the fields and the trees
rushing by and were talking.

"I don't believe a word of it."

Incredulous at the familiar voice, Jason snapped his head right and
Weed his left. Standing there with his head stuck through the drawing-
room curtains and a most wide and wonderful laugh on his face was
the President of the United States.

Jason and Weed got quickly to their feet. They spoke almost in uni-
son.

"Good evening, Mr. President."

Jason could tell that a couple of men were behind him but he did not look at them. He looked in fascination at the President.

"Just making a bed check," the President said, and laughed again uproariously. Then his head popped out, the curtains came to again and he was gone.

Jason and Weed waited a moment, then sat back to their drinks.

"Yeh, he always makes a tour of the train the first night out," Weed said with the offhand and somewhat superior air of one who has been on these trains before. "He walks through all twenty-four cars and ends up in the engineer's cab. He chews the fat with the engineer and then walks back the twenty-four cars to his on the end."

Jason looked out the train window and felt a sense of wonder. He felt also a pride in his own land that a man like that, a good man, was its President.

He felt one more thing. He would like to have shaken his hand but he was glad he had been thoughtful enough of the President, whose hand must get pretty sore from having to shake hands so often, not to stick his out. It was a minor point but he was very glad he had not stuck his hand out.

Very late that night Jason lay awake in his upper berth thinking of the man in the end car.

"God bless the President of the United States," he said to himself.

He had not said that prayer since as a child his mother had taught him to say it at bedtime for the man of the great office, the man far away none of them had ever seen. The personnel of the prayer one asked God to bless had varied from night to night, depending on which relatives were in distress of some kind or another, which members of the church in illness, moderate illness or the kind they called "at death's door" (Jason used to wonder: "Does death have a door—and what is that door like?"). But, where others came and went, the President of the United States was always on the list. But after all those years of prayer for him Jason had never until tonight seen a President of the United States.

Jason hoped the President was getting a good night's sleep in the end car. He drifted into sleep himself to that sweet cacophony of wheels spinning on rails.

The great train rolled on through the night and across the fields of the Republic. Breaking like a hurled javelin over the tracks of the Baltimore and Ohio through the undulating lands of Maryland, the rocky hills of West Virginia, the rich flat farms of Ohio . . . throttling its way across the surge and sweep of America . . . America unsurpassed.

whistlestop

"Hightower," Ward Weed said, cocking a leg on the drawing-room couch, "I want you to be responsible for waking me. Trains make me sleepy and I'll need to have someone to wake me when we get to the tank towns. I tell you what you do. You got the schedule of stops there?"

Jason indicated an affirmative. He had the schedule all right, a thick mimeographed thing listing all the stops in the thirty-three-day cross-and-recross-the-country trip, hitting twenty-six states of the Union.

"I tell you what you do," Weed said. He dug the heel of his shoe into the drawing-room couch and his face lighted happily as he succeeded in ripping loose some threads. "Wake me ten minutes before we get into any town where the President's speaking. You got that straight now? Wake me up ten minutes before we hit the town. Be sure you don't wake me any sooner—or any later. Ten minutes is exactly what I need. You got that real straight now, Hightower?"

And Ward Weed sacked out.

Jason mentally added the duties of a human alarm clock to those of carrying the photographer's bags, getting material for captions and research, writing this material up, and air-expressing the undeveloped film along with the captions and research at every opportunity. As he did so he remembered that World War II epitaph in couplet:

> *Here lies the body of Lieutenant McSnooties*
> *He died in addition to his other duties.*

Jason looked at his watch. It was 3:02 P.M. He looked at the schedule of stops. The first one was at 4:05 at a town called Frenchman's Knob, Ohio. He left the room, strolled happily up and down the train peering around, and at 3:55 came back, reached down and started shaking Weed.

"Ungh . . . Huc . . . Ahp . . . Wherarwe?"

"Ten minutes out of Frenchman's Knob," Jason said. "Frenchman's Knob, Ohio. Why-oh-why-oh-why-oh."

Weed sat up in the lower berth of the drawing room, rubbed his hand flat across his face and spoke an obscenity. He got up and went into the lavatory and Jason could hear various sounds of splashing and gurgling. When the photographer came out his wavy brown hair was wet and combed carefully. He dug down into a bag and got two 35-millimeter cameras and put them around his neck. They could feel the train beginning to brake down.

"All right, grab those two bags there and let's go," Weed said.

"Yassuh!"

The excitement of this great land voyage, Jason told himself, of seeing the magnificent sweep of the United States of America, of seeing one of its great manifestations—a candidate for high office, and that candidate being the President of the United States, going to the people imploring their blessing—was so all-encompassing as to overshadow anything, even if he had had to clean the heads. Jason picked up the heavy leather bags containing film and extra cameras and slung one over each shoulder. He followed Weed out of the drawing room and down the passageway. They had to walk eight cars aft, in a tide of correspondents moving the same way, before they reached the car where the door would be opened. It was opened already, the steps were down and a cluster of correspondents was waiting wedged in there, straining like leashed hound dogs on the scent, for the train to slow enough for them to jump out. Over the heads of the cluster Jason could see a few hundred people gathered on the station platform. The men had their sleeves rolled up and the women wore short-sleeved cotton-print summer dresses. Their faces looked lined and weather-marked. Red farmer faces. The heat from the platform came up into the air-conditioned train and assailed the waiting correspondents.

"All right, let's hit the deck up there," one of the correspondents in the back of the cluster rasped impatiently. "Piss or get off the pot."

The train was slowing enough now and the correspondents started peeling off. Jason followed Weed out. The photographer, carrying only the two light-weight cameras, came down in easy running gait on the platform, no break in stride. Jason, carrying the two heavy bags, hit it heavily, stumbled a moment, but caught himself before he plunged to the concrete. Weed and Jason joined the wave of correspondents moving rapidly to the rear of the train, fast-stepping, almost running. The people also were moving forward, more slowly and less hectically though in anticipation, to the place they estimated the last car would stop. When it stopped they surged politely forward to a point ringed by the Secret Service men, lean, athletic, good-looking, quiet and self-assured men, who had leapt off quickly. In a moment the President came out on the platform and a cheer went up.

As the President talked, Weed moved through the crowd shooting the faces of the people, and Jason followed him. Weed was a good photographer and he worked swiftly and without most of the people being aware that he had photographed them until Jason stepped up and asked their names. The two bags were very heavy and Jason felt his shirt soaked in sweat, and hot sweat running down his neck and inside his shirt. When Weed took a picture of someone Jason stepped up, and squeezing his arms against his sides to keep the bags from falling off, got the person's name and occupation and sometimes a comment about the President, for or against. Since the film would go to New York undeveloped and he would never see any of the pictures until they appeared in the magazine, Jason had to keep extremely careful check on the number of the frame Weed was shooting to match the caption with the frame. Otherwise he would end up identifying Joe Smith as Harry Jones and there would be hell to pay. A 35-millimeter roll has thirty-six pictures or "frames" and Jason's captions would go, "Roll 10, Frame 25—Jim Smith and Mrs. Smith and daughters Almira and Betty and son Eugene watch the President speak— 'He's for the farmer and I'm for him,' Smith said of President—Smith is farmer near Frenchman's Knob, Ohio." Jason had to work swiftly himself and he must not get in Weed's way or even approach the subject until Weed was through with him, lest the subject become artificial and pose. It was a skillful technique and accounted for *Vital* photographers getting pictures, revealing pictures, that other photographers did not get.

Despite the bags and the sweat, and the fast working, Jason felt good to be seeing these people and talking, if briefly, with them. They were good faces. The good people, the great people when they are really good or/and great, Jason thought as he saw the faces, the wonderful country faces. They seemed less involved, less complicated, certainly less frantic, less jerky of movement and compulsive of voice than the people of the great city. The man on the train was out to get their votes. Politics, Jason thought, is at once the highest and the lowest art known to man. The highest in its holding of the ultimate power —the power of governing—where from its acts man would be trampled down or elevated to a higher glory. The lowest in the hypocrisy and the lies of the politicians, of all of them, even the best of them. Not a one but who employed, to a greater or lesser degree, hypocrisy, the misleading partial fact, or even lies, and frequently not realizing it himself, so convinced of his own rightness, and goodness, his adversary's wrongness and evil, had he become by constant reiteration of both.

Now and then there were some cheers at something the President said. Then the speech was over. It was only a fifteen-minute stop. The President had gone back inside, the Secret Service men were climbing lithely aboard. Presently came the whistle warning everyone to get aboard. In three or four minutes then the train was starting up. Weed and Jason hurried with several other correspondents to catch it. Jason could feel the bags banging, smashing, against his ribs. As the train moved out he swung aboard. It was going fast enough by then that he wasn't sure he would have made it if he had been five seconds later. He leaned out the vestibule window and saw the patches of farm people lapping over from the track to the station platform. They were beginning to break up. They had seen the President of the United States and that was something the children there could tell their grandchildren, if the world was still around then for anyone to tell anybody anything, or if the tyranny had not conquered and wiped out all American history so that no child in Frenchman's Knob, Ohio, would ever tell any grandchild about any American President. And Jason wondered: Do the people here, deep in the embracing land, realize the threatening tyranny?

The great train fled on. Over the tracks of the B & O, the Chicago, Burlington and Quincy, the Chicago, Rock Island and Pacific. Mitchell, Huron, Shoals, Loogootee . . . Table Grove, Adair, Swan Creek, Roseville, Little York . . . Anita, Wiota, Marne, Walnut, Avoca . . . through the limestone and sycamores of Indiana, the Indian mounds and Lincoln country of Illinois, the great seas of golden wheat stroked in the winds of Iowa and stretching as far as eye could see . . . the variety and infinitude of the blessed land.

the four-day man

People, especially men people, differ enormously in this matter. Some can go a week, some a month. Some can scarcely go twenty-four hours without showing definite spastic symptoms. Some, on the other hand—a familiar example is the case of the religious, or at least some of them—can go a lifetime. Many authorities in the field have elaborated the reasons for these differences in the human, but since this is a work of character rather than an endocrinological treatise we shall not investigate here the scientific and medical reasons which the interested reader can get so fully these days in any properly stocked library. It is sufficient for our purposes to say that the difference in the need varies spectacularly. In Ward Weed's case he began to get decidedly nervous if he went more than four days.

Now the photographer had been a whole week cooped up in this train and the symptoms of his nervousness and irritability were beginning to engulf the drawing room shared by himself and Jason. Far from enjoying this benevolent, expenses-paid look at the sweep and grandeur of America, Weed was ravaged and almost consumed by his frustrations. He did not see the golden gorges of Indiana bedecked in their haunting and tendriled vines; he fidgeted. He did not even look out at the great Mississippi when they crossed it from Illinois; he pared his nails. Where others stood at the vestibule windows he did not even glance out at the cloud-battened wheatfields of Iowa spilling in awesome spectacle to the far horizon; he sat restless and moody in his drawing room with the blinds down and for his vista a descending bottle of Scotch. His frustration broke surface in a score of ways. He snapped at Jason much more even than usual. One day he went into a frightful tantrum because Jason awakened him twelve instead of ten minutes before a whistlestop. Another day he had an outburst of temperament because Jason had left a sliver of toothpaste in the washbasin they shared. Weed was as sloppy and slovenly a man as could be imagined in respect to the state of any room he occupied. His suits, shirts and underwear were flung all over the drawing room and he did not even have diplomatic relations with the coat hanger. Not to mention the meadows of fingernail and toenail slivers which decorated the drawing-room floor from his incessant habit of trimming his fingernails and toenails. From the fit over a half-inch stain of toothpaste the extent of his frustration could be seen. It was getting worse by the day. A couple of times through the campaign trip the train stopped overnight in some town in order to give the gamy correspondents a chance to get showers. Ward Weed had begun to look forward to this overnight stop as a sailor three months at sea to making port, and for the same reason. The first overnight stop was still, however, some days away, and Ward Weed was in a sweat of deprivation.

One of the principal sublimations for sex is talk. You can be fairly certain that anyone who talks, talks, talks is sublimating sex. Sublimating talk is the most boring and sometimes downright maddening talk the world knows, and unfortunately most people who talk have to have an audience. It would be wonderful if these people could just sit in a room by themselves and talk but there are very few people who can do this. Most have to have a body of some kind—often it makes no difference what kind, since the body is hardly permitted to speak— sitting there. Weed tried to sublimate his frustration by talking, talking, talking to Jason. Weed's complete roster of conversation was as follows:

1. Women
2. His war experiences.
3. His high IQ.

He never talked about a single thing other than one of these three things.

Between whistlestops Weed would lie in his lower berth and go on for hours on one or another of this trio of topics, and Jason, lying in his upper berth, had to listen. After all, he had to live with the creature. They were stuck together for four weeks and five days in the same drawing room on this train and it would be hellish if they didn't get along at least moderately, hellish both for themselves, or at least for Jason, and for the story. Jason's only small consolation was that generally he did not have to look at Weed performing these monologues, since most of the performances took place berthed. The recumbent position and Weed's everlasting going on brought him in mind occasionally of the great founding traditions of psychoanalysis. The only trouble was, he had the melancholy thought, he was not getting paid for his role in the duo. Sometimes it would be over the fold-down table and a bottle of Scotch but usually it was in the recumbent position. In whichever position, Weed had an interesting habit while talking: paring and cleaning his fingernails with an eighteen-karat-gold snap-shut manicure device he always carried with him and usually had out.

First Weed tried talking about women, since that was what his mind was always on these days on the train. Weed's talk on this subject dealt exclusively with his victories in the field and over the enemy. It was like an unending serial with the same two characters: the manly male and the luscious, abnormally beautiful female who collapses before his manhood. This itself is not an unusual conversational trait of the male sex. The only way in which Weed's accounts stood out was the fiercely anatomical detail of his depictions. Jason had never heard anything like it. He would start with the undressing—of someone, sometimes it was the ravenous girl who undressed him—and proceed in almost intolerable detail through every gesture, movement and sound made by the fortunate creature. Weed's talk was a superlative oral example of what Jason called "The Swift School of Fiction," by which he did not mean the good Dean but the distinguished Chicago meat-packing company. The designation was an allusion to the relentless anatomical detail employed by adherents of this school in description of scenes relating to sex, as anatomical as running a steer through the slaughter yards and then quartering this good animal into his various parts. For Jason such an approach to sex served only to annihilate all sex desire, and how anyone could consider such scenes excitative any more than would be a manual on "How to Slaughter and Dissect a Cow" was beyond him. He preferred some mystery to be left to sex, and indeed considered this one of its most exciting enchantments, but he realized that this was a very old-fashioned approach to this important subject and even led people to suspicions that the person who held it was probably a sexual pervert. Anyhow he felt that way. Who wanted to go to bed with a big slice of red porterhouse? All Weed's interminable accounts did was to make Jason go almost mad and to think at times he couldn't stand it another moment. Then he hit upon a device to save his sanity: This was to try to outdo Weed in vocal virility. That was a pretty ambitious device but Jason made a try. He would have gone out of his mind otherwise, being cooped up here with him all the time and listening to him go on about women. From the moment he put the device into practice Jason found things, if not heavenly, a good deal more bearable. Once the photographer completed another lengthy, exampled recitation of his virility with a thought.

"Hightower," he said from the lower berth, "why did I have to draw you on an assignment like this. I'm lying here thinking just how different matters would have been if I'd been assigned as my researcher three or four of the other sex I could name."

Weed habitually referred to Jason with the proprietary "my researcher."

"Ward," Jason intoned from the upper berth, "have you ever had two women at the same time?"

"Not really," Weed hedged. "Sort of, I suppose you'd say, but not really."

"How do you mean, Ward, 'sort of'?"

"It was in Japan. Town of Yokosuka. The night I came ashore in the first wave of the occupation. I sort of fooled around with a couple of them. It was more one after the other though."

"Oh, that's not the same thing at all," Jason said exclusively. "I'm talking about at the *same* time."

"Look here," Weed said irritably, "just what do you mean, at the *same* time?"

"Don't you know how to do it?" Jason said innocently.

"Now see here, Hightower," Weed said angrily, "just what the hell are you talking about . . ."

"Well." Jason sighed heavily. "It's this way . . ."

Jason had a limited experience in the field but he had the powers of improvisation of a person who can play the piano by ear the first time he sits down to the keys, and forthwith he plunged into an orgy of anatomical detail. Since this book is intended for the most conservative living rooms, or at least for the most conservative bedrooms, we will spare the reader the major meat of these details. And say only that Jason spoke geometrically of writhing thighs, of heaving bellies, of panting breasts, until finally Weed cried out.

"Stop it! Godamit stop it! Stop it now, Hightower!"

Then, presently, Weed would resume his own descriptions. But as the days passed on the train, and the distance from his four-day limit and hence the strain within him grew ever greater, the photographer discovered that these depictions, being so graphic, served only to heighten his desire and frustration, so that he began to give up talking about women and turned to his other subjects. Such as his war experiences as a photographer-correspondent. Across the panorama of the states of the Union the whole battle for the Pacific was refought island by island in that drawing room, Kwajalein, Tarawa, Saipan, and the other names of glory on most of which it appeared Weed had gone in approximately an hour ahead of time to clear the way for the first waves of Marines. Jason wondered if any man since Julius Caesar or Sergeant York had undergone as much front-line battlefire as his companion of the drawing room.

When he had exhausted momentarily the great subjects of women and war, Weed talked about his IQ.

"Actually it's a handicap," he said, "having an IQ of 155."

"God in heaven," Jason said, impressed. "Is that your IQ?"

"Yeh," Weed said. "One five five. Sometimes I wish I didn't have it. Sometimes I wish I was a jerk like everybody else. Having an IQ of one five five makes you extra sensitive to things."

"I should think so," Jason said, audience-like.

"You have to have things other jerks aren't even conscious exists."

"I can readily imagine," Jason said.

"You aren't satisfied with the second-rate," Weed said. "With an IQ like that you gotta have the best."

"I can certainly see how that premise follows the first premise."

"You notice how I never drink red label Johnny Walker? I gotta have black label."

"I see what you mean," the audience said. "It's really entirely logical."

"Actually I'm not really satisfied unless I have a seventeen- or twenty-five-year-old Scotch. But you can't get that at just any ginmill you happen to walk into anywhere around the United States like I'm always doing."

"I understand it is made in limited quantities," Jason said. "Also such IQ's being rare those remote places probably don't get many calls for it, hence don't stock the finer stuff needed by these higher IQ's."

"Tailor-made suits," Weed said. "I'd be really *unhappy* in a ready-made suit."

"They often don't fit too well," the audience gave back agreeably.

"I haven't paid less than two hundred dollars for a suit in years," the photographer said. He took no notice, as is true of all talk talk talkers, of anything the audience said. He just wanted it to indicate, from time to time, that it was there. Jason could have said "Wamnosket" a few times each time and it would have been as well. "Women."

The wheel always spun full circle. Everything came back to, there was no helping it, Women.

"What was that?" Jason said.

"I said women. You know what women are, don't you? Same way there. She's gotta be really first-class. I don't take anyone to the beautyrest arena who isn't absolutely first-class. I won't do it."

"No reason you should," Jason said. "You're stuck with your IQ and you gotta make the best of it."

"Don't get me started talking about women. Godamit to hell!" Weed suddenly turned savagely on Jason. "Didn't I tell you I didn't want to talk about women?"

"I'm sorry," Jason apologized. "I won't bring the subject up again."

"Just watch it," Weed said angrily. "Godamit to hell! When do we stop overnight in that place?"

"Day after tomorrow night," Jason said.

"Two more nights alone." Weed sighed heavily. "What's the name of the city?"

"Broken Bow."

"How big is it?" Weed said, suspicious at the name.

Jason, in the top bunk, picked up the schedule of stops lying on his chest. "Two thousand four hundred and forty-three persons."

"Two thousand four hundred and forty-three!" Weed burst out in an incredulous fury at the size of the town. "Great God Almighty! What are the odds in a jerk town of that kind of me getting someone really first-class!"

"Well, Ava Gardner came from a little town in North Carolina," Jason said encouragingly.

"That was a fluke," Weed shot out angrily. "One in a million. A sweepstakes winner. A thousand-to-one shot. Two thousand four hundred and forty-three persons!" he again burst out furiously, as if unbelieving that any place so small existed on earth. "Why in the name of *decency* couldn't we have stopped overnight in some place that had people in it."

"Well, the only real purpose of the overnight stop," Jason said, "is to give us all a chance to get showers so that the train will be habitable for the rest of the trip."

"Well, Jesus Christ in a basket," Weed screamed in outrage at this illogic, "don't they know that *cities* have showers too?"

"Well, I suppose even though you usually won't accept anything but the best," Jason said soothingly, "there are times when anyone is obliged to take the best that's available."

"A philosopher, eh? Well, I tell you this much, son," Weed said savagely. "I won't have gone this long without since I was hitting beachheads in the Pacific."

Jason braced himself for a recapitulation of the Pacific war. However, Weed kept course.

"I know myself pretty well," the photographer said, "and I have discovered this about myself: I need a woman at least every four days."

It was the first Jason had heard about Weed's four-day cutoff period and he was intrigued by the precision of the figure. "That's extremely interesting," he said. "I imagine you must be pretty virile. But tell me. How did you arrive at the figure of four days?"

"By experience, stupid!" Weed exploded. "Actually I like it a lot more often but I'm not really thrown off my stride until four days without it. When four days pass and I haven't had it, every part of me is affected—physical, mental, emotional, professional."

"Professional?" Jason said. "How does it affect the professional?"

"How in God's name would it affect the professional in the case of a photographer," Weed said with extreme irritation. "I don't take nearly as good pictures, that's how, stupid."

"Well, I suppose sex does relax almost anyone," Jason said.

"Yes, but I have a definite, essential *need* for it," Weed kept himself in a special class. "Right now, for example, I'm just focusing and clicking the shutter, that's all. I'm not really *getting any real pictures because I am not penetrating to what I am doing*. I've tried to figure it out and I'm convinced the need has something to do with my IQ. I believe that the higher the IQ the greater the *need*."

"It's an arresting supposition," Jason said.

"It figures," the photographer said. "A man with a superior IQ is going to *need*, he's going to have *as an absolute necessity* for, what a man with a cheap IQ would like but can do without and not make much difference in his usual slob life. If I don't have it at least every four days," Weed repeated grimly, "I'm in trouble. Real trouble. Hightower, do you realize it'll be *twelve days* since I've had it?"

"It's a long time all right," Jason intoned, adding: "I mean in your special case of course."

Jason heard Weed shifting restlessly on the berth below.

"Ten minutes till the next stop," Jason announced.

"What's the name of that town?" the photographer asked.

"Kennesaw Landing, Iowa," Jason said.

"I don't mean that, I mean the overnight stop."

"Broken Bow." Jason would not have thought it would be such a difficult place-name to remember.

"What was that population figure?"

Jason repeated it.

"Two thousand four hundred and forty-three!" the photographer shouted in fury at the town. "Well, I'll guarantee you this, Hightower. I'll find *someone* in that town. I'll find the best that's available and I'll take it. You hear that?"

"Isn't that what I just said and suggested and recommended a little while ago, you ignorant, boorish son of a bitch?" Jason said. However, he said it to himself.

Aloud he said: "Tell me, Ward. How do you propose to go about finding the best in Broken Bow? Not that I doubt you'll find a way."

"You damn right I will," the photographer said. "Just stick around, son, and watch Weed in action. Weed in the field. What's the name of that town again?"

"Broken Bow."

"Broken Bow and Ward Weed will have reason to remember each other," the photographer said ominously.

Weed reached roughly for his copy of the mimeographed schedule which had been issued to all correspondents on boarding the train ten days ago and turned the pages noisily until he reached a short paragraph headed "Broken Bow." In tones to suggest those of an elderly Atlantan reciting a sympathetic biography of General Sherman he read aloud:

"Arrival: 6:10 P.M. Overnight stop. Buses will be provided to take correspondents desiring showers from train to high school gym. Following showers buses will transport those correspondents interested to the Broken Bow Country Club, where a program of refreshments and entertainment will be provided by the Broken Bow High School P.T.A. group and students. Train departs 7:10 A.M.—*sharp*—following morning."

" 'Refreshments and entertainment,' " Weed said with utter revulsion. He got out of the berth and picked up a camera. "I can imagine what *they* will be. Well, sir, I know what refreshments would entertain old Weed and transport him hither and yonder. 'The Broken Bow Country Club'!" He said the phrase as if it were the most obscene calumny. "A town of two thousand four hundred and forty-three people that has the nerve to have a country club!"

"They're all over the nation these days," Jason said expertly, climbing down from the upper. "The lower classes have got on board."

The train started stuttering to a stop.

"Boy, I'll bet that's the joint all right," Weed said savagely. " 'The Broken Bow Country Club'! The Pie Tee Ay! Probably three old-women chaperones to every young girl under forty-five. Well, I'll guarantee you one thing: old Weed will get *something* in that jerk town."

"I have," the photographer's audience said, as he followed him down the corridor, "every confidence in you. You repulsive cretin." The last three words he said to himself as he flung himself onto the platform at Kennesaw Landing.

The sound of the train's wheels turning over on the rails mingled with the sound of phalanxes of typewriters batted at furiously to form the symphonic motif of the campaign train. Over the tracks of the C B & Q, the C R I & P, the Atchison, Topeka and Santa Fe. Tobias, Ohiowa, Strang, Ong, Edgar . . . Esbon, Lebanon, Athol, Kensington, Agra . . . Sugar City, Manzanola, Rocky Ford, Swink, Las Animas . . . pacing off where the Conestoga wagons pitched along in Nebraska, past the spot in Kansas that is the exact center of the country, over the fearsome white torrent of the Arkansas rushing down the mighty gorges of rock carved in Colorado by aeons of hungry time . . . the grandeur and the dust of America.

sweet land of liberty

Jason was standing at the rear of the crescent-shaped crowd of about six hundred on the railroad tracks when he saw the hand of the man in front and slightly to the right of him arc back in pitching position. The man was a southpaw and his hand went far back, paused cocked, and was just ready to whip forward when Jason reached out and with a quick movement plucked the tomato from the hand much like plucking one from the vine.

The man's head snapped around, its weatherbeaten, red-leathery features startled. While the man watched, his mouth ajar and his face in disbelief, Jason took an enormous, noisy, slurping bite out of the tomato, the juice running down his chin. It was a good, vine-ripened tomato, doing without which was one of the true hardships of living in New York where you never got them, and Jason wished only he had some salt to go with it.

"A very superb specimen of a tomah-to, my good man," Jason, giving the vegetable the effete Eastern pronunciation, complimented the hopeful pitcher. "Definitely of blue-ribbon quality. May I inquire: Is it off your own acres?" Jason took another large noisy bite and more juice dribbled down his chin. "Much better employment of the tomah-to," he said through the fullness in his mouth, "than in the face of the President of the United States. Doesn't show quite the proper respect for the office and all that sort of thing, now does it, my friend? Oh. I was trying to remember whether a tomah-to is a vegetable or a fruit? Could you illuminate the question?"

Looking still startled and now quite abashed as well the man turned abruptly and disappeared into the crowd.

What a country, Jason thought. What a wondrous, wonderful, fascinating country, where a man could throw a tomato at the President of the United States.

So wonderful there was room even for savages. Is that, Jason wondered, another definition of democracy?

The great train sped and slowed, stopped and started. Over the tracks of the St. Louis-San Francisco and the A T & S F. Mustang, Tuttle, Amber, Chickasha, Cement . . . Tulia, Happy, Canyon, Dawn, Hereford . . . Wagon Mound, Optimo, Watrous, San Jose, Santo Domingo . . . past oil derricks fingering the skies of Oklahoma, across the plains of Texas where beyond the windows wakes of white dust stirred behind the herds of white-faced cattle jostled rump to horn, through the distant mesas of New Mexico punctuated only with yucca. The empty lands and the rich lands.

virility on the ninth green

The sun was still blazing angrily at 6:10 P.M. when precisely on time the campaign train steamed into Broken Bow. The town lay in a valley ringed by blue hills. About a third of the population of the town was waiting on the station platform as the train moved gingerly in. The campaign train always entered a station very slowly to avoid killing several dozen children who might be wandering on and off the tracks, an occurrence which would have been very bad publicity for the party. Lesser events have lost an election. As the train was slowing down, Weed and Jason jumped off onto the platform with the other correspondents. Out of the air-conditioned train they were swallowed up in a pall of dead, blazing heat.

"The black hole of Calcutta," Weed bawled out in hearing of several citizens.

"Must be the way those hills close the town in," Jason said.

"Yeh, you're pretty observant all right," Weed said. "It takes a really ace reporter to see those hills there."

Jason thought suddenly and for the first time in real earnest just how much he was beginning to dislike Weed's company and wondered how worse it could get. They were only a third of the way through the trip.

The President spoke a few minutes, the third of the population of Broken Bow listened politely and clapped hands a few times. *He* had gone out to beseech *them* and this defined the United States of America. From their watchful faces not a man alive could have predicted how they would vote come November or how many votes if any the words of the man speaking up there would change: and unless they so pleased they did not have to tell anyone what they were thinking about anything and for this silence nobody would ship them off to northern snowwastes or put them behind barbed wire and in fact not a soul need ever know how they voted, and this, Jason thought, was the United States. Where was her equal? Weed shot lightly and even before the President had finished speaking he had shot all he intended to.

"Let's go back and get our junk," he said to Jason, "and avoid the subway rush hour."

They picked up their dopp kits and changes of underwear and shirts and wandered on back out and got seats with other correspondents, also clutching dopp kits and clean clothes, in the bus waiting alongside the train. The bus was a big yellow thing with big black letters on its side, "Broken Bow High School."

"Isn't this quaint though?" Jason heard the grayish-haired, matronly-mannered woman columnist Irene Priestly say from the front of the bus. "Isn't this the grass roots though?"

"Listen to that whore," Weed said. " 'Isn't this quaint though?' " he mimicked her voice. " 'Isn't this the grass roots?' "

When the correspondents were all aboard, the bus rolled away through the little town. A few people were walking along the streets and they stopped and stood looking curiously at the familiar bus with its unfamiliar cargo, of strangers from the large world outside, as did a man mowing a front lawn. The smell of new-mown grass rose sweetly through the windows, a crisp happy smell Jason had all but forgotten and it was good to have it now and in one time-obliterating instant swept him back to a childhood in which this was one of the smells one knew; a long-lost smell. Feeling good, and yet a little lonely, lonely for something nameless and faraway in time and gone forever, Jason lifted his hand and waved quietly out the window to the man mowing the lawn. The man waved back.

The high school was a new-looking building of yellow brick, and the principal himself was on hand to greet the correspondents and lead them personally through the building to the gymnasium and the boys' showers. To lead all except one, the woman columnist, for whose convoy a woman teacher was on hand to take her across the basketball court to the girls' showers on the other side. In the boys' showers the correspondents started undressing. Their bodies, Jason noticed, looked mostly soft, waxy-white and lumpy and most of them had emphatically too much weight, lardy, rippling white fat, in the gut and on the bottom. Weed was an exception to this prevailing physiognomy. His body looked lean, hard and tanned and in excellent condition. Weed was what went under the word "glamorous," in looks and in manner. The correspondents piled into the showers and soon exultant squeals and the happy slick sounds of soaping on bodies were filling the air. Jason stepped into a shower, adjusted the nozzle and took the burst of spray full and stinging in his face. It was incarnate bliss after a dozen days without it.

When they had finished their showers and dressed, Jason and Weed wandered out onto the lawn in front of the schoolhouse. It was astonishingly green considering the heat. Last light was beginning to disappear over the darkened hills and the first stars made their entrance through the skies beyond. There were two school buses now drawn up in the driveway alongside the lawn. When the last of the correspondents had appeared the principal spoke in the twilight. He had a drawling, warm and friendly voice.

"Gentlemen," he said. "Gentlemen—and lady," with a small laugh, "those of you gentlemen wishing to return to the train, would you be so good as to step into this bus?" and he indicated one.

"And gentlemen, those of you gentlemen who would care to partake of the refreshments and entertainment which have been provided for your pleasure at the Broken Bow Country Club by the P.T.A. assisted by the students of Broken Bow High School, would those of you gentlemen so desiring please step into this bus," and he indicated the other one. "May I add, gentlemen, that we are more than honored to have the members of the world's most famous and able press corps— the White House press group—honor our town by spending overnight here, that we are particularly honored to have any and all of you who so desire to attend the affair at our newly completed country club, and that if there is anything at all that any of us starting with myself can do to assist you during your all-too-brief stay here, we will each and all of us in Broken Bow consider it a most distinct honor if you will but make your desires known to us."

"I've got a desire I'd be honored if he'd assist," Weed said with reasonable quiet to Jason where they stood alongside on the lawn. "Do you imagine the bloater would mind doing a fast pimp job for me with one of the ladies of the Pie Tee Ay—or better still with one of his young students?"

"And now, gentlemen," the principal was saying, "if you'll come along to your respective buses. This one for the train," he repeated. "This one for the affair at the country club."

"I'm going to have an affair at the country club," Weed said. Suddenly he reached in his pocket and dug out three rolls of film. "Oh, Hightower. See if you can get these shipped off tonight. If you have time after you've done that, try to come on out to the"—and Weed laughed briefly—"Broken Bow Country Club."

Jason thought of telling the photographer to shove the three rolls of 35-millimeter high-speed Ektachrome film up his ass. Instead he took them and started for the bus that was going back to the train. He had just decided that the one thing he had to have was an evening apart from Weed, even apart from the same room he was in, the same building. He had just decided, while standing there on the lawn of the Broken Bow High School, that without that evening alone he would probably be incapable of spending twenty-one more days with Ward Weed. He would get the film off and then he would spend the evening walking around town, having a beer in a bar or, if the town lacked that, a chocolate malt in a drugstore, and he would get in bed early so as not to have to look at Weed again until the following day. Jason had a great and most specific need for a certain amount of privacy, and in recent days this need had been sorely pressed.

As it turned out the town had no bar. In the field of beer and liquor the state practiced local option and the citizens of Broken Bow had opted against these beverages. Jason went into the only drugstore in town and had a chocolate malt. He enjoyed sitting in the drugstore, where things went lazily and people were polite with a natural politeness. And it was the best chocolate malt he had had since he was a child.

He was in his berth on the train by 10:00 P.M. It was such peaceful ecstasy being alone in the drawing room, to have it free of Weed's brawling torrent of words about himself, the room becalmed as the sea after a spitting storm, that he went promptly to sleep, his last thought being: How wondrous to go to sleep without the ape here, and to sleep until sweet dawn . . .

He was awakened by a strong, finger-digging hand shaking him violently by the shoulder.

"Hightower! Wake up! Wake up, Hightower!"

Jason sprang up in his berth, calculating from the urgency of the voice that something very serious, such as the assassination of the President of the United States in Broken Bow, had occurred. He looked down into the face of the photographer Ward Weed.

"What's happened?" Jason said.

"Hightower!" Weed shouted. "Hightower, it's all taken care of! I've been laid!"

Perhaps no other single thing irritated Jason so much as to be awakened prematurely from sleep, unless in emergency, and of all nights and by all people as tonight by Weed. And at the heard reason for the awakening he looked down upon the face of the photographer with a savage incredulousness. The face was beaming. More, it was clutched in a look of smug satiation.

"What time is it?" Jason bit out.

"Three A.M."

"Three A.M.! Jesus Christ on a bicycle, what's the idea of waking me up at three A.M.!"

"Because I knew you would want to know," Weed said. "God, it was so wonderful I knew you couldn't wait until morning to hear it. See how relaxed I am now? Brother, it was great! Just great!"

Weed spoke without interruption for forty-two minutes, giving the blow-by-blow account to Jason with an admixture of gusto, euphoria and always surpassing virility.

"It was something! We tooled on out there in that damn school bus, about twenty correspondents coming along for laughs. All the time the high school principal, he came along with us, kept singsonging about how everyone in Broken Bow wanted us to get a good impression of the joint and how he hoped we all had a good relaxing time. 'Our country club probably isn't much compared with what you world-traveled gentlemen of the Fourth Estate are accustomed to,' he said, 'but we here in Broken Bow are proud of it.' 'The Fourth Estate'!" Weed said. "I hadn't heard that one in years. 'Particularly are we proud,' said he, 'of our fine little golf course, even if but nine holes. I am but sorry you gentlemen cannot stay over tomorrow to try it. We think we have the finest little greens you'll find just about anywhere.'

"Well, we got there finally and who should we find waiting for us but one dozen—exactly one dozen—high school girls who had been candidates in the high school beauty contest which was run off last week. The beyoo-tees of Broken Bow! Nothing but the finest for us gentlemen of the Fourth Estate! A dozen girls, their dozen mamas and another dozen or so even older old bags there to chaperone *them* and to see to it, I take it, that while we had a good time we didn't have *too* good a time. I suppose they had heard more than one thing about us world-traveled gentlemen of the Fourth Estate! You can see right away, I hope, the problem old Weed was up against.

"The club was actually a pretty neat little job for such a hick town as this. Surprised me right off. A clubhouse, a swimming pool, one tennis court and the nine-hole golf course the principal kept running off at the mouth about. When we got inside they started serving us all punch. Punch! Non-alcoholic punch! Can you imagine a *country club* without drinking whiskey? Why, that's why the things exist in the first place. Well, we tasted the sickening stuff—I almost spewed mine out on one of the old cows standing by me, it gagged me so—and they actually had a five-piece band there. 'Those that so wish,' said the high school principal, 'please pleasure yourselves with these young ladies who are waiting to dance with you.' 'Pleasure yourselves!' " Weed exclaimed. "Brother, was I just ready to pleasure myself!

"I stood there on the sidelines watching these slobs off the train dancing—if you can call it that, I wouldn't—with the high school beyoo-tees. It was the damndest thing you ever saw. It was like a whole roomful of Draculas and Cinderellas. I wanted to do a little picking and choosing before rushing headlong into things. You'd have been amazed, son, how sharp-looking some of those girls were. They all looked like they'd just been scrubbed and bathed and had bath powder dusted all over their firm young bodies and they were all wearing exactly the same thing, frilly white evening dresses—evening dresses!—and they looked good enough to eat including the icing. I would have guessed all of them were certified virgins. I kept looking as they danced by and finally I saw her. I mean I picked out the one. You can be sure of it, son, and this is something for you to remember, in any dozen girls there'll be one that stands out. Something about her. You gotta be a photographer really to tell these things. I picked her out and tapped the shoulder of some fat near-sighted slob from the New York *Times,* a pencil-pusher who had better been hacking away at his typewriter instead of dancing with something like that so far out of his class here in the grass roots of America.

"We danced around and got to talking and it turned out she had won the beauty contest—no surprise to me, just confirmed my judgment. She was Miss Broken Bow. Miss Broken Bow! She mentioned the Leica I was carrying, so I had to tell her who I was. Well, sir, you should have seen the charge that gave her. 'Oh, I read *Vital* every week,' she frothed at the mouth. 'It's my *favorite* magazine.' Then she cooed on: 'Mr. Weed, I bet you'd like something besides that punch.'

" 'Well, what do you have in mind, Diana?' I asked her. Help me God, that was her name, Diana.

" 'Just let's get our punch glasses and I'll just show you,' she said.

"We filled a couple of punch glasses with that grapejuice with the sickening smell and then she led me downstairs to a basement. The locker rooms were downstairs and there were two closed doors. I wouldn't have believed this unless I'd seen it with my own eyes, but each door had a picture of a leg on it. The leg on one door was big and heavy and had hair on it. The leg on the other door was very slender and hairless. Isn't that the damndest thing you ever heard of?

" 'It's in there,' she said, nodding to the door decorated with the hairy leg. 'Daddy's locker. It's open. Everybody trusts everybody in Broken Bow. Why don't you just go get it?'

"She gave me the locker number and I went on in and opened up, and sitting there among the jockstraps, like a lily in a cesspool, was a bottle of Jack Daniel's. Jack Daniel's! And black label at that. So! I took it back out.

" 'Daddy's got very good taste,' I said.

" 'He's a pretty good Daddy all right,' she said. 'I'm Daddy's favorite and he lets me do pretty much what I want. I think anything I did would be all right with Daddy because, you see, I'm his girl. There's nothing eating at Daddy.' So help me, that's what she said, and something about it sounded pretty odd but I let it pass. I aimed now not to get her scared or anything like that. You see, I didn't know her then.

"She smiled, and by God, Hightower, you've never seen a smile like that. I don't think she had a filling in her mouth. She was the cutest little package you ever saw and she looked so damn innocent in that frilly white evening dress and all I was surprised to know she even knew what Jack Daniel's was and I thought probably if she did just the smell of it would knock her out. We went outside by the swimming pool. It was very dark there and more so under the umbrella at the table where we parked. And guess what she did then? She took the two glasses of grapejuice over and poured them in the swimming pool and came back and filled the glasses with Jack Daniel's. I knew right then that I had hold of something here. It is not every girl who will pour grapejuice into the swimming pool instead of just tossing it on the grass. It takes class to do that.

"Well, we just sat there talking awhile and guzzling at the Jack Daniel's. The funny thing was it didn't seem to affect her a bit. I don't think I've ever seen anyone that Jack Daniel's didn't have some effect on. As a matter of fact I felt it a lot more than she seemed to.

"And you know what we talked about? All we talked about was the train here, which she asked me about, and what her life was like in this town here, Broken Bow. She said she supposed they didn't do very much compared with the life I lead. All they did she said was to go to school and church and the drugstore downtown and the football games, where she was a cheer leader, and now since it was finished recently they came out to the country club. She said she supposed I wouldn't consider it very much but she liked it all right and she had never had any desire to go to New York or any place like that when she got a little older. She said she liked it right here and she had a lot of fun at the country club here. The townspeople looked upon it as a big deal to have a country club.

"Well, sir, with her talking like that I began to get discouraged. I mean, it's when the girl starts to talking about going to New York to try things out, when she talks about wanting to get away from all this, and such lofty crapperoo, that you know she's the sort that's imaginative and might let you squeeze in as a manifestation, shall we say, old sod, of her imagination. So that when Diana began to talk about loving it so much in Broken Bow and never wanting to go anywhere when she grew up and liking the life here and the country club and all, well, that began to classify her to me as a girl there wasn't much doing with. You see how this follows, I hope.

" 'Yes,' I said, pretty weary with all this junk about how sweet and nice the country club was, 'the principal said you had a nice golf course. The old goat really laid it on about how those greens were just about the finest little greens you would find anywhere. He talked about it so much I think I could draw you a picture of it with my eyes closed.'

"I said all this in a pretty weary tone, and I figured I'd got hold of something truly conservative or even reactionary here, and was about to say I had to get back to the train to take some more pictures of the President, who of course was in bed by that time. Then she spoke up, and there was just something in the way she said what she said.

" 'Why do it with your eyes closed?' she said. 'Why not see them?'

" 'See what?' I said.

" 'The greens,' she said. 'The ninth hole is just over the little ridge there.'

"I caught my breath just a moment, I still wasn't sure.

" 'Daddy's the Chairman of the Greens Committee,' she said then.

"Daddy! I was beginning to feel it was odd as hell the way she kept dragging in Daddy. I've gone in for psychology quite a bit as you may have noticed and I was beginning to have an idea or two. But I didn't say anything about that. But then all of a sudden it came over me that the thing to do was definitely to have a look at that ninth green.

"We got up and started walking across the yard around the club and pretty soon we went over the ridge and there the ninth hole green was. It was pretty dark and in the distance you could barely see the lights of the club.

"Well, sir, we sat down on the green and just looked at those hills beyond it. They were darker than the sky and you could make out their outlines. She started telling me about the school pageant that was coming up next week. Jesus Almighty, I thought. The school pageant!

" 'It's from history,' she said. 'It's about the Lewis and Clark Expedition and I've got the lead. I play the part of Sacajawea, who was their Indian guide. I wear this white doeskin Indian costume. It's the first thing of this kind I've ever done and it's pretty interesting. Daddy likes the idea of me going out for things like this pageant.'

"Daddy! Well, sir, Hightower, I don't know how it happened. I don't know what came over me to tell me that however things seemed, this was all just sitting there ready and ripe as grapes in May. But then it hit me and I knew. You always know. We never said a word about it. Never at any point did we say one word about it. We were sort of lying back on our elbows on the green and she was jabbering away about the pageant and how she played Sacajawea in it. I put my arm behind her and then I put my hand inside her dress. She never stopped talking.

" 'You know, Mr. Weed,' she said—she called me 'Mr. Weed' even then!—'I think I enjoy playing Sacajawea in this pageant even more than I enjoyed winning the beauty queen contest . . .'

"And she kept talking about the pageant. You would have thought I had not even touched her little finger much less that I had my hand where I had my hand. She kept on rattling away about the pageant and her being Sacajawea in it. While I . . . .

. . . .

"Well, sir, you can imagine what was going on with me, two weeks deprived. Then I took my hand away from her breast and down under that frilly white dress and . . . .

. . . .

" 'There are a lot of lines to learn, you know, Mr. Weed,' she said right then. 'That's what's been the hardest part. There are five hundred and forty-four lines that I've been having to learn.'

" 'I don't think I could ever do it,' I said.

"I never mentioned anything else or made the foggiest reference to what I was doing, and somehow I had the feeling, instinct I guess you would call it, that the one thing I must not do was to *talk* about what I was doing, that that would break the spell, and that as long as nothing was *said* about it, everything would be okay with her and she would do anything, anything.

"Both of us, you see, were talking about the pageant. Neither of us mentioned anything else, least of all what we were doing, and all the time . . . .

. . . .

. . . . "

Weed went on in unmerciful detail.

" 'So far, Mr. Weed,' she said right then, and gave a little laugh, 'I've managed to memorize two hundred and sixty-five lines.'

" 'Very good progress,' I said, beginning to . . . .

" 'Daddy's helped me to memorize them,' she said. 'Daddy's so wonderful at helping me in everything and letting me do what I want and he really spoils me I guess you'd say but I think he wants to spoil me, he's such a wonderful Daddy, Mr. Weed.'

"Sigmund Aloysius Freud! I thought. And all this time . . . .

. . . .

. . . .

. . . .

. . . .

. . . .

. . . . "

Weed spared not a moan nor a gasp. "Well, sir, I'd never had anything like it. My God, she made those slick babes in New York that I've had more of than I can count, she made even the best of them seem like the inside of a Kelvinator. They just can't do it like she did it. Maybe the reason is they're too slick and too self-conscious and they're thinking too much about doing it, about the *idea* of doing it. She didn't think, she just . . . I wouldn't have believed it. I was flabbergasted. You know something, Hightower. There must not be any real women left in New York. They are all out here in the provinces. I've never had a one that could stand up—lie down, I guess I should say," Weed said with a hearty laugh, "with Diana of Broken Bow."

The photographer laughed shortly. "Every time I think of that sweet little thing, with those fresh rosy cheeks and that sweet young breath and that innocent look . . ." Weed paused the briefest moment. "Do you suppose she could have been a nymphomaniac? And that damn Daddy talk. I don't know what to make of it even now. A psychiatrist probably could get his hands into something there." Weed gave another short laugh. "Not as interesting, though, as where I got mine."

Jason, revolted and infuriated beyond all measure and memory, looked closely at Weed. Was the story true? He wasn't sure but he thought it probably was. Weed looked too satiated for it not to be true. It is the one look in the world which you cannot fake. It was true, and Jason made up his mind right then and there that he loathed the photographer, and suddenly the decision came over him: He would get back at him for that story. Somehow, some way, he would get back at him. He had never thought about "getting back" at anyone before but he thought it now with this unbearable, this authenticated bastard.

"I never did it before on a golf green," Weed said triumphantly and euphorically. "It was a completely new experience. And it was just like the principal said. It was the finest little green I ever played."

The light went out. Jason slumped back into his berth. Right now, he thought as he went off to the two hours of sleep which were all he would have before having to get up to cover the President of the United States at yet another whistle-stop, he would like to kick his teeth in. Not the President's. Weed's.

The great train clattered proudly over the ever-changing land. Over the tracks of the A T & S F and the Southern Pacific. Rimmy Jims, Winona, Ashfork, Pan, Peach Springs . . . Mojave, Monolith, Tehachapi, Earlimart, Pixley . . . Rogue River, Gold Hill, Wolf Creek, Glendale, Riddle . . . between the sandstone spires and deep-sculpted canyons of Arizona, above the stony headlands of California's coast, around the hillsides of forested Oregon. From sea to shining sea.

the oldest of campaign pictures

The great train rolled on. Making about twenty stops a day. Twenty times a day Jason, Weed and the other correspondents aboard jumped off, hurried to the rear end of the train, and attended to the reportage to the nation and the world of the President's words and of the people hearing them before, in November, deciding the President's fate. The train, rolling on across the roll-call of the states, seemed isolated, suspended, a microcosm apart. And yet more a part of the country than anything. Jason was fascinated to see and be on a campaign train, and was swept up in its enormous pulsing vitality. All aboard worked furiously hard, pushing themselves almost beyond man's endurance. The President worked hard. He was making fifteen or twenty speeches a day. Sometimes it was to only two or three hundred people gathered on the tracks behind the last car. Sometimes it was to several thousand in the municipal auditorium of some city where they pulled in at night. When he wasn't jumping off at the whistle-stops Jason spent a good deal of his time in the press car. The correspondents worked hard. Getting on and off the train so many times a day, jumping down while it was still moving, running to the back, taking notes, jumping back on, often again while it was still moving, writing stories, plus walking the eight, ten or a dozen cars some of them were from the press car and the dining car and the club car. All the work and all the high nervous tensions, and some of the correspondents were pretty old and tubby. They took punishment but they seemed to Jason to thrive on it. He was amazed at how some old white-haired goat of a correspondent could leap off a moving train and land every time on his feet and running, and never a break in his stride, as sure-footed as a Sierra Nevada goat. Jason liked the correspondents very much. They were the least pretentious and most honest people he had ever been with. The correspondents worked hard, especially the wire-service correspondents, who filed on every stop every speech: Somewhere across the nation or around the world some paper was going to press and wanted the latest, the very latest. *Nothing but the very latest would ever do,* the swift-clattering wheels seemed to say. Fresh injections of the dope of excitement were needed hourly.

Jason lay on his back in his upper berth, listening to the train move over the land and his feet resting of necessity on some of the bags of Weed's photographic gear stored there, lay looking at his feet. He wiggled his toes and thought what a marvel of construction was the human body. With a body like that man was bound to win out, sometime.

The train braked down. Jason looked at his schedule. Athens, Oregon. He swung his legs over the berth and dropped to the floor. Weed was putting a couple of cameras around his neck.

"Pick up those bags," the photographer said.

The hands of Jason, which had just started out to do this very thing before Weed had spoken, froze for a moment, then . . . continued on their way and picked them up. He slung one over each shoulder, each shoulder bending perceptibly under the weight.

"Yassuh!" he said. "All ready, Marse Weed."

"Very funny," Weed said.

As the train moved across the country, the photographers covering the President had begun to get pretty desperate to get something different on him. At first the pictures of him speaking at the little towns handled it, establishing the new fact that the President was out campaigning. But when that fact had been established, and reëstablished, and established and reëstablished some more, by pictures of the President speaking from the rear platform of the train, the photographers began to get restless and nervously anxious for something different. So much so that by the time of Athens they arranged with the President's publicity people to have that oldest of campaign pictures, to wit: the President holding a babe-in-arms. It may be the oldest but it is always good at least once in each campaign trip and the photographers, as is often the case in the profession, were desperate.

The baby, who was a little ten-month-old object, was dutifully handed up to the President on the rear platform. The photographers, scrambling and jostling each other loudly and frantically for position and banging each other about with their bodies and now and then, supposedly inadvertently, with their cameras, started shooting away. The President smiled and the dumfounded child looked up at the strange man.

"Tickle it, Mr. President!" one of the photographers yelled in a wheedling voice.

"Give us a big smile now, Mr. President!" another bawled.

"Look this way now, Mr. President!" still another photographer barked.

"One more there, Mr. President! That's right . . . there . . . That's right!"

"Hold it around this way, Mr. President!" another shrieked frantically.

"Now do something with it, Mr. President!" another instructed.

"Say something to it, Mr. President!" a photographer ordered.

Presently the poor child was screaming at the top of his tiny but forceful lungs. Not because of the President of the United States, who was very good with babies, a thing or its absence which any baby can sense almost instantaneously and, not having as yet amassed the inhibitions which fill the lives of all adults, reacts very clearly to, but because of all those jabbering apes jumping up and down in front of him, howling and bellowing and snarling and screaming and with the most twisted demoniacal looks on their faces, holding big black monstrous and terrifying instruments up in front of his face.

"Why, the bastard's crying!" a photographer roared. The child's mother looked around at the speaker. "Smile kid!" the photographer screamed.

"Tickle it again, Mr. President!" another commanded. "Make it smile . . . That's it . . . that's it! Hey now, don't shove *me,* you son of a bitch. I was standing right here before you ever *thought* of coming over here . . . Smile, Mr. President! Give us a smile now! That's right, Mr. President! That's it! That's it!"

The terrified baby screamed at the top of his tiny lungs. The towns-people looked on in amazement at this performance, their mouths agape, their eyes wide and astonished at a power (the photographers') on one hand and a subservience (the President's) on the other they never dreamed existed. The baby screamed and screamed. Jesus God, the President thought with a heavy inward sigh. He kept smiling. Finally the mother got her baby back. Snatching him to her bosom she fled the hell out of there.

The whistle of the great train sounded ghostily through the curves in the mountains. Over the tracks of the Great Northern, The Chicago, Milwaukee, St. Paul and Pacific and the Northern Pacific. Snohomish, Sultan, Goldbar, Index, Skykomish . . . Potlatch, Onaway, Deary, Helmet, Santa . . . Big Timber, Pompey's Pillar, Bighorn, Rosebud, Zero . . . up through the great mountained timber line of Washington, past the dam-leashed power of Idaho's rivers, along the slender beauty of the tamaracks penciled tall against Montana's sky. Under the wide skies, across the rolling rivers, through the lovely lands.

mister gloom

There were many famous by-lines in the press corps accompanying the Presidential campaign train but none so distinguished as that of Augustus Balfrey. Augustus Balfrey was a syndicated columnist. The columnists, of course, are the elite of American journalism. Theirs are the names best known to readers of American newspapers. They have the largest audience. They of all the practitioners of the craft of journalism have access to the most innermost citadels of news. They share the confidences of senators and of cabinet officials. They speak with the greatest profundity. They have the most faithful followers. They are courted most, more slobbering is done at their feet by people of real rank, civilian and military, than perhaps is the case with any other figures on the American scene. They have the greatest power of all figures in journalism. They receive the largest salaries. They can write as they please. And of all the columnists in America none ranked higher or had greater fame than Augustus Balfrey.

All columnists have a specialty in the form of some "line" or general approach their column follows. It is upon this line that their great fame is erected.

Augustus Balfrey's line was Gloom. Gloom and Doom.

Virtually every column of Augustus Balfrey's was a paean to gloom. Reading his column, "Balfrey Speaks," was like reading the more dire parts of the great Book of Revelation. Alongside Augustus Balfrey, Ecclesiastes spoke like the Marx Brothers or a member of the Optimist Club. Augustus Balfrey saw nothing in the scene around him to prompt any emotion but despair for the United States of America. For this country's future he felt the blackest forebodings. All was dark and impending disaster of the most terrible and cataclysmic sort around every corner every day—his was a daily column and thereby of necessity the despair and gloom had to be daily. It was difficult to see how anyone who read his column could with any sense of self-respect refrain from jumping out the nearest sixteenth-story window, particularly if he had any connection whatsoever with the United States government. Augustus Balfrey was a master of the prose column and the gloom was made even more ominous by the manner in which he almost invariably began his column:

> None of this has as yet been made public, and indeed there is some question if it ever will be officially, since the Administration fears the calamitous reaction and even panic of the American people if it were, but this reporter has learned that we stand on the furtherest thin edge of the dark abyss of extinction . . .

Or:

> Official Washington refuses to talk about it but on the highest and most impeccable authority this reporter can now state that the final disaster is at hand . . .

This approach was bound to put the fear of God in a Bowery drunk, suggesting or even baldly stating as it did that Augustus Balfrey's dire forebodings were based on information of unquestioned accuracy available exclusively to him and that the general daily news available to everyone was calculated to lull into a false sense of security and well-being and furthermore was based on the most unadulterated pap. It is difficult to see how a man reading Augustus Balfrey's column could avoid hopping the first plane to Moscow and taking out his first citizenship papers, or whatever it is one takes out there, as a means of getting on the crest of the wave of the future while there was still time.

Jason had long been one of the forty million readers of Augustus Balfrey's column and indeed agreed deeply with Balfrey's main line that this country was in mortal danger—the only thing he doubted was whether daily invocations of gloom and doom constituted the best method of dealing with the danger. But it was with the greatest excitement and anticipation of meeting, or at any rate seeing close up, this distinguished name that he learned he was aboard the campaign train. His face, of course, being carried daily in his column, was familiar to everyone including Jason, and there was no reason why Jason when he saw him could not just go up to him and strike up a conversation—or, who knows, maybe they would run into each other having a clubby drink in the club car. Newspapermen are the most democratic people in the world, Jason had learned already from his brief sojourn in the pastures of journalism, nobody stood on rank, and there was no reason at all why any moment now he might not find himself in a conversation with the famous and "influential," as they always said, Augustus Balfrey.

When three weeks went by and Jason did not see the famous man he began to wonder where in the world he could be. A train, after all, has limited space. He could, of course, take all of his meals in his room, though this hardly seemed likely, and, if he were a teetotaler, he could pass up the club car, but to Jason there would appear to be little point in his being aboard the train unless he were to emerge once in a while to see and hear the President speak to the people at the whistlestops. But Jason, though keeping a close eye out, had not once seen him. One day in the press car he politely inquired of the correspondent for the New York *Times*, a mild-appearing, quietly dignified and fiercely incorruptible if subdued man by the rememberable name of Lucas Brown. Jason figured if anybody would know, this or anything else, it would be a *Times* man.

"Well," Jason said pleasantly and as casually as he could make it, "I see that Augustus Balfrey is aboard."

And Jason looked at the mimeographed list of correspondents, which he had brought from his drawing room for purposes of making the inquiry casual, as if he were just glancing over the list and had caught Balfrey's name. One thing he had learned, if you were going to be a newspaperman you must never show a shred of respect for rank or names. Newspapermen hated that.

"Yes," the New York *Times* correspondent said.

Jason considered this reply rather laconic, at least for his purposes, so he pursued.

"That's curious," he said. "I haven't noticed him around."

"Balfrey's around," the New York *Times* man said.

Well, one thing you could say about a New York *Times* man, Jason thought, they certainly didn't waste words. This was a refreshing change, in any event, from certain of the correspondents who wasted about 125 words per minute.

"Strange," Jason said. "I haven't seen him at any of the whistle-stops."

"Nothing strange about that," the New York *Times* man said.

Jason waited for him to elaborate but he did not. Therefore Jason decided he would have to switch to the direct question approach, however reluctantly. No man could avoid answering a direct question.

"Why isn't there anything strange about it?" he asked courteously and with the respect due a representative of the nation's greatest newspaper.

"It isn't strange that you should not see Augustus Balfrey at the whistle-stops," the *Times* man said, "for the explicit reason that Augustus Balfrey never gets off at the whistle-stops."

It was a fine example, Jason thought admiringly, of the crystal-clear, declarative sentence of which any good *Times* man was a master.

"Oh," Jason said. "That *would* explain it, wouldn't it," he said pleasantly.

The *Times* man apparently saw nothing in this statement which required a response.

"I would think one would see him at least in the club car," Jason said. "Or perhaps it is that Balfrey does not drink."

"Oh, yes," the *Times* man said. "Balfrey has been known to take a drink."

"I would think one would see him at least in the dining car," Jason went on doggedly. "I suppose Balfrey has to eat like all other humans— or, for that matter, all other animals."

"Or for that matter, vegetables," the *Times* man corrected him. "Balfrey eats all right."

Well, sir, Jason thought, a New York *Times* man must certainly be better at getting information than giving it. Which is probably what made New York *Times* reporters the best in the world, Jason thought, and how awful it was when the reverse was the case, and this was true in the profession more often than you would think: Jabbering reporters.

"Well, I'm glad to hear that," Jason tried a light tone. "Wouldn't it be a scandal if a man as well known as Augustus Balfrey died of starvation on a Presidential campaign train."

"Oh, I imagine the nation would somehow find a way to carry on," the *Times* man said.

Encouraged by Jason's heartily laughing reaction to this sally, the *Times* man now came a little to life.

"When Balfrey dies it will not be of starvation," he said. "It will be of atrophy of the marrow."

"What was that?" Jason said. He was not familiar with the disease and thought perhaps he had not heard precisely. This was entirely possible, since the *Times* man talked in a remarkably subdued voice, as well as in the most monotonic voice Jason had perhaps ever heard.

"I hand it to Balfrey," the *Times* man said.

"Is that so?" Jason said interestedly. "What is it you hand to him, sir?"

The New York *Times* man was twice Jason's age and Jason felt the "sir" was warranted and fitting both for this reason and the fact of the great paper he represented. He was wrong.

"Please don't call me sir, if you don't mind," the *Times* man said. He said this in a very subdued and quite friendly voice and with an undertone of pride and self-respect. "I'm a reporter."

"Of course," Jason said.

This exchange seemed to have broken the ice, as they say, a bit between them, and the New York *Times* man spoke what was for him virtually a paragraph of gushing.

"I hand it to Balfrey because he interviews Balfrey so successfully to get material for his incestuous column. I hand it to Balfrey because his mental pores can absorb from the atmosphere exactly what he needs, without the humiliating necessity of asking others questions or even of observation of any great amount. I hand it to Balfrey because as a syndicated columnist he never has to *ask* anybody anything—he *tells* them. I hand it to Balfrey because he is a craftsman of prose and can and does turn out one of those columns of his in a maximum of thirty minutes' work a day. I hand it to Balfrey because he has it made as does no one else in the mighty profession of journalism. I hand it to Balfrey."

The *Times* man, after a pause from such excessive talk, added more.

"I will state to you Balfrey's schedule. It is unvaryingly exact: He sleeps in his room on this train until exactly 11:00 A.M. He then has breakfast in his room, he shaves and he dresses carefully. At exactly 12:12 P.M. he enters the club car and has three martinis on the rocks and talks with the correspondents the while his mental pores jiggle and function around. At exactly 1:10 P.M. he goes back to his room, and from exactly 1:15 P.M. until exactly 1:45 P.M.—never a minute more— he writes his column. It is always first draft, he never changes a single word, and if you have seen his prose and how smooth and craftsmanlike it is you will realize how sublime is his mastery of his chosen métier. At precisely 1:45 P.M. he leaves his room, brings his column down to the Western Union man and it goes out datelined ABOARD PRESIDENTIAL CAMPAIGN TRAIN. At precisely 1:50 P.M. he returns to his room and takes a three-hour nap. At precisely 4:50 he arises, shaves again—he has a heavy beard—and dresses. At precisely 5:30 he enters the club car and has three martinis—this time not on the rocks, and not with lemon twist, olive or pearl onion, just the martini. At precisely 8:00 P.M. he goes into the dining car and has dinner. At precisely 9:15 P.M. he returns to the club car and has two brandies with the correspondents. At precisely 10:30 P.M. he goes to his room, where I presume he reads—what, I'm sorry to say, I do not know, for I have never been in his room—and then goes to bed."

Jason said nothing for a while, so profoundly impressed was he both by the precision and triumph of this schedule and by the *Times* man's knowledge of its detail and his extremely orderly and craftsmanlike documentation of it.

Now Jason could hardly wait to meet Augustus Balfrey. Armed with this schedule it should be no problem. Indeed it was a miracle that he had not run into him thus far just by the operation of the law of averages. The only explanation must be, he thought, that his own schedule of eating, drinking and general existence aboard this train had been so highly erratic, certainly in that respect as different as could be from Augustus Balfrey's.

Jason felt the train slowing down. He looked at his copy of the schedule of stops and saw that the town was Moscow, Montana. He got up and started down the cars to wake Weed and pack-mule out the camera bags. In the second car beyond the press car he ran into the photographer headed this way. He was carrying only a single 35-millimeter camera slung around his neck.

"Never mind getting the bags," Weed said in lordly tones. "I've decided I've been overshooting. I'm going to skip this one."

Jason turned back and headed for one of the jump-off vestibules. He could see the faces on the station platform moving by and got glimpses of straw hats and sunbonnets and short-sleeved dresses and long-sleeved blue-denim shirts rolled up—it was an uncommonly hot day for the area. When the train slowed enough he jumped off with the other correspondents. A well of heat came up and smashed him in the face. With the other correspondents he walked rapidly to the rear of the train. The people now moved over onto the track. About five hundred of them, farm-looking people, the weather-etched farm faces. They were polite and respectful and without anyone telling them to left a little semicircle of respectful space between themselves and the rear end of the train where the President would come out and nobody pushed anybody. This semicircle just below the President was where the correspondents always stood taking notes. Jason decided not to stand there but wander around on the fringes of the crowd. Maybe he could pick up a few enlivening quotes for his research, and anyhow he wanted to see these people. He stepped over some tracks and moved toward the rear of the crowd, keeping to its outer edges. He took a clockwise look at the scene before him. A silver-painted water tower labeled "Moscow" rose to his left. Down the track he could see a grain storage elevator. Next he could see the town street that ran by the station and on it a row of one-story frame buildings. Jason read some of the signs in front of them: "Eats," "Moscow Hardware Co.," "Moscow Feed Co.—Larro Feeds" . . . His eyes came back across the people. A strong cheer was going up. The President was coming out on the platform of his train car. Then the people were very quiet, listening, chins tilted. The faces were browned and lined and open, very open faces. Now and then they laughed at something the President said, they clapped approval, and a twangy voice from deep in the crowd yelled encouragement. Jason moved around on the edges of the crowd, but always watching it. He was so engrossed that he bumped into a man. He turned and looked, murmuring apology.

He was an astonishing sight. He was resoundingly fat, tubby fat, with a sallow, heavy-jowled white face that looked almost Louis-the-Fourteenth-powdered alongside those of the townspeople and farm people. The most amazing thing was that he was wearing a heavy tweed jacket and dark gray flannel trousers, both of casual elegance, and a pink oxford-cloth shirt. The heat on the tracks was all but intolerable to Jason in his thin sport shirt and paper-thin dacron trousers and he would have thought anyone wearing tweed and flannel would have been courting disaster. On the contrary. Not a crystal of sweat stood out on the man's sallow fleshy face. All the same the tweed jacket and flannel trousers and the pink shirt made a screaming contrast to the overalled men just beyond them. The man had a very jolly face—it occurred to Jason he would make an excellent Santa Claus—and he smiled when he spoke to Jason.

"Isn't this folksy though!" His voice was decidedly British and Jason guessed he must be a correspondent for something like Reuters or the *Times* of London. There were five or six correspondents from foreign soil aboard the Presidential train. "I don't believe we've met," he said pleasantly. "There are so many of us on that train, aren't there? My name is Augustus Balfrey."

Jason was thunderstruck and hoped it didn't show too much. He had not even said, "I'm Augustus Balfrey," but, "My name is . . ." There is all the difference in the world in those two ways of saying it and which it is can tell you considerable as to the character of the speaker. It was as if someone had said, "My name is Harry S Truman," or, "My name is Dwight Eisenhower," as though this statement would provide identifying intelligence to the person in front of him. It was clear now to Jason why he had not recognized the famous columnist on the train. The Augustus Balfrey of the flesh was so different from the Augustus Balfrey whose picture was carried as an inset in his column as to seem another person, or at best the "before" part of an extreme "before-and-after" set of photographs advertising a reducing tablet. The Augustus Balfrey of the flesh was decidedly older and a huge amount fatter, more bloated, heavier-jowled and vein-cheeked. But perhaps the most striking difference was that while the picture was highly serious, even grim, in keeping with the temperament of the column Augustus Balfrey wrote, the man in the flesh was as jolly as could be imagined.

Jason had been going around the edges of the crowd clockwise, Augustus Balfrey had been going around it counterclockwise. And they had bumped into each other at almost exactly twelve o'clock—on the tracks straight down from which the President was speaking. Jason shook Balfrey's proffered hand.

"Isn't this folksy though!" Augustus Balfrey repeated in exclamation. "Isn't it grand! I'm so glad I got off here. It should be very good for The Column. Aren't they *magnificent* faces though? Look at those faces! There you have the authentic grandeur."

A man nearby spat out a glob of tobacco juice.

"Just magnificent!" Jason exclaimed agreeably.

"It renews one, you know," Augustus Balfrey went on. "I mean, getting away from the studied slickness of the East, especially those capitals of the calculated gesture, the carefully chosen and motivated word—I speak of course of Washington and New York—and plunging into the midst of these earthy people, tied as they are to the soil, from which I suppose in the last analysis all comes, wouldn't you agree? I don't mind confessing to you that I'm absolutely *hypnotized* by these magnificent folksy faces."

As Jason stood in awe-full regard of Augustus Balfrey's gift of rhapsody, the columnist let his eyes rest on one face in the crowd, then moved to the next one, and the next one . . . about ten seconds of the most intense concentration on each face.

"You know what the greatest danger is in a profession such as yours and mine?"

How charmingly democratic of him! Jason thought, to bracket him professionally with the great Augustus Balfrey. He promptly warmed to the great man.

"Well, no, I don't believe I do," Jason said.

"The greatest danger in a profession such as yours and mine," Augustus Balfrey said, "is that we will get *cut off*."

"Isn't that so!" Jason agreed warmly.

"We really ought to get out amongst the *people* more often," Augustus Balfrey said. "There's really nothing that I can think of that's more *imperative* in a profession dedicated to reporting and interpreting the nation and its people. But I find it so *terribly* difficult to get away— don't you?"

"Oh, yes, indeed," Jason said, warming still more. "*Terribly* difficult."

"We get so busy in our busy little worlds," Augustus Balfrey said, "that we think we don't have time to go back to our real fount of vitality."

Balfrey's eyes brightened in discovery at the phrase. Jason looked eagerly at him, the eager audience.

" 'Our fount of vitality,' " the columnist repeated, tasting the sound the phrase made and finding it not wanting. "There's something in that for The Column," he mused. "You know, that's what this is really. Everything we are is gathered right here on these railroad tracks. These are the *people*. Without them we die as a nation: Look at those *faces*, I tell you!"

Jason looked.

"Have you ever seen more magnificent, *simple* faces! Some people may call them ignorant because they haven't seen the latest Broadway shows and do not wear dinner coats every night or serve the *Grand Cru* Château Mouton-Rothschild at dinner. Some people may look down upon them as hicks—how I hate that word hicks. I hope you do?"

"I detest the word," Jason said, and added, "Mr. Balfrey." How happy and excited and secure he felt to be taken into the confidence of such a man.

The famous columnist hesitated, looking at Jason. What he saw apparently pleased him or at least did not displease him.

"You may call me Gus," Augustus Balfrey said.

"Thank you very much," Jason said eagerly.

"I say to you that they are not hicks," Augustus Balfrey continued, moving his arm. "Or if they are, then that word is a proud sobriquet. I say to you that whatever true aristocracy we have in this country, you see it now assembled on these dusty railroad tracks . . ." Down those same tracks the President of the United States was speaking but Augustus Balfrey's voice was not loud enough to drown out that of the nation's chief executive. It only made the President's words unintelligible. Jason found himself remembering irrelevantly how the great columnist had more than once criticized the President quite severely, but withal like a stern taskmaster to a child, in his column. "You know I truly think—and I say this to you—that the only last thin shred of chance we have is to go back to our *roots* here to replenish ourselves, to pluck from here the sustenance without which this country will not stand and is headed for decimation surely as we stand upon these railway tracks. To pluck it from the truly great of this nation: You see them here. These great, *simple* people."

"Oh, indeed," Jason agreed. He was most anxious not to say anything that would offend this wonderful, famous man he could now call Gus.

"*This* is America," Augustus Balfrey said. "Not New York. No, nor Washington. No, it is instanter here where we stand on these humble

railroad tracks. That water tower over there! That grain elevator down
there! See how it stands like an exclamation point to the word America!
That legend over there: 'Eats!' What poetry of the people in that word!
The people here *are* America. Not the slick chicks of New York and
Washington. How humbled I feel! How reverent in the presence of
these people and their objects! You know, I cannot tell you how happy
I am that I decided to get off here, it was some sudden sure inspiration,
some inexplicable but irresistible and most certain impulse, and I know
what The Column tomorrow will be. It will deal with the discovery of
America in Moscow—Moscow of all places! Moscow, Montana, what a
dire, ironic twist that will be! how effective for The Column—and with
how, unless we all discover what I in such humility discovered today in
Moscow, Montana, unless we renew ourselves in the discovery of these
true people here and their shrinelike folk objects, such as that sign
'Eats,' we are headed for imminent annihilation from that land of whose
capital this village stands, the defiant namesake . . ."

So absorbed had Augustus Balfrey become in his subject and in the
delivery of it, and in all the surrounding folksiness familiar to nine out
of every ten Americans but so new and strange to him who wrote daily
and with such brilliance about this country, and in such hypnotized
fascination had Jason become enveloped in listening to and in watching
Augustus Balfrey, that one fact of the landscape, aside from the folk-
object water tower, the exclamation-point grain elevator and the proud
sobriquet "Eats," escaped both the famous columnist and Jason. It was
only as Balfrey's generous, tublike body and his eyes moved ever clockwise in describing these touchstones of the nation's heartland, Jason's
body and eyes following him all the way, and moved beyond "Eats" to
"Moscow Feed Store—Larro Feeds," which rose just across from the
station, and continued clockwise until they rested at six o'clock, that is
to say, straight ahead, at the end of the campaign train, that they noticed this detail in the landscape . . .

"Jesus Christ on a bicycle!" Augustus Balfrey suddenly broke off his
rhapsody on roots. "The train's moving!"

Jason looked, and he was thunderstruck. Yes, the train was starting
to move very, very slowly away from them. What was more important,
it was a good fifty yards away from them. And what was really critical,
between them and it stood five hundred of the magnificent, simple people of America.

Augustus Balfrey, however, kept his head. In crisis he showed himself a man of decision and action, and Jason thought about this quality
in him even as he displayed it, even as he roared out in tones of command:

"Follow me!"

With a mighty thrust of his fat, bloated tuglike body Augustus Balfrey plunged into the backs of the simple people. They were of the

slow-moving sort as in any small farm community, and some of them stood stupidly in place waving gently and with a certain nostalgia at the train starting away, so that Augustus Balfrey was forced to extend his arms like pudgy flailing oars to clear a channel through them on the track toward the train. Like an aroused, waddling icebreaker the columnist plowed through the crowd, spilling people to the right and left of the tracks. Fortunately many of them were old and spilled easily.

"Out of the way, hicks!" he yelled when someone did not move fast enough.

He plowed on, Jason coming behind in the channel the icebreaker was clearing.

"Move, yokels!" Augustus Balfrey yelled, sending a simple old man of about seventy-eight sprawling leftward of the track.

"Clear a path, you bloody rubes!" he screamed.

Spilling the simple people to the left and to the right of him Augustus Balfrey, with Jason hot behind, finally was through the crowd, so that between him and Jason and the train moving out stood now only unobstructed track. But now the pace and the heat, which was frightening, were beginning to tell on Augustus Balfrey. He was much too generously proportioned a man for so much and such vigorous and concentrated exercise, and Jason, pulling alongside him now that they were through the crowd, could see via his peripheral vision the columnist's red, veined, purpled, bloated and swelling face and hear his panting like a polar bear which had awakened to find itself a hitched member of the twenty-mule Borax team plowing across Death Valley in California on an August day, and no wonder, the martinis and food he stoked in and never any exercise save the air-conditioned walk from his bedroom on the train to the club and dining cars, and right now Jason would imagine that heavy tweed jacket and those heavy flannel trousers Balfrey was wearing did not help. It was very difficult to say but to Jason it seemed that the train, gathering speed, was enhancing the distance between them and it, or at best that they were not shortening that distance. Jason and Augustus Balfrey gave a fresh burst of speed.

"Second wind!" Jason cried out encouragingly. "Keep going, Mr. Balfrey—I mean Augustus—I mean Gus! You'll get your second wind any time now!"

"Jesus Christ in an airplane!" Augustus Balfrey gasped. "I can't get stuck in a savage wasteland like this. It'd take us two days to get out of this hell-hole to civilization!"

"Just don't talk!" Jason said, giving the order to the famous man as delicately and discreetly as possible. "Please," he added respectfully. "Save . . . your . . . breath . . ."

Jason felt his own lungs almost bursting. He was in comparatively good shape and size and youth and he could readily imagine what must be happening to those of Augustus Balfrey. Even as he ran, Jason's mind faced the problem. If it had been a matter only of leaping on the rear of the last car they might make it. Up ahead now Jason could see the rounded great shield of the President of the United States hanging on the rear of that car. Yes, with the last car they would have a fighting chance. But no one was allowed to get on the last car. That was the President's car and it was guarded fore and aft by Secret Service men who would regard such an entry in the light a stagecoach driver of the old West would regard a tomahawk-brandishing Sioux coming alongside and leaping on his dashing horses. No, the last car would be impossible, there would be no refuge there. Even on the next two cars—occupied by the White House staff—the vestibule doors were kept closed. Not until the fourth car could they get on. There the steps were always kept down until the train was out of the station for any late-starter correspondent running to catch it. My God, Jason thought, it was absolutely hopeless to make the fourth car. He probably could have made it himself if he could have gone on but he could not desert a famous man who had just invited him to call him by his nickname. Possibly on the second or third car someone might, if they got there, see them running alongside and open up. But that was the best they could hope for. He tried to communicate the situation to Balfrey, who not having been off the train before might not know the drill.

"Fourth car!" he said. "Got to get to fourth car."

"Nonsense!" Augustus Balfrey panted back. "Last car."

"President's!" Jason gasped out, trying to save his diminishing wind for running as opposed to discursiveness.

"Nonsense!" Augustus Balfrey repeated more irritably as if there were any question of his being received anywhere, including in the personal railway car of the President of the United States. "President's car!" Balfrey said stubbornly.

They beat down the cindery track behind the Presidential car.

Now suddenly Balfrey began to holler.

"Augustus Balfrey!" Augustus Balfrey hollered.

He repeated the cry.

"It's me—Augustus Balfrey!" he shouted angrily. "Open up there!"

And: "Augustus Balfrey!" savagely. "Open up there I say! It's Augustus Balfrey!"

A distant memory came to Jason of the columnist's having once described the chief executive, among other, more disparaging depictions, as "a wardheel politician with a wardheel mind." It seemed to Jason, in his approaching daze, that Augustus Balfrey's shouted name was quite the worst possible distress signal and that if they did reach the rear of the car they might easily, on recognition, get their knuckles pistol-whipped off it while scrambling up. They beat on and on toward the rear car. Suddenly . . .

Suddenly—and Jason could scarcely believe his eyes and thought the intense heat and the exertion must have brought on a mirage— Jason saw the President of the United States. Did he imagine it? Did he imagine the President was smiling? Standing there on the rear platform alongside the President he thought he saw another man, who of course would be of the protective Secret Service. Did he imagine all this?

"Come on, Augustus!" the President of the United States yelled gleeful encouragement. Or so Jason thought he heard. With the combination of the heat and his pounding heart he was not really sure of any of his senses right now.

Mirage, imagination, or reality, the vision and the yell gave hope, and Jason and Augustus Balfrey called upon their lungs for their last tucked-away corner of air. In one mighty, final burst they leapt forward and reached the back of the train. The steps were down. With their last bitter ounce of strength they flung themselves upward, Augustus Balfrey in the van. Jason saw strong arms reach down and grab for the great columnist and give a great yank. Jason, to help, gave Balfrey a mighty push by his tremendous bottom and he went aboard like a jet pilot using his ejector seat in an emergency. Then Jason could feel himself being pulled up.

Gasping for air, and not having enough as yet even to speak, Jason looked in stupefaction at the scene around him: Balfrey lay in a collapsed, gasping heap on the platform. Above him stood the President of the United States. He was smiling. Jason finally got air just sufficient to stammer out a torrent of apologies and he all but genuflected. The President smiled more broadly.

"Nonsense," the President said. "You made it, that's the point. Young man, you must have run the quarter-mile in school—or walked a plow."

The President of the United States looked down upon the fallen columnist with a smile of tempered compassion.

"And as for Augustus," he said with that smile, "I could not afford to let anything happen to him. For I could not possibly conduct my office without him. I read Augustus each morning without fail. There is nothing to spur one on to new deeds," the President of the United States said happily, "quite so much as reading daily what a son of a bitch one is."

Suddenly Augustus Balfrey could be seen to be coming to life like a beached walrus doused with water. He raised up on his elbow. He looked up and around him and spoke.

"It will come as no surprise to me to discover I have gravely, in every likelihood permanently, injured, by overstraining, my heart."

He spoke in utter gloom.

Day and night the train pulsed through the Union. Over the tracks of the N P, the C M S P & P and the Minneapolis, St. Paul and Sault Ste. Marie. Heart, Gladstone, Hebron, Glen Ullin, New Salem . . . Granite Falls, Sacred Heart, Danube, Olivia, Bird Island . . . Prentice, Ogema, Chelsea, Stetsonville, Unity . . . through the fat grainlands of North Dakota, along the unnumbered lakes of Minnesota, through the green-rich dairy country of Wisconsin. The wild lands and the tamed lands.

goodness

"Anyone done Gilbert's overnight?" someone would ask in the press car.

The correspondents would look around at each other. "No . . . Nope . . . Not tonight . . . Nobody, I guess . . ."

"Okay, I'll do it."

Twice daily one of the correspondents, in addition to filing stories for his own paper or wire service under his own name, would file a story under Gilbert Justice's by-line and give it to the Western Union man at his counter in the press car to send to Gilbert's paper. The correspondents took turns doing it. They all on the train knew Gilbert Justice's style long since and would imitate it very adeptly. Gilbert Justice used a lot of phrases like "rip-roaring speech," "the President accused So-and-So pointblank," "in a hell-for-leather speech" and the like, and whoever wrote Gilbert's story that day always worked plenty of phrases of this sort in. So adept were they that not an editor on Gilbert Justice's paper ever suspected that it was not Gilbert Justice himself who had written the story. To this day the publisher of that paper is not aware that he has carried scores of stories under the by-line of Gilbert Justice but written by some of the greatest correspondents in America, by by-lines far more famous than was Gilbert Justice's.

Gilbert Justice was sixty-two now and he was a good-natured and friendly man, especially after the first two days out. For twenty-seven years now Gilbert Justice had been the Washington correspondent of a Midwestern paper. It was an afternoon paper, so that two stories had to be filed daily. The overnight for the early editions of the paper next day. And the mid-morning filing to catch the late editions. Gilbert Justice had been covering campaign trains for twenty-seven years, clear back to Herbert Hoover, but in the past eight of these years he had not, except for the first two days out and the last two before the train got in, filed a single story from a campaign train. But not once had an expected story missed getting to his paper.

Jason thought how good newspaper people are really. He had never met better-hearted people. He strolled back to the drawing room to wake Weed for Wampum, Wisconsin.

Gilbert Justice? From the second day the campaign train hit the road, until the second day before it pulled back into Washington, Gilbert Justice, he was stone-drunk.

Majestically the great train wound back over the country. Over the tracks of the New York Central and the B & O. Three Rivers, Homer, Ypsilanti, Dundee, Temperance . . . Petrolia, Bruin, Foxburg, Lucinda, Tiona . . . Scio, Belmont, Friendship, Olean, Salamanca . . . Along piny lakeside dunes in Michigan, past the red-breathed vapors of steel mills in Pennsylvania, crossing the E-ri-e Canal in New York. The inexhaustible faces of the land.

the deadhead redhead

At the little town of Potawatami, New York, an interesting thing happened. One would hardly have expected anything interesting to happen in Potawatami, because it was the next to the last stop on the thirty-three-day cross-and-recross-country trip and by now everyone was so bushed and frazzled and had his ears so full of political speeches that nothing short of an attack by the President on his own candidacy would have roused anyone, and if the President was going to make a major pronouncement of that sort he certainly would not choose the town of Potawatami, New York, as the place to make it. Potawatami's population was 1,843. The stop at Potawatami was the fourth of the day and a very brief one—ten minutes—it was scheduled for 11:00 A.M., and for the rest of the day the train would highball it for the last stop, which was New York City, where it was due at 6:00 P.M. for a massive rally at Madison Square Garden at 8:00 P.M. Then the train would end in Washington. New York City has a population of 7,891,957. Everybody on the campaign train was harboring what energy remained after the brutalizing month's cross-country train trip for Madison Square Garden.

Particularly from the point of view of the *Vital* photographer-reporter team covering the campaign train today's stops could scarcely have been more unimportant. It was too late to catch anything for this week's issue, and by next week's issue anything shot now would be so

old as to stand no chance whatsoever of running. Since day before yesterday, in fact—the last day on which picture takes could be got to
New York in time for this week's issue—Ward Weed had not even
been bothering to shoot. He did, however, carrying a couple of loaded
cameras, make it a point to get off the train each time it stopped for a
speech by the President and go around to the rear of the train. He did
this for protective purposes—protective of himself, that is. Though
the Secret Service was batting 1.000 in keeping Presidents alive since
its assignment to this function, in the typical close-the-barn-door-after-
the-horse-has-bolted spirit of the American Congress, following the
assassination of McKinley, anything could always happen around the
President of the United States and there were always a few nuts rattling
loose around the country. If the President of the United States should
be slain on the back of the train while Weed was sacked out in his drawing room a few cars away, the reaction of the managing editor of *Vital*
magazine to this stimulus would be a thing of dimensions Weed did not
care to contemplate. Potawatami was situated thirty-nine miles from
Buffalo, and as the train drew near the little town someone in the press
car remarked in melancholy tones that Buffalo's chief claim to fame was
the fact that it was there that President McKinley had been assassinated
in 1901. Weed got off all right when the train drew into the station.

As for the other half of the *Vital* team, he had seldom even bothered to get off the train in the last couple of days. Jason Hightower was
not tired of looking at or listening to the President or the whistlestop
crowds but he was heartily sick and tired, beyond anything he would
have believed possible in respect to another member of the human
race, of looking at and listening to his colleague Ward Weed. He had
estimated his own reserves of endurance to the fifth decimal point and
figured he had just barely enough patience left to make it to New
York City and the end of the trip, provided he stayed out of Weed's
sight and company to the maximum extent possible. One way was not
to get off at the whistlestops, when Weed had to get off even if he didn't
shoot. These moments were peculiarly pleasant for Jason to the point of
a fine feeling that for their duration Weed was not even physically on the
train.

Jason had been reading heavily in the books he had brought along
but had scarcely cracked until now because of being busy and of his
absorption in the train and in the country seen from it and when it
stopped at the towns. But in the last two days he had pleasurably read
or sampled *The Unquiet Grave* by Cyril Connolly, Baudelaire's
Les Fleurs du Mal, Edith Hamilton's *The Greek Way,* Gauguin's *Noa
Noa,* Ovid's *Metamorphoses,* P. C. Wren's *Beau Geste,* and what he considered the greatest of all man's writings aside from certain portions of
the Bible, Plato's *Dialogues.* At the present moment, as the train
pulled into the steamy station of Potawatami, New York, Jason was

perusing *The Penguin Book of English Verse,* which he held comfortably in one hand while gustily chewing an apple he held in the other and had brought last night from the dining car. Since he was wearing nothing but a pair of undershorts and had not shaved in a couple of days, in consideration for the sensibilities of the good people of Potawatami, who might be somewhat stirred and strained to see such an apparition on the Presidential train and even on this account prejudicially cast their votes against the candidate the train carried—Jason knew enough about politics to know that the slightest little thing, even an obscure unpleasant feeling from a remotely related, slight, really forgotten incident, could change a vote, and he liked the President and did not want to turn votes against him by any untoward action of his— he pulled down the shade as the train came to a stop. Not before, however, a cluster of past-middle-aged ladies and gentlemen, who from the Sunday-best dress and ribboned badges they were wearing appeared to be the official reception committee for the Presidential train, had got a shocked glimpse of an unshaved, nude but for jockey shorts figure, sitting at one of the train windows, chewing an apple and reading (anyhow, Jason thought reassuringly, they're the local party politicians so nothing could change *their* votes). In the darkened room Jason switched on the light and with a happy sigh resumed his apple and the poets.

The train had barely come to a full stop and Jason had scarcely taken one more bite and turned one more page and was just reading with satisfaction and approval and a certain excitement of communication the clown's song from *Twelfth Night*—

> *O mistris mine where are you roming:*
> *O stay and heare, your true loves coming,*
> *That can sing both high and low.*
> *Trip no further prettie sweeting.* ·
> *Journeys end in lovers meeting,*
> *Every wise mans sonne doth know.*
>
> *What is love, tis not heereafter,*
> *Present mirth, hath present laughter:*
> *What's to come, is still unsure*
> *In delay there lies no plentie,*
> *Then come kisse me sweet and twentie:*
> *Youths a stuffe will not endure.*

when he heard a rustle at the drawn curtains in the doorway of the drawing room, looked up, and saw impaled upon the curtains a human head, the loveliest and the reddest-haired head he had ever seen sticking through the curtains of a train drawing room. He put down his apple and Shakespeare.

The head, confronted with the rather disheartening vision that Jason was at the moment, did not panic. That pretty mouth, with its rather full, bunched lower lip painted in a soft hue, said only: "Oh, I'm terribly sorry to disturb you"—and promptly withdrew.

It was Jason who nearly panicked. Leaping to his feet he stuck *his* head through the curtains into the corridor. He moved so swiftly that the girl had barely started away.

"Hey, you there!" Jason said.

The girl turned.

"Come back here," Jason said smartly.

Meantime behind the curtains he had hastily reached for his trousers and was pulling them on. Simultaneously he with one hand zippered his trousers up and with the other zippered the curtains down.

"May I be of any help to you?" he asked.

She was absolutely stunning and she looked about seventeen. She was the bud about to burst into bloom. She wore a button-down boy's oxford-cloth shirt, a light blue cardigan cashmere sweater, and a dark blue tailored skirt, and no hat. She was a vision of youth: she had wide blue eyes and quick lithe movements and spoke riotously of youth in all its fragrance and of the flawless-fleshed nymph leaping through some shadow-and-sunlight forest glade. But above all her hair: It was that rarest of hair colors, a truly red red and all full of lights. She came back and followed Jason into the drawing room. The first thing she looked at was the face-down book, and as no true intellectual can help from doing she picked it up to see what Jason had been reading. It is by such things that the true intellectual characterizes anybody.

"Oh, poetry," she said. She said it in a tone that implied Jason's reading of the work immediately characterized him to her and in a favorable way. "You read, do you?"

"Yes, I know how to read," Jason said.

The girl laughed, a low gurgle. "Isn't it a coincidence that I'm using this very book in a course I'm taking in English Lit. It's my favorite course. That and Political Thought. What an interesting coincidence."

"An immediate bond," Jason said warmly.

"I'm very interested in politics," the girl said. "There are not many things in this world more interesting than politics, are there?"

"Only one or two," Jason said.

"Politics must be very interesting to you and you must know a lot about it, being a political correspondent."

She spoke very respectfully to Jason, who after all was a member of the world's most famous press group, the White House press corps.

"Indeed it is," Jason said, not going into the fact that he was a quite temporary member of this great press corps and that even as such his chief function was carrying a photographer's bags. It would take too much time to elaborate these intricate distinctions to the visitor.

The visitor turned over some more of Jason's books scattered on the drawing-room couch.

"Why, *The Unquiet Grave*," she exclaimed happily, and looked at Jason in a manner that suggested his possession of this volume further characterized him to her, and most favorably. "I think this may be my favorite book of all. It's my night-table book."

"What kind of book?" Jason asked.

"My night-table book. The one book I keep on my night table and read every night before going to bed. I read only one paragraph of it at a time. It's the one book that should be read only in paragraphs, don't you think? And I have a favorite paragraph in it. Here, let me find it for you."

She leafed knowledgeably through the pages until she came to it and she read aloud: " 'From now on specialize; never again make any concession to the ninety-nine percent of you which is like everybody else at the expense of the one percent which is unique.' "

Her voice had the timbre of girlishness and the ring of vitality and eagerness and it was a very alive thing to hear.

"Don't you agree," she said, putting the book back, "that that is one of the profoundest truths ever spoken, and spoken as beautifully as truth was ever spoken?"

"Well!" Jason said. "You speak very well yourself. And may I say that you read beautifully."

One of Jason's standing precepts in regard to that large subject of the handling of women was, in the case of a beautiful woman, never never to praise her for her beauty—this she would feel smug and superior about if you mentioned it, having heard it so interminably—but instead to praise her for her qualities of the mind, for which she was probably never praised if she was beautiful, for her intelligence and related qualities.

It never failed to work. Even now this beautiful and astonishing creature—who had descended out of God knew where, quite possibly, Jason felt, from right where He was—blushed becomingly.

"That's very kind of you," she said. "I'm very interested in matters of this sort. What a coincidence that we seem to like the same books."

"There is hardly a stronger bond between two persons and I am not sure I believe in coincidences," Jason said profoundly. "If things happen, there must be a reason."

"Perhaps," the girl said thoughtfully. "But oh . . ." She seemed to catch herself. "I've got so interested here that I almost forgot why I came. I'm from the Potawatami Presbyterian Normal College."

"What was that name again?" Jason said.

"The Potawatami Presbyterian Normal College."

"Oh, yes, indeed," Jason said. "I've heard of it. It is said to be a very fine little religious institution."

"You're a liar but a most polite liar and it is at least little and it is most emphatically religious," she summed the institution up. She laughed a moment. "I think the Potawatami Presbyterian Normal College must be the only school left in the United States where the girl students have to be in by eight P.M.—eleven P.M. on Saturdays."

"Well, in any event that leaves a good deal of time for reading." Jason tried to look for the bright side of anything.

"And little else," the girl said. "I'm supposed to be studying to be a teacher. But what I want to do is to go into journalism. We have a pretty considerable journalism course at Potawatami Presbyterian Normal. You cannot get a major in journalism but you can get a minor, and that's what I'm doing."

"Welcome aboard," Jason said fraternally.

The girl smiled. "Listen," she said, "what I'm here for is this. When we heard this train was coming through here, the journalism professor worked up a project for the journalism students. He decided we would go to the train and ask all the political correspondents who their personal preference for President in this campaign was. The idea was that this poll would probably get the college some publicity and it would also give us journalism students experience in interviewing and also a chance to meet the correspondents at least long enough to see what they looked like."

"They generally have two hands, two feet, two eyes, two ears, one nose and one mouth," Jason said. "The really good ones have two noses and the really bad ones have two mouths."

The girl smiled and opened her notebook. "This is anonymous but we're supposed to put down the name just to make sure we don't duplicate. Do you mind giving me your name? It won't be published."

The assumption here was that it would not look quite proper if the correspondent for a given paper favored for President a different candidate from the choice of his newspaper. Of course most newspapers are Republican and most reporters on these newspapers are Democratic, the correlation doubtless being one of economic status.

"Jason Hightower," Jason said.

"Your newspaper?"

"*Vital* magazine."

The girl looked up and an expression of thrill touched those heart-catching features. "Oh, *Vital* magazine!" she trilled. "How exciting that must be!"

And suddenly, so thrilled was she, she burst out: "You know, my great ambition is to work for *Vital* magazine."

"Is that so?" Jason said.

"Oh, I'm sorry," she said. "I shouldn't have said that. It sounds climbing and . . . well, *utilizing*. Though I didn't mean it that way— and anyhow a good reporter isn't supposed to discuss himself."

"Don't let that trouble you," Jason said. "So many discuss little else."

"Now about this interview," she said firmly, pressing her lips together, "whom do you favor for President of the U . . ."

The train gave a lurch. It slammed them momentarily against each other. Then they had righted themselves.

"The train's moving!" the girl exclaimed.

And so it was.

The girl wheeled, turning for the door. And as suddenly as the lurch an absolute and passionate determination came over Jason that he must not, his life depended on it, let this creature get away. He had no notion why he felt this and indeed no time to determine why. Already she was halfway through the curtains.

"Your notebook!" Jason exclaimed desperately. "You've forgotten your notebook!"

That stopped her for a moment, and Jason could feel the train pick up a tiny amount of speed. He grabbed for something to give her.

"Oh, that's *my* notebook," he said.

She looked down in confusion at her hand holding her own notebook. "I've got mine," she said a little shrilly. "How do you get off this train!"

"But I haven't given you my reply as to whom I favor as the next President of the United States of America," Jason said, making the sentence as long as possible.

"Never mind that now!" the girl shrilled desperately. "Show me how to get off."

"Quick!" Jason said. "Stand aside!"

Brushing past her to lead the way, Jason, barefooted and barechested but wearing trousers, started down the passageway, she hard behind him. He saw a couple of correspondents coming toward him and managed to run into them, the train swaying like it was, like a destroyer ramming a pair of submarines. The two men snapped back against the side of the train like struck tenpins, lurched, and the glasses with lenses thick as a telescope's which one of the two men was wearing hurtled to the floor.

"Goddamn it to blue bastard hell watch where you're going!" the glassless correspondent shouted violently.

"Be so good as to watch your language, my good man," Jason said. "This young lady is from the Potawatami Presbyterian Normal College, the local institution of higher learning in the town we are just departing," he drew that one out redundantly, "and she is not accustomed to hearing the abnormal language with which you have just befouled this passageway."

Beneath him Jason could happily feel the increase in the r.p.m.'s of the wheels.

"Oh, I'm terribly sorry," the profane correspondent apologized abjectly. "My apologies, Miss. I didn't see you." From the thickness of the lenses of those glasses which lay on the floor she must be no more than a blur to him even now, Jason thought.

"Just watch it, you hear . . ." Jason started in to make an issue of it.

"For god's sake let's forget it!" the girl screamed, startling everybody. "Get me off of here!"

"See the language you've driven this young lady to," Jason said to the correspondent. "Now if you'll be so good as to clear the way . . ."

Another sixty seconds were fortunately lost as the correspondent bent down and retrieved his glasses. As the correspondents stood aside, flattening themselves almost at attention against the sides of the narrow corridor, Jason resumed his plunge down it. The girl almost pushing him, he reached the door. He fumbled a few precious seconds with the handle, then opened it. He was ecstatic to see that the vestibule steps were up. If the steps had been down she probably could just have made it. He saw the platform rushing past ever faster. He fumbled clumsily with the vestibule door and finally got it open and the steps down. He breathed a sigh of relief. By now the train was running past the end of the platform at a good twenty miles per hour . . .

"Sorry," Jason said.

Before he knew it the girl with almost a plunge had swept past him, was on the steps and was about to leap off. Lunging instantly against her, Jason jerked her violently back. Then they both stood, panting heavily, watching a landscape that was now fields rushing by beneath them.

"Have you lost your mind?" Jason yelled against the wind and the sound of the wheels turning over fast, gathering real speed now.

"But I'm supposed to be in by eight P.M.!" She was almost whimpering.

"The only way you would have been in at eight P.M.," Jason said, "would have been in a basket."

They stood, silent awhile on the steps, getting their breath back as now the train poured through the countryside.

"Well, anyhow," she said finally, "I can get off at the next stop." She looked at her watch. "It's eleven-twenty now. I'll get off at the next stop —I guess they'll stop at Silver Creek. That's fifteen minutes away. Do they stop there?"

"No."

"Angola? That's the next town."

"No," Jason said. "The train does not stop at Angola."

"Derby?"

"No."

The girl, her eyes widening, looked at him for several moments in the gathering silence.

"Then *when*," she said, "*is* the next stop. *When* and *where* is the next stop?"

"Six P.M.," Jason answered the first part of the question.

She looked up at him, her eyes growing very wide.

"New York City," he answered the second part.

She was silent for quite a while. Then she gave a very deep sigh, which made her pert breasts go forward under the sweater then recede. "Well." She sighed very deeply. "I guess I'm in for it."

She was truly disheartened. Who can look at a beautiful seventeen-year-old red-headed girl disheartened and not undertake to cheer her up? Not Jason certainly. That was all in the world he ever had in mind —cheering a poor depressed young girl up—as he was to remember later. He had suggested they step back up into the vestibule and they did and it was then and there that he spoke those words.

"Now just look at it this way"—he could even remember exactly the one thing he had in mind that would probably cheer her up the most of anything in the world he could possibly say—"now just look at it this way. I have a philosophy about these things," he said with the right to ponderousness and declamation that the several years and the male sex and the profession he had on her he felt gave him. "The philosophy—and how often it has worked out in experience!—is that what at the time may seem the worst thing that could happen to you turns out to be the very best thing in the world that could possibly happen to you. The founder of your church," he said, to give her a touchstone, "had somewhat the same philosophy. Calvin believed in fatalism and predestination—essentially, that every act is meant to be . . ."

Recklessly Jason plunged on. "Now it is obvious to me that you have a bright future in the profession of journalism."

Jason had been right as rain. The transformation was instantaneous. The worried look was replaced by a pair of much interested blue eyes looking up at him.

"Why do you say that, Mr. Hightower? How do you know it?"

"By the way you asked your questions a little while ago when you were interviewing me. It was done with a skill which, considering your inexperience, was not much short of astonishing."

"How kind you really are, Mr. Hightower!" she said, forgetting that she had only had time, due to her absorption in Jason's books, to ask one question. Women—even quite young ones—have such a convenient lapse of memory where their ambition is concerned, an asset which serves them beyond measure.

"I'm not kind in the slightest," Jason plunged on. "I'm just stating a fact. You see, the main business of a reporter is to ask questions, conduct interviews. You agree with that don't you? Isn't that what they teach you in the journalism classes at Potawatami Presbyterian Normal College?"

"More or less I guess," the girl said.

"Well, whether they teach it to you or not it's the truth. The definition of a reporter is a man—or, in your case, a woman—who asks questions and conducts interviews," Jason said in the manner of an old pro giving the young and hopeful but confused and uncertain the benefit of his hardy experience. "And you do it with a skill worth commenting on."

The girl was now completely interested. She was not even any more looking outside at the landscape which was so swiftly taking her away from the town where she had to be in by 8:00 P.M.

Jason knew he was being ever so reckless, that he was about to commit a kind of professional rape upon an impressionable seventeen-year-old girl, and he had a definite premonition, a visitation, that while very often recklessness does not have to be paid for in this life, all pious opinion to the contrary notwithstanding, that somehow this piece of recklessness would have to be cashed in. How he knew this he could not have said. He only knew that he knew it. But even knowing it, and even knowing that he knew it, he could not help himself.

With abandon he plunged on.

"Now look at it this way. First you want to be a reporter. Right?"

"Oh, very much, Mr. Hightower. More than anything."

"Second, someone who is, I say this with no false modesty, qualified to judge your talents or absence of them in connection with this ambition, has stated, having observed you in action, that you have decided talents in this direction. You understand?"

"Yes, Mr. Hightower." She spoke now with meekness and almost with humility.

"Now I come to point three, or four, whichever it is. To the reason why your having got caught on this train may turn out to be the best blessing in disguise that ever happened to you, may indeed change your entire life around," Jason said with about as much recklessness as one can practice.

The girl looked up in adoration. Jason took a sigh and did it.

"I work for *Vital* magazine. You have said you want to work for *Vital* magazine more than anything else in the world. By your missing getting off—in which case I could have done nothing since I wouldn't even have known your name by then . . . By the way what is your name?"

"Lilleba Ericsson."

"Lilleba Ericsson," Jason repeated. "Lilleba Ericsson! What a sweet-rolling name! Lilleba. I never heard that one but how sweet it is. What does it mean?"

"It's Norwegian for 'Little Baby.' My people came from Norway."

A Norwegian redhead! Jason caught his breath in startlement and wonder at his prize. He took a deep breath. "I shall not forget that name." He took an even deeper breath and said it. "By your missing getting off this train, well . . . when you graduate next spring you come in to see me in New York and I'll fix you up at *Vital*."

He had said it. The girl's mouth hung open. Her eyes grew very wide. She was thunderstruck.

"At *Vital*?" she finally found speech enough to utter hoarsely. She was thrilled almost to the point of fainting.

"*Vital* magazine," Jason repeated, feeling that at this point simplicity made the most dramatic effect.

So gratified was he with her response, and even more with himself in the role of distributing such largesse, that the potentially frightful consequences of his act of articulation which he had felt so definitely in premonition only a moment ago were now completely obliterated from his mind and memory. Because what he had said made her so happy, he now felt absolutely nothing except wonderful.

"You really think I could work at *Vital*?" the girl said incredulously. "What do you *need* to work for *Vital*, Mr. Hightower?" she said, unable fully to believe, take in, comprehend, her great good fortune, her blessing-in-disguise from having got stuck on the train.

Jason looked at her. He felt he had never seen anything so lovely. "I have often wondered," he said, "but whatever it is you've got it."

Jason straightened up. He felt, as one does who distributes important largesse, like standing up.

"Do you really think I have a future in journalism, Mr. Hightower?"

Jason looked at her. "I am convinced," he said, "that you have a truly sensational future in the profession. And now, there's only one little problem. What to do with you until we get to New York City."

"Is that a problem, Mr. Hightower?" she said uncomprehendingly.

"Of a sort," Jason said gravely. "You see, nobody not cleared by the Secret Service is supposed to be on this train."

"But surely, Mr. Hightower, they wouldn't think a student from Potawatami Presbyterian Normal College . . ."

"It's a rule," Jason rather loftily cut this logic off. "The Secret Service can't afford to take the remotest chance. If some outfit were going to try to bump off the President they would probably choose someone of the description you've just given, someone from a place like Potawatami Presbyterian Normal College, someone . . . How old are you?"

"Eighteen."

"Eighteen." Jason caught his breath. ". . . someone eighteen years old and innocent and American-looking and from Potawatami Presbyterian Normal College, who couldn't possibly do it. That would be the exact person they would choose. Anyhow, how do *they* know you're from Potawatami Presbyterian Normal? For all they know that might be a tale told by some mob's moll, some mob bent on wiping out the President of the United . . . Do you have identification?"

She fumbled, made nervous by Jason's ominous tone, in her purse. "It's here . . . here somewhere . . . Here!"

She pulled out a card and handed it to Jason.

"Come with me," Jason said, "and we'll see Gordon Ellison."

"Who's Gordon Ellison?"

"A Secret Service man. A kind of a friend of mine. Wait right here."

He returned to his drawing room long enough only to whip on his shirt and shoes, came back, and she followed him meekly through the cars. When they reached the press car he found a seat for her. She looked fascinated at the sight of so many major-league correspondents working away. Several of the correspondents looked up in a reciprocal fascination before forcing themselves back to their work.

"You wait here," Jason said. "I'll go see Ellison."

Jason went on through the cars until he got to the Secret Service car. He found Ellison and explained the situation to him. Ellison smiled in amusement. Jason showed him the card which identified the stowaway as a student at Potawatami Presbyterian Normal College and carried her picture. Ellison whistled at the picture.

"How old is she?" he asked.

"Eighteen," Jason said.

"Eighteen?" Ellison whistled again. "Okay. But I think you probably better bring her down for a look."

Jason went back and fetched her down to the Secret Service car. She looked extremely thrilled to be in these precincts. Ellison very courteously and with somewhat mock formality looked from her to the picture, comparing.

"Matches," he said formally. "May you have a good time in New York City, Miss Ericsson."

"Thank you, thank you very much, sir," she said, half-nervous, half-thrilled.

Jason returned her to the press car. He told her to wait and went down to the drawing room. Weed was there snoring away. He remembered with some satisfaction Weed's words to him of the night before.

"Hightower, I've had it. The moment we leave that last stop before New York I'm sacking out until we hit the city. Be sure not to wake me until just ten minutes before we get in. You got that?"

"Yassuh," Jason had replied.

Now Jason tiptoed out and went back to the girl.

He spent the day with her, talking, having lunch, talking, talking,

talking. It was delightful beyond words, like spending a day with an unexpected angel who had just dropped in from a pretty mauve cloud. An angel with a mind, too, it became ever clearer as the hours fled away, the train streaked for New York. They got going quite a communication of ideas and they ranged with much scope and rather voraciously through the centuries of man's ideas, beginning with the early Greeks and extending into the century that was their own. As the train streaked for New York there passed between them the names and ideas of Hesiod, Pindar and Socrates, of Virgil and Ovid and St. Paul, of Augustine and Aquinas, of Villon and Milton, of Dryden and Herrick, of Swift and Shakespeare, of Verlaine and Montaigne, of La Fontaine and La Rochefoucauld, of Balzac and Baudelaire, of Thackeray and Dickens and Stendhal and Shelley and Melville and Tolstoy (how great was man, Jason thought, to have produced such!), and they were backtracking in time and getting into Lao-tse and Chuang-tse when the time of their day ran out. Seldom had Jason so enjoyed talking with a human being of this one's sex, youth and physical attraction. From time to time Jason checked the drawing room. Weed was still sleeping away and he took care not to awaken him. At 4:30 he went down, and shaking him vigorously, almost viciously, woke him.

"Weed old man!" he screamed in his ear.

"Ugh . . . unh . . . ugh . . . ump . . ."

Jason shook him with both hands until his head was bouncing, and shouted at him some more. "Weed, old man! I've got something to tell you I know you're dying to hear so I just had to wake you up, old man!"

Thereupon Jason launched into a description of the girl and all her charms and of how she had got stuck aboard. Then he paused. And then he said:

"Weed, old man. I borrowed Lucas Brown's room. You know Brown, the *Times* man. A good man, but never mind that. I took her in there and I said honey, take off your dress. She took it off. I said honey, take off your slip. She took it off and stood there in her panties and bra, the most beautiful thing I have ever seen, eighteen. I said honey chile, take . . ."

For forty-two minutes Jason went on in a detailed description which almost exactly paralleled Weed's at Broken Bow, except more so, a blow-by-blow account. It is unprintable. Weed hated for any male researcher out with him on a story to make any time with a girl. He considered it a peasant usurpation of his exclusive *droit du seigneur*. He squirmed on his bunk. Jason went on, and on. Not until the train was ten minutes out of its last stop on the long, long trip, ten minutes off the island of Manhattan, did Jason conclude his account.

"Oh, Weed," he said then, "if you want a look at her I'll bring her by here when we get off—right now, in fact."

"Yes, do that," Weed said urgently. "Then you can help me with these bags. Bring her by right now. I want very much to meet her. We might go for a drink somewhere together—my apartment maybe . . ."

The train was slowing down. By the time Jason got back to the press car it was pulling into Grand Central Station.

"Let's go, kid," he said.

They got up and walked forward. The train came to a stop just as they reached Jason's car. Weed was standing in the vestibule and when he saw the girl his eyes almost popped out of his head. Jason took her right on past him and onto the platform and they started walking down it.

"Hey," Weed yelled after them. "You! Hightower! Come back here and pick up these bags. Come back here immediately! I said, *Come back here and pick up these bags!*"

Jason looked slowly as a grazing cow back over his shoulder.

"Pick them up yourself!" he yelled happily. "Jerk."

Then, turning and taking the girl by the elbow, Jason propelled her on down the platform.

"What was that?" she said. "Who was that?"

"That joker? Oh, he's my photographer. That thing about the bags is a little joke between us. Heh, heh."

Slowly the great train neared the end. Over the tracks of the Pennsylvania. Down through the stacked factory-land of New Jersey, along the duck-blind salt marshes of Delaware. Down through Maryland.

the nature of greatness

As the President stepped off the train at Washington, all of them following him, he came to a respectful stop, facing the music as the welcoming band burst into that thrilling tune played only in the President's presence, "Hail to the Chief." That song which so incarnates the best of American politics, having somehow in it the thing of choosing a man freely and setting him in chosen trust at the head of the country. And then the title "Chief"—not tsar, not king, not dictator, not commissar. And Jason thought: What a great and mighty thing is the Republic!

What manner of thing had there ever been like the United States of America! It is a great nation. It is a very great nation. As nations go, as governments go, it is one of the most honest and perhaps the most high-minded ever to erect itself upon the lands of the earth. It had its faults but on balance it was the best there was—it was the best there had been. And now at last its moment had come. As come it must.

For to every great nation its fateful moment of destiny comes. And everything that that nation is rides on that moment. But this time, most fearful of all fearful things, not just this nation but all mankind, all its future, all freedom and all decency of men today and for a thousand years to come rode on this moment. And it seemed to him that all history past, present and future, all the gods in heaven and all the millioned souls of mankind who had trod this earth throughout immortal time stood still, leaning over the ramparts of other worlds, to witness the outcome of this battle which would fix forevermore man's fate.

And he thought also: It is not enough for a nation to be great only by the measure of a given time which is past. For as it never stops giving its rewards, greatness equally never stops collecting its price. To retain its greatness a nation must ever rise to new demands upon that greatness. If this nation did, it would survive, and with it man's freedom. If it did not, this nation, and liberty with it, would perish. The United States of America would be great or it would fall.

This nation fall! Jason thought of the massive threatening tyranny just over the circle of the earth, none greater in the annals of man's ancient quarrel with tyranny, and thought with a quick fear in his vitals of its potential clutch upon these free mountains, these towns and cities, these proud fields of liberty, liberty's land he had just spanned. And, something tearing in him, but also something rising in him, he saw the tyrant's soldiers, faces of hardness and mercilessness, bestriding this land. Did this people even realize the very real possibility of this? May the Republic awake! he wished devoutly, he prayed, in a love, a deep, deep love for this land. Thinking:

America! Accept that fruit of greatness proffered to but a few peoples in all time's chronicle of valor and cowardice. Reject it, and see not only your downfall but the downfall of the dreams and hopes of free men everywhere, striving . . . for what? For the right to call their souls their own, and the right to put food in their mouths. Is the Tibetan less your brother for tending goats on a distant mountainside? Is not the man in Indonesia, the man in Africa your brother? And what does one do toward a brother? Shall not the wealthy brother share his bounty, of things material as well as ideals spoken, with his less favored brother? What kind of brother is it who will let his brother go in rags— rags either of tyranny, under whatever name, or rags of deprivation and hunger—while he has bounty of clothes and food and freedom? America! Arise and take up thy cross or surely the day will come when *thou* cryest out, and no man answers. Thy time is at hand; the trumpet is sounding for *thee;* hear it even now! And the river crossed on some distant plain in Asia or Europe will become—unless you halt it with your courage and your compassion—the river crossed in Ohio. Where are the men to halt it? Where are the men to succor the besieged everywhere in their hour of peril and need? Where the men who stood ready . . . what was it the colonists said? . . . to stake their lives, their fortunes, their sacred honor on the fateful issue? Nothing less would avail. Where the men today who would stake these?

Was the quality of the men still there, as of old? Men who held honor first, liberty above all? He believed so. The land, perhaps all it needed was a voice. The voice of America had once been Jefferson's and Samuel Adams', it had been Jackson's and Lincoln's, it had been Theodore Roosevelt's and Franklin Roosevelt's. Names of hope and of defiance to tyranny. The land was there, great as ever, and needed only a voice. And he thought: What greater subject had writer ever had to hand than the mid-twentieth century United States of America, upon whom history, in its ways, had now chosen to depend the fate of all men alive and to live.

CYCLE THREE

THE MOST
UNUSUAL BUILDING
IN THE WORLD

11

Ingredients

The ingredients whose mixture we wish now to relate included an ambition of Paisley Fairlamb's; what might be termed a non-ambition of Henry Gaskin's; a hotel registration book; and Crystal Bidwell's abiding interest in her subjects.

These forces—three human and one material—were all set into play whose end no man could foresee by the fact of a young lady's thoughts turning where they must. And even, behind that, the match that so unawarely ignited it all was a simple thing indeed: a visit to Henry Gaskin by his relatives.

Paisley Fairlamb's one reigning ambition was to be assigned to the Paris bureau. Which city, she had become convinced as a consequence of her "third year" of schooling there, was really the only city in the world to live in. It was an ambition which in the normal state of operations at the magazine she would never realize, since she had majored in foreign affairs in college.

Henry Gaskin's non-ambition was wedded bliss.

Henry Gaskin sat in his apartment listening to his records, having a drink and trying to snatch a few moments of peace before they burst in ecstatically from another day "on your fabulous, fabulous city, Henry," as his aunt so distressingly put it. How rash and headlong had been that impulsive act of generosity and loving-kindness when, having received a really handsome gift from his aunt in the form of one dozen home-canned fruit jars of a sensationally hot sauce, intersticed with peppers so satanic they almost took off a layer of tongue, Gaskin, who had a passion for hot peppers and was constantly on the look for ever hotter breeds, had sat down immediately and invited them—never dreaming they would accept, for his aunt and uncle had not passed over the borders of Massachusetts in fourteen years—to spend "a few days" (miserable mistaken generosity and generality—"a few days"!) with him in New York. All thoughts of loving-kindness and generosity should be slept on overnight, he thought rather bitterly, as he began to consider his problem.

Having relatives visit you in New York is always a thing of doubtful wisdom. One gets in a rather set routine in New York and it is appalling how much relatives can upset this routine. Far more, for some reason, than if you live in a place, say, like High Point, North Carolina, and have your relatives visit you there. The reasons are probably two in number. One is that you live in an apartment in New York, and relatives find it far easier to take over, as it were, your apartment in New York and with it your life, than they would in the house you would probably inhabit in High Point. The second is that relatives visiting you in New York are much more inclined to expect you to lay on quite a program of entertainment for them in a city which has somewhat more to offer in this direction than High Point. Most inhabitants of Manhattan find a visit from relatives quite a trial. This time it was more than that. And just an uncle and aunt at that. And even so, had they stayed only the week they had threatened, matters might have been different.

Last night, however, his dear ones had announced cozily to Gaskin—and indeed rather in the attitude of conferring a special dispensation on their nephew—that they were enjoying his hospitality, his apartment and, in general, the rich store of activity, entertaining and educational, that New York had to offer so much that they had decided to do it up right and stay a second week.

"There's so much to do in New York, Henry!" his aunt had bubbled. "We haven't *begun* to exhaust the possibilities."

"Yes," Gaskin said. "That would take a long time, I'm afraid," he said as diplomatically as possible. "It's hard to get *everything* in New York in on just one visit, isn't it?"

"Well, all we can do is try, isn't it, Henry?" his aunt trilled with a gay laugh that pierced right through him. "If there's anything Stephen and I have it's *time*. And after all, Henry, Stephen and I only get to New York once every fourteen years."

"Thank God," Gaskin said. He said this to himself.

Gaskin's problem, though he truly loved his aunt and uncle, for they were good people, was that for an entire week he had been leading a life not only a hundred percent chaste toward Paisley Fairlamb but hardly even seeing her, so much had he put himself out to entertain his beloved uncle and aunt during their week—so much so, indeed, that this very fact, their enjoying it so much, probably led to their decision to stay over. It made one think of what Mr. Proust said about selfish altruism being the only fruitful kind. Paisley had a school friend visiting her, so that there was no asylum to be had there. He was a quite miserable man, what with the nerves twinly exacerbated by his relations and the deprivation of Paisley. For in the months since the night of the house-pet lion, Paisley Fairlamb had become, so to speak, Henry Gaskin's chief source of supply. Not by any manner of means his only one, but the chief one, the central one. Gaskin was almost unaware himself how much he was seeing her. These things do slip up on one. And the habit grew. And life ground on.

Next morning at the office the first thing he did was to sail out a triple formation of paper airplanes centered with typed messages appropriated from some of his poetical reading reflecting his rather surly and frustrated mood. They read:

> *Weep on! and, as thy sorrows flow*
> *I'll taste the luxury of woe.*

> *I shall never be friends again with roses;*
> *I shall loathe sweet tunes.*

And finally:

> *Since all the good we have rests in the mind,*
> *By whose proportions only we redeeme*
> *Our thoughts from out confusion, and doe finde*
> *The measure of our selves, and of our pow'rs;*
> *And that all happinesse remaines confinde*
> *Within the kingdome of this breast of ours:*
> *Without whose boundes all that we looke on lies*
> *In others jurisdictions, others pow'rs,*
> *Out of the circuit of our liberties.*
> *All glory, honor, fame, applause, renowne,*
> *Are not belonging to our royalties,*
> *But t'others wils, wherein they are onely growne:*
> *And that unlesse we finde us all within,*
> *We never can without us be our owne,*
> *Nor call it right our life what we live in:*
> *But a possession held for others use.*
>
> > *I agree with the astute and*
> > *acute Samuel Daniel*
> > (*signed*) *Henry Gaskin*

It didn't help too much. For, settling back to his desk, his frustration and surliness so welled up in him that he made an instant decision. He picked up his phone, dialed his own apartment, and informed his guests he would be working very late on a story, he had just been told by the copy editor, probably until 2:00 or 3:00 A.M., and rather than stumble over them at that hour in his one-room apartment he would probably take the hotel room near the office which, a lie, he said the magazine kept permanently for late workers. The lie was classifiable as a white one in the sense it was told to spare the feelings of his blood kin. Immediately after hanging up he dialed Paisley Fairlamb down the corridor.

"I'm taking a night off from conducting the sightseeing bus," he said. "This deprivation is making me highly irritable and cross. Can you break off early, say at four o'clock?"

"Four o'clock?" Paisley said. "That's pretty early." Really, however, she felt a delightful little thrill at this dependence on her.

"It can't be too early," he said. "And please don't play hard to get at this critical juncture. Let's drop it all at four and see what feelings we can rustle up one toward the other."

"All right, let's rustle them up," Paisley said deliciously.

At four o'clock the two colleagues left the building and Gaskin guided them by the shortest route to the Grigsby Hotel. It was near the office and he could hardly wait. Gaskin marched with an offhand yet quite self-possessed air up to the desk, grasped the pen the desk clerk gave him and wrote in a reasonably firm hand:

"Mr. and Mrs. Harrison Duckworth—Stamford, Conn."

"Caught in the city," he said vaguely to the desk clerk in explanation of the absence of luggage. He expected next that they would ask payment in advance. "I'm from *Vital* magazine," he added, only because the magazine gave a good deal of custom to the Grigsby.

"Oh, that's all right, Mr. Duckworth," the desk clerk said with uncommon courtesy. "We've been expecting you."

That sounded a little strange but Gaskin decided not to go into it. It is often better not to go into things that sound a little strange. Also his mind was alive, concentrating, and very nearly vibrating now on more incipient and less strange, more tangible and less shadowy matters.

At the room on the eighth floor Gaskin tipped the bellboy, who had done nothing but carry the key, unlock the door with it, and turn on the lights, a dollar bill. Considering he had had no luggage to carry, this was generous enough to get a thanks even from a New York bellhop. The bellboy left and Gaskin and Paisley surveyed the quarters.

It was a very large room, a very nice room.

"I'm going to have a bath," Paisley said briskly. That was an ordinary enough statement. It was the next word, given in that healthy, explicit manner of Paisley Fairlamb's, which lifted her into class. "First."

Harrison Duckworth was a tremendous Puritan. He was the most moral, Puritan person on *Vital* magazine. By Puritan we mean of course that he didn't tell his wife—or anybody else—whenever he slept with a girl from the office. He did it on the sly instead of openly, which meant of course he was a good Puritan.

In the *Vital* building Harrison Duckworth closed the door to his office and locked it from the inside. First he went into his closet and pedaled for fifteen minutes on his Exercycle—he always put in a session pedaling the Exercycle before taking a girl out. It improved his circulation and raised his temperature of masculine athletic self-approval. Then he dismounted, came back into his office and sat down in his Do-More executive-model chair behind his enormous double-executive-size desk. He reached over, picked up his phone and dialed four digits. Presently he said into the mouthpiece: "I'm leaving," and hung up. He stood up, took his topcoat and hat from the clothes tree, put them on, picked up a small suitcase, left his office, went down the corridor, turned into the elevator bank and pushed a button. Within a minute the door of one of the elevators slid open. Duckworth walked into the empty elevator. The door closed and simultaneously as the elevator started its swift plunge from the top, thirty-fourth floor, Duckworth saw a small red light flash on on the elevator board. He could see it was for the thirty-third floor and he was pleased with the precise timing. The elevator stopped smoothly at floor thirty-three and a young lady walked in. They spoke to one another formally and, as the elevator resumed its plunge, stood on opposite sides of the cage without forther conversation. In the New York manner, Duckworth did not remove his hat. When the elevator stroked to a landing Duckworth let the girl pass out first, waited the fraction of a moment, then followed her out. Her high heels clicked an exciting, erotic tattoo across the lobby. He kept his pace slow, following her casually, until about ten paces were between them by the time she passed through the revolving door. Out on the street Duckworth maintained the distance as both headed up the cross-street toward Fifth Avenue. She traversed Fifth, walked uptown two blocks, then turned east into another cross-street. Not until they were on this street did he overtake her. They stood on the walk which passed by great St. Patrick's Cathedral. He waved down a taxi.

"The Grinzing Restaurant," he told the hackie.

"You got me, Mac."

"Three two three East Seven-nine Street."

Within a quarter-hour they were walking into the restaurant. It was a dark restaurant with Austrian food and sighing violin music.

"A booth in the back," Duckworth said to the head waiter.

Immediately they were seated Duckworth ordered a dry Manhattan for himself and a martini for the girl. Then they had one more round of them and then they ate. Duckworth ate rather rapidly. The girl, to keep pace with him, did not finish all her meal. They had coffee and left. Duckworth flagged another taxi. Inside the cab he told the driver: "Grigsby Hotel, between Madison and Fifth on . . ."

"I know where it is," the driver interrupted.

At the hotel Duckworth got out first, helped her out, paid the taxi and followed her inside. A bellboy came over and took his small suitcase. While she lingered in the lobby Duckworth walked up to the desk.

"I believe you have a reservation for Mr. and Mrs. Harrison Duckworth."

An expression of surprise passed across the hotel clerk's face.

"Duckworth?" he said. "Did you say the name was Duckworth?"

"I believe that's what I said," Duckworth said in bell-tones which carried the first warnings of impatience, just enough to stimulate the hotel clerk to put a "sir" on his addressings to him after that.

"Yes, sir, we *did* have a reservation in the name of Mr. and Mrs. Harrison Duckworth . . ."

"*Did* have?" Duckworth broke him off. "Listen, I've no time for games. I reserved a room here this morning."

"Are *you* Harrison Duckworth, sir?"

Duckworth's face flushed. "Listen . . ." he started.

"Well, that's an interesting coincidence, sir. A man and his wife with the same name as yours registered earlier this evening."

"Listen to me carefully now, you," Duckworth said with cold savagery. He had a temper at times like this, as almost any man would. "I don't know what this is all about but *I'm* Harrison Duckworth and *I* want *my* room."

"There must be two of you, sir," the clerk said, a little frightened now. "That is to say," he added hastily, "two Harrison Duckworths . . ."

"Listen, do you have a room for me or don't you?" Duckworth said savagely.

"Well, we're pretty crowded"—the clerk looked at Duckworth's face —"but one moment, sir."

The clerk disappeared briefly, then returned, smiling broadly.

"Well, sir, you're in luck. I thought for a moment there I might have to ask the *other* Harrison Duckworth to come down here and straighten this out. But I *do* have one room left. What a coincidence. It's on the same floor, as a matter of fact it's . . ."

"Never mind!" Duckworth shouted savagely. "I have neither time nor understanding for this foolish talk. Give me a pen!"

"It's right there in the holder, sir."

Duckworth ripped it out.

"Well, I'm glad we could accommodate you, sir. Of course it's a connecting bath . . ."

"Connecting bath!" Duckworth's head shot up violently from the registry.

"I'm sorry, sir, terribly sorry, but it's all I have. We're very crowded right now due to so many of our long-time clients not having left for Florida yet for the winter. Been so pretty in New York, you know . . ."

"Never mind! Never mind!" Duckworth said savagely. "I'll take it."

He registered fiercely: "Mr. and Mrs. Harrison Duckworth—Stamford, Conn."—put the pen not back in the holder but slammed it down on the desk.

"Front!" the hotel clerk barked harshly to the bellboy, to work a little of his off, and banged the desk bell brutally.

Duckworth followed the girl into the elevator. "If there's anything I hate it's to share the bathroom—with *anybody*," he said as the elevator started up.

Back down in the lobby the hotel clerk pulled the card out of the registry pad and was about to file it when his eyebrows came up sharply.

Holding the card he walked into the little pigeon-sized slot where the telephone operator sat.

"Now that's what I call a *real* coincidence, Myrtle," he said. "*Two* Harrison Duckworths on one night—and *both* of them from Stamford, Connecticut. Must be Duckworth country up there . . ."

Harrison Duckworth was rather restless. Tossing, turning, twisting.

"Joy," he said. "That *Vital* expense account book you left in the bathroom. I put it on the dresser."

"What was that, Harrison?"

"I left it on the dresser. The expense account book."

"Expense account book?" Joy Morehouse said. "I didn't have any expense account book. And if I did, well . . . Harrison I may look to have an IQ of eighty-four but I would hardly take an expense account book to the bathroom at a hotel to make entries. Not at a time like this."

"I guess that's so," Duckworth said slowly. "I did think it rather odd."

"Shall we get some sleep, Harrison? And then see. I'm so sleepy."

"Yes, let's do that."

An hour later Harrison Duckworth was still wide awake, listening to taxi horns and his own rather disturbed mind. He could hear her rhythmic breathing, sleeping like a baby. Youth, he thought savagely. He got out of bed very quietly and felt and tiptoed his way to the bathroom in the dark. En route he felt along the dresser and found the expense account book and took it with him. Inside the bathroom he closed the door very carefully, then switched on the light. He opened the book. He stared at it in disbelief. Then he stared at the opposite door leading into the other bedroom. He closed the book, hesitated, then stuck it in the pocket of his bathrobe. He turned out the light and went back to bed.

Harrison Duckworth did not sleep well that night. In fact he hardly did anything well. In fact he hardly was able to do anything at all. Such is the mind's power, galvanic or impotizing as the case may be, over the body. There is something in what the Christian Science people say, nobody can deny that.

Next morning in the office Harrison Duckworth did something very unusual. Instead of waiting until he ran into him in the corridors, he took the extreme measure of dialing Henry Gaskin direct and asking him to drop by his office—at once. Gaskin at the moment the phone rang had been engaged in his favorite sport of sailing paper airplanes out the window on Fifth Avenue below, and which he felt almost beatific doing this morning. He put the phone down, put a sheet of copy paper in his typewriter, centered it carefully, typed out the Drydenian legend—

Ah how sweet it is to love,
Ah how gay is young desire!

folded it into a craftsman's airplane and walked over and sailed it out the window. Then he went on down the corridor whistling a Rodgers and Hart tune. He entered the vice managing editor's office, casting upon his superior a pleasant smile.

"Close the door, Henry," the vice managing editor snapped, "and sit down."

The writer took a seat beside Duckworth's desk while the vice managing editor looked at him carefully.

"Well, how's everything going, Henry?"

"Oh, about the same," Gaskin said. "No broken bones—that I know of." A sort of distant curiosity attached itself to his very relaxed feeling. Never except on the most serious business—such as sending a man out to a bureau or promoting him into exile on The Thinking Desk—did Duckworth summon anyone into his office like this and, particularly, start talking like this. However, Gaskin felt so euphoric after eighteen hours in Room 823 of the Grigsby Hotel that nothing short of the big bomb could have rocked him.

"Well, I'm glad to hear it," Duckworth was saying. "How did you sleep last night, Henry?"

"What was that?" Gaskin said, uncertain he had heard correctly.

"I said, how did you *sleep* last night."

"Oh, heavenly," Gaskin said, his eyes going off with a look of satiation. A most beatific smile rounded his face for a moment. "I'm not sure I ever slept better than last night."

"I imagine."

"Why? Do I have red circles under my eyes?"

"Not that I can see from this distance, Henry. But of course you're a good three feet away."

"Shall I come closer?" Gaskin said facetiously. He really felt terrific.

"Never mind the wit, Henry." For the first time then Gaskin noticed that Duckworth was playing with something, turning it around and around in his hands. With its green color and from its size he was able to identify it easily as a *Vital* expense account book.

"Catch, Henry."

Gaskin was mildly startled as the expense account book came sailing toward him. However, he fielded it neatly.

"Look inside, Henry."

Gaskin did so. "Now where could I have lost that? Did you find it in the corridor?"

"Not exactly, Henry. In the bathroom."

"Oh, the head. I must have taken it in there to do my accounts. Saving time you know."

"I realize you're always so busy, Henry, and that's very commendable of you to save the company's time like that. However, I didn't mean the company bathroom. I meant the Grigsby Hotel bathroom."

There was a profound silence. Gaskin heard dimly the humming noise of the city thirty-four stories below.

Then Gaskin said calmly: "Yes, I was a little late last night and took a nearby hotel. It was kind of the hotel to return it here. Thanks very much, Harrison." He started to get up.

"Sit down, Henry."

Gaskin sat back in his chair.

"Henry. How long has this been going on?"

"What is that, Harrison?"

"False registry at hotels."

"Well, I don't know if I'd call it that."

"Never mind what you would call it! That's what the State of New York calls it."

"Oh, is that so? I never knew."

"You haven't answered my question, Henry. Try not to be devious, will you? How long has this been going on?"

"Oh, ten years I'd say. Give or take six months."

"Ten years! Have you ever used my name before?"

"Never."

"Whose have you used?"

Gaskin thought a moment.

"I said, whose have you used."

"I'm thinking, Harrison."

In a moment Gaskin spoke. "Henry B. Stendhal, John C. Calhoun, Arnold Bennett, Jason Hightower, Eli Watt, Oliver H. Perry, Montgomery Shanks, Jeremy Bentham, James Bowie, Sam Clemens, Steve Crane, Samuel Adams, John Masefield, Ted Dreiser, Benjamin Harrison, I. M. Pindar, Franklin D. Hoover, C. Mather, Theodore S. Eliot, Frank Villon . . ."

"I get the picture, Henry. You're *positive* you've never used my name?"

"Positive. I never forget a name."

"Apparently you remember too many. Henry, don't you realize you can go up to that place on the Hudson for this on two counts? Do you know what the penalty for fornication is?"

"Is there one?"

"It's five years."

"It would be interesting to see them undertake to enforce that one," Gaskin said pleasantly.

"And for false hotel registry, the second count, five years more."

"Well, maybe the sentences will run concurrently," Gaskin said pleasantly. "That's the usual practice, I seem to remember from my police reporter days."

"Listen, Henry. If it's all right with you, let's don't have any witty horsefeathers about this."

"I don't want any, Harrison. I never do."

"It's just that my wife was a little upset last night, seeing that some-one with our names had registered before us. You know how women are about these things. Women can get upset over nothing whatsoever. I suppose you understand this about women, Henry?"

"I understand—perfectly," Gaskin said.

"And especially if she's your wife. That gives them more license to get upset over nothing, I suppose they feel. You understand this about one's *wife,* don't you, Henry?"

"I understand—perfectly," Gaskin said.

"And, Henry."

"Yes, Harrison."

"It might be just as well if you didn't use my name again. There are so many names in the world."

"I understand—perfectly," Gaskin said.

"Now you can tool your ass on out of here. Have a nice day, Henry."

"Likewise, Harrison."

Harrison Duckworth sat thinking about last night. He grew so irri-tated that he went over and locked his office door, went into his closet, mounted his Exercycle and pedaled furiously for fifteen minutes, head down and leaning into the nonexistent wind, trying to work the irrita-tion off.

Back in his office Henry Gaskin stood looking out the window. His mind was filled with nothing but that beatitude. And abruptly he felt a great surge of sweetness for his aunt and uncle, who, in a manner most indirect, had made this possible. Had been the catalytic agent for it. He thought of phoning his aunt and thanking her for being a catalytic agent. Then thought better of it. It might confuse her. He just sank down and down, and up and up, into the warm cocoon of his euphoria, beatitude—happiness.

Suddenly he turned back to his desk, got out a piece of copy paper, slid it into his typewriter, centered it and typed out a Campionian mes-sage for the crowds below. It read:

> Mocking kisses alike, powt with lovely lip.
> Thus drowned with jollities, their merry daies doe slip.

He made it into a very fine airplane, and walking to the window, sailed it out with a feeling of blessing, like a god from Olympus above, on the crowds below and of goodness and good will for everyone. A little less, perhaps, for Harrison Duckworth than for the rest of the hu-man race.

Then, so swiftly, another ingredient was added. Two weeks later, after he was settled nicely back in his apartment, Henry Gaskin left the building with Paisley Fairlamb on a routine date. The coals of passion were still there, but not raging as before, only nicely banked. The raging passion almost requires obstacles to be overcome and, aunt and uncle gone, there were none particularly now. They strode pleasantly along together toward Fifth and then north up it, pausing now and then to look in a window. They looked in at all the china at Plummer's, then into the windows of Van Cleef and Arpels and Bergdorf Goodman, then, crossing over, swung down the east side of Fifth, going south. They looked in the windows of F. A. O. Schwarz, which Gaskin liked very much doing, and in those at Tiffany's, where it seemed to Gaskin that she lingered slightly longer than at the other windows—well, one would at Tiffany's. She turned away, rather reluctantly, Gaskin fancied. And they continued on. They looked in the leathery windows of Mark Cross, the windows of Buccellati, and the windows of Jensen's, and then they achieved Cartier's, and she stopped and they looked in there. And still she looked. And she looked. She really seemed keenly intent. And suddenly it hit him about like one of those swinging balls used to wreck buildings and right in the back of the neck. And then she was turning and saying rather archly, "Hank, I've got a surprise for you."

"Well, I like surprises, like most of the human race," he said, but even then he had just a very slight sense of foreboding. "What is the surprise?"

"Hank," she said, so sweetly. "You don't *tell* surprises. You *spring* them."

"I see," Gaskin said. "Well, spring away."

"Come with me."

And actually taking his hand, like a little child—or like a lamb to —well, he would never forget that walk, especially reconstructing it all in retrospect—she actually, literally, led him up Fifth to 57th. Across town on 57th Street to Park. Up Park to the Eighties. About a twenty-five-minute walk for two people in good health, which both were, and the shadows deepened down the canyons. Past a doorman who said, startling Gaskin, "Good evening, Miss Paisley!" into a well-shined, Tudor-style foyer, into an elevator where Gaskin was again startled, in the identical way, by a bald man wearing a dicky and an upturned stiff collar behind a royal blue vest and who exclaimed identically, "Good evening, Miss Paisley," though a little more quietly than the doorman— after all, the latter was an outdoor man—and up, up. The elevator stopped smoothly, they emerged into a tiny space belonging to one apartment only, Paisley rapped three times, the door opened, and standing there were a handsome, gray-haired man and an attractive, gray-haired woman, both well dressed, both smiling pleasantly—paternally, Gaskin thought—upon him, and the smiles even broadening when Paisley said:

"Hank, this is Mums and Daddy."

The next month was a very busy one for Henry Gaskin. He was about as busy as the Secretary General of the U.N. during a crisis amongst the nations, and for a not unlike reason. He was seen to be going out a good deal with Crystal Bidwell. Bidwell and Gaskin! And he still saw a good deal of Paisley. Toward the end of the month, on a Friday the night of which he had another date with her, Paisley was seen to go into Crystal Bidwell's office and there spend quite a long time—behind a closed door. When she emerged she had a dazed, faraway look—dazed *and* happy, ecstatic.

That night over dinner at one of those candly places on West Fourth Street, Paisley, while they were having a dessert of chocolate mousse, reached over, affectionately took his hand, and in that peculiar, particular manner when people have to, if that is the phrase, break news that is a delight to themselves and a misery to the receiver of it, said: "Hank, guess what? I've been assigned to the Paris bureau!"

"You've what!" Gaskin licked a piece of chocolate off his lips. It tasted very good.

"Yes. Crystal told me today. Isn't she wonderful, though? And isn't it great! Isn't it wonderful!"

"She's great and it's wonderful," Gaskin said, looking far away over her shoulder. What he saw there in the candle-glow was the ghostly image of Crystal Bidwell, face touched with a soft and rather wry smile.

"Let's go call Mums and Daddy and celebrate, Hank. Or shall we just celebrate ourselves?"

"Why, which would you prefer?"

She looked very warmly and quite coquettishly at him. She really was a very feminine little thing.

"Ourselves, Hank."

It was very good, with that urgency behind it. In fact Henry Gaskin wondered a bit if he had been too skillful for his own good in mixing the ingredients. No, he thought. It is good. But it is not that good.

And thus it came about that Paisley Fairlamb ceased to be Henry Gaskin's main source of supply. It had been pleasant, and no regrets. On either side. It had been a very close call, for Hank Gaskin, to getting his non-ambition.

12

The Third Beatitude

The most immediately distinctive thing about Alvin Creech, before he had opened his mouth, the first thing to engage the newcomer's eye, was the way the multitude of little piglike hairs curled like a luxuriant bower out through his shirt from his stomach, at which latitude of his body he always had one, often two, and on special occasions as many as three—never more than three—buttons opened. At times he also had one or two open at a lower latitude—he scorned zippers—but always at that of his stomach. Alvin Creech never wore either undershirt or T-shirt, so that there was nothing to impede that lush growth from bursting from his stomach in full flower.

Thus the initial visual stimulus. Where sounds then entered personality the great distinctive thing about Alvin Creech was his belch—or we should say, belches. He belched a very great deal, all day long. They were very interesting sounds, varying as prodigiously in pitch and volume as the myriad instruments of the full New York Philharmonic, and in duration. Quick little piccolo belches, medium-sized French-horn belches, and bass fiddle and percussion belches big, loud and long enough they could be heard through the wall into the next office and halfway down the corridor through his open door. That was a long corridor.

Alvin Creech was an exceptionally fine specimen of a species which insofar as we know has never been well defined and scarcely isolated. This is not strange since the species is very new upon the land. But in its short existence it has had spectacular success.

Alvin Creech was a New York Rustic. Let us have a look at this breed.

It might help to get at it if at the outset we should describe the New York Rustic by contrast.

The run-of-the-mind American youth coming to the great city of New York to make his way, fame, fortune, and who knows, a dyed East Side model or two or even a Greenwich Village amateur whore, swiftly assumes the dress, mannerisms, expressions (both facial and verbal) and attitudes of those around him. He undergoes a metamorphosis as complete as any in the animal kingdom. He soon discards his double-breasted, wide-lapeled, padded-shoulder coat for the single-breasted, three-button, narrow-lapeled, padless-shouldered jacket made famous by the firm of Brooks Brothers, and he commences to call it a jacket instead of a coat. His shirts become of the button-down-collar type. He discards the wide-brimmed hat for the narrow-brimmed one, the wide tie for the narrow one. He stops putting cream and sugar in his coffee and learns rapidly to look down upon all who do. His expressed opinions change in a manner quite wholesale and he embraces the value that the most hallowed experience known to man, more precious than rubies, is the stiletto remark concerning someone and if in his presence at a party more precious than emeralds, and the value that the snide remark is the highest flowering of conversation. Even his accent changes somewhat and particularly his verbal expressions. He begins to say neye-ther instead of nee-ther, and, I haven't the foggiest. This pattern is nothing new. People have always conformed to their environment, always feared more than anything to run against the mob. The only difference here is that the poor deluded fellow thinks of himself as a nonconformist, for in New York conformity consists in whole of a most inflexible noncomformity.

The New York Rustic does none of these things. Quite the contrary. Far from changing his dress to conform to those around him, he cultivates the difference. Far from undertaking to improve his twangy, nasal accent, he emphasizes it. He talks more Southern at cocktail parties in New York than in Georgia, more hillbilly Arkansawan than in Pea Ridge. In fact in Pea Ridge they might have a hard time understanding him.

It hardly needs remarking that all of this tends in one direction alone and is so calculated: to make the New York Rustic stand out from the crowd.

The New York Rustic—who might also accurately be termed the professional rustic—is never a stupid person. That is the fatal mistake more than one operator who considered himself a shrewd judge of character and a deviously clever fellow to boot especially in in-fighting has made shortly before he went down for the count with a rustic stiletto twanging between his shoulder blades. We will set forth as a general proposition here that the New York Rustic—and his breed increases— is the most dangerous and absolutely ruthless back-stabber in all of American business, with a cunning agility that would excite the admiration of the most advanced practitioner of the art on Madison Avenue, and we wish heartily to advise anyone within range of these writings who may have one in his office, not for a single minute, in mortal danger of his very position, to drop his guard around him, to be misled or lulled by the twang and the hillbilly language. In passing, we might observe that one of the more fascinating and curious—and quite often deadly— errors made by the Easterner in general and the New Yorker in particular is that the man from another part of the country with a twang, a drawl, a Southern accent, slow rate of speech, or anything different from his own clipped, frantic and compulsive manner of handling the mother tongue, is somehow a sub-cretin and hardly knows which way is up and which sideways let alone his arse from third base. The enormity of this delusion on the part of the Easterner in general and the New Yorker in particular operates as a fabulous advantage, possibly the greatest, for the man with the drawl, twang or Southern accent from another part of the country. He would not for the world have him think otherwise. But one would think the Easterner or the New Yorker of his own accord would learn. Why they do not we do not know, for personally we do not consider the average Easterner or New Yorker—some of our best friends are Easterners and New Yorkers—inferior in intelligence to people from other parts of the country. Perhaps it is that there is nothing more difficult for the man who feels a superiority which happens to be nonexistent, fanciful and without foundation to learn than that it is nonexistent.

And so, Alvin Creech. He was a very shrewd man and a very intelligent one. Despite the pig's hair, the belches, and even other arresting attributes: He wore a shirt several days and the blackened neckband could be seen from most angles. Creech always had the writer sit by him at his desk while editing his copy. He smoked cigars and there were ashes eternally dribbling over him, shirt or trousers or both. You could instantly you entered his office tell he smoked cigars, even if one was not at the moment in his mouth. The air was filled almost to the gasping point with their pungency, and besides, the Maxwell House coffee can which he used as an ashtray, having long since thrown into the wastebasket the expensive bronze ashtray the magazine provided for editors at this level, customarily contained a dozen or so wet cigar stumps. Creech never bothered to empty the coffee can. When it got full he brought a new one from home. Sometimes he blew, not deliberately of course, cigar smoke into your face—immediately brushing it considerately away, often in your direction. Perhaps due to his cigar consumption Creech cleared his throat a good deal while editing copy, and to save time, for he was an extremely busy man, since he saw and edited every single word that went into the magazine every week, instead of going to the head, which would take time, he spat into his handkerchief —fortunately a large job, for he used imported (from his native state) red bandannas that must have been a yard square. Curiously enough he was very fastidious in some ways, e.g.: He believed very much in keeping the fingernails clean. "If there's anything that disgusts me," Creech had said more than once, usually while cleaning his own nails with his letter opener, "it's to see someone with dirty nails—it's the most loathsome, revolting, disgusting and downright *dirty* sight I know of," he would say—as a hunk of dirt popped out from under his nail onto a piece of copy or a writer's lap. For purposes of dental hygiene he kept a box of toothpicks on his desk and for an hour or so after returning from lunch had one in his hand picking his teeth diligently with it and then expelling with his tongue and upper lip, like a rocket launcher, the morsel of steak, lettuce, Camembert cheese, spaghetti oiled thickly in clam sauce, or, most usually, a sample of his two favorite foods, which were Chinese food and apple pie—the latter he always took with *both* a slice of cheese and two dips of ice cream, for he was a tremendous Eater— either out on the desk, where it was usually though not always, if it were an exceptionally large find, invisible in the pile of papers, or, swiveling in his chair, into the wastebasket or sometimes vaguely toward the writer sitting by him—not deliberately, of course.

Some people felt that Alvin Creech was a slob. It is a harsh word. We don't like the word. We hate to use the word because to us the Slob is the horror of our times. The professional hillbilly. We never would use it except that Alvin Creech used it about himself. Frequently, and what is more, with the keenest pride.

"I," how often have I heard him say, "am a slob. Uppercase that S. I am a Slob. And I am proud of it." He then gave a long belch before continuing. "Guess I just wasn't brought up ay-feat. Guess I'm jes' stuck with what I am. I am what I am and that's what I yam," he would say humorously. "No opportunity to go to Hay-vard, or one of those places. Guess I'm just a slob, like a hundred million other good Americans."

Alvin actually knew grammar and syntax as well as Fowler and practiced them with first-rate craftsmanship in his editing. Speaking, however, was sometimes a different matter. He was a walking lexicon of hillbilly phonetics. He said things like "I'll be gol-danged if I know," "I reckon," "not enough to wad a shotgun," "You ain't a wolfin," "I swan," and "tarnation." One would have thought he had arrived yesterday from his native state. To which, in point of fact, he had not been back in the fifteen years since coming to work for *Vital*.

He had a fat belly, a fat face and fat porcine lips, and bore an actual physical resemblance to a pig, or rather a hog. The comparison would not have offended him. On the contrary he was very proud of his nickname "Razorback." Was it not the nickname of his state? A razorback, for the edification of such of our readers as may not have had the opportunity of being brought up on the farm, as was Alvin Creech, is a very distinctive species of hog. However, you never want to stand in the way of one when he is about to charge. They do charge. Creech was proud of anything that emphasized his rustic air. Indeed he had turned his origins to great value. He added unmistakable distinction to the *Vital* office and no one who had ever known him even briefly ever forgot him.

But what made Razorback Creech into a real man of distinction was the fusion of his rustic traits with his British background gained from a tour in the London bureau. Mixed in with his hillbilly phrases were such Britishisms as "chap," "bloody," "ruddy" and "I say." It sounded pretty curious sometimes, the combination. In addition, all of Creech's clothes were British. Good Savile Row British. From their creaselessness and bagginess and their stains of various sizes they looked as if they were treated to a visit to the dry cleaners about once every six months: but they were British. He wore a British homburg that had cost him $100 U. S. and that had not been cleaned and blocked in the five years he had had it: but it was unmistakably British. His shoes may never have been shined: but they were without any hesitation British. His general appearance and personal habits packaged into the clothes from Savile Row made for a combination that it took longer than five minutes to forget.

The copy editor was not a bad guy. We should hate for our readers to gain that impression. He did ride close herd on the writers. However, it must be said that his was an extremely tough, trying and responsible job, seeing every word that went into the magazine, and it is never pleasant to have to deal with writers, who have such warped points of view about their own work. No one, even those who were not wildly fond of him—and it must be said in fairness to Creech that the majority of these were writers, and we have yet to find a writer who considers his editor anything but a horned fiend devoted to mutilating the texture and singing, surging quality of his writing at every turn—ever questioned Razorback Creech's professional abilities. He was an enormously able copy editor. It was a job both highly skilled and highly responsible and he could not have held it for a day without being very very good.

No. As we see it there was only one valid failing Creech had. This was that he mistook gentleness in a man for weakness; that he interpreted the least evidence of sensitivity in a person as softness. It was very curious that Razorback Creech, being such a shrewd man, should make a mistake in that area of judgment, of all areas. Curious—and ironic. For one of the writers was a man named James Bernstein. James Bernstein was not merely gentle. He could easily have been the man the Lord Jesus Christ had in mind when He spoke the Third Beatitude.

The world can be divided broadly into two groups of men: the personality projectors—those who throw their personalities around, bouncing them like a squash ball off the various walls of any room they happen to be in; and the quiet men. James Bernstein was one of the quiet men.

James Bernstein was an egghead. He was a sensitive man, and a gentle one. His feelings were not violent on many subjects. All that James Bernstein asked of the world was the one thing which the world will never give anybody, which was to be left alone. Despite the absence of this gift he made out all right, for he had great self-sufficiency, and was not bored if things were not hopping all the time, being able to find other things within himself. He had never done any harm to anyone in his life, certainly never any intentional harm.

To say he was one of the quiet men is not to say he was a dull man. The two are not the same at all. Actually he was very pleasant company, one of the few extant any more with whom one could carry on a conversation instead of a battle of monologues. It was just that Bernstein would not compete for the floor—not that he resented it in the slightest when someone wanted to do all the talking. However, if someone wanted to converse rather than to establish petty conversational triumphs, Bernstein was a very pleasant man to have lunch with or to drop by his office and kill off an hour's time.

He was an almost unbelievably well-read man, without throwing this around either. You could know him for years and never know this fact about him unless you happened to get started talking about books. Bernstein never started any such conversation himself. He did not drop the names of Baudelaire, Rimbaud, Stendhal and La Rochefoucauld into the conversation, as the egghead generally does in the way others drop names of famous Hollywood stars or big New York names. But if you got to know him and got to talking about books, it soon began to dawn upon you that there was almost nothing James Bernstein had not read. Unbeknownst to Bernstein, Hank Gaskin once bet a tutor from St. John's College (the Annapolis one), whom he had met through Jason Hightower—who had mentioned casually to Gaskin the man's reputation for being remarkably learned—that he could not bring up any historical subject, any book that had ever been written, any system of philosophy, any poet, composer, author, scientist whom or which Bernstein was not familiar with and could discuss intelligently. The professor tried for an hour, in a supposedly casual visit to Bernstein's office with Gaskin. The next day Gaskin, never being entirely sure how Bernstein would take the matter of the bet, dropped by his office and tried to give him half of his winnings.

"After all you earned at least half of it," Gaskin said.

Bernstein was quietly amused by the bet and not at all vain about it. He was, in fact, not vain about anything. But he politely declined the fifty.

"It's good of you, Hank," he said, "and very generous. But I never think of knowledge as something to make a profit on. If I happen to have a certain assorted amount of it, anybody could have, except that I have happened all my life to read quite a bit. Thanks, however, for the offer. That was an interesting chap you brought by here."

Gaskin ordered a book for which he paid fifty dollars and a few days later, after the rare-books store had found it, he left the copy of the 1620 edition of Pindar, with the emblem of the Prince de Conde on the binding, on Bernstein's desk. That Bernstein accepted, considering it a very sweet thing to do on Gaskin's part.

For he was a sweet man himself. There are not many men in this world one would use the word "sweet" to describe; indeed the word has even gone out of fashion as pertains to women, who nowadays would probably resent it applied to themselves. But James Bernstein was one of them. None of this was in self-consciousness. He did not out of any moral reasons go about his day or the life he lived, never in his life had said to himself, "I will not be evil," "I will not be calculating." It was just that these qualities would have shaped up to him as being a little silly, as depriving man of life rather than enhancing it, and as being no way civilized human beings should behave one toward the other. In short, he considered the human being inviolate: No one is to try to do anything *to* someone else. *Nobody* is to try to do *anything* to *anybody:* That would have been Bernstein's coat-of-arms had he had one.

Professionally James Bernstein had reached as far as he ever intended to, counted on, or probably could go in life, which was a "writer" on *Vital* magazine. He was as competent as the next practitioner of this decidedly specialized, skilled and rather curious art, and a good deal more so than most. He had been doing it for about ten years now, in various departments of the magazine, at the moment National Affairs.

He had not inherited much of the earth. He did have two acres in Westport, where he lived with a wife who was also a gentle woman. They had two children, a girl six and a boy eight. The children were very fond of their father, who seemed to them to understand their world much better than anyone else they knew, including other children.

In physical size, appearance, and indeed general approach to life, James Bernstein was as keen an antithesis to Razorback Creech as one could imagine. Bernstein was a small man, small-boned, running to decided thinness, five feet five and a half inches, usually carrying no more than one hundred thirty pounds. He was a neat man, and "considerate" would have been another adjective to apply to him. James Bernstein never snapped at a researcher—he took the rather unusual point of view that they were always doing the best they could; never joined in a sprint to get a just-vacated seat in a commuter train; never jostled anyone aside at a busy store counter. As a result it took him longer to buy something than almost anyone else; he stood more than was normal in commuter trains; and occasionally researchers were a little lax when working with him. James Bernstein was aware of all these things but he did not consider their lack important, or the gaining of them worth the price. And as for the researchers, any laxness on the part of some was more than compensated for by the extra hard work, extra digging other researchers would do without being asked to for Bernstein in appreciation of a writer who did not shout at them and of a man who did not try to beat them down simply because they were of a different sex from his.

To some James Bernstein may have appeared a bland person. To this we say: One should always ask: What kind of people are these bland people inside? The bland person, so appearing, all of his real life being inside him, perhaps there are worlds there which would arrest and surprise him who would explore.

One further comment: The feelings of James Bernstein were not terribly attitudinized on many subjects: But one of these was boorishness, which he disliked in any form.

One of the most interesting of all aspects in the evaluation of character is the interpretation a good many people in this world place upon gentleness in a person. We speak of the interpretation which identifies gentleness as synonymous with softness. It is perhaps the greatest single mistake of all mistakes made in character judgment. What makes the mistake interesting is the almost-hundred-percent wrongness of it. With very few exceptions gentleness in a person, and especially in a man, is the clearest barometer in the world to a person of true inner, good toughness. A moment's thought on the part of anyone would reveal the obviousness of such a correlation. It is only the bully who has to shout and bluster, to push people around, from the very reason that he has no inner toughness, no true fiber of his own, and the bullyness, the bluster, the pushing are but substitutes for this lack. He who has true inner toughness feels no need to bully, swagger or raise his voice, or to push people around. One would think that after all these thousands of years people would learn this. If not from their own experience, from history, whose strongest figures are gentle men. From Jesus Christ to Albert Schweitzer this has been so, and no one would think to call Jesus weak or Schweitzer soft. In fact each had/has more true manhood in his little finger than all the bullies, all the blusterers, all the pushers-arounders, all the run-over-other-people specialists who have ever defiled the sweet earth: The earth which would be sweet without them.

Still, men—and very intelligent men otherwise too—persist in mistaking gentleness in a man for weakness. And where they see the gentle man, getting out their cleavers to let him have it. It is an awful mistake. Many a bully has learned it too late, to the point, some of them, of paying quite unexpectedly with their lives for the lesson.

The Lord, we repeat, must have had James Bernstein in mind when He spoke the Third Beatitude. The only trouble was that thus far, at any rate, James Bernstein had not inherited much of the earth, although he had certainly lived up to his part of the beatitude if the Lord had not —thus far—to His. Sometimes the Lord takes a little while to live up to His. You cannot rush the Lord.

If we may speak of an attitude in such a personified way, Creech's toward James Bernstein had been going on for some time now, and fur-

thermore it had become increasingly intensified. Without getting technical to a point that may bore the reader, we wish to say that there were
dozens of little ways in which Creech, in his own rustically Svengalian
manner, could accomplish this purpose with no one except himself and
the victim of it ever being aware of what he was doing. He could, for
instance, make a writer rewrite a caption, a textblock or a head more
times than were necessary if the purpose were only to get the best caption, textblock or head. These were rewritten such a great deal at *Vital*
anyhow—a writer had been known to spend half a day on a two-line
caption and most of a night on a three-line, sixteen-character head before the copy editor was satisfied—that it would have been difficult to
prove that in the instance of a given writer Creech was making him do
more of it than was demanded by solely professional considerations.
There were numerous other subtle weapons available to Creech, such as
the order in which he edited turned-in copy and thus the time when a
given writer got to go home—the copy editor could regulate and vary
this by hours. Even normally copy was not necessarily edited in the
order in which it was handed in: a certain section of the magazine going to press earlier, Creech might naturally edit the copy for that sooner
than copy which was handed in earlier for a section which was going to
press later. The copy editor had many subtle weapons. And yet when it
began to happen toward him, a writer knew it, whereas other editors
and even other writers would probably not even have the slightest suspicion of it. All this called for a master of the little tyranny.

It had gone on for weeks now. Motivation? Well, none other, actually,
than that suggested above: Creech's conviction that the man, being
gentle, was weak, soft, and hence a natural object for the instinct in him
which had to be given exercise every now and then, the instinct and almost irresistible need, in Creech's case—even the devil has his needs,
one of them having been to tempt Eve to tempt Adam and so start all this
—to bully someone, to push someone around.

Thus it came to pass that James Bernstein found himself spending
unusually long sessions sitting in the chair alongside Creech's desk
while Creech slashed away at his copy, which by that time had probably
already been rewritten three times anyhow.

"Nah! Nah, Jamesey," Creech said one day, gripping a pencil. Little
belch. "Tarnation! This ain't *a*-tall what I-yuh told ya." Medium-sized
belch. "Now let us give just one more bloody try to get across what I
mean."

Creech belched. The Long Belch, beginning deep in his stomach and
bursting over Bernstein on its way down the corridor. Aarpp—ppp-ppp-
p-pp-ppp-ppppp-pppp-up!

"Ya see here. This here is cryptic," said Creech, using one of his
favorite criticisms.

Creech slashed out a line and wrote in something else.

"It's also in the wrong place. It don't march forward in orderly sequence. I hope you know what I-yuh mean. The bloody thing don't track," he said, using another favorite criticism.

He drew a heavy red circle around the corrected sentence and then a long and heavy, waveringly vertical line transposing it to the next paragraph. Sitting back the copy editor regarded the mutilated copy. He got out a toothpick from the box on his desk and started picking at his teeth.

"I'll be gol-danged, I-yuh just don't seem to be able to make myself clear to you, Jamesey. Yore copy sure seems to be getting mighty cryptic lately."

He leaned back in his chair, and lit up a cigar.

"You don't smoke cigars, do you, Jamesey?" Creech said, sending a stream of heavy cigar smoke toward Bernstein. He made the motion of fanning it away. "Didn't mean to blind you. I-yuh reckon I-yuh couldn't see you for a moment there."

He leaned deeper. Bernstein could see the pig's hair curling out of his stomach. Then, leaning forward, Creech slashed at the copy yet some more. It was not long before it was unrecognizable.

"Take this back and run it through yore typewriter again, Jamesey boy," Creech said—it was the fourth time. He belched. "And oh, Jamesey. Drop this by the copy room on yore way, will you? Give you a little ruddy exercise."

Bernstein took his own copy and the other copy, went by the copy room to leave the latter and took the former back to his own office. His office, being on the east side of the building, did not have as spectacular a view as those on the south—looking out over the soaring midtown skyline; or those on the west—looking out over Times Square, the Hudson River, and especially on the great ships coming and going to the far-away, beckoning places of the earth. But it did have an arresting view straight downward, of Fifth Avenue and the coursing crowds. Bernstein, leaning a little out, stood watching the specks moving up and down the avenue. From here the eternal hurry was not so apparent, only dark, tiny objects which must be alive since they were in motion, an almost swaying, hypnotizing motion. It was three o'clock. It was at that exact moment that James Bernstein, looking far down, admitted it all into his mind.

He admitted into his mind the intelligence that Alvin Creech had decided to do things to him. This had really never happened before to Bernstein and for a while he simply stood there and with full calm examined the fact and in particular examined the type of mental operation that would be behind it. He was not naïve. But he did not like to think of his fellow human beings as having such natures, such motivations. He would go an awfully long time before admitting even to himself the fact of such qualities in a given person.

He turned from the window and went out into the corridor and got a Coke from the machine and walked around the corridors drinking it. He took his time at this, then returned to his office, stuck a piece of copy paper into his typewriter and rewrote the textblock in line with the suggestions—if you could call them that—Creech had made. Finishing it he pulled it out of the typewriter, stood up and had started out of his office to take it down to Creech's office, when the phone rang. He hesitated. Then he stepped back and picked it up.

"Bernstein, whenerya gonna get that bloody copy down here?" The voice was not hard. "Whater ya doin' with it, eatin' it? I thought I showed you pretty clearly what you should do. We're putting out a magazine this ruddy week as well as next week, and the next and the next, ya know."

Bernstein waited a moment before speaking quietly. "I was having a Coke," he said. "I'm coming down now."

Two clicks—a heavy and a normal one—were heard on the line.

He strolled with the copy down to Creech's office. He laid it on the desk and turned to go.

"Where ya goin', James? Don't ya like my company?" Belch. "Sit down while I-yuh have a look at yore bloody composition."

Bernstein took the seat by Creech's desk.

Alvin Creech, holding his cigar in one hand and the copy in the other, leaned back deep in his chair to read it. He read very slowly, puffing out great billows of cigar smoke in the general direction of Bernstein. Then he started shaking his head.

"Naw, naw, *naw*. I swan, this ain't what I-yuh tol' you *a*-tall. Whilickers, Bernstein!" Belch. "Don't you understand bloody English? When I tol' ya that . . ."

Bernstein stopped listening to the twangy voice, which rolled on, and he did not look at the porcine face. Bernstein's eyes looked at only one thing.

They looked, as if magnetized there, at the great bower of curling pig's hair growing out of Creech's fat belly—never more so than in the position he now sat, tipped back deep in his chair and with three buttons of his shirt open at navel-level.

". . . ain't it *a*-tall," the twang was saying. Belch. Belch. And now the great Long Belch rolling upward—Bernstein could see the movements like heavy sea waves of the folds of flesh around Creech's belly —and then bursting profoundly, Aarppppp—pppppp-p-p-ppp-pppp-ppppp-ppppp-pppp-up! "Bernstein, ya oughta know better'n this by now. Gol-dang it, this ain't even *near* what I had in mind, what I-yuh *tol'* ya as plain as anything, even *wrote* for ya . . ."

The writer's hand shot out. It was an electric movement. And it was followed immediately by the most terrified and terrifying scream those corridors had ever heard. It sounded like someone having his fingernails pulled.

"Let go of me!" the voice screamed in terror, and in faultless English. "Please . . . let . . . go!"

Bernstein had a bulldog's grip, a whole lavish fistful of that bellyhair. We have never experienced it and so are only guessing, but we would imagine that one of the most painful experiences that a man can undergo, is to have a great clump of hair, pulled with violent strength— and without anesthetic—from his belly by someone who will not let go but is pulling him onward and upward only by those hairs. We are only imagining this, but the terror-stricken screams which erupted from Creech would seem to suggest that we are imagining fairly accurately.

He screamed and he screamed. For indeed Bernstein was literally holding the fat torso of the copy editor up by the handle of his stomach-hair. And Razorback Creech was grunting like a pig and screaming like a stuck one. When at last Bernstein let go, Creech fell back in his chair in collapse, like a man who has just undergone some extreme traumatic shock. The writer stood a moment over the panting porcine form of the editor. A form which was grasping its belly with both hands and moaning quite horribly. He spoke quietly:

"Creech, I have used up both cheeks where you are concerned. Let me therefore apprise you: Don't ever again push me around just to be pushing me around."

And, having committed the sole act of violence of his life, James Bernstein turned and walked quietly out.

After that Razorback Creech and James Bernstein got along fine. Bernstein returned, from this lone detour, to being gentle—with everybody, including Razorback Creech. And never again did Creech try to push James Bernstein around. He should have been grateful to Bernstein, for he had taught him—at the cost, to be sure, of a certain amount of physical stress, but after all one of comparatively brief duration—an enormously valuable lesson if he could only apply it in general.

Men make the mistake and nations make it. At this stage of man's moral evolution they are mortally incapable of assimilating what is called by the name of the general principle, this one to wit being:

Never mistake gentleness for softness.

The incident also proved it was just as Our Lord said in the Third Beatitude, especially with a slight, reverent addition to it, reading as follows:

"Blessed are the meek: for they shall inherit the earth. Sometimes they inherit more of it if they give the Lord a slight assist."

Matthew 5:5. King James (Bernstein) Version.

13

The Seasoning of Jason Hightower: Vinegar

All of the photographers on *Vital* magazine were men of extraordinary talent. A *Vital* photographer was as distinctive from the common garden variety of newspaper photographer as is the designer of sets for a Broadway show from a house painter. But there was one *Vital* photographer who held a distinction possessed by none of the others. She was a woman.

Vital was in no sense prejudiced in the matter of hiring women photographers. Its only standard was the Greek one of excellence. But for some reason or other there have not been many really great women photographers. Probably no more than three or four since the camera started. This is strange considering the enormously revolutionary consequences of the camera—the effect of motion pictures, for example, on the daily lives of the masses, and even more, of the television screen, these two alone, and *Vital* magazine might honorably be added to this list, fairly determining the clothes we wear, the cars we drive, the food we put into our mouths, even the values we hold and the thoughts we think—and women having this admirable tendency to want to have their oar in in anything revolutionary. As to why women have been so shy of the profession of photography the writer will leave to someone working on his doctor's dissertation at some place like, say, the Stanford University School of Journalism. In any event, nothing could testify more to Georgia Dewey's high professional ability than the fact that she was the only woman photographer on the staff of *Vital* magazine. She was not hired because she was a woman. She was hired because she was very good.

It was not Georgia Dewey's only distinction. Besides being *Vital's* only woman photographer she was also its most aggressive one. She was spectacularly single-minded. Nothing was of any importance whatsoever to her in life except the picture, and she would go to any lengths to get it. She never failed to deliver. When Georgia Dewey was assigned by *Vital* to cover an event, she almost completely took the event over to the point it sometimes seemed the event was taking place not for its own sake but merely as a vehicle for the operation of her camera. She did not merely penetrate, or surround, the story. She devoured it. She left her subjects almost in a state of nervous collapse. If it was an essay "in depth" on a wedding, which the magazine decided to do once, Georgia stayed so close to the couple with her camera as to show everything short of the wedlock's consummation and left the newly-weds almost ready for the divorce courts. Once her coverage of a Harvard commencement almost disrupted those customarily awe-inspiring ceremonies. In full view of several thousand people Georgia dashed up and down the aisleways in Harvard Yard, popped up like a jack-in-the-box now behind now in front of the distinguished commencement speaker during his gallant, and not very successful, attempt to deliver his address over her opposition (she almost completely obliterated the poor man from the audience's view during the climax of his speech, with the result that something he had long meant to be ringing and possibly historic was entirely lost), and in general so actively shot the ceremonies that she became their central figure, the myriad graduates, their mothers, wives, sweethearts, uncles, aunts and cousins being unable to keep their attention on anything except Georgia's incessant revolutions over the ivy-clad and hallowed Yard. The powers of Harvard were so upset that afterward that university's president wrote the editor-in-chief of *Vital* the only letter of its kind this tolerant man had ever felt compelled to dispatch—a hot, official protest at "the performance, and I use this word in the theatrical sense, of *Vital*'s photographer at the solemn ceremony of commencement, which this young lady for the first time in the more than 300 years of this notable event at this institution single-handedly came close to turning into a Roman carnival." The letter shot Georgia's standing with *Vital*'s editors even higher. It demonstrated once again to them her unquenchable initiative.

Nothing was sacred to Georgia Dewey when it came to getting the picture. Nobody, in her view, had any right to hide anything. The concept of privacy of any kind she viewed as undemocratic and vestigial of feudal, that is, pre-camera, times. She considered that her 35-millimeter camera had the right of entry anywhere on earth. Perhaps due to this assumption, it came very close to having it anywhere. She had photographed settings where no camera had ever previously been allowed: the inside of an insane asylum (the director of which was later fired for allowing the pictures); the private living quarters of one of the royal houses of Europe, where no commoner much less a Leica had ever before set foot; the first pictures of a new bomber, which she brainwashed the Air Force into letting her take; the first pictures of life inside the monastery of an occult religious order, where previously neither woman nor photographer had ever trespassed. Georgia stopped at nothing to get the picture and she oftentimes got pictures other photographers, even *Vital* photographers, could not get. This did not make her popular with the other photographers. To be explicit, most of them loathed her. She did not care the slightest. Quite often other photographers were infuriated at her. She took their fury as a compliment. Once she had been assigned to the same bureau as Montgomery Shanks. At one point during their tours of duty there, the picture editor dropped Shanks, who was an extremely good photographer, a mild note from New York suggesting that Georgia seemed to be getting better pictures than Shanks. Shanks was so livid he could hardly speak. He could write, however—or wire. He fired back to the picture editor a cable which stated:

RE YOUR LETTER. GEORGIA POSSESSES A PIECE OF EQUIPMENT I DO NOT. SHANKS.

The implications of this charge were not wholly spiteful. Granted that Georgia had great initiative anyhow. But the power differential between great initiative and the piece of equipment to which Shanks referred can be of great magnitude indeed, the latter being frequently sufficient to obtain a picture that great initiative alone could never hope to obtain, men being what they are. To come to the point here and say forthrightly what it might take two pages to say roundabout, Georgia Dewey was not beyond hitting the sack with someone to get a picture. An Air Force major general, the governor of a Western state, the president of a fairly large corporation and a select number of other figures of comparable rank had received Georgia's reward for getting her in to take pictures customarily forbidden but which it was in their power to allow. Lest one, from this, abstract a misleading picture of Georgia's character, it should be stated hastily that Georgia never made any crass, articulated deals of this kind. But there are other ways besides crassness for passing a worthwhile message along. A woman has eyes which by a glance here, and a body which by a gesture there, can provide all the articulation required. There was one more fact: Georgia had never distributed her reward to any except those of the ranks, or comparable ranks, mentioned above—general, governor, corporation president. There is one fact more: She had never, not once in her life, gone to bed with any man without having a definite photographic purpose in mind. Georgia Dewey was a woman of enormous single-mindedness.

Georgia Dewey was young considering her professional attainments. She was twenty-eight. She had about her a decided air, of carriage and of complete self-assuredness. Her face was overlaid with a kind of permanent warning system, an alert expression which suggested she could take care of herself whatever the situation, that no one was going to slip up on her and had best not try. It was a rather full face, on the sensual side, with full lips, a face not pretty but exotically arresting and even exciting and with a wondrous, smooth, light olive complexion. Her brown hair had strands of blond in it—natural, not dyed. Her features were regular, with a small nose slightly upturned. She was five feet three and three-fourths inches tall and just verging on plumpness, which she had taken to treating by an hour's hard and expensive exercise each day in one of those New York sweatshops dedicated to keeping the female body within bounds. She considered this daily hour a professional investment and as a matter of fact deducted it on her income tax return. She spent a great deal of money on clothes. She considered them a professional investment as well. She had the taste of a couturier, and even on Fifth Avenue women—women, not just men—would turn to look at this beautifully dressed woman, and, for a moment before passing on into the throng, speculate as to who she was. She was as turned out as if a personal maid worked over her two hours every morning.

It was curious that with her rather exotic looks and her style, there seemed something just faintly gross about her. It was perhaps not so curious that this quality enhanced the excitement men felt around her. Perhaps they felt it offered promise; they were mistaken. When one was seated across from her, in conversation, from time to time one got a glimpse of her thighs, which had the olive smoothness of her face. One had the feeling the glimpse was deliberately allowed. Indeed there seemed not a thing Georgia did of which she was not always, every instant, entirely aware—no move made, no word said, out of the unthinking impulse. This awareness, with the self-sufficiency and discipline it implied, the knowing exactly what she wanted and what she was doing, was unbreachable. If they were real, she had very firm, molded breasts. In the exquisite sweaters and dresses she wore they always stood out, each very clearly, and independently, defined. There was not a man on *Vital* magazine who could have said whether or not they were real, though the amount of speculation may be imagined. Many had tried but none had been allowed—there was no one on *Vital* magazine, after all, who could get her in to take a picture. All in all, Georgia Dewey was a woman who induced in any man who was around her very long an almost senseless rage—but that specific, very rare kind of male rage that incites in the man the desire to rape. Not just to go to bed, but, literally, to rape, to brutalize, to breach the unbreachable and set it screaming in ecstasy, in pain and above all in surrender. She had inspired this emotion in a number of men who were customarily very mild creatures, had never before known such an emotion, and were shocked to find themselves capable of it.

Thus *Vital*'s only woman photographer.

Along about April, the editors of *Vital* felt challenged to do a picture essay "in depth," a favored phrase around the magazine, on a powerful force which was at work in the land: the congressional investigating committee. Two or three of these committees had leapt into a sensational prominence, such as at times to infect a third of the nation to sit the day long in front of its television sets watching the committee in session, in an almost hypnotic fascination and an audience-size hitherto reserved for more important events such as the World Series or a heavyweight championship match. The problems involved in doing the story were very formidable. The workings of the committee were not at all picturable, the usual test for whether a story was to be done. Men sitting around tables seldom are. The public sessions themselves were, of course, spirited and therefore picturable. But all of America was seeing these daily on its television screens. In line with the legend on its masthead, "An eye seeing the world from *inside*," the magazine wished to get something Americans had not seen; it wished to show what a congressional committee actually was, what put it together, its *inner* workings. It was one of those stories so important, since so much in the news, that it had to be done, its absence of picturability somehow overcome. It was a prize but extremely difficult assignment. It would require great imagination and aggressiveness on the part of the photographer. Georgia Dewey was assigned.

For a researcher to complete the team, Georgia Dewey would ordinarily have been given one from *Vital*'s Washington bureau. As it happened, two members of the bureau were in the throes of some kind of virus, and the remaining members were almost inundated just in handling the regular and always increasing, in these times, Washington coverage. Therefore it became necessary to assign a researcher from New York. Jason Hightower was assigned, partly because Crystal Bidwell had tentatively in mind assigning him to a regular tour of duty in the Washington bureau before long and wished first to test him out in those pastures. "Anyhow he needs seasoning," Bidwell told herself— "seasoning" being another favored phrase at the magazine as applied by the editors to what the researchers needed. "A political story should help season Hightower." Partly he was assigned because Georgia Dewey enjoyed the reputation among the researchers as going away the most difficult photographer on the staff to work with—a signal accolade, considering the divalike aspects of many of her colleagues, and the researchers dreaded being sent out with her. "Hightower wants taking in hand," Bidwell told herself.

"Jason," Crystal told him sweetly in her office, "I have a great swatch of news for you. You're going to get a very wonderful assignment—a story that will take almost a full month in Washington. Aren't you pleased?"

Jason really was. He had always felt a man should take a good look at Washington sometime as part of his general education. He had never felt this so strongly that he wished to finance the education himself. With the company footing the tuition, however, an entirely different complexion was cast on the matter.

"Why, that's fine, Crystal," he said. "I appreciate your thinking of old Jason." He was quite surprised that she had. He had never regarded Bidwell as one of his friends in court around here. The thought filtered through his mind that in all fairness he would have to slightly reassess the bitch.

"I thought you'd like it," Bidwell said sweetly. "It's a very choice assignment."

"Indeed it sounds like it," Jason said expansively. "By the way, what is the assignment?"

Crystal explained it. "I should warn you that it's a very difficult assignment. It's to do a full-scale essay on a congressional committee—in depth. With a capital D. This will really take you behind the scenes in Washington, Jason."

"That's delightful," Jason said, warming to the bitch. "I've always wanted to discover first-hand if senators and congressmen are as cretinish as everyone claims they are. It doesn't seem possible since the Republic still stands, and I'm inclined to think it's all propaganda, whose, I haven't the slightest. Probably novelists and playwrights. It's always popular to beat a congressman about the head. It's part of the price the public extracts for the privilege of serving them. Well, well. Who's the photographer?"

"Georgia Dewey," Bidwell said sweetly.

"Georgia Dewey!" Jason let out an abrupt shout. "That fat-assed shrew?"

Crystal smiled sweetly. "Now, Jason. *Quel* ungallant."

"Ungallant!" Jason exclaimed. He had already decided not to reassess Bidwell at all. "Why, that pedigreed shrew wouldn't recognize gallantry if you rubbed her nose in it. Jesus Christ in jeans, Crystal. What have I done to deserve being assigned to a month with that bitch?"

Bidwell gave the sweet smile which reflected her intensive enjoyment of these attacks on her fellow female. "Now, Jason," she said. "Georgia is a very good photographer. She may be just a trifle difficult at times . . ."

"A trifle difficult!" Jason exclaimed. "My God, what an understatement that one is. Why, she thinks a researcher is her personal lackey. I mean, more than most photographers around here do. She thinks a researcher is supposed to kiss her ass three times a day and twice before breakfast."

Crystal gave a sweet, immaculate smile. "Now, Jason. I think if you take the right attitude you can learn a lot from Georgia. It should be good discipline for you."

"Discipline!" Jason exclaimed. "Discipline for being a galley slave. That's all the discipline you can learn from Georgia Dewey."

Crystal gave a deliberate sigh. "Well, Jason, I think you know me well enough to know I never force anyone to take an assignment. That would be rather silly, wouldn't it? But I feel I should remind you that this is an unusually important assignment. I don't want to scare you but. The editors consider it one of the more major stories we've done in a long time. It is also, as I've said, a very difficult assignment. Considering all this, it means something that we've tapped you for it. It reflects our faith in your potential. You have much to gain if the story turns out well. And, I don't wish to scare you but: To be perfectly fair with you I should add, much to lose if you should fall down on it. Of course you won't do anything of the sort," Crystal interpolated with the smile a schoolteacher might aim at a hardened pupil.

She paused for breath then continued. "Besides this, the assignment should be a great education for you. It should provide excellent seasoning—with a capital S. With the government so important in things these days, a spot of Washington is almost *de rigueur* for any reporter. Now that I've got through all that windup," Crystal said, smiling instantly again, "I will say that you can turn the assignment down if you wish. I'll have no *personal* recriminations against you. However, I feel I should tell you that it won't enhance your chances of a regular bureau assignment if you turn down a month's tour in one. It shows, well—shall we say, lack of initiative? And, Jason. There's something else. This is a picture magazine after all. The photographer is the heart of this magazine. For a researcher to turn down an assignment because he isn't personally overjoyed in the company of some particular photographer . . . well, it doesn't show quite, shall we say—the right spirit. Do you think, Jason?"

"Not often enough," Jason said. "But I am right now. Even if the photographer is Georgia Dewey?"

"Even if it's Georgia Dewey," Crystal said briskly. "After all, Jason, *Aucun chemin de fleurs ne conduit à la gloire.* That's a French saying meaning, 'No flowery road leads to glory.' "

"None does here certainly," Jason grumbled. "All right then. I'll go to Washington with the fat-assed bitch."

"And, Jason."

"Hunh?"

"Jason," Crystal said sweetly. She had a very sweet and feminine voice. "It isn't all that fat. Now you'd better draw some expense account money. *Toujours gai.*"

Jason and Georgia Dewey flew down to Washington the next day. Georgia had 484 pounds of excess baggage in twenty pieces, half photographic and half clothing equipment. Jason hauled it from the building to the three taxis he had hailed while she stood over him, as though keeping a suspicious eye on a redcap whose honesty or carefulness she didn't trust, to make sure all of it got in. At La Guardia three pro-

fessional porters handled it. Georgia left it to Jason to finance the tip-
ping and the eighteen-dollar taxi fare out. When they got in the plane
she took the seat by the window and sat silently until the plane was
aloft.

"Do you mind if we don't talk going down?" she said the moment
the seat-belt, no-smoking sign went off. "I'm extremely tired. I want to
sleep. And I want to think about a concept for the story."

"At the same time? That's fine with me," Jason said, lighting a cigarette. "I've always got a few concepts I can think about myself."

"Do you mind not smoking?"

"What was that?" Jason jerked around.

"I'm extremely allergic to cigarette smoke."

"Oh. Is that so?" Jason said. He took one last deep drag, then ground
the freshly lighted cigarette out savagely in the arm ashtray.

She turned her face toward the window. Most of the way down, her
eyes were closed. Jason doubted if she was sleeping. He had first noticed when he was about ten years old that when people were really
sleeping their mouths were open a little, they made little grunting noises,
little globules of saliva collected in the corners of their mouths, something unromantic of the sort. No one slept like Dewey was pretending
to sleep here. Her mouth closed just so, that fairy-princess-in-repose
expression, and the most delicate little swells of those sharply etched,
cashmere-capped twin peaks. He was glad when the plane landed. He
was a little nervous, probably from having to give up the smoking habit
so unexpectedly.

Three rooms had been reserved for them in the Mayflower Hotel in
Washington. One room for Georgia, one for Jason, and one for Georgia's extra equipment. They checked into the hotel shortly before dinner, their piled-up baggage in the lobby looking like the equipage for
a large conducted tour of the continent. It took four bellhops and a
half-hour to get them and the equipment checked into their rooms on
the eleventh floor. Although all the luggage except one suitcase was
hers, Georgia made no move to tip the bellboys who were standing
there shuffling their feet, not quite holding their hands out. Finally
Jason angrily took out a ten-dollar bill and tossed it among them like
a piece of red meat to a pack of bird dogs.

"Fight over it," he said savagely.

When the squad of bellboys had departed, Georgia turned to Jason.
"Oh . . . what is your first name again? I'm sorry, I keep forgetting."

"Oh, I understand," Jason said. "I've been used to that all my life,
don't give it another thought. It's a very, very difficult name to remember. It's almost impossible to pronounce and there are probably not
more than two other persons in the world with the same name. Jason."

"Oh, yes. Jason. Jason, do you mind if we don't have dinner together this evening? I'm rather tired and I want to concentrate on this

story. It's a very difficult story and I want to spend the evening alone with it. I want to try to get the concept of it. I think I'll just have some chicken sandwiches in. Do you mind awfully?"

"Mind awfully?" Jason said. "Why, I'm shaken. Shaken, I always say. No, seriously, that's fine. I happen to have a date with the first secretary of the Soviet Embassy."

Georgia looked very closely at Jason. "You do like to try to be funny, don't you? Good night, Jason."

"Sweet concepts," Jason said, bowing out.

The first thing he did when he got into his room was to have two cigarettes. He was dying for both of them. My God, he thought, it's going to be appalling in itself just not to be able to smoke around her for a month. He took a shower and went out and started walking down Connecticut Avenue. It was a fine spring night and he walked all the way, asking directions a couple of times. It was the first thing he wanted to see in Washington. If he had a hero, it was this one. Walking up the steps he could see the great brooding figure above him. He went on up slowly, his eyes on it all the way, and stood for perhaps fifteen minutes watching it. Then he turned to read the words engraved into the marble walls. One side had his favorite, The Second Inaugural . . . "Both read the same Bible, and pray to the same God; and each invokes His aid against the other. It may seem strange that any men should dare to ask a just God's assistance in wringing their bread from the sweat of other men's faces; but let us judge not that we be not judged." Then he looked at the figure again. He found himself thinking, "If he had lived, I wonder how things would be in the South today. I think this would be much more one nation, had he lived." Suddenly he was thinking of the fact of Death, a fairly rare thought with him and always with one effect —to make him determine to live, while life was here. If he was sure of one speculation about the future, it was this, that when old he would regret not the things he had done but those he hadn't. Immortality would be fine if it happened to be there—some day he would have to sit down and decide once and for all if he believed in it or not, and about ten more years of living, he figured, would bring him to the right stage of development to tackle that great sound barrier . . . Immortality would be fine if it happened to be there, but what a tragedy if it wasn't and man wasted what man was certain of.

He walked back down the steps. Down the Mall he could see stars hovering over the Washington Monument. He walked along the reflecting pool then on over to the Tidal Basin, the sweet smell of the cherry blossoms carried to him on the soft night wind. He sat on the grass bank by the water for a while. Many of the blossoms had fallen to the ground and he thought momentarily of scooping some of them up and taking them to Georgia as a gesture of some kind. He didn't consider it seriously—the cow would probably think he was trying to suck up. He did

gather some up, however, into a sack made by knotting the four corners
of his handkerchief, and took them back to the hotel, where he filled a
glass with water in the bathroom, dropped the blossoms into it, watched
them floating pinkly there for a few moments, then took the glass in
and set it on the stand by his bed. He went peacefully to sleep.

Next morning Georgia loaded Jason up before they started down
to the Hill. For one of his hands she gave him an extremely heavy
metal-reinforced case containing extra cameras, flashbulbs and film;
for the other, the heavy strobe lighting units. For his neck she gave
him another heavy leather case containing more photographic equipment. Also for his neck she gave him two extra 35-millimeter cameras.
Of his available booms that left only his feet free, Jason calculated,
and he needed these for locomotion. Around *her* neck Georgia carried
one 35-millimeter camera and one Rolleiflex. Of course she had to be
free to work.

"We won't do much shooting today," Georgia explained briskly.
"Today I just want to familiarize myself with the settings. But there's
nothing to be lost by having this along in case something turns up. It
certainly won't hurt to have it along."

"I hope not," Jason said glumly, staggering a little as he wedged his
way into the taxi.

They "familiarized" themselves with the settings by sitting in on the
morning session of the committee, then meeting the committee "staff,"
who were expecting them. The research that had come up from Washington had stressed the staff as the real heart of any congressional committee—a staff of investigators headed by a chief counsel. The chief
counsel, a man by the name of van Claven, seemed a little suspicious
of the whole idea of the story, as if their getting too close to the evidence might hamper his investigations.

"What a stuffy, unsophisticated creep that van Claven is," Georgia
said over their lunch in the Senate dining room. "He could be a problem, except that we'll just by-pass him. I never believe in dealing with
flunkys. I always deal with the top."

The top was the chairman of the committee, Senator Jonas J. Coddington, the senior senator from a New England state. After sitting in
on the afternoon session they went up to meet the senator. He was a
very tall, angular, almost cadaverous man with graying hair, deep-set
eyes and a twang. Jason imagined that Cotton Mather must have looked
a little like that. A month ago not ten Americans outside his own state
could have told you who Senator Coddington was. Now his had become
the most frequent name on the front pages of the nation's newspapers,
and every line of his face, every intonation of his twangy voice were as
familiar to every television viewer in America as the creature for thirty
years across the breakfast table.

Georgia was dressed very smartly in a tailored, expensive black suit without a blouse. When she introduced herself the senator gave her a close look, and she looked him right back. Jason got a good impression of the senator. He made a quick judgment that his Cotton Mather aspects stopped with his looks. He seemed very male, as if he still looked upon a good piece as one of the sweeter things of life. This is a quality that the man who has it can tell in another who has it as surely and as quickly as he can tell the color of his eyes, how, Jason didn't know, he only knew it was infallible. Jason felt the senator belonged to the tribe which liked women, a tribe getting closer to extinction by the year and more and more being considered perverted, and Jason had a very favorable impression.

"Oh, yes, Miss Dewey," the senator was saying. "They told me *Vital* was doing a story on the committee." He looked down at Georgia and beamed graciously. "Will you please do me the favor of letting me know if I can be of any help at all to you?"

"Why, that's very kind of you, Senator," Georgia said. She smiled winsomely. "You may count on my doing you that favor. I'll be around for a while and I'll let you know."

"You do that," Senator Coddington said, looking closely at the photographer. "And who is this?"

"Oh, I'm sorry," Georgia said. "This is my researcher—Jason Hightower."

My researcher, Jason thought furiously. He smiled and wedged one hand free from all the equipment he was carrying to take the senator's hand.

"How do you do, sir," he said. "I carry the bags."

"Well"—the senator beamed—"it must be a pleasure to carry them for such an attractive young lady as Miss Dewey."

"Why, aren't you sweet, Senator," Georgia said demurely.

"It must be a real pleasure," the senator repeated. He laughed generously. "They *pay* you for associating with this lovely young lady?"

"Yes, they insist on paying me," Jason said. He joined in the laughter. "They're very strict about that. Not that a lovely young lady like Miss Dewey isn't a real pleasure—I imagine."

The senator shot Jason a glance, but the young man was smiling blandly and he seemed like a nice young boy. He guessed he was wrong. "Yes, a real pleasure I can imagine," the senator said. "Well!" He turned to Georgia. "Just remember what I said. Anything I can do!"

"Oh, I won't forget, Senator," Georgia said.

When they were going back to the hotel in the taxi, Georgia turned crisply to Jason. "Now you listen to me," she said. "I've been with you just long enough to realize what a smart aleck you are. But keep it out of the story, you understand? I won't have you messing things up with Senator Coddington. He's too important to this story. You understand that?"

Jason yawned. He felt pretty bored right at the moment. "Listen," he said, "do you mind if we don't talk going back to the hotel? I'm extremely tired."

And he leaned back against the seat cushion and closed his eyes. He actually went to sleep.

"Hey, Mac," was the next thing he knew.

He opened his eyes. The taxi was in front of the hotel and he was alone in it.

"The lady went on in," the taxi driver said.

"Oh," Jason said. He started to get out.

"Mac," the taxi driver said. "You wouldn't just mind paying me, now, would you?"

Jason stopped, hunched in the doorway. "You mean she didn't pay you?"

"Nope," the taxi driver said. "You expect her to?"

"No," Jason said. He paid the driver off and went on in the hotel.

Just as Crystal Bidwell had predicted, the next several days were an education for Jason. They were also extremely long and busy days. He discovered just how much Georgia gave herself to a story. She was untiring. She shot incessantly, everything. With her camera she set about to bore into the operations of the committee staff. The committee they were shooting was looking into tax frauds. The elements of the investigation included accusations of improper influence, of payoffs in high places—Jason was amazed at the trifling nature of the "payoffs," here a television set, there a Cadillac, here a free vacation, as against the benefits received—and of a number of doubtful-appearing characters floating in and out of the story like ambitious derelicts trying to insinuate themselves into favor at the royal court. Georgia took thousands of pictures tracing the operations of the staff leading to this evidence, to these strange characters in the Capital play. Jason lugged her bags and extra cameras around and took copious notes for captions and research. He had never seen Capitol Hill and he was so fascinated to see it that even Georgia's empresslike attitude toward him for the time being hardly grazed him. They started to work very early in the morning—it seemed that Washington was a much earlier-to-work city than New York—they worked until seven or so in the evening, and after that Georgia usually went to the darkroom in the Washington bureau office to see how her pictures were coming out.

One night when a week had gone by he went back to the bureau office with her and joined her in the darkroom while she developed that day's take and printed up some of the frames. It was a very tiny room, pitch-dark save for a spot of dark red light glowing up into her face. As they stood at the sink waiting for the blowups to emerge in the developing solution, Jason felt some definite emotions coming up in him. With some tongs she was gently agitating the solution. Somehow in the darkness the red light and the strong chemical smell of the developer seemed as suggestive as drawn shades and Femme perfume. Jason moved imperceptibly. At least he thought imperceptibly.

"Hightower," she said. She did not move a fraction and her hands did not stop sloshing the solution. "Stop that filthy nonsense."

Jason was stung. "What the hell are you talking about?" he said.

"You know what I'm talking about," she said, starting to lift the pictures from the developer to the hypo. "Stop rubbing up against me."

"Rubbing up against you!" Jason said in outrage. "Jesus Christ Almighty in a teakettle!"

He turned angrily and started forgetfully for the door.

"Don't open that door, you stupid ass," she snapped. "Haven't you even sense enough to know you'll ruin the pictures?"

Jason stopped, frozen. He was trembling with anger. He stood almost flattened against the door, so as not to contaminate her, until the pictures came out of the hypo. It was ten long minutes. The minute the pictures were fixed he flung the door open and started to flee.

"Oh, Jason," she said.

"What is it?" He turned sharply in the doorway.

"Will you order me a sandwich from that place downstairs. Chicken —white meat—no lettuce, no mayonnaise, just a little butter—unsalted if they have it—on white bread, untoasted."

He dashed down the corridor of the empty office, stopped at a phone on one of the desks, rang the restaurant downstairs in the building, and to the girl who answered spoke in a shrill female voice: "*Vital.* Now get this straight, you hear? One chicken sandwich, white meat all the way through, leave off all lettuce, be sure there's not a scrap of mayonnaise in the sandwich, spread on a little butter, unsalted—if you don't have any send out and get some, there must be an all-night store somewhere in this town—put it on white bread, and be sure the bread is absolutely fresh. My name is Georgia Dewey. Got that? Georgia Dewey. Now *Vital* does a lot of business with you clowns down there and I want those specifications for my sandwich carried out to the letter. You hear? Now I don't want any nonsense out of you. You hear me? To the letter."

He slammed down the phone and left the building.

"That bitch," he said aloud on his way to the Mayflower. " 'Stop rubbing up against me'! That scrofulous bitch."

"What was that you said, Mac?" the taxi driver said ominously, slowing down.

"Oh, not you." Jason waved his hand in imperious rage. "Drive on. Drive on!"

After that Jason stopped going with her to the darkroom. It was as if she never even noticed this; she said nothing. The only remark she made about the evening was made in the taxi en route to the Hill next morning and concerned the sandwich.

"You know," she said, "I feel a little odd this morning. I think it must have been that chicken sandwich. I thought it tasted rather strange. That's odd, because chicken sandwiches are usually the one safe thing, which is why I try to eat them on the road."

"I know how it is," Jason said, "you've got to be pretty careful on the road here in Washington. You haven't been drinking the water, have you? Personally I never drink the water in these uncertain towns on the road."

"You're really impressed by your wit, aren't you?"

"It's about the only thing that ever amuses me," Jason said.

"How fortunate," she said, "that it amuses one person."

She looked out the taxi window.

Jason decided he wouldn't let her ruin his Washington trip. So he took to spending his nights alone rambling around the city. He saw the Library of Congress, the National Gallery of Art, the Washington Cathedral, the Archives Building—where he stared down keenly at the Constitution, the Declaration of Independence, the Bill of Rights— the Washington Monument, the Jefferson Memorial, and went pedal-boating in the Tidal Basin. But his favorite pastime was to sit in Lafa-yette Park watching the White House across the street and playing a game with himself, which was to try to imagine exactly what was going on inside there at the moment. "Is he sitting in a chair trying to figure out what he's going to do about the farm problem—or is he brush-ing his teeth? Is he thinking what a son of a bitch that senator is for not backing his program in Congress—or is he wondering if it'll be a pretty day for a walk tomorrow?" Jason found himself playing this game with a good deal of fascination in the soft April night of the nation's capital. "I wonder what he's doing right now. Gargling? Or trying to figure out what we should do about Soviet Russia?" He reflected on the dual nature of those who govern: Their own human attributes, daily and familiar to them as any other man's to himself, and their vision of themselves, an image fashioned each relentless day, both by their own seed of greatness or of weakness and by the great god chance, in his-tory's awful spectrum. Now surely was one of those fateful periods of history when the spectrum lighted up. The light bore down more closely. The stakes were a world, and a hundred years from tonight, the lives of ten billion souls would follow a course resolved a century before by what went on tonight, and last night, and tomorrow night be-hind those softly lit columns across the street.

He thought of that sound of the people which surely must be pounding like tumbrils in the ears of the man across the street. That sound summarized, so ever increasingly, by the word *gimmee*. It was a time for sacrifice and the people called *more*. It could make cold chills run up and down your spine just to think about it. One could almost mathematically demonstrate that unless this people went almost immediately into something very like an orgy of sacrifice it would be swept away —and far, far sooner than anyone thought—to join the gluttons and spineless of history, swept away before the tyrant who was even now battering at the door, ready to install his proconsul in that building across the street. This sacrifice had passed the point of being optional. It was demanded if we were even to be around a few years from now. It seemed to Jason that we were like a man in an overloaded, swamping boat who knows unless he casts his excess baggage overboard he will drown and not live to enjoy it anyhow—and yet, in his insensate greed, hangs on to it.

Jason looked and thought he saw someone come out and stand for a moment on the portico, between the columns, then turn and go back inside. It was like seeing a ghost of history. And looking at that house and all its meaning stretching back into a history never once craven when the chips were down, he thought there was a thing it would be judicious of all tyrants to engrave across their consciousness or perhaps put upon a piece of paper and read each morning before breakfast, to wit: *Don't count the Americans out yet.*

He and Georgia managed, for the sake of the story, to stay on speaking terms and even worked hard and well together, for the sake of the story. But their communication pretty much stopped right there. Sometimes they would have a quick sandwich together at night—Georgia had stopped eating chicken and turned to eating the even safer peanut butter and watercress sandwiches—but that about did it for their fraternization. Then it came about, after about two weeks, that Jason had seen almost all of Washington there was to see at night. One day he decided he would break down and ask her to dinner. After all, he told himself chivalrously, he ought to make an effort here. Maybe if he took the first step, she would turn out to have a lot more humanity in her than met the eye. It was often that way with people, he told himself sententiously, they only wanted to be reassured, and if you could show them they had nothing to be suspicious of in you, that you were not trying to do anything to them, you found them really very nice. It was up to him to be big about things by taking the first step and trying to understand her, which was probably the only thing in the world she needed to come around. It was true of almost everybody, Jason told himself, feeling expansive and tolerant.

It was the end of the day and they were taxiing up Pennsylvania Avenue, bound from the Capitol to the hotel.

"Well, Georgia," he said with a friendly smile. "How are the pictures going, do you think?"

She was looking out the window on her side—they were passing the National Gallery of Art—and in response to his question she held up a hand indicating silence. After two weeks with Georgia, Jason was used to this gesture. It meant that she was going through some train of thought she didn't want disturbed. At first it had irritated him almost beyond endurance. Today, however, he was not going to be upset by anything she did. He would meet her nine tenths of the way, and the other tenth if necessary. He understood the human foibles of someone like Georgia Dewey—she was insecure or something like that, probably went back to deep in her childhood, traumatic experience or something, and so on and so on—and by being above being irritated or angered by them he would disarm her and bring her around. The taxi passed the National Archives ("What Is Past Is Prologue"), the Justice Department and the Post Office Department before Georgia turned her head back from the street and inclined it slightly toward him.

"You were saying?"

"I was saying," Jason said pleasantly, " 'How are the pictures going?' "

"Like swill," Georgia said. "I can't seem to get inside the damn story."

"Get inside it?" Jason said in surprise. "Why," he said encouragingly, "I thought you had dug a Holland Tunnel inside it. I've never seen a photographer work harder. It's been wonderful how hard you've worked, Georgia. You've been shooting everything in sight—the work of the committee staff, you've followed a piece of evidence through, you've . . ."

"All that is just so much swill," Georgia impatiently interrupted this paean. "Oh, it'll be good enough to fill out the story. But it's not enough even to make the story run. There are no really great pictures anywhere in there. What I need is one great sequence with something doing, some action in it. That will carry the story and the bilge we've been shooting can fill it out. But I don't have the sequence."

"Yes, I understand the problem," Jason said solicitously. "I certainly can understand it and appreciate what you're trying to do."

The taxi turned up Fifteenth Street. "Listen, Georgia," he said in friendly, and even risingly enthusiastic tones. "I've got a hot idea. Why don't we forget all about the story tonight and have dinner and maybe go dancing? How about that? I've been casing Washington and for this burg I've found an acceptable place out northwest. In my judgment you've been working too hard, much too hard, you're tired and what you really need," Jason said avuncularly—he was beginning, all by himself with absolutely no encouragement, to feel terribly friendly toward Georgia, "is to get your mind off the story. Doubtless by backing away from the story you'll come up with . . . with"—Jason hesitated

—". . . a concept for that sequence." He turned eagerly toward her. "Why don't we give *you* a night off—if anyone ever deserved it *you* do—have dinner and . . ."

"Not a chance, Junior," Georgia broke him off. The taxi was passing the Treasury Building. "I'm having dinner with Coddington."

"*Senator* Coddington?" Jason said dumbly.

"Do you know any other Coddingtons on this story?"

"No, I guess not," Jason said, slumping back in his corner of the taxi.

"You know," Georgia said, "behind that Yankee down-East twang of his is one of the sharpest minds you've ever seen. If you think he's a potato farmer you don't know your ass from third base."

Jason sat up again in the cab. "You're having dinner with Coddington?" he repeated stupidly.

Georgia looked at him. "What's wrong with your hearing, Hightower? I said Coddington. Senator Jonas J. Coddington."

"Oh," Jason said, slumping back again. He felt a little numb, eaten out.

"You think you got it straight now?" Georgia said. "You know, of course, that Coddington wants to be President."

The taxi was passing the White House, which may have been what reminded her.

"President of what?" Jason said.

"Of the United States, simpleton. What's wrong with you?"

"He'll never make it," Jason said with sudden savagery. He probably said that because he was angry with Coddington for keeping him from dinner with Georgia. His lofty friendliness of a few minutes ago had evaporated out the taxi window. "I can tell you right now," he said, "that Jonas J. Coddington will never be President of the United States."

"My God, who the hell do you think you are after two weeks in Washington?"

"Well, let me tell you," Jason continued. "I know this much about American history. The United States no longer elects fools for Presidents. We used to now and then, but things are too serious now. No fool can any longer be elected President of the United States. Now Coddington is not a fool. But he is too obvious and I will go further and say that no obvious man can any longer be elected President of the United States. That is about the only respect in which the nation has improved," he said grumpily.

"My, my," she said. "Two weeks and you're Walter Lippmann, Jr."

"I can tell you this," Jason said. "If you're having dinner with Coddington because he might be President, you're wasting your time!"

"My God, what's wrong with you?" she said. "Have you completely lost your mind? Of course I'm not having dinner with Coddington because he might be President. For one thing the election isn't for three more years. If I were going to have dinner with him for that reason I wouldn't have it now. I'm having dinner with him because of the story, stupid. As chairman of this committee we're shooting the story on he is an extremely powerful man. He can really help us."

"I just hope you're right," Jason said grouchily.

"And let me tell you something. Coddington *could* be President of the United States. But what is more important, he *thinks* he could be President. He likes publicity. He needs good publicity."

The taxi pulled up to the hotel and stopped. "That proves what I said," Jason said, making no move to get out. "That you're having dinner with him because he might be President of the United States."

"That may be why he's having dinner with *me*," Georgia said. "That's not why I'm having dinner with *him*."

"It's all the same thing," Jason said casuistically. "My point is that you're having dinner with him because he might be President of the United States. Now whether that's your specified reason has nothing to do with it. If he did not want to be President of the United States he would never have asked you. This point is so clear. I hope you see that?"

"For Christ's sake!" Georgia said. "What difference does it make! This is the damndest conversation I ever heard of. The national election is three years away, nobody has even mentioned Coddington for President . . ."

"But that has nothing to do with the point I was making," Jason said. "Georgia, it's as logical as anything in the world . . ."

"Jesus!" Georgia said, almost in a scream. "Let's get out of here!"

As they walked into the lobby she said, almost to herself, "You know, I think I'll try for a cover on him."

"I don't think it would ever run," Jason said discouragingly.

14

The Seasoning of Jason Hightower: Sugar

Jason ate alone that night. Although he had eaten alone very happily most of his nights in Washington, having counted on dinner tonight with Georgia he felt lonely for the first time since he'd come to the Capital.

He ate alone the next night and the night after that—her dinner engagement with the senator appeared to have become almost a standing thing—and by this time he was so miserable he could hardly get the food inside him. The third night he stayed up reading *Phaedo* and *Theaetetus* erratically and helping himself, less erratically, to a bottle of J and B. It was 1:00 A.M. when he heard Georgia come in next door. He waited a few minutes, then left his room and went to her door and knocked.

"Who is it?"

"Old Marse Hightower."

She opened the door. "Oh, you. Hello, Hightower."

"I thought perhaps you'd like one for the bed."

"Oh." She sighed querulously. "Well, all right. Just one then. I'm extremely tired. Order me a little Dubonnet. Do it from your room, will you? I want to get undressed."

"Why, surely," Jason said.

He went to his room and had a cigarette, both to give her time and because it would be the last one before he got back to the room. Whenever that is, he found himself thinking suddenly—and ambitiously. Then he phoned room service for some ice and a glass of Dubonnet. Then he picked up the bottle of J and B and, by habit, his pack of cigarettes. Then he remembered he wouldn't—or couldn't—need the cigarettes. However, they were already in his pocket so he left them there. He went on down to her room and knocked.

"Just a minute," she called out.

It was a long minute. When she opened the door she was wearing a Chinese red dressing gown. It was silk and it was stunning. The order came and he handed her the Dubonnet and mixed himself a thick Scotch. He flopped into the easy chair across from the one where she sat.

"How was Coddington?"

"You know," she said, "the more I see of him the more I realize that man may be headed places, all of them up. Stranger things have happened in this country than Jonas Coddington becoming President. If he plays it very carefully. President Jonas J. Coddington," she said. "It even sounds right, doesn't it?"

"Not to me," Jason said. "I can't see it."

"Well, let's don't get started on that again. The point is, I think he can help us a lot on this story."

She sipped, very barely, at her Dubonnet. "What I really need is to go out with the investigators on an actual operation. Van Claven won't give me permission. He says it's too ticklish, it might endanger the investigation. He's so stuffy it's pitiful. Well, of course he takes his orders from Coddington. He's just a flunky—that most pathetic of

flunkies, the one who doesn't realize it. I think the senator is about ready
to pass him the word."

At that moment Jason was treated to something that startled him.
Georgia, sitting in the chair across from him, crossed her legs. Under
the silken garment for the barest flash of a second Jason was treated
to a glimpse of her thighs and for the most minute fraction of a second of that which, when all has been said, holds all men everywhere,
eternally has and forever will, in subjugation. Jason was just slightly
tight but not so tight but what, with the glimpse and with her talk about
Coddington, everything he had ever heard about Georgia Dewey came
rushing in one great flood tide into his consciousness.

"Oh," he said. "Well, I'm glad the senator is going to be co-operative."

"He hasn't promised yet," she said. She was barely sipping even
at that damn Dubonnet, which, Jason thought, is about as alcoholic as
a Coca-Cola. She's so damn careful, he thought. So damned disciplined,
so figured-it-all-out. "As a matter of fact I haven't asked—yet. You
mustn't rush these things. How well I do know that. It's all a matter of
timing, you know."

"Oh, is that what it is, timing," Jason said.

"Sometimes I think timing is the most important thing in the world."

"Is that so?" Jason said. "I'm glad to learn that. I'm always trying to
learn things like that. 'Timing is the most important thing in the world.'
That will be the thing I've learned for today."

"By tomorrow night," Georgia said, looking at Jason over her
Dubonnet, "I think he may be ready for me to ask."

"Jesus Christ," Jason said with sudden anger. "Are you having dinner with the old goat again tomorrow night?"

"Of course I am," Georgia said in a demonstrated surprise at Jason's
reaction. "What's wrong with you?"

But then once more she crossed her legs, once more his eyes, in that
microscopic moment of time allowed him, telescoped up her olive,
smooth-as-a-face thighs. Suddenly it made him angry.

"Georgia, don't look now," Jason said. He swallowed the rest of his
drink, stood up, lit a cigarette and blew out a long stream of smoke in
her face. "Don't look now but your thighs are showing. And that ain't
all, kid. Good night."

Picking up his bottle of J and B he turned and walked out of the
room, leaving her batting smoke out of her eyes.

She never made any reference to that evening. But there was a difference. He began to notice the difference the next day while they
were driving down in the taxi. She was less sullen than she had been
since the story started. In fact she was almost friendly with him. He felt
suspicious.

"Let's sit in on a hearing this morning, Jason," she said. It was the first time she had addressed him by his given name. "I have to get some hearing shots sometime. I might as well do it while I'm waiting to see what Coddington says about me going out with the investigators. Is that all right with you?"

He was flabbergasted at her asking whether anything was all right with anybody except herself. Then it came over him like a vision why she was being civilized for a change. She obviously didn't understand decent treatment. The bitch probably mistook it for a cringing weakness. She was just the type to make that colossal error. She did understand what happened last night. He should have known it. It confirmed one of his basic beliefs, which was that women interpreted excessive consideration in a man as weakness, that what they really want, and love, is being taken in hand, cuffed around—at least they want strong shots of this admixtured with consideration. The whole sex, he thought, is essentially masochistic. Heretofore this had been only an intellectual belief with him, and only last night, however unwittingly, had he tried it out in practice. He felt a high glow.

"Sure," he said crisply. "That'll be fine, Georgia."

At the hearing Jason sat in the press section while Georgia bounced up and down the room shooting pictures. The spectators gave almost as much attention to her as they did to the witness. She was strikingly dressed in a black dress with half-dollar-sized Chinese red buttons all the way down the front. Chinese red appeared to be one of her favorite colors, Jason thought. Jason imagined most men looking at her would imagine themselves unbuttoning these buttons, which act of imagination, he reflected, was the buttons' sole *raison d'être*. If they only knew, he thought. When he was not thinking, himself, of the olive thighs beneath that dress and imagining, himself, his hand holding the smooth, frangible weight—and now in the hearing room in the Senate Office Building Jason turned, squirming, and shot his eyes off Georgia, anywhere—when he was not thinking of this, Jason spent most of the hearing while Georgia was shooting observing Senator Coddington on the courtlike rostrum up above the witness.

"Who's the fancy broad with the big tits?"

The question had been spoken directly into his ear, indeed he had felt the mouth which spoke it against his ear. Turning, Jason cast a long look upon the reporter sitting next to him.

Jason put his mouth against the reporter's ear. "What paper do you represent?" he whispered crisply into it.

The reporter put his mouth against Jason's ear. "What in hell has that got to do with it?"

Jason put his mouth against the reporter's ear. "Will you just answer the question, please?"

The reporter put his mouth against Jason's ear. "The New York *Times,*" he said. He sounded irritated.

Jason leaned close to the *Times* reporter's ear. "I just wanted to find out what newspaper had a representative who would ask a tactless question like that. I might have expected it from one of these sensational tabloids. I must say I'm surprised to hear it from a fairly decent rag like the *Times*."

The *Times* reporter put his mouth against Jason's ear. "What the hell's the matter with you? I asked a simple question."

Jason put his mouth against the *Times* reporter's ear. "What was the question? I forgot. Say it louder."

The *Times* reporter, very irritated, repeated it. "I said, 'Who is the fancy broad with the big tits?' "

The witness at the table directly in front of them and three or four of the senators who had not been following the testimony too closely looked up, startled. The *Times* reporter looked fiercely down at the press table. Presently the hearing resumed.

Jason leaned over and put his mouth against the reporter's ear. "It's my wife."

The *Times* reporter, blushing heavily, put his mouth against Jason's ear. "I'm sorry, old man," he said with profuse apology. "I didn't know."

Jason put his mouth against the reporter's ear. "Just be careful next time, will you? I know everybody does it, and I should be used to it, but it still offends me to hear total strangers discussing my wife's tits. How would you like it if someone came up to you and asked you about your wife's tits? Particularly if you didn't know him? If I wasn't so understanding about it and you were with any other paper than the *Times,* which I happen to like, I'd bash your face in. But they are pretty tits, aren't they?"

The *Times* reporter, abashed, gave Jason a curious look and went back to taking notes on the testimony. Jason went back to watching Coddington. As chairman, Senator Coddington sat in the middle of the rostrum, the chief counsel and the committee members of one of the two political parties to his right, the members of the other party to his left. The senator had a very deliberative, judicious manner, of a man who realized the overriding importance of fairness toward a witness, whoever he might be, whatever the accusations against him. Jason liked Coddington more and more. The chief counsel, who was a brilliant young lawyer, despite what Georgia said, asked most of the questions of the witness. Only now and then did Coddington interpose a question in that slow, twangy voice of his. Jason made a note for his research: "Coddington asks few questions but these are shrewdly to the point. No jerk, Coddington." He looked up from his notes and back at Coddington. And now Jason saw: Those deep-set eyes were resting on something across the room. Jason followed the line of vision. Then he looked back at the senator: he was smiling softly. Jason followed his line of vision back again: The same soft smile, it could have been a duplicate of the senator's, indented the face of Georgia Dewey. Jason made another note: "Cadaverous, nose-voiced Senator Jonas J. Coddington, the tail-loving Puritan from New England."

Georgia covered the afternoon session, as well, but they left early. After they had started up Pennsylvania Avenue Jason found out why.

"Jason, why don't you drop me at Garfinckel's and keep the taxi."

"Garfinckel's?"

"I've got to buy a dress."

Jason couldn't imagine why. She had worn something different almost every day. Ten pieces of that mountainous amount of luggage she had brought from New York were personal not photographic equipment.

He didn't see her again until next morning, when he picked her up at her room. It was the first time since they had come to Washington that she seemed happy. Her eyes glowed in triumph.

"Well!" she said as they were taxiing down to the Hill. "We're in. Coddington agreed to everything last night. I'm going along with the investigators."

"That's fine," Jason said. "When do we do it?"

She turned to him. "Jason," she said. "Coddington is sticking his neck out for me on this. It's a very big thing for him to let me go along. It's very secret and very touchy. They want to keep it as small as possible. I'm awfully sorry about it but that means you can't go."

"Oh, I understand," Jason said magnanimously. She had never been so solicitous about him. He felt very successful. Then he decided something else. He lit a cigarette. "When are *you* going?"

"Tonight," she said. "And tomorrow night. I'll be gone two nights." She smiled softly. She said nothing about the cigarette. What she said was: "I hope you don't miss me too much."

He felt something jump in him. "I'll try not to," he said. He smiled mysteriously. Then he added: "But hurry back, will you?"

She looked at him, smiled with remarkable softness, and he felt the jumping again as she said, her voice equally soft, "I really will, dear."

He was surprised to find himself so restless from the moment he awakened next day. He stayed restless. He couldn't shake it off. He felt very alone in the city and felt the day would never get through. He tried something he almost never did, which was to go to a movie. He couldn't sit still and left after half an hour. Then only a few minutes later he found himself going into another one. The same thing happened. About six o'clock he went back to the hotel and started drinking in the Mayflower Men's Bar. He didn't want even to put eyes on any other woman. He drank and wondered what was happening between Georgia and himself. It was certainly strange, he felt, but something had come about. How odd the ways of human relationships! he thought as he drank on. The other was just a mannerism with her, a defense, plus the natural human instinct to get away, with another person, with what the traffic would bear. It was just a matter of straightening their relationship out, of shifting the axis to the point she understood that his natural decency was not to be taken as synonymous with any toleration of being squashed around like a cupcake. Now that it had shifted, mighty vistas opened to him. He kept on drinking and did not eat. He remembered very vaguely going up the elevator and knocking on her door, of there being no answer, of realizing she hadn't got back, of making his way into his own room and just managing to get his clothes off before falling into bed. It was bright daylight when he awakened and was thinking instantly of her.

To give her time to sleep, considerately, he had breakfast, shaved and took a shower and went out and took a long walk. By the time he got back to the hotel it was noon and he went up and knocked softly on her door. She answered it in her dressing gown—a different dressing gown, this one of pure white, also silk, also tailored, also stunning. He noticed she had on no make-up and that she didn't need any. She was radiant.

"Oh, Jason. Come in."

When he followed her into the room he saw she was having breakfast. Suddenly she whirled ebulliently to him.

"Jason!" she screamed so suddenly he was startled. "I got them. They're wonderful. I've got it!"

"You've got what?" he said dully.

"The pictures! I got the pictures I wanted!"

"I'm very glad, Georgia."

"It was just like a raid . . ." she said excitedly.

He sat while she finished her breakfast and told him about it. She ate greedily, little pieces of toast and now and then of scrambled eggs clinging to her lips. She seemed highly sensual, and slightly gross to him. He found himself incredibly excited. Watching her he hardly listened to her account of the "raid."

She finished breakfast and sat back for another cup of coffee. She looked at him over the top of her cup. "You know," she said, "I think the story's about done. A few loose ends to clean up and we've had it. Now that that's that . . . Jason."

In her voice, in his spoken name, was a tone he would not have thought her capable of a few days ago. It was sweet, the word was sweet. She was looking at him in a way that made something tremble around in the pit of his stomach.

"Jason," she was saying in that tone, with that look, "now that the story's almost over, there's one other thing." Again she waited, looking at him. "Jason. You seem to have been rather disturbed on this story —by something."

"Disturbed by something?" Jason said quizzically. "I can't imagine what. I'm disturbed all the time by the way everything is in the world but I can't think of anything more than usual that's disturbed me."

"Can't you, Jason? Can't you, if you really think hard? Hard, Jason," she repeated, looking at him, and, he felt, at his body. "Hard, Jason. Hard." He felt dizzy.

"Jason," she said very softly. "I think you've been rather disturbed by . . . well, Jason, by the fact I have a body."

Jason looked keenly at her. He felt extremely heady.

The phone rang.

"Let's forget it, shall we, Jason? Let's forget the phone."

"Yes, let's do," he agreed hastily. He could hear his own voice shaking. "Let's forget the phone."

She waited until it had stopped. "I was saying—I think you've been rather disturbed. And I think you deserve something, Jason."

She put down her cup. She stood up. She never took her eyes off him. As he watched she undid the belt of her robe. The belt fell away loosely to either side. Always watching him, her hands moved to where the robe joined, and using both hands she slowly pushed the folds back and let the white garment drop to the floor. It made a small silken rustle.

The light came in through the curtains of heavy gauze in back of her and held her in the glow of noon. He caught his breath at her voluptuousness. She was odalisquian. The breasts firm, the nipples pink— pink, he thought, as the cherry blossoms. The belly flat. The hips wide and the thighs seeming long for her height, giving her an hourglass figure, and all of her golden, olive golden, and against the gold a curling reddish bower. She was a vision in the morning glade at Fontainebleau, out of some impossible magical dream, and his heart pounded wildly within him.

He could not remember doing it. But suddenly he realized he was standing up and that all of him stood poised toward her.

"Oh, my God, honey. Oh, darling. How I've wanted this. Oh, yes, how right you are, I have been disturbed. Do you realize how I've dreamed of you, of this . . . Oh, how I've wanted you, sweet, sweet honey . . ."

His voice was quivering, he could feel his heart beating insanely in his chest, he felt he might pass out from excitement. He took a step toward her.

"Stop right there, Hightower."

Her voice was as hard and rasping as a hoe against concrete. He checked, frozen.

"Now, you son of a bitch, get the hell out of here. And remember never to tell me again that my thighs are showing."

Her eyes were flashing. Her whole naked flesh seemed to quiver with anger and with triumph. He stood unbelieving. Then all at once he believed it, and where disbelief had been came a savagery so consuming that for one wild, insane moment he took a half-step forward with the intent of ripping her with his fists, of smashing that smug, triumphant face, of grabbing her and choking her until her tongue should pop from her mouth. In the intensity of his feeling he almost blacked out. Then he was back. My God, he thought, coming a little to himself, this must be how people get murdered. This is the authentic homicidal impulse . . .

He had to get out of here. With a violent movement he turned toward the door, his heedless arm sending a table lamp catapulting against the wall. He was there without knowing how he had got there and had opened the door.

Standing there, one hand raised to knock and the other carrying something, was the cadaverous figure of Senator Jonas J. Coddington.

Startled, Jason looked up at the towering frame. Those eyes in their cavernous sockets looked down at him. For one moment in time the *tableau vivant* was fixed, like a clip from a motion picture reel: Jason with his hand on the doorknob; the senator with his hand, knotted into a loose fist for knocking, raised into air. Transfixed, Jason looked up at the senator; the senator's eyes looked down at him. Then slowly the senator's hand came down. Jason fought back his gasping breath. The door was only partly open so that the senator could not see into the room. Then everything came back to Jason. Sanity came back.

"Senator Coddington!" he said. "What an honor this is. I believe you know Miss Dewey, sir?"

And with one mighty gesture Jason flung the door wide, at the same time flattening himself against the wall so as not to impede the senator's view.

"Jonas!" the photographer shrieked wildly to the cadaverous, gray-haired man.

"Jonas!" Jason said mockingly.

"Jonas," Georgia was saying. She scrambled frantically for the robe at her feet. "I'm so glad you came. I believe you met Jason Hightower, my assistant."

"Assistant!" Jason said in outrage. "Just listen to that vain cow."

The senator, a man, Jason imagined, not easily surprised, seemed amazed and rather perplexed at the look he was being afforded at these unfamiliar mores. He turned to Jason.

"As I believe I observed before, young man," he said, "they actually pay you for the privilege of, uh"—the senator stole a glance at Georgia, who was fighting her way into her robe—"associating with this lovely young lady?"

"Yes," Jason said cheerily, "we actually get paid for it. Amazing they'd insist on doing that, isn't it, Senator? It just shows you how paternalistic *Vital* magazine is toward its employees. I doubt if there's a more generous company . . ."

"Get out of my room!" This disquisition on the company's benevolence was suddenly shut off by a hellish scream. It was the voice of a cheated fishwife. Then she screamed an explanation toward the senator. "This young man was trying to rape me!"

"Rape!" Jason yelled back incredulously. "Why, the woman's obviously mad. As if anyone could rape a cow like that. Why, she's got pasterns like Man o' War, sir," Jason said to the senator. "And withers like Seabiscuit. As you can see."

Georgia let out a bloodcurdling shriek. "Throw him out, Jonas!"

"Throw him out, Jonas!" Jason mimicked.

"My dear," the senator said quietly into the uproar. "I don't know quite what's going on here. As a member of the world's greatest deliberative body part of my job is to keep myself well informed, but apparently I'm far from up on all the modern practices. I just came to bring you this. I phoned up but there was no answer. I was about to leave when the clerk—recognizing me, since I suppose I have a small amount of notoriety these days—said he was quite certain you were in. He was only too helpful. I just came to bring . . ."

The senator's voice trailed off. He walked over and upon the foot of one of the beds set the most enormous box of flowers Jason had ever seen.

The senator stood there a moment uncertainly. "I think the best contribution I can make here," he said judiciously, "is to withdraw."

He bowed to Georgia, then turned and walked in dignity toward the door. His hand on the doorknob, he hesitated, then turned to Jason. He shook his head. "Life is a very interesting thing, isn't it, my boy? It is always interesting to see what each new day will bring forth."

And he was gone.

Jason looked for a moment at the closed door. Then he turned toward Georgia.

"Well, I'll be dogged," Jason said in the tones of a hillbilly. "I'll be double-dogged. You know something, Georgia. I've changed my mind. If he ever does run for President, Senator Jonas J. Coddington can count on one vote. He can count on the vote of Jason H. Hightower. Didn't he handle that well, though?" Jason said with the dispassionate air of a man making an observation on some cursory, passing event.

"Get out of here!" It was a shattering noise. "Get out of this room—quick!"

Jason, feeling much better now, and certainly thoroughly calm, decided not to conclude his visit just yet. He felt like talking over the recent events in a pleasant, relaxed conversation. He came back, dropped in one of the easy chairs and slouched down with his head on top of it. He yawned and stuck his feet up on one of the twin beds and cocked and crossed them comfortably.

"Georgia, tell me one thing . . ." he said easily.

"Get out of that chair!" It was a horrifying scream. "Get out of my room this instant!"

"Listen, my dear," Jason said quietly, "it's all right with me whatever you do . . ."

"All right with you!" she screamed. "Don't you 'my dear' me, you perverted imbecile. Who do you think you are . . ."

"Now just what do you mean by perverted?" Jason asked with interest. It would be interesting, he felt, to see what she meant. "Do you mean it in the classic sense, in the homosexual sense, in . . ."

"Quiet!" she let out a piercing yell. "Stop talking! Shut up and get out!"

"Georgia, all this melodrama is hardly necessary. I recommend you simply calm yourself . . ."

"Melodrama! I'll show you some melodrama!" She leapt for the phone. "Get out of here immediately or I'll call the house detective."

"I imagine they have a few in this place," Jason said. "They need them. Georgia," he said quietly. Her hand was on the phone. "Now listen to me, Georgia. I'm just curious. I've got a mind like . . . well, I'm curious. Can I help that? I'm just that way. I just like to know. Now." Jason recrossed his feet on the bed. "Now, tell me one thing and I'll leave."

He looked up at her. "Why do you hate men?"

Slowly her hand slid off the phone. She stood there, tortured, he would imagine, wrathful, angry at . . . God, what was she angry at, Jason wondered. The world? Herself? She spat it out: "I'll tell you why I hate men. I hate them because they're superior. Most of all I hate them because they have dirty minds, dirty, filthy little minds. Do you think I don't know what they say about me? Do you think I don't know what every photographer and half the other people on that magazine say? That Georgia Dewey sleeps for her pictures! That's what they all say. You want to know something else? All those filthy-minded men who talk, you know why they talk? Because I won't go to bed with any of *them*. And you know why else they talk? Because they know I'm a better photographer than all but three or four of them. But they can't stand that. They can't stand a woman being better! They have to blame it on what's here . . ." and she pointed, in an angry, scornful gesture Jason would be long in forgetting, to the golden crown between her legs. "Sure I do it sometimes. But it also just happens I'm a better photographer than most of them. I'd be better than most of them if you put a chastity belt on me and threw the key away. And they know it. But they'd never admit it. They have to say, 'Georgia Dewey gets pictures because she's got that thing.' Sure, I hate men. I hate them because they can't admit a woman can be as good as they are."

She stopped, breathing very heavily.

"Georgia." Suddenly, and he was very surprised at the emotion, everything in him went out to her. "Georgia," he said even more quietly. "Take it easy, will you, Georgia. You sound like Susan B. Anthony. I don't think it's as bad as you say."

"The hell it isn't. You're not a woman and they don't talk about you and that's why you think it isn't bad. Well, I'm a woman and . . ."

She was on the bed, sobbing. "I'm a woman and I've never done it for . . . for joy, Jason. It's always been for a reason. Never for joy."

She raised up on the bed and looked at him. Her robe hung loosely around her, her eyes were bloodshot, and the woman who looked so smart and desirable there with her camera in the Senate hearing room now looked an utter slattern. She looked at him. The expression was gross. It was almost obscene. And yet, somehow, it was very, very pleading. If he felt anything now, it was certainly not desire, not in the slightest. It may have been compassion.

"Jason. Oh, Jason, what's wrong with me?"

Jason recrossed his feet. "What's wrong with you," he said, "is what's wrong with millions of women in this country. You said it yourself. You've never done it just because you wanted to do it. It was always with calculation—the same way that most women in this country, maybe in lesser degree but essentially the same, do it, for every calculating reason in the world and never for itself, the only way it's any good."

He felt very sanctimonious. But he believed it.

"Jason. Come here, Jason."

He smiled. "I'm not coming anywhere, Georgia. I've heard that she-wolf cry at least once too often. Now let's discuss this some more . . ."

He was really very interested, almost like an anthropologist stumbling across a fascinating new tribe. Jason had never seen anything like Georgia Dewey and he was absorbed.

"Now, look at your problem this way . . ." he said.

"You know what *your* problem is?" she interrupted. "You talk about things too much. Everything's in the mind with you. You worship words." She got up off the bed. "If you won't come here I'm coming there."

And she came toward him. As she did her robe fell away from her once more, but this time not by design. She kept coming on.

"Georgia," Jason said hastily, "don't you think we ought to talk about . . ."

But then his mouth was closed. And it came to pass that he knew, in that way which infallibly, in a woman, distinguishes the real from the pretended, that in the twenty-eighth year of her life and in room 1136 of the Hotel Mayflower in Washington, D. C., Georgia Dewey had passed into the realms of joy.

This was because, once there, Georgia Dewey, in joy as in photography, was a woman of great initiative, spectacularly single-minded.

They finished the story in about a week more and went back to New York. They worked very, very little during this week and if the truth were known could have skipped about six days of it, as far as the story was concerned. The Room Service department of the Mayflower Hotel noticed that suddenly the two people in rooms 1136 and 1138 were having nearly all their meals in, often with very choice, expensive wines. The eleventh-floor maid noticed that the people in these two rooms hardly ever left them.

In New York, Georgia and Jason were received in triumph. It was a magnificent story. Two weeks later it ran for ten pages and a cover. The cover was of Senator Coddington. The cover slug read: "Puritan Senator Takes Out After Tax Corruption." Some people said later that it was this cover which started the Presidential boom for the fine senator from New England.

Crystal Bidwell called Jason into her office to let him know what a splendid job he had done.

"Jason! *A chaque saint sa chandelle!* French for honor to whom honor is due. You're to be especially commended, Jason, for being such a good soldier. Between you and me I know that Georgia Dewey, though of course an excellent photographer, is . . . well, shall we say, difficult?"

"No," Jason said soberly, "I don't think we shall say that. I found Georgia quite delightful."

"What did you say?" Bidwell said, astonished.

"The truth is," Jason continued, "that there's no photographer I've ever worked with that I enjoyed more."

"Oh," said Crystal. She sounded rather disappointed. She looked at Jason very closely.

Jason Hightower's eyes had a far, faraway look. "Crystal, I didn't know it at the time but I realize now how right you were. The assignment was just as you predicted. It was so seasoning. With a capital S."

15

The Utility of Futility

The magazine had been intending for some time to do the lead, but each time in recent weeks some less dull story had come in to crowd it out. This week, however, there had been no town in Oklahoma wiped out by a tornado, no island in the Pacific obliterated by the test firing of a hydrogen bomb, no beloved old British family doctor turning out to be the murderer and quaint incinerater of twenty-three elderly lady-patients at Brighton. So it had been decided to go after the agricultural crisis as a lead. One of the many fine things about farming was that there was almost always an agricultural crisis if you happened to need a lead. All week now *Vital* photographers had been caroming up and down the land shooting things on and about farms. The story encompassed drought in some regions, and the photographers had gone after the always-available cracked earth, with maybe a cow's skull on it—there was a river bed in Texas which had been dry and cracked for seventy-five years, but this if anything increased its effectiveness; big crops and trouble-making surpluses in other areas (that plenty can be a problem is perhaps the most terrifying aspect of our age), and the photographers had gone after wind-lashed fields of grain and stuffed grain elevators; the question of parity, and the photographers had gone after the sessions of a congressional agriculture committee the members of which consistently managed in the same breath to scream for economy in government and to bluster for maximum price supports; and there were always the close-up faces of farmers, which were always "grizzled." There wasn't really much different even *Vital* photographers could do in an agricultural-crisis story. Nevertheless the magazine went after the crisis about twice a year. "After all," as Harrison Duckworth once said, "where would we be without agriculture?"

Gaskin hated it when he caught the story. A little after 10:00 A.M. Creech, the copy editor, buzzed him on the phone from his office at the other end of the corridor, gave him the word and said that it was going for a five-page lead.

"Oh, Christ in a teakettle," Gaskin received the happy news.

"Charity Cabot is the researcher," Creech said. "I suggest you get together with her."

"I suggest I'd like to get together with Charity Cabot," Gaskin said. Creech joined Gaskin in a small spurt of laughter.

10:05 A.M. That was a comfort, anyhow, having Charity Cabot for the researcher. In these days, Gaskin reflected philosophically, we must never fail to thank God for small blessings. Gaskin liked working with Charity Cabot. She was very proficient at her job, did not spend all her time battling the male sex as woman's natural enemy, and did not feel, as he felt some of the researchers felt, that she had constantly to throw her personality all around the offices and up and down the corridors by way of periodic shriekings of the vocal cords and whinnying bursts of shrill, hysterical laughter. She had a brightness and energy that were natural, never compulsive, with eyes full of light and a face fresh and listening, and the world had not got to her. It was very refreshing to be around her. Gaskin got up from his desk and went down to the National Affairs bullpen, where the researchers sat. Her desk was stacked high with thousands of contact prints, hundreds of blowups and a stack of research literally a foot high. Gaskin, standing by her desk, groaned profoundly.

"It looks like you and me got stuck down on the farm. I just got word from Razorback." Gaskin sang a little ditty, loud enough that several of the researchers looked up from their work:

> *"How you gonna keep them down on the farm*
> *After they've seen New York . . ."*

Charity Cabot smiled up at Gaskin, whom she liked. She considered him a very proficient writer, very professional and not given to quibbling over every little point as if every word he wrote were the *Lysis* of Plato.

"Like to see some of the blowups," she said, "for atmosphere?"

"You mean rippling fields of grain, cracked earth, grizzled faces?"

Charity Cabot laughed. "You couldn't be more right." Nevertheless she flipped through some of them for him.

Gaskin sighed majestically. "I suppose I shall have to start reading, a little bit. Don't give me too much. I don't want to get confused by knowing the story too well."

Charity Cabot smiled and picked up a folder that was not, Gaskin was happy to see, too thick. She had done her work well, having gone through that monstrous pile of research and selected material for the writer to read instead of dumping it all in his lap.

"This has part of the file from Washington giving the general picture," she said, "and one dispatch from each of the major farming regions giving the general picture there."

"That's the ticket," Gaskin said, "the general picture. The big thing is to stay away from the detailed facts."

He took the folder and cruised back to his office.

10:20 A.M. He put on a stack of Hindemith records, wedged his huge frame deep into his chair and cocked his feet on his desk, opened the folder, sighed pretty profoundly, and started in reading. It had the usual stuff he had come to expect in agricultural-crisis stories and he kept yawning prolifically. If it hadn't been for the music he would have gone fast asleep—this was why he always played someone jazzy like Hindemith when reading research of this nature. He was about a fourth of the way through it, his mind wandering enormously, when he saw Charity standing in the doorway of his office. She had a mountainous pile of pictures in both arms.

"We're going in to lay it out," she said brightly. "We were pretty sure you would want to come along."

Giving another sigh, Gaskin pulled his oversized body up out of the chair, pretended to stagger a moment. " . . . Reading agricultural research has this odd tendency to make one dizzy . . ." he said, and then made it to the hallway, where he joined Charity and the National Affairs editor, Dockery, who was chuckling throatily. Together the three of them trooped down the length of the hall to the managing editor's office.

"Oh! We three kings of Orient are," Gaskin sang.

"Bearing gifts we traverse afar," Dockery sang.

"What gifts," Charity said. By that time they had reached the door of the managing editor's office. They paraded in.

10:40 A.M. The managing editor of *Vital* magazine was its one authentic genius—genius, true genius, as opposed to talent, of which the magazine had such a disproportionate share. Among other things it was he who personally selected every picture and read every word that went into the magazine. There he stood now, with his shirt sleeves rolled halfway up his arms, his tie off and smoking a cigar. If you hadn't known who he was you would have taken him for the proprietor of a hardware store in a small Midwestern town. He was that unimpressive on sight. He was of medium height, had thinning sandy hair, a cherubic face with slightly puffed, slightly veined cheeks; only the eyes were any key to the world in him. The eyes were restless, almost jumping at things; they bulged a little, and this set-forward position seemed to give them a peripheral vision manyfold that of a journeyman pair of eyes. Otherwise he could have been anybody, instead of the man who more than any other single person, more than any other fifty persons, made the magazine what it was. Everybody on the magazine was scared of him in more or less degree. Now he stood slumped and half leaning against a waist-high, yard-deep shelf that ran the entire length of the office, which was enormous. The shelf had built-in lighting devices for illuminating color transparencies; it had a squawkbox fitted with switches, one for each of the senior editors, and it was otherwise bare. It needed to be for the space required to lay out a story from the vast number of pictures *Vital* photographers shot on an assignment.

Dockery, as part of his job, had done a proposed layout of the story. This, with any of the department heads, was nearly always only a formality. The managing editor, like any good genius, customarily had other ideas. Now he looked at the proposed layouts and laid them aside. Then he sat down at the shelf. Charity Cabot leaned over his shoulder, and stayed in that position for fifteen minutes. This was the process known as "soundtracking" and it had been devised to save the time of the managing editor, who was one of the busiest men in the United States of America and had to make literally hundreds of decisions a day. While the managing editor flipped the pictures, rapidly or not so rapidly depending on their appeal to him, Charity got in three, four, or eight or ten words on what the particular picture was about.

When they had gone through the pictures the managing editor pressed a button, which brought one of the assistant art directors into the room. The managing editor then proceeded expertly to lay out the story in a way radically different from the way Dockery had laid it out. When it was all over he had chosen for use some twenty-nine pictures out of the almost six thousand that *Vital* photographers had shot for the story. The assistant art director scooped up everything—the contacts, the blowups, the discarded layouts, the new layouts—and went away. Then the managing editor turned, puffed twice on his cigar, leaned back against the shelf and spent fifty-five seconds talking with Dockery, Gaskin and Charity about the approach the story should have.

"Ump . . . grunt . . . uhg . . . Zow . . . muh . . . wah . . . zumow . . ."

Dockery, Charity and Gaskin then left. They went on down the hall and stopped in for a few minutes in Gaskin's office. Hindemith was still raging away.

"You have any idea what he meant?" Gaskin asked methodically.

"Well, I think . . ." And Dockery said what he thought the managing editor meant about the approach to the story, that is to say, what "pitch" it should have.

"I think . . ." And Charity Cabot said what she thought the managing editor meant. It was somewhat different from what Dockery had thought.

"Well, I think . . ." And Gaskin said what he thought the managing editor meant. It was quite a bit different from what either Dockery or Charity had thought.

This conference was necessary because the managing editor of *Vital*, while an imperatively brilliant man, was also to the common mortal almost entirely inarticulate. He talked in jerks of phrases, almost spasms. A newcomer to *Vital* never had the remotest notion of what he was talking about. After a while of working at the magazine you began to learn very slightly the key to it. It was like learning Sanskrit. The whole alphabet was different. It involved not only sounds but also gestures—a shrug of the shoulder meant one thing, a quick flicking of the hand outward another. But no one ever fully mastered it, either the vocal or sign language, even people who had been there years. Hence, on emerging from his office, the department editor, writer and researcher together tried to figure out exactly what the managing editor had in mind. It was a canny business. Sometimes they hit it. Sometimes they missed it by a mile. But there was nothing to do but try. It would have been unthinkable to walk back in and ask simply, "Now precisely what did you have in mind, old man?" Besides, it wouldn't have done any good. You still wouldn't have understood. You had to do it by trial and error. But to keep the writer from having to do any more extra work than he usually did anyhow, this conference was almost invariably held.

When the interpretations were at variance, as was usually the case, the three tried to compromise them into something that the managing editor might have had in mind. Dockery, Gaskin and Cabot did that today. Then Dockery and Cabot went back to their desks and Gaskin was left alone with Hindemith. He decided right now he would rather be alone with Sibelius, so he put the Finn on.

"Sibelius," he told himself, "is better background for doing a story on the United States agricultural situation than is Hindemith. More pastoral, cousin."

11:25 A.M. It would be another hour, give or take, before photostats of the layout came up and Gaskin would know how many lines he had for the opening page and how many for the two spreads. He spent the time reading, more or less, the remainder of the research Charity had given him. He had rarely read anything so boring. But he was a professional writer, and a highly competent one, and he could do this story or any other story. It was past noon when he got the stats. He could start writing any time now, but first he did a few things around his office. He put on some more records, adjusted the Venetian blinds and the polka-dot chintz curtians so the light wouldn't be so harsh, rearranged the two pillows on the leather couch, adjusted a picture or two on the wall and sharpened some pencils. The O.G. (Office Girl) would sharpen your pencils for you if you left them in the Outgoing box, but Gaskin had been accustomed to sharpening his own pencils from his newspaper days and it was one luxury he could never adapt to at *Vital*, having someone else sharpen your pencils. He adjusted excellently to all the other luxuries.

By the time he had accomplished these various self-appointed and unnecessary chores it was past twelve-thirty. Gaskin knew from experience that a lead of this sort would see him in the office until midnight at the very minimum and quite possibly until the hours of Sunday morning.

It didn't seem possible with the comparatively small number of words to write, but Gaskin knew from experience just how possible it was. He decided to go out to lunch rather than start now and have the work interrupted. He knew also from experience the thing to do was to take a long lunch in which you forgot about the story. He did this with three other people from the office, all of them beforehand having three martinis by way of anesthetization to things in general. Somehow, though, today he could not stop thinking about the story. Everything he ate reminded him of it, the chicken "supreme," the boiled potato, and the peas of that naked sickening bile-green tint peas have when served in New York restaurants and that pebblelike consistency—all reminded him of it, since every last bit of it came from a farm, somewhere. Even during the martinis he could not get away from the story, for staring down into the sheeny liquid, which today somehow looked like watered gasoline, he kept watching the pearl onion, and he remembered that that, too, originally came from a farm, somewhere, sometime. He felt unaccountably restless. Who can say why certain moods come upon man?

3:00 P.M. Back from lunch Henry Gaskin readjusted the polka-dot curtains and rearranged the polka-dot pillows, sharpened a few more pencils, then put on some Tchaikovsky and started in writing the text-blocks and captions. Gaskin was a fast writer and it rolled along, if not very merrily. The layout, after being photostated, was changed a couple of times with consequent modifications in the length of some of the text-blocks and captions. He rewrote them to fit the space. Then he wrote the heads. He had the whole hated thing done by six o'clock, which was very fast time for this size story. He turned it in to the copy room for typing, then went down to see the copy editor, to tell him he had done so and to find out when he probably would be edited.

"Not until after supper," Creech said. He wouldn't have been caught dead using the word "dinner" for the day's concluding meal. "I-uh got a bloody lot of copy here 'fore yores, as you may see." And he nodded to his Incoming box.

"In that case I'll just see myself down to the Eagle's Nest. I shall gaze narcissistically at my reflection in the top of a martini."

6:15 P.M. Gaskin wandered over with some people and had three martinis, which he needed after doing that story. He was feeling pretty good with the story in and was hopeful it would be edited soon enough that he could make one or two interesting-sounding parties he knew about tonight. The story had two barriers to hurdle—the copy editor and the managing editor—but Gaskin was hopeful. Hope springs . . . After the martinis he walked lightly back across the street with some fellow workers and took the elevator to the editorial offices on the thirty-fourth floor.

7:15 P.M. They proceeded to the next feature of the Saturday night ritual, the serving of dinner in by the management. To some this was an act of consideration, to others an act of canniness to keep the staff from wandering out for drinks and never returning. The great elegance both of the dinner and of the men who served it—there in front of the AP ticker, which is the Book of Life, constantly pouring out on an endless roll of yellow paper the idiosyncrasies, vicissitudes, and the dark evils of our mad world—made the customers who filed by to eat it —noisy, bleary-eyed, ink-stained, disheveled, shirt-sleeved and tieless —look like Bowery bums who had by some ghastly mistake got into an impossibly high-powered soup line.

"Fattening us up for the kill, mates," Gaskin used to say of the Saturday night dinner.

Gaskin and several of the others ate in his office, using the desk, the armchair and the couch. By eight o'clock the big meal was all over. Gaskin had another cup of coffee and sat waiting for the call.

While waiting he picked up a book he had been reading, the writings of Lao-tse and Chuang-tse, and read:

Smugs are those people who having heard what their teacher says, feel very, very satisfied and very pleased with themselves. They think they have learned the truth and do not realize that there was a time when no material universe existed. The snugs are lice on the bodies of hogs. They choose their abode in the long mane and hair of the hogs and believe themselves to be living in a grand palace with a big garden. They hide themselves in the corners, armpits, breasts and legs of the pigs and think that they are living in security. They do not realize that one day the butcher may come and rolling up his sleeve begin to lay hay under it and set fire to singe the pig, and both themselves and the pig will be scorched to death. This is to live within the limitations of their own choice. These are the snugs . . .

His phone rang and he grabbed it up.

"Pull yoreself on down hyere, Henry," the copy editor said. "I want words with you."

8:35 P.M. The copy editor, who in Gaskin's opinion was an authentic snug, had a number of changes to suggest.

"This hyere is cryptic," he said. "Now this hyere part needs some changin' around hyere . . . This I think you ought to rewrite completely. Try running the whole thing through your typewriter again, all right, Henry?" asking one of the rhetorical questions which were his chief means of communication.

"Do I have any choice in the matter?" Gaskin said, asking one of his own.

The copy editor took out his red bandanna handkerchief and mopped his face.

8:55 P.M. Gaskin took the batch of yellow flimsies down to his office. He put on some Berlioz—the composer he favored when he was doing the copy editor's changes—and worked an hour or so making them. Then he put them through the copy room for retyping. Then he waited. He was beginning to feel a drum-drumming in his ears, a cadenced beat-beat which went: *Where will I be ten years from now?* He picked up his book and read:

> The mountain trees invite their own cutting down; lamp oil invites its own burning up. Cinnamon bark can be eaten; therefore the tree is cut down. Lacquer can be used; therefore the tree is scraped. All men know the utility of useful things; but they do not know the utility of futility . . .

His phone rang.

"Sashay on down hyere, Henry."

10:25 P.M. Gaskin went down to Creech's office and sat by while the copy editor went over it again. Sometimes the copy editor liked to be alone when he was slaughtering a writer's copy but ordinarily he liked for the writer to sit there and watch him do it. Three guesses why. The copy editor made some penciled changes here and there then leaned back in his chair, scratched his hairy belly and belched generously.

"Bloody good feed tonight," he said. "Now be a good boy and drop this by the copy room, Henry. On yore way out."

The snug had a buzzer which would fetch someone from the copy room to pick up copy but he was fond of using writers as messenger boys. The snug was very considerate of the copy-room people.

"Anything I can get you?" Gaskin said.

"Not right now thank you very much however, Henry," the snug said.

"You're welcome," said Gaskin. "Let joy be unconfined."

Gaskin took the copy and dropped it by the copy room and went back to his office.

10:55 P.M. He put on some Puccini, the composer he favored when his copy had got through the copy editor and had only the managing editor to get by. He picked up Chuang-tse and read:

> As to what the world does and the way people seek happiness now, I do not know if such happiness be real happiness or unhappiness. I watch the world rushing about with the crowd to seek happiness, and see something

seems to drive them along. Yet they all say they are happy. I have not participated in their happiness or unhappiness. Is there, after all, such a thing as happiness or unhappiness?

I consider inaction as true happiness, while the world regards it as great misery. It has been said, "Perfect happiness is the absence of the striving for happiness: perfect renown is the absence of concern for renown."

He got up and went to the window and stood watching the lights of Manhattan outside. His eyes swung in a rhythmic arc from the lighted living towers to the artist's concept on his wall of New York as the city would appear fifteen minutes after an H-bomb had been dropped on it —then back to the present towers which just out the window rose in dark grandeur to the sky.

"Think it over, Henry, 'fore you jump."

Gaskin turned easily. It was the copy editor and he was laughing. Just a shade ghoulishly, Gaskin fancied. Creech had a keen sense of humor if the jest was his own. He had just stuck his head in the door, on his way somewhere, and now had gone.

Gaskin lay down on the couch and read awhile:

He who would be the ultimate guide of the world should take care to preserve the original nature of man. For duck's legs, though short, cannot be lengthened without dismay to the duck, and a crane's legs, though long, cannot be shortened without misery to the crane. That which is long in nature must not be cut off, and that which is short in nature must not be lengthened. One should not worry about changing them. It would seem that humanity and justice were not part of the nature of man! Yet from the time of the Three Dynasties downwards what a commotion has been raised about them!

He got up and wandered restlessly around the National Affairs bullpen. Charity Cabot was busy checking his copy for accuracy, putting dots over the words, so he didn't bother her. He went in and talked with Dockery a little bit. Then he went back to his office. He looked at his watch. Then he remembered that the liquor would have been broken out and went down and got some Scotch. Pretty soon nearly everyone had a glass by him while working or in his hand if wandering up and down the corridors.

11:35 P.M. Gaskin went back to his office. He put on some Debussy and read some more:

There is no greater injury to one's character than practicing virtue with motivation. . . . A man feels a pleasurable sensation before he smiles, and smiles before he thinks how he ought to smile.

He went to the window and stood watching. The city had a warm glow below him and down there he could see what appeared an infinitude of people. The theaters had just emptied and they would be on their way to night clubs. Gaskin imagined he could hear their gay chatter. Within a radius of five blocks from where Hank Gaskin stood there must have been a hundred night clubs. How this city wears on the nerves! he thought. And how this office does! He thought of how prodigal the magazine was in everything, including its use of one's talent, using but a fraction of the talent of each. Group journalism! he thought. He turned and his eyes lighted upon the picture of the devastated city. He turned back to the window and to the great avenue and the milling people on it. *What will I be doing ten years from now?* the sing-song went, beat-beat, hammer-hammer, in his mind.

Suddenly, while standing there, Gaskin had an idea. He had never done it at night for some reason—probably because you couldn't see the results—but it occurred to him to do it tonight. He walked over to his desk, put his glass down and picked up a piece of copy paper. He started to shape it. Then it occurred to him to write something on it. He put it in his typewriter, centered it with excessive care, and wrote in letters with no caps

what am i doing here?

He shaped the sheet of paper into an elegant airplane and carried it to the window. He stood there a moment, then sailed it out. He watched it fluttering down for a few yards, then it disappeared in the darkness. He looked at his watch—it was 11:45. At almost this moment his phone rang. It was Creech and his voice had an edge to it. When it did he usually forgot all about the rustic accent and the British expressions.

"Come on down here, Henry," he said. "Come on into the managing editor's office."

11:55 P.M. Gaskin went on down the long corridor and into the vast office. Dockery was already there and so was Creech. The managing editor had his head cocked back and to the side—a position with which Gaskin was familiar—and was making a few gestures.

"Ump . . . grunt . . . Ugh . . . Zow . . . muh . . . Wahr . . . zamow . . . eeph . . ."

Dockery, Gaskin and the copy editor went out. They went into Creech's office. The copy editor looked quite worried. The three of them conferred on what the managing editor meant. One thing was clear, he didn't like what Gaskin had done. As usual, each of the three had a different interpretation as to what the managing editor wanted. The copy editor, however, had known the managing editor longest, dealt with him far more than either Dockery or Gaskin, and so was considered to have mastered his language, sound and sign, more closely, at least, than anyone else. Therefore his interpretation was accepted and Gaskin went back to do the whole thing over.

Before sitting down to his task he put on some Respighi, his favorite composer when he had to do over what the copy editor had approved but the managing editor didn't. Also he decided to launch another airplane before getting started. He centered the copy sheet in his typewriter and wrote

> i wonder if i'll be doing this same thing ten years
> from now. and if so why i will have lived.

He shaped it, walked over to the window, launched it, watched it disappear into the dark void, and returned and sat down to his desk to rewrite the entire story.

3:00 A.M. He felt as if corn and wheat were coming out of his ears, not to mention Scotch. He had got up from time to time to freshen his drink; by now he was going fairly much on nerves alone. By now, also, he loathed agriculture to a point he would gladly have seen every farmer in America hanged and quartered like one of the hogs on his Iowa farm.

At three he did have it finished. Finished again. He put it through the copy room for typing, waited and wandered around, passing the time drinking, then finally returned to his office. After a while he got another phone call. It was the copy editor. His voice was still on edge though not so much so as before.

"Come on down here, Henry. The managing editor's office."

3:45 A.M. Gaskin went on down. Dockery was there again. The managing editor was holding one of the textblocks and gesturing at it.

"Zeep . . . Muh . . . Yonka . . . Ugh . . . Grunt . . . Zirial . . . Naph . . . Angh . . ."

The three men left and went into the copy editor's office to confer.

"I think," said the copy editor, "Cy means that this here business about the corn crop in Wisconsin is given too much bloody emphasis. Also, in this textblock, he means, I think, he wants a little history of the drought in the Southwest. Got it clear, Gaskin?"

"Rigidly," Gaskin said. "It's one of the clearest things I have heard in the last five years."

Gaskin went back to his office. He dug through the research trying to find something about the history of the drought in the Southwest. He couldn't find it. He went down to Charity Cabot's desk. She was on the long-distance telephone checking with a stringer in Idaho about some point in the story. He waited until she had finished.

"We got anything on the history of the drought in the Southwest?"

"The what?"

"History. Big Cy wants some history."

Charity looked through her stack of research. She couldn't find any-thing. She called up the Morgue and asked them to send up what they had on the subject. In twenty minutes a young man brought up eighteen thick folders labeled "Drought" and dumped them on Charity's desk. They contained everything but a copy of *The Grapes of Wrath*. Char-ity and Gaskin plowed through the folders until they found something historical. Then Gaskin went down to his office and worked it into the textblock. This part occupied eighteen words.

5:00 A.M. He took the rewritten textblocks directly to the copy editor and started to leave.

"I say, don't be in such a ruddy hurry, Henry," Creech said. "Don't you like muh-eye company?"

"No," Gaskin said. "Not at this hour."

"Have yoreself a seat right here, Henry. How you feeling, Henry old boy?"

"I'm beginning to feel insecure, Alvin. Very insecure, old boy."

"Well, we all do sometimes."

"We bloody well do, old boy."

The copy editor went over Gaskin's copy, made some minor changes and initialed it. Then he handed the copy to Gaskin.

"Now just be a good boy, Henry, and drop this here by the copy room. That's a good boy."

"Yes, sir," said Henry Gaskin. With his hand dirtied from typewriter ribbon, newsprint, et cetera, he gave a British-type salute. They are the most elegant in the world.

5:20 A.M. Gaskin trudged down the corridor to the copy room, carrying the two pieces of paper and singing some lines from "God Bless the Bas-tard King of England." He left them there for typing and went back to the layout room to get another drink. Carrying the drink he wandered down to the National Affairs bullpen. Charity Cabot was having trouble getting dots on a couple of points—the amount of acreage left fallow in America under the government plow-under program of 1934; and the amount of wheat harvested in all history in the state of Kansas. On the first point she had called and got out of bed the Washington bureau member who had worked on the story there. He in turn was routing various members of the Department of Agriculture out of bed all over the city of Washington to see what they knew about it. They were try-ing to find some holdover from the early Roosevelt days but there were not many of these around any more.

"Why don't you call Henry Wallace?" Gaskin said.

He was joking, but Charity Cabot's eyes lighted up. There was no-body a *Vital* researcher wouldn't call. And there was no hour when she wouldn't call him.

"Why, that's a wonderful idea, Hank. He lives somewhere near here, doesn't he? Connecticut or something like that."

She picked up the phone and dialed the Morgue. "Would you get me Henry Wallace's present address and if possible phone number. . . . What's that? . . . The one who was vice-president of course. . . . Vice-president of what? . . . Of the United States. . . . And before that he was Secretary of Agriculture . . ."

In a few minutes Gaskin could hear Charity's voice. "Hello, Mr. Wallace? This is Charity Cabot of *Vital* magazine. I'm terribly sorry to awaken you at this hour, but . . ."

5:25 A.M. Gaskin wandered away. He ambled up and down the corridors talking to people and refreshing his drink from time to time. Then he returned to his office. He was worn to a nub. And he had drunk a great deal of Scotch whiskey. He opened the book and read some more:

> To be united is to be parted. To be completed is to be destroyed. To be sharp-edged is to be blunted. To be in an elevated position is to be criticized. To do is to impair. To be eminent is to be plotted against. To be stupid is to be taken advantage of. Alas, is there anything in this human world that we can regard as sure?

He had just looked at his watch—it was 5:30 A.M.—when he got a call from the copy editor.

"It's all through Cy," Creech said. "I just thought as how you might like to know, Henry."

"I do like to know," Gaskin said. "I really like to get that news, old man. Thanks ever so much for conveying it. Over."

5:35 A.M. Gaskin let the phone drop back into its cradle. Now he would wait around for any checkpoints Charity had—questions of accuracy. He walked over and looked out the window. He could see the first edges of light on the far horizon. The buildings were turning to high silhouettes and the streets far below were empty. Then down the otherwise empty avenue—he thought of the crowds of hours earlier—he saw two people walking. Lovers undoubtedly, he thought, caught up in the dream of being all alone on the late streets of New York. That was one thing love made you do in New York, walk its late streets. Suddenly Gaskin went to his desk, got a sheet of copy paper, centered it in the typewriter and wrote

> maybe i ought to quit and do something

He made it into an airplane and went over and sailed it down. It floated down easily into the dawn and the empty streets of the city.

He continued freshening his drink. Pretty soon Charity came down with her checkpoints.

7:15 A.M. They had finished with the checkpoints and were sitting in Gaskin's office while he had a last drink. Outside the dawn was coming up red, and inside Beethoven's Ninth Symphony was coming out of the speaker in the corner. Gaskin felt very bushed. He was sitting in his chair and he looked at Charity Cabot seated on the couch. Even she looked a little tired but she still looked very young and very pretty. He thought of asking her about ten years from now. Then it occurred to him that the question might be cruel put to someone so young, so pretty, to a girl. He just asked, "How do you like it here, Charity?"

She smiled a little at him. "Well, it means no Saturday night dates. What is that song?"

" 'Saturday night is the loneliest night in the week,' " Gaskin said. He knew all the popular songs for forty years back.

"Saturday night isn't lonely here," she said. "In fact, not lonely enough. But I guess I like it here. I like most of the people."

"Me, too," Gaskin said. He had had a great deal to drink. "I like the people. 'Saturday night,' " he sang it a little, " 'is the loneliest night in the week. For that's the night that my baby and I used to dance cheek to cheek . . .' Charity."

"What?"

Suddenly the fury and the frazzle of it hit Hank Gaskin. "Charity, you got any carbon paper?"

"What do you want with carbon paper at seven o'clock on Sunday morning?"

"Never mind," Gaskin said. He added cannily, "I'd just like some."

She went out and found him some and left it. "Excuse me," she said, "I'll be back."

7:40 A.M. While Charity went to the ladies room Gaskin read from his book:

Do you realize how one's character is lost and where knowledge leads? A man loses his character through the desire for fame, and knowledge leads to contention. In the struggle for fame men crush each other, while their knowledge is but an instrument for scheming and contention. These two are instruments of evil and lead one away from the moral life . . .

He got out a sheet of copy paper. He centered it as exactly as he could and wrote

i not just ought to. i am.

He thereupon thoughtfully added an admonitory passage from his book for the benefit of some passer-by known only to God, who on the gay streets below might catch up the wisp of paper,

> Human life in this world is but as the form of a white pony flashing across a rock crevice. In a moment it is gone. Suddenly waking up, all life is born; suddenly slipping off, all silently creep away. With one change, one is born; with another, one dies. Living creatures moan, and mankind weeps. Remove its bondage, slip off its skin-carcass, and curling up, where shall the soul of man go and the body go with it? Is it perhaps on the great journey home?

He made it into an airplane, then walked over to the window. He hesitated a moment. Then he let go. Down, down it sailed, caught now by the breeze and borne upward, then descending again into the early light. He did not wait to see it land. He went back to his desk, got out nine sheets of the carbon paper, got some flimsies from his desk drawer and stuck the whole thing in the typewriter. He wrote, "Dear Messers . . ." and wrote on the names of the managing editor, the vice managing editor, the two assistant managing editors, copy editor and several of the senior editors. "I herewith tender, if that word is not too cryptic, my resignation. I am tired of the agricultural situation. The first time I wrote it I wasn't so tired but the fifth time I rewrote it I was very tired. So I'm quitting, and good-bye all you bastards." He signed it "Uncryptically yours, Henry Gaskin."

Gaskin pulled the batch out of his typewriter, removed the carbons, and carrying the ten copies started going down the corridors. The offices off them were deserted now. He walked first into the office of the copy editor. He carefully placed a copy in the roller of the typewriter so it would be sure not to get blown away. He started to get up and go into the next office. Suddenly he saw the telephone on the copy editor's desk. Somehow the telephone stirred something in him. Maybe it was that the copy editor was always calling him on it and usually with unpleasant news. Stealthily Gaskin's hand reached out and took the phone tenderly. Then suddenly he gave a mighty jerk and the phone came leaping off the wall, loosening some plaster with it. To Gaskin's ears it was a sound joyous as the angels' song to the shepherds at Bethlehem. He got up and went into the next office . . . then the next. In each he left a copy of his letter of resignation. In each he separated the phone from its moorings. He went back to his office. Charity wasn't there. Probably she was looking for him. He sat down and wrote her a note he had gone home, so she wouldn't worry. Then he noticed he had one copy of his resignation left. He tried to make an airplane out of it. Being on flimsy paper it made a very poor one but anyway he walked over and fluttered it out the window. It seemed to go up and keep going instead of down. Then he left the office himself—by way of the door, not the window—borne outward on the strains of Beethoven's Ninth Symphony, which there hardly seemed any point in turning off. It was 8:23 of a Sabbath morning.

As always Gaskin never remembered what happened. The next facts he knew came over him very slowly. He was awake. He was lying on a bed. He was in a very dark room, black. But he knew the bed was a strange one. Now he felt thoroughly in command. It was a situation of unfamiliarity very familiar to him, one which he had handled a good many times before.

He started going through the drill. He got up and felt his way to the window. He pulled up the Venetian blind. A flood of light burst into the blackened room, almost blinding him. He must have been looking directly into the sun. It shot a formidable, jagged, splitting feeling through his head, like a sharp clean ax splitting timbers. He waited only long enough to see in a flash that the scene below was nothing he could identify—there was a boulevard and quite a bit of traffic. Then he plunged the blind closed again. His head felt a little better in the blackness. He stumbled his way back to the bed. There must, he figured, be a phone by it. Every hotel had a phone by the bed. He fumbled around by the bed. His hands found a small table. On top of it he felt a lamp. He was very careful not to knock it off. His hands crept cautiously around the top of the table. With a spring of joy inside him they rested on something cold and familiar. He lifted the receiver from its cradle.

"Room service," he said.

"Por favor?"

It was a very pleasant day in Mexico City, and he saw a good many things he had never seen, including the Pyramids of the Sun and the Moon. Monday night he took an overnight plane which set him back down at Idlewild at 8:00 A.M. He went directly to the office. He would be taking the hi-fi, the records and somehow the enormous couch. The chintz curtains, armchair and pictures he would leave—he might take two or three of his favorite pictures. He walked in and sat down to his desk and commenced to clean it out. Then he noticed that his typewriter had a note in it. He leaned over and read it. It said, "Call me—Charity."

He phoned her. "I'll be right down," she said.

She came on down. She handed him a sheaf of papers. He looked at the first one—it was the original of his letter of resignation. He looked beneath—they were the carbons.

"I couldn't do anything about the phones," she said.

He looked up at the girl. For a while he didn't say anything. Then a soft smile broke over his face and he said quietly, "Why, thank you, Charity." He stood up. "Well, I guess I'll take off my coat and tie. How about lunch?"

"I'd love it," Charity said. "I really would, you know."

He looked at her. She looked back a moment then left. Gaskin sat down on his couch. Actually he knew she meant well. But he was not sure whether or not he was glad she had done it. He thought about it for quite a while but he was never sure. Some day, somehow, some way he would make his move in this world, to do something about it all. The time seemed not now, but he felt, more clearly than he had ever felt anything, that the time would come. Once more he read in the book he had been reading:

> *I have Three Treasures;*
> *Guard them and keep them safe:*
> *The first is Love.*
> *The second is, Never too much.*
> *The third is, Never be the first in the world.*
> *Through Love, one has no fear;*
> *Through not doing too much, one has amplitude of reserve power;*
> *Through not presuming to be the first in the world,*
> *One can develop one's talent and let it mature.*
> *If one forsakes love and fearlessness,*
>   *forsakes restraint and reserve power,*
>   *forsakes following behind and rushes in front,*
> *He is doomed!*
> *For love is victorious in attack,*
> *And invulnerable in defense.*
> *Heaven arms with love*
> *Those it would not see destroyed.*

My life is being used, he thought. *That must stop.* Meantime he would have a long lunch today. He got up and tacked up the pink couch schedule and signed himself up for the 3-3:30 period. He turned and found himself looking at the picture of New York destroyed. Then he went over and put on someone he always chose at times like these. Bach.

16

Excellence Through Sweat

John Marshall Reasoner was head of *Vital* magazine's Nature Affairs Department. Actually, except for one researcher, Reasoner *was* the Nature Affairs Department. He fulfilled the functions both of editor—deciding and planning what stories the department would cover and laying the stories out once the pictures were in; and of writer—writing the textblocks, captions and heads for the stories which the managing editor selected to run. Most Nature Affairs stories were short—a page and two half-pages usually, sometimes a little more, and very rarely a "picture essay" of five or six pages. It was a minor department of the magazine. The department, some people felt, really should have been called the "Unnatural Affairs Department," since so many of the stories dealt with animals in acts of deviation from their species: a house-pet lion, a bloodhound nursing a kitten, a penguin sitting up in the seat of an airplane en route from Antarctica and to all appearances quite keenly enjoying the scenery.

Johnny Reasoner had ability and several times had been offered a larger position on the magazine. By now he might almost have been something like National Affairs editor if he had so chosen. He always succeeded in talking his way out of any offer of promotion. "I like it where I am," he explained. He had no ambition to move out of his circumscribed world into bigger and more powerful ponds in the magazine. He preferred writing about animals to writing about human beings. He apparently was going to spend the rest of his life composing little groups of words about unlionlike lions, undoglike dogs and unpenguinlike penguins.

People were a little scared of Johnny Reasoner. He had an acid tongue. His voice was very even in pitch, and the words came out as if clipped with a straight-edge razor. He was contemptuous of cant or pretense in whatever form and whenever he encountered it made no attempt to conceal this contempt. On the contrary, he was highly likely to show it by way of some short but acid-dipped phrase of sarcasm. Then people would give that slightly scared, slightly uncomfortable laugh. There was something about Johnny Reasoner that made you feel he saw completely through you, saw every trait of pretentiousness, pose or vanity you had, and had utter contempt for it. And yet Johnny

300

Reasoner was not an unpleasant person to be with. He made what is called "interesting" company. Probably this was because, although he never made small talk, he was fluent of phrase, highly read on a great number of subjects, had an extremely quick mind, and what he said was intelligent and provocative of thought. And his sarcasm was often —though not always—accompanied by a short laugh which took a good deal of the sharpness off. The sarcasm and the laugh, combined, seemed to be saying: "Don't try to fool me. I will not sit still for it. I can see through your motive. You are like everybody else is: you have your motives."

But Johnny Reasoner would have been the first to include himself in this sweeping characterization of the human race.

Researchers moved around a good deal at *Vital,* department to department, and new researchers were always coming in. Johnny Reasoner had a sense of humor and one place he often displayed it was with a new researcher in his department. At a point when they were well into their introductory talk, she sitting in a chair by his desk while Reasoner, leaning back in his with his right leg cocked on the desk, fluently oriented her into the workings of the Nature Affairs Department, he would casually reach into a drawer of his desk and get out an icepick he kept there. Continuing his smooth talk about how the Nature Affairs Department sought out the unusual manifestations of ducks, geese, lions, apes, whooping cranes and lesser adjutants, Reasoner would toy easily with the icepick. Now very casually, leaning forward slightly from his powerful torso but never breaking his talk, he would begin to draw the point of the icepick lightly over the area around the knee of his right leg. This extracted no special notice from the girl, or scarcely a thought, since many people have some kind of manual habit when talking—toying with their glasses, doodling on a piece of paper, rubbing the eraser of a pencil on the back of their ear, and the like. At the most she would have a mild thought that an icepick as a tool for such usual mannerisms was rather unusual. But that would be all and she would continue to pay close attention to Reasoner's delineation of the department in which she was about to commence work. Reasoner speaking:

". . . By this time I've come to expect an animal to do just about anything that a human being does, along with a good deal more. We've certainly had animals doing just about everything. Really to surprise me in this department there would have to arrive on this desk a picture showing a Bengal tiger dancing with Queen Elizabeth at a garden party at Buckingham Palace while holding a Pimm's Cup in his free paw. You couldn't expect a Bengal tiger to have very good manners, of course . . ."

The girl would smile broadly. And at this point Reasoner, never looking at it, but continuing to talk to the girl, would very slowly raise the icepick over his shoulder in throwing position, then . . . Then, with a swift and skillful, pantherlike movement, flip it. The icepick would land, stuck and quivering, in his stretched-out right leg.

"EE-ee-ee-ee-ow-ow-ow-ow-ow-oh-oh-oh-oh-ee-ee—ohp—ohp—oh —oo—oo—oo-oop-oop——ee—ee—ee—eee—ohm—ohm—ohm— oop—oop—ee—ow—oh—ee—ohh . . ."

The gasping screams of the thunderstruck girl would ring through the office. Then Reasoner would casually reach forward and pull the icepick out of his leg. Reasoner had extremely powerful hands but even he would have to give a strong, tensing pull to get the icepick out.

The researcher's reaction was invariably, whether openly so or quickly, partially, suppressed, one of surprised horror. Along with, when she recovered the power of intelligible speech, some such exclamation as:

"Oh my God, you scared the wits out of me . . ."

"Oh, I didn't know . . ." and an embarrassed silence.

"Oh, I didn't know you had . . . had *that* . . . I'm so sorry . . ."

"I didn't know you had a wooden . . . that is to say . . . I mean an . . . artificial leg . . ."

In June, 1941, John Marshall Reasoner was graduated from Harvard College with a *summa cum laude* in American history. He also had by that point in time an appointment as a Rhodes scholar. He was aiming for a career in teaching in one of the prep schools of the East, with the intention if he was good enough of eventually being headmaster of one of these schools. He was dedicated in a missionary sense to the idea of training young minds; it seemed to him the greatest and most rewarding thing in the world a man could devote his life to. He never got to Oxford, because the war broke out. He did, however, get overseas, to the Italian theater. He went as a second lieutenant of infantry and a platoon leader. It was in this capacity, while leading a night reconnaissance patrol on the lower slopes of the hill of the monastery at Cassino, that he caught the large-sized fragment of 88-millimeter which at once changed all the teaching plans. He knew this instantly when he woke up in the field hospital and discovered that his right leg was gone at a point about four inches above the knee. He was certainly not going to drag the manufactured replacement for that leg around in front of a pack of teen-age boys who would, they could not help themselves, identify him always in terms of that replacement. This may not have been true, but since Reasoner believed it was, it was as effective as if it had been. Since he could not be what he wanted very much to be, a teacher in a prep school and eventually if he was good enough headmaster of one, he did not care a great deal what specific means of livelihood he took on. It was a curious frame of mind for him, who had always known exactly and passionately what he wanted to be, to find himself in a position of choosing one of several dozen different things to be, with an equal feeling of dispassionateness, objectivity and lack of involvement or care or interest about them all. He got into *Vital* quite by chance. When he went back for one more year of school, in the springtime a representative of the magazine came around and talked with some of the students about the possibilities of employment at the magazine. Reasoner was one of them, and a month later was offered a job. He had worked as a researcher in various departments and finally had been given the Nature Affairs Department as his own.

Reasoner was very competent professionally, as noted above. He had the utilitarian, craftsman's philosophy, by the mid-Twentieth Century all but extinct in this country, of becoming a master of whatever one's trade happened to be. Over the years he had mastered so well the field of journalistic ducks, geese and apes that he could spot a *Vital*-type Nature Affairs story instinctively, so that it was seldom a story he suggested for coverage was not shot, and once shot, seldom it did not run. When the story was in, he was also a master at writing the kind of headlines, captions and textblocks *Vital* liked for its Nature Affairs stories, so that Johnny Reasoner required perhaps less rewriting than any other writer on the magazine. He had mastered all the types of leads *Vital* favored. For example, if the story concerned a goose doing something ungooselike, the lead might run, "Most geese are so and so. But the goose in the above picture is different from the way all geese are supposed to be. This goose . . ." He was very good at his job.

Johnny Reasoner was married. He had been married for nearly ten years now. He had married shortly before going overseas, a girl by the name of Alice Motherwell he had known for about a year. Their decision to marry had been brought on, or at least advanced, by the fact Reasoner was going overseas. Alice had disclosed to him that she was pregnant. Alice's family, unaware of this compelling reason for it, had opposed the marriage. The real basis for their opposition was never stated but a less astute man than Reasoner could have sensed it readily. His father was a teacher in a high school in a small town in Iowa and neither socially nor financially were the Reasoners at all up to the Motherwells, who had to pay especial attention to these matters since Alice was an only child. Alice's father, who owned a paper mill in New Hampshire and was quite certain Reasoner was after his money, was much too shrewd to mention these real grounds when, stalling for time and counting on time, distance and war to wipe out all plans for marriage, he had tried to talk them into waiting. Instead, taking Reasoner aside, he had put the entire matter on the shrewd grounds of compassion.

"Do you think it's quite fair to Alice," he put it straight to Reasoner, "getting married so soon before you go overseas? Suppose something should happen to you? Suppose—I don't like to talk about this, Johnny, but I think we have to face reality here—suppose you should be, well, mangled in some way. Would that be quite fair to Alice?"

When Reasoner came home the way he did, Alice's father at least had the satisfaction of telling his daughter "I told you so." That is one of the satisfactions of life and it was savored somewhat by the owner of the paper mill in New Hampshire.

Alice Reasoner was a good wife. A *good* wife. Everyone knew that and everyone said that. Everyone talked of how great a sacrifice it must be for her and how wonderful she was with Johnny and how understanding and had been from the day he came home. If there had been a nation-wide contest conducted by the *Ladies' Home Journal* to select "The Most Understanding Wife of One of Our Boys Who Came Home Missing a Part" the contest would probably have been won by Alice Reasoner. Everyone knew she was the sweetest woman in the world.

Johnny Reasoner knew all about this talk. His own feeling about his wife was different. He hated her with a passionate hatred. His reason for this was twofold. First, in the few days of their marriage they had before he went overseas, she unfolded to him reasons for marrying him that were somewhat at variance with those she had outlined before the wedding. In the three weeks previous to the marriage, she related, she had slept with five different men, one of whom was himself, and this proclivity had so frightened her she decided she should be married; the other prompting for this decision, she told him, was the fear she had become pregnant from one of those five men, and in one way or another all the other four—two of them were married already —were ineligible to marry her. That left Reasoner. She was not sure she was pregnant but she *could* be. There wasn't time to be sure before he went overseas, hence she had had to act. She made it all sound very logical from her point of view, as doubtless it was. One woman's point of view is another man's hate. Reasoner had refrained from divorcing her immediately because he could not face handing the triumph of the divorce to her father—he hated himself for this weakness but it was there. Fortunately there was no pregnancy, so that he at least did not have to face the acquisition of a child bearing his name whose father could have been any one of four other men. He had made up his mind that if a child were born he would insist on two things: a divorce, and custody of the child. The other reason he hated his wife was that since his return she had built an entire way of life out of being the good wife to such a returned-with-something-missing husband as himself. She never told him this—they had no real communication by which this or anything else could be told. He did not need to be told it. She had set out to make herself into the model of the patient, understanding, *good* wife. He knew it and loathed her for it. And she had succeeded very well, as everybody said so frequently. Johnny Reasoner never performed a motion or breathed a syllable to lead people to change their ennobled opinion of his wife.

As to why Johnny Reasoner did not divorce his wife, that is a natural question for the reader to ask. Perhaps it was that there is an optimum time for divorce—with Reasoner it had certainly been the time of those disclosures from his wife following their marriage—and that once this point is passed, people, however mismated, seldom get a divorce, certainly not unless one of them meets someone else with whom he or she falls violently and helplessly in love. But this is only a speculation. The writer can only say that there was no single answer to the question. He can only answer the question with a question: Why do millions of couples with nothing in common—and, yes, many of them despising his or her partner in marriage—why do millions such, and many of them most intelligent people, continue to remain married? If the reader can answer that question—the writer cannot—he will have his answer as to why Johnny Reasoner continued married.

Johnny Reasoner had made up his mind to one thing, which is more than can be said for either member of many such couples. If he ever found a woman who passed one particular test, he would undertake to divorce his wife and marry that woman. He never expected to find such a woman, so the question remained largely academic to him and he expected it so to remain throughout his life. Nevertheless the very fact the decision existed, ready for implementation in the unlikely event of the one condition being fulfilled, helped, along with the keen discipline he possessed, to keep him going.

Johnny Reasoner was a man of surpassing discipline, knowing that he could not live without discipline, particularly as he was now constructed. His discipline was manifested in many areas—physical, mental and emotional. Physically, for instance, over the strain of dragging that mechanical leg around, from which often even on a cold day sweat would break out in a thousand little beads on his brow. Mentally, in a highly ordered mind. Emotionally—emotionally as will be seen if the reader will read on.

Johnny Reasoner's most striking physical feature was the great muscled power of that part of his body above his waist, which came from swinging that leg. His chest seemed like some enormously powerful dynamo and his arms and hands suggested great strength and power.

He had sandy hair, his face had a few freckles, and his eyes were blue, quiet and cold-looking.

People did have one compensation they could always fall back on for feeling Reasoner's penetration into themselves and for his acid commentaries on what he found. They were able to feel sorry for him because of his leg, which served the worthy twofold purpose of making them feel like good, compassionate people and also of making them thank God that Reasoner had the artificial leg and they didn't.

Johnny Reasoner was a man of a certain inner violence, barely inner, for it hovered always near the surface. People suspected something of the sort in him. What it was they did not know. They only knew it by a vague kind of fear they had around him. But how dangerously near to the surface the inner violence lodged, no one knew. No one except Johnny Reasoner.

One day a new O.G. stopped by the office. Her name was Tammy Rhinelander. She was exactly one half the age of Johnny Reasoner, who was thirty-six.

The lowliest cog in the great *Vital* machine was the "O.G."—Office Girl. The O.G.s' job was to keep the Incoming boxes filled and the Outgoing boxes empty. They delivered things around the office—copies of dispatches from the bureaus, story lists, newspapers, interoffice memoranda. You could see them moving pertly up and down the corridors carrying these things, or, where the load was great, pushing supermarket baskets containing them. They also sharpened pencils for the ranks of writer and above. Researchers had to sharpen their own pencils. It was one way of getting into the *Vital* organization and most of the O.G.'s aspired to be researchers themselves.

As a class the *Vital* O.G.'s were so fetching as to make the Rockettes look rather sallow. There was something rather saucy about them. Grooming and general appearance, as well as of course intelligence, were factors considered in the hiring of O.G.'s, so that they turned out to be decidedly decorative as well as useful. For another thing they were young: seventeen to twenty years old. For another, it took a physically fit girl to be an O.G. and her work kept her that way. The O.G.'s did a lot of walking. Once one O.G. had worn a pedometer for a day just to see how much. At the end of the day the pedometer showed that she had clocked seven miles, all of it up and down the corridors. Their fitness stood out in the office, since it didn't take any to be a researcher or a writer or any other editorial employee on the magazine, and many of these, especially the writers, went years with no exercise to speak of. Yes, as a class the O.G.'s were girls of exceptionally good health and posture. Many of them actually glowed, particularly when compared with the writers, a rather ashen and waxy, lumpy lot, and "O.G. watching" was as popular with *Vital* males as bird-watching with those of Boston. They were some of the pinchablest girl-flesh in the City of New York, but they were never to be pinched. They were the only off-limits females on the magazine: their age being one reason, and another being that there were so many attractive researchers around that it wasn't necessary to have them on-limits.

One day a new O.G. came to work for *Vital,* who, because of her

good health, surpassing posture, her figure, her gait, and other appealing attributes, from that very first day excited an unusual amount of
attention on the part of the other employees. Her name was Tammy
Rhinelander. In every detail she was of unusual aspect. She must have
been a good five feet eight inches tall and her bones were thoroughly
covered. When she entered your office the forward view was something
to make you stop whatever you were doing, and when she left your office the aft view was a thing for you to continue the study until she had
disappeared around the corner to the next office. She had a sinuous
walk and her eyes lingered significantly on you. She gave the men of
the magazine a rich subject for discussion in those great periods of idleness which the nature of the magazine afforded. Much argument centered on the question of whether her forward or aft view was to be
preferred. It was certainly six of one and a half-dozen of the other,
which, though most of the writers and editors tended to favor her forward view, her bosoms being without question the most voluptuously
full-bodied, robustly almost overpowering healthy, and entrancing that
the corridors of *Vital* had seen in a long time. She looked about nineteen. Facts about her built up gradually, a little item gleaned here by
one writer, another there by another, and these items all pooled so
that a picture of her began slowly to emerge. She was not nineteen. She
was eighteen. She had attended Vassar College and must have been
very precocious to graduate so young from that fine old institution of
such rigorous standards scholastically. So that her physical assets were
not her only ones. She had a brain. As if she were not richly enough
endowed already with these talents, she also appeared to be an heiress
of sorts. She was the only child of the president of a carbide and carbon
firm which had its national offices in New York and had a practice of
distributing those rich, built-in-capital-gains stock dividends to its upper
personnel as a way of getting around the income tax. Plainly, Tammy
Rhinelander did not work as a means of keeping body and soul together. She was working, in point of fact, because of a certain ambition
with which she was intensely fired.

In connection with this ambition Tammy liked to get into conversations with the writers in their offices. This was very easy, since her O.G.
chores called for her to stop in each writer's office at least a dozen times
a day.

Now if there was anything the O.G.'s were not supposed to do it was
to get into conversations with writers. On coming to work for *Vital*
each O.G. was given a thorough heart-to-heart talk by Crystal Bidwell, who had charge of the employment, care and rearing of O.G.'s.
The talk had one basic theme:

"O.G.'s should be seen and not heard—and not seen too much at a
time. All of your actions and movements should be discreet—never
interfering with the operation. You see, the writer has to think a good

deal. That is the nature of writing. So he mustn't be disturbed. He might
be in the midst of a telling thought. Fifteen seconds at one time is the
longest you should ever be in a writer's office. And above all don't get
in the habit of *talking* with them."

Despite this injunction Tammy, who did some of her own thinking
too, was quick to discover two things for herself. One, that the writers
had a great deal of idle time. Second, that they were as anxious to put
their telling thoughts and even their work aside to talk with her as she
was to talk with them. As for discreet movements, it would have been
impossible for her to make one had her life depended on it. But given
her structure, that was certainly no fault of hers.

Tammy's reason for wanting to talk with the writers was that she
wanted to be a writer herself. That was her ambition, and for it she
would have traded all her beauty, intelligence and her father's money.
She had the notion many have that the way to be a writer is to talk with
a writer. It is not. But after all she was eighteen. The writers at *Vital*
were not the kind of writer Tammy Rhinelander longed to be, but at
this stage in her life the word "writer" encompassed almost anyone
who put one word after another. And her physical endowments, and
that air of youthful fresh-limbed ripeness she gave off, would have made
any writer alive discuss with her writing or anything else under God's
bright heaven that she might care to discuss.

Soon Tammy had developed the habit, when she dropped into a
writer's office to deliver copies of bureau dispatches or newspapers or
shapened pencils, to linger and chat a little bit. She was new enough
that Crystal Bidwell had not yet caught up with her and this habit. However, Tammy was very considerate not to interrupt the writers in their
work.

"You look very busy, Mr. Gaskin," she would almost always considerately say before lingering.

"Not at all, Tammy," Gaskin would say, immediately shoving his
work aside with both hands. "Nothing we do here is of such value
that it should be allowed to interfere with more important things, such
as intelligent conversation. Well, how have you been?"

"Oh, pretty well, thank you, Mr. Gaskin," Tammy said. "I've been
working on this short story."

"A short story, eh?" Gaskin said promptingly.

"It might develop into a novella."

"A novella, eh?" Gaskin said encouragingly.

"It might even turn out to be a novel."

"A novel, eh? Well, if Sagan can do it, why not Rhinelander?
You're if anything more attractive hence that much better equipped to
be a writer of fiction."

Tammy giggled. "Why, how *galant,* Mr. Gaskin. But I hope you realize I'm serious. I want to be a serious writer. I get tired, between you

and me, of people thinking I'm just a body. I want to be a serious writer."

"We need them," Gaskin said. "Nothing we need more."

"This short story or novella or novel," Tammy said. "I'm rather excited about it. I don't think anyone has ever done anything on this subject. It concerns life at a girls' college."

"Derivative, I assume?" Gaskin said. "A *roman à clef?*"

"Somewhat, naturally," Tammy said. "It concerns a girl student who falls in love with the president of Vassar."

"Oh, a novel of lesbianism?" Gaskin said.

"Oh, I'm changing that part of it, Mr. Gaskin," Tammy said. "After all it is fiction, even though a *roman à clef.* I've changed the president into a man."

"Do you think the change wise?" Gaskin said. "I don't think we've had any novel of a young girl falling in love with a woman of seventy. That would be a new theme, which is what makes a novel these days —to find an entirely new, untried theme. Sagan has built a mighty reputation on being the first novelist to explore and ravage the theme of a teen-ager falling in love with a man with gout and hardening of the arteries. I wouldn't reject out of hand, if I were you, the theme of a teen-age girl and a seventy-year-old woman college president falling in love."

"Isn't it a little bizarre?" Tammy said.

"Isn't nearly every novel today a little bizarre?" Gaskin said.

"Well, maybe so," Tammy said.

"A new theme!" Gaskin exclaimed. "That's the ticket. From Homer and Aeschylus until today writers have dealt with the ancient and timeless themes of love, of man trying to overcome, and the like. But now we have entered a new and thrilling era in writing. The era of new and ingenious themes. I understand there's a novel coming out which concerns a love affair between a homosexual white man amputee syphilitic from Birmingham, Alabama, and a blind Negro girl with polio from Southampton. There's real plot for you. A new theme! That is the thing to seek and search for."

Tammy smiled. "Mr. Gaskin," she said, "it's nice of you to talk with me. I think I learn about writing from talking with you."

"Nobody," Gaskin said, "learns a thing about writing from talking with anybody. However, it's nice to talk with *you.* Any time, Tammy."

One writer at *Vital* asked Tammy to dinner to discuss writing. She accepted heartily. You can imagine the writer's surprise when Tammy's mother joined the pair of them, so that the writer actually had to talk about writing. Her mother, Tammy explained, was thoroughly behind her ambition to be a writer. After that, however, no other writer asked Tammy to dinner. Still, everybody continued to look at her in the office more than anybody else was looked at. This continued to be true

even though Tammy Rhinelander had now been working at the magazine for a full two months, which continuation was unusual at a place
like *Vital,* where the novelty of a given beauty newly employed was
ordinarily quickly supplanted by the novelty of another given beauty
more newly employed.

Unlike most of the writers and editors on *Vital,* Johnny Reasoner
did not pay even the customary visual homage to the O.G.'s who entered his office several times a day. The O.G.'s were always coming and
going and there were always new ones. Some of them were enough to
excite fleshly thoughts in Thomas Aquinas, the way their sweet and
saucy little behinds flounced out of the office. Reasoner paid them no
attention, nor was he even tempted to. Years back Reasoner had got
all settled in his mind. Before he went into the Army he had been a
young man somewhat more lusty than average and he had satisfied this
nature as much as the next young man if not more. In the long months
of recuperation and rehabilitation—how he loathed that word "rehabilitation"! it was as bad as the word "charitable"—following the
occurrence on the slopes of Cassino he had done a great deal of thinking on the changes that would be necessary in his life. In orderly fashion he had taken up the sections of a man's life one by one and had
come to terms with them. For example, his career: He had made the
orderly decision previously described to give up the idea of teaching in
a prep school. In regard to sex, he had made another orderly decision: he would get the minimum he could get by with from his wife
and if anything interfered with that he would get it from professionals,
and to tell the truth he made little distinction between the two. This
decision was made with complete unemotionality and an entire lack of
self-pity. It was a practical decision. Reasoner knew he could not have
stood even a suggestion of pity or even sympathy, and he knew, as
surely and instinctively as he knew about the boys at the prep school,
that no woman would be able to dissociate her concept of him from the
kind of man he physically now was. Once having made the decision
Reasoner never looked back. He was never tempted. He would not
have been tempted so much as to look at any woman at the magazine,
not if she had paraded six times a day into his office wearing nothing but
a garter belt and black stockings. This attitude gave Reasoner a really
singular distinction on the magazine. He was sealed off there, having
reached the understanding with himself.
One day Reasoner was sitting at his typewriter doing the textblock
for a story on a duck in North Carolina which refused to go in the
water. His office was in an unusually quiet section of the building—
stuck off in a corner of the thirty-third floor—and with his back to the
door and his fingers resting lightly on the keys he was gazing out the
window at the New York skyline. It was one of those magic days of

April that sometimes fall like an incantation upon the great city, somehow for a moment—a day—making the eyes and the heart look upward, mind and memory forget the soot and the blowing trash and the
frenzy, and giving the city an air almost of fragrance, almost, and this
is very strange indeed, of peace. Reasoner's mind wandered from the
story and was enveloped in the goodness of the day, the air in the lofty
heights coming in gentle scent through the opened window—it was the
first day of the year he had been able to have the window open—and
spangled shafts of sunlight shot from the sky like sweet arrows hurtled
down the granite canyons. He thought about the great city, its peopled
acres, those millioned souls seeking along its asphalted defiles, seeking . . . what? Quick fortune, easy thrill, waiting around the next
building-windy corner, but always waiting, for what they hardly knew,
for something quick perhaps, something easy—and even if it came
bringing more despair than ecstasy, like everything quick, everything
easy? Waiting: for what? A fame which was forgotten tomorrow and
was worth nothing today? An excitement which passed even as it was
grasped? A glimpse of rootless glory snatched away more quickly than
the slide in a kaleidoscope? Drawn, sucked here from the prairies and
from the mill towns, to wear suits with narrow lapels and unpadded
shoulders, black sheath dresses, to have their hair cut with the injunction to the barber never to use clippers only scissors, to learn and embrace the values of eye shadow and the debutante slouch. And all for
what? For a greater cup of happiness than was to be found at home?
Was happiness greater here than if he had stayed in Iowa, or was it less?
And how did one measure happiness? And was the pursuit of it so hallowed in the Declaration of the Republic a proper goal for man—could
he ever lose himself in the seeking for happiness, or having it for a
measure of life only plunge deeper, deeper into the dark tunnels?
Must man above all else reject the pursuit of happiness, saying to himself that the one certain way never to find happiness was to record the
search for it on any escutcheon as the goal of life? Then for what must
man strive? What goal? What purpose? Why *was* he here? Surely not
to rush around as were nearly all of the millions below these fortressed
towers as if motion itself would provide some kind of answer. Life must
hold something better than that. Should a man suddenly quit everything he was doing and go off and be a Schweitzer? Or was that too pat,
that the helping of man was the purpose of man? Then a Thoreau?
Not to help man as a goal, but to find, develop one's self? Perhaps that
was it. The Greeks said it. The Greek poet Hesiod said it: "Excellence
through sweat," that is the goal of life. Jesus Christ said: "Do unto
others as ye would have them do unto you." That was all right, too.
Nothing wrong with that. One, of course, did not preclude the other.
The first really embraced the second, for only man in excellence—inner excellence—can help another. Let us start with what Hesiod said:

"Excellence through sweat." That was it. That was the whole purpose of life and embraced everything.

Not in a long time now had Reasoner had such thoughts and he felt surprise at having them now. Was it the day, the rare April day, the first good day since December? He did not know. He found his fingers moving on the typewriter keys and, looking, saw that he had written two lines:

> The purpose of man: Excellence through sweat.
> The greatness of man: Defiant against all evil, coping with the obstacles and the hardships and the bitterness that are the very nature of life, never surrendering . . .

"Do you like writing about ducks and geese and apes?"

Reasoner looked around, startled. He pulled the sheet of paper explosively out of the machine, without using the roller, crumpled it and dropped it in the wastebasket. My God, for privacy! he thought. He glanced angrily over his shoulder. Standing there, just putting into his Incoming box an envelope—one of the shocking-pink-colored envelopes imprinted with the word URGENT in large black capital letters which were used in interoffice communication—was a girl who was obviously a new O.G., or at least one he hadn't noticed before. Reasoner was first of all irritated with himself for being startled. Then he was irritated at her, whoever she was, for startling him. The two irritations came in that order, a thing significant to Reasoner's character. He was not an easily startled man and he did not like it. The girl did not make much of an impression on him one way or the other. This itself was extraordinary, at least from the girl's point of view.

Johnny Reasoner took one swift look at her, a look which hardly registered her looks, or at most registered them as something entirely objective, such as registering the fact a certain quarter horse in yonder pasture was a fine specimen of the breed, and snapped out: "What was it?"

Tammy Rhinelander smiled upon Reasoner that smile of hers that people felt was significant but wasn't and which always—always— worked. "I was just wondering, do you like writing about ducks and geese and apes? Not a very significant question, I suppose," she said with that smile, lingering.

"You suppose right," Reasoner said. He turned sharply back to his typewriter, his back to her, stuck in a fresh sheet of paper and virtually attacking the keys started writing the textblock for the story of the duck that didn't like water.

He did not see Tammy Rhinelander's shrug. He did not see her sinuous walk, supple hips moving, when she left. He did not see into her mind and read there the surprise and interest at a most unusual experience for Tammy Rhinelander, which was: This was the first man at *Vital* to rebuff her. This was the first writer there she had failed to impress. Not only that. This was the first man to rebuff her anywhere any time in the eighteen years of her life.

The experience being so unusual, Tammy Rhinelander was not at all abashed or discouraged by it. On the contrary. Its very unusualness whetted her interest in the Nature Affairs editor and writer. She was tired of things being always so easy. It gave him one immediate distinction among all the writers she had encountered at the magazine. And one thing more: She had seen what he had been writing on the typewriter, what he had torn out so explosively. And seeing, had seen into the man.

In the succeeding days Tammy Rhinelander made it a special point to drop by Reasoner's office even when she had nothing to deliver. She could always be checking on his Outgoing box, and seeing if he had any pencils to sharpen. On these visits she made repeated attempts to engage Reasoner in conversation. She got nowhere. The attempts each lasted a very short time, and consisted of no more than a very few words on each side. They went like this:

"Well, nothing Outgoing this morning, I see, Mr. Reasoner."

"You have excellent vision."

And Reasoner went back to the story he was doing.

And:

"Mr. Reasoner. Do you have any pencils that need sharpening?"

"If I do, I'll put them in the Outgoing box—as usual."

And Reasoner went back to the newspaper he was reading.

And:

"Mr. Reasoner. What kind of animals are we doing this week?"

" 'We?' "

And Reasoner went back to writing about a penguin which the National Zoölogical Park in Washington was keeping in an unrefrigerated habitat, that is, outdoors, as an experiment.

And:

"Well! You look as if you had a hard night last night. Hangover, Mr. Reasoner?"

"Do you regularly offer these unsolicited observations on people's appearance?"

"Oh, I'm sorry. I hope you don't mind, Mr. Reasoner. It's just that I'm, well, interested in people."

"Oh, are you?" Reasoner said.

She thought she detected the faintest show of interest on his part and so unusual was this that she plunged in. "Yes, I really am. You see, I majored in psychology at Vassar . . ."

She was sorry the instant she said it. It was a terrible thing to say.

It was so blatantly naïve. It was such an opening for someone like Reasoner. She knew what was coming and she wished she could disappear into the floor. He just looked at her for a moment over a dispatch from one of the bureaus he was reading.

But that was all he did. Without making any remark at all he went back to the dispatch. She felt it was an act of kindness, but as toward a child, and this did not make her feel better.

Tammy Rhinelander was a member of that breed of persons upon whom resistance acts as the keenest spur: the breed, by the way, which has always accomplished almost everything that has been accomplished in this world. The quality is most generally found among those who started out at about the age of two having to fight for everything they got. In this respect Tammy Rhinelander was an exception to the breed. She had always had everything she wanted, her family being in one of the really upper strata, both socially and financially, in New York. (She had conducted an on-and-off rebellion against the values of this society, one instance of it being getting a job as an O.G. at *Vital*.) She had a built-in mechanism that made her go after what she wanted, the more so if the object presented a resistance to her possession of it. If he had set out with the one goal of making himself supernally attractive to her, Reasoner could not have done better than by being the almost unapproachable person he was. Tammy Rhinelander's reaction was unhesitating: She stepped up her interruptions of the head of the Department of Nature Affairs.

Reasoner let it go on a week more. Then one late afternoon she came into his office, said something, he was curt as usual, she picked up the contents of his Outgoing box and left. Outside his office, going down the corridor, she glanced at the shocking-pink interoffice URGENT envelope which had been the only thing in the box to see who the addressee was so she could deliver it. When she saw the name she came to a halt in the corridor. On the outside of the envelope, opposite the *To,* was written in strong copy-pencil-black letters:

Miss Rhinelander

She looked fixedly at her name on the shocking-pink envelope. Then she looked at the word URGENT. A feeling of anticipation began to race through her. Nothing very concrete as to the envelope's contents suggested itself to her. She walked on down the corridor a little way and stopped at the drinking fountain. She felt a kind of tingling and the sensation being enjoyable wanted to prolong it. She delivered some more of the copies of bureau dispatches she was carrying around to various offices. She lingered talking with two or three of the writers. They were eager as always. She found herself much less interested than usual in talking with them. She found in herself an astonishing, almost

irresistible desire to talk with Johnny Reasoner. The fact that he had
resisted her seemed hardly enough to account for the strength of this
desire. But she could not imagine anything else that would really account for it. Yes, she could: She *felt* something about him. What it was
she could not say but thought part of it must be that he was not a carbon copy of everybody else in the world. She kept putting off opening
the envelope. Then finally she knew she could wait no longer. She felt
a desire to be alone when she opened it. She went on down the corridors until she found an empty office—someone on vacation. She closed
the door and sat down behind the desk. She looked out the window
and saw beyond her the lights of Times Square just beginning to crayon
the sky. She turned back and opened the pink URGENT envelope.

Inside was a sheet of the thick white copy paper used at the magazine. It was folded three ways like a letter. She unfolded it and held it
up. There was very little writing on it and what there was was typed
and centered roughly on the page. She read:

> *To:* Rhinelander
> *Fm:* Reasoner
> Peddle it somewhere else

Tammy Rhinelander looked at that injunction reposing there in the
middle of white space. Her eyes widened, looking at it so intently.
Abruptly she laughed. She sat very thoughtfully for a long while, occasionally reading the four words again and each time laughing, a quiet,
bemused laugh. Tammy Rhinelander was a very strong-minded girl
and she intuitively placed an interpretation on the note that someone
less strong-minded might not have placed. Her interpretation began
with the idea that an emotional reaction of any kind is always, from a
woman's point of view, to be preferred to indifference. Women are very
curious people anyhow. The effect of the note on her, far from being
one of freezing or even disheartenment, was to send her already abiding interest in John Marshall Reasoner, and her keen curiosity about
him, soaring into the upper regions. It is very difficult to overcome anyone, and especially a woman, who takes points of view like this. Finally
she crumpled the shocking-pink URGENT envelope and tossed it in
the wastebasket. The note she folded many ways and tucked between
her breasts. There was plenty of room for it there.

As she got up to leave the office a passing thought suddenly occurred to her. The thought was that she had never seen Reasoner outside of that office of his. Never seen him get up and walk around the
office as most of the writers did when they were doing stories. Never
seen him leave his chair. And she thought: He must be a man of very
strong nerves. This thought increased her attraction to him.

The next day Tammy Rhinelander began her winter-week vacation. Reasoner scarcely noticed her absence, except to note briefly that his note apparently had worked. The day Tammy Rhinelander returned to work, as she started down the corridor a woman who had an air of being very busy and as if people were always wasting her busy time came up to her.

"I've been looking everywhere for you," she said irritably, as though the girl had been deliberately hiding. "Crystal wants to see you."

The woman was Crystal Bidwell's secretary.

"Well, come along," the woman said with the air of one who feels herself required to take everything efficiently in hand if anything is ever to get done in this inefficient world.

Tammy Rhinelander followed the secretary on up to the next floor and into Crystal Bidwell's office.

"Tammy," Crystal said, blinkering her smile. "Sit down, will you, my dear. Tammy. I've got some news for you I'm rather just inclined to believe will make you . . . well, shall we say pleased, my dear? Tammy. You're going to be a researcher. There's an opening in the Nature Affairs Department and we're putting you there. Well, what do you say?"

The following morning Tammy Rhinelander showed up at Johnny Reasoner's office. He was reading the New York *Times* looking for ideas for Nature Affairs stories. She just stood there waiting for him to recognize her.

"Did you want something?" he said finally.

"No, thank you, Mr. Reasoner," Tammy Rhinelander said. "I'm your new researcher."

Reasoner looked up mildly from his paper. "Let's not be quite so humorous so early in the morning, Miss Rhinelander."

"Oh, I'm not being humorous, Mr. Reasoner."

Reasoner took one look at her and immediately put his paper down. He picked up his phone and dialed Crystal Bidwell's number. Yes, she said, Tammy Rhinelander was his new researcher. Well, goddamn it to hell, why hadn't he been told? It was a hell of a way to run a railroad for the girl just to walk in and announce it herself. What in the name of Jesus God was going on around here? No one else on the magazine would have dared to speak like that to Crystal Bidwell. Reasoner was good enough at his job, and careless enough if he lost it for the reason of being frank, that he could, and the fact of the matter was, Crystal Bidwell, though in a superior position, was a little scared of Johnny Reasoner. What was more unusual, Crystal actually apologized. She had tried to reach him yesterday to tell him but he had apparently gone home early.

Reasoner hung up the phone. He sighed heavily. "Wonders never cease. Draw up a chair, Miss Rhinelander. Now I suppose I'll have to tell you something about the workings of the Nature Affairs Department . . ."

Pretty soon Johnny Reasoner reached down, and pulling open a drawer of his desk, brought out an icepick.

When it happened she started. But there were no gasps, no yells, no squeals. Then she laughed and it was not a nervous laugh. From long experience, beyond any possibility of being fooled, he knew that other kind of laugh, the nervous laugh.

What she said was: "That is a very neat trick, Mr. Reasoner." Then she leaned over, curious as a cat. "I've never seen one before."

And she looked. And then she did something no woman had ever done: She felt the thing. The fingers lightly on his artificial leg seemed at once very far away and yet somehow penetrating up into the very marrow, and, yes, the spirit, of John Marshall Reasoner.

When her fingers lifted he said: "Would you like a drink?"

"I would, very much."

They went to a bar near the office but seldom patronized by office people. It was in a basement and there was no elevator. Going down the steps Reasoner held onto the rail and made the quick, heavy swings which he had mastered so well so long since and which had given him that powerhouse of a torso. She walked down with him and there was no consciousness in the air that she had to slow her pace to his, although she did. Not that she had tried to hide the fact of the slowness, but as if it were natural.

Their talk flowed easily, but without compulsion. There was no embarrassment over silences. The feeling of being comfortable together was immediate. And they did not have to drink a lot.

They had been very long over the first drink when she said quietly: "You know that icepick act of yours. You know what it means, don't you?"

He was amazed not only not to feel anger but a strange and quickening amusement. "No, I don't know," he said. "You tell me. After all you majored in psychology at Vassar."

"It's your way of taking out your feeling of violence. That's what it is."

He felt a wild amusement. "That's pretty profound," he said, smiling. "You're a pretty profound girl."

"And that reminds me. That sarcasm of yours. That's part of the same thing."

"Oh, is that so?"

"You know what I think it all is?" She took a deep breath. "It's a false virility."

" 'False virility,' " Reasoner said happily. "What an ingenious phrase that one is. Did you learn that one in the Vassar psychology course?"

"No, I just thought it up right now," she said. "You've got this feeling of violence in you and you take it out in the sarcasm and in the icepick throwing."

He looked across at her and he smiled, and it was a good smile. "Perhaps you're right," he said. "Perhaps you are. I'll try taking it out in another way. You gather what I mean, of course? So that the virility will not be false."

People were very surprised at how Johnny Reasoner suddenly began to sweeten up. Everybody in the office noticed it. His sarcasm all but vanished. He was suddenly a very considerate and soft-spoken man, even his voice seeming to change; it was no longer taut and clipped, it took on a soft and easy modulation. But no one thought to remark the timing, that the change had begun about the time he got a new researcher.

Then a couple of months later, the office, which did not shock or surprise easily, suffered both emotions on learning that Reasoner and his wife were getting a divorce. It wasn't very difficult for Reasoner. An even better position than being the patient, understanding, *good* wife was being the *abandoned* patient, understanding, good wife. They were even more surprised and shocked when, one month after the divorce came through, Johnny Reasoner was united in wedlock with Tammy Rhinelander. People could hardly talk of anything else.

"That poor dear sweet Alice Reasoner," they said and chattered. "That brute of a husband of hers, that ingrate. After all she gave up for him, the way she cared for him like a slave over all these years, he runs off—well, not literally, since he *couldn't* run," they said and sniggered, with smug, sly cruelty, laughing slightly, slyly, sniggering, "he *goes* off with that rich hot-pants Tammy Rhinelander, that little bitch half his age. Well, I'll bet you *that* one doesn't last long." They said this last hopefully.

The Rhinelanders from their triplex across from the River Club were highly enthusiastic about John Marshall Reasoner. They thought him a wonderful man—a man of quality—and the best thing in the world for their daughter, who heretofore had been decidedly flighty. He had such a *settling* effect on her.

The change in Reasoner was very obvious to people in the office, and his happiness. Some were very disappointed and chagrined that a man with an artificial leg could be so happy. They had felt sorry for Johnny Reasoner and they were angry at him for taking this right of theirs—to feel sorry—away by being so happy and making such a great marriage. Johnny Reasoner knew how they felt and knew they talked, but far from caring, from the vantage point of his new compassionate attitude toward everybody and everything, felt quite sorry for them. Coping with life; striving for excellence: These are the only things. The other is outside the man who does; does not touch him.

And oh, yes. Reasoner took his icepick home to his new apartment and put it in the kitchen drawer—for chopping ice. He also put in an application for a teaching job at The Choate School.

17
The Bet

Life is altogether a thing of chance. Man controls his destiny only within the awful framework of chance. It is all that is allotted him, lest he be god. A momentary whim sets in motion the frightening machinery of fate, and because when he is twenty a man is slighted, an empire falls when he is fifty: the man may be one of history's chosen, one of those deputized by history to do its business. A stray slice of shrapnel pierces a plane and the man in it who may have been President and changed the destiny of a nation or even of the world passes instead into engulfing eternity; the easy-smiling, forever tolerant hand of chance reaches out effortlessly to touch another. A word, a sentence, fall from lips unable to resist the spite of a wisecrack, and a career of greatness is laid to ashes even as the suspirant syllables find air. Life is altogether a thing of chance. And no part of life more so than the coming together of two human beings.

On the whim of a wager this destiny was cast . . .

Montgomery Shanks, who believed in sportsmanship and fair play up to a point, even offered odds. For as he himself put it so generously to Henry Gaskin: "If Montgomery Shanks can't make it with a woman, nobody can."

Henry Gaskin pondered this Euclidean thesis for a moment and more or less agreed. "Yes, Monty, I know. In fact I find it very hard to convince myself that you couldn't, since your abilities and attractions in the area are so well known. There is just one thing that convinces me you didn't."

"What is that?" Shanks said.

"The fact that you've admitted you didn't. That is the greatest proof in the world."

"I see what you mean," Shanks said. "I guess you do find it very hard to believe, don't you?"

"Very hard," Gaskin said. "It's like learning that Don Juan was a eunuch."

"Very funny," Shanks said. "Your humor, Gaskin, never fails to charm. Well, it's a fact. I might as well admit it. I failed." And he repeated, looking off into space, "If Montgomery Shanks can't make it with a woman, nobody can."

Then he offered the very generous odds. It was quite gallant of Gaskin to refuse them.

"No," he said. "That would be being a cad. A thing like this has to be an even bet. I couldn't face myself otherwise."

"Well, we surely don't want that to happen," Shanks said. "We certainly want you to be able to face yourself, Henry. All right it's an even bet then. A hundred do?"

"That will be fine," Hank Gaskin said. "Just about right to make it interesting."

"It's the only thing that will," Shanks said confidently. "Henry, you're not going anywhere. Believe me, if Montgomery Shanks can't . . ."

"'. . . make it with a woman, nobody can.' Yes, I know," Gaskin said. "Then it's on from now. I've got two months, is that understood?"

"Yes, since I had just five days that will make it about even," Shanks forced in some generosity. "However, two months or two years, you're going exactly nowhere, Henry."

"We'll see," Gaskin said.

"And by the way, Henry?"

"Yes?"

"This is honor bright, remember that."

"Honor bright," Gaskin said. "I wouldn't lie about a thing like that. I couldn't face . . ."

"'You couldn't face yourself.' Yes I know, Henry."

If there was one man in New York who believed in the evils of monogamy, or even in going too much with one girl, that man was Henry Gaskin.

"There are so many entrancing varieties of clover in this world," as Gaskin said, using one of the pastoral metaphors of which he, who was such a city boy, was so fond, "I can never understand how any man of intelligence and parts can possibly find true spiritual satisfaction in eating the same strain all the time, when if the world is meant for anything—and sometimes I wonder if and what it is—it is meant for man to explore in all its many-hued variegations. To settle for the lone explorations, well: It's really, when you come down to it—well, the only word for it is unnatural."

There was nothing unnatural about Henry Gaskin. He believed, frankly, in women. There are worse things to believe in, for it is, at least potentially, a field so highly and humanly communicative, offering —potentially—rewards so sublime as to inspire the remorse of the gods that they were not born men. And it was rather refreshing to find a man interested in the human things in these days when men seem interested in almost nothing save such non-human endeavors as getting the next job up in the company, and making more of the root of all evil, striving ever harder so they can die off nice and early and leave all that money to their wives, who can then go off and have a good time in Florida, Venice, and that sort of thing. Henry Gaskin had no interest whatsoever in getting onward and upward in any company, possibly because he had, and intended to have, no wife who would push and prod him to do that both to make more money and from the strain of making it, more poisoning than the deadliest virus, die off and leave her with all those nice trips to make.

"Monogamy?" as Henry Gaskin was fond of saying. "It is our leading evil, the author of half our miseries and three-fourths of our frustrations. And this is the reason why, this is the heart of it all: It is the one thing above all which, killing one's personality as it of course inevitably has to do—the very word suggests that—stifles everything man is."

Armed with these beliefs, it was with a clear conscience that Henry Gaskin, who had no intention of having his personality seriously tampered with, started in to date Charity Cabot.

Henry Gaskin had worked with Charity Cabot on several stories, and in particular they had established a certain empathy during the Manhattan agricultural crisis, when it was she who kept—he couldn't say saved—his job for him. Gaskin knew little about Charity Cabot, but keeping it in a detached way, he could admire her. Her pleasantness, which seemed a very genuine thing consisting of a true interest in human beings rather than the usual forced mechanical thing that passes counterfeitly for communication in this world; her professional, self-respecting efficiency; the sense of intact neatness and awareness she gave off, in a word, her general air. But he was also somehow aware, even before talking with Shanks, of her strong moral convictions, her quietly forceful and self-assured belief in the things in which she believed, and of such peculiarities as her never drinking. Henry Gaskin and Charity Cabot were hardly two persons one would expect to get together.

Theirs constituted as "proper" a series of dates as could be imagined. They went to plays mostly, occasionally an opera or the City Center Ballet and great Balanchine and hauntingly fetching Tanaquil LeClercq, Melissa Hayden and Maria Tallchief, those goddesses of the slender star. She was especially fond of ballet. But mostly they talked.

Rather imperceptibly and over a period of some weeks, a strange thing began to happen. Gaskin began to notice how enormously comfortable he was with her. After a considerable amount of exposure to her company he could not deny the fact that she wore extremely well. Extremely well. He was delectably surprised. To spend much time with a woman solely in the non-physical areas—well, while in no way condemning this half of the human race for the fact (if one had to condemn anybody it could only be Nature), he had found it to *be* a fact in his experience that it was not the most richly rewarding expenditure of time available on this earth. But this young lady! They spent really a good deal of time together and, to paraphrase John Paul Jones and Franklin Delano Roosevelt, he had not yet begun to get tired of her. This left him really impressed, for he had always believed in spreading himself with an almost crashing thinness where women were concerned. Though he was not—being a passionately careful man in such matters, who believed in an awful lot of looking, and more, before you leaped, if ever—ready to admit that he was in love with Charity Cabot or really anywhere near it—the phrase "in love" rather terrified him anyway, on principle—he did feel, in about his third subconscious, the highest he would ever permit the distant thought, that he was closer to that terrible condition with her than he had ever been with anyone. No, he had not yet begun to get tired of her. This left him quite impressed. It also left him a little frightened. He felt, if he were not careful, it really might slip up on him at almost any time. "In love"? No. But there was that business of being so highly comfortable with her, and on this Henry Gaskin placed a higher premium as an absolutely essential ingredient of "in love" than do most.

Their conversation? Well, it ranged far and wide. But it had a pattern. It had a pattern. Two or three short samples of it over a period:

I. "Henry, do you want to devote your life to pursuing that? Is that *enough* to *devote* your life to?"

"Well, not entirely," he hedged. "I don't think it's the only thing now. Now what makes you think I think it's the *only* thing. I haven't indicated or showed that with you, have I? After all, you can see how much I enjoy the City Center ballet. I practically led the claque the other night."

"There are a lot of things besides *that* in this world, Henry."

"I don't deny it. What, for example?"

"Well, religion."

"Oh, I can't see that religion has done much for the world," he said blithely. "There are a lot of religions in this world and I suppose most people belong to one or the other of them. Still we have hunger, we have wars, and we have people screaming and scratching, and clawing and clobbering at each other. Oh, I can't see really that religion has done much for this besotted world," he said casually.

Far from repelling her this attracted her—as it might a missionary. Fresh meat for conversion to the faith. There is little point, after all, in saints talking with each other.

"Then what *do* you believe in?"

"I suppose I have what you might call a negative belief. I believe in people not jumping on each other."

Her eyes became wide.

II. Again, another night:

"What you said the other night. Is that the same as believing in the intactness of the individual? In his inviolability?"

"I would say so. So long as one's inviolability doesn't hurt oneself. I don't think it's exactly enough to go through life having nothing but inviolability."

"Then you mean a willing violability?"

"Even more. An eager violability."

"And in selection. You believe in selection, in selectivity?"

"Very much. Instinct—or the mind—or both, have little other reason for being."

"Then how does one judge? What is the dividing line?"

"Ah, that is the greatest mystery of the human heart. The dividing line of violability. There is some sense, I think, that tells one. But who has ever been able to define it? I know of no way to articulate it."

She waited a moment. "I think it is a matter of *concentration*. Where one's energies are to go. We are given so much energy, and no more. So much *will* and no more. It is a frightful thing to waste that energy, that will, on anything not worth eagerly spending it on."

"But that is almost to say, 'I believe in the essential sadness of the human heart.' That life is mainly a thing of sadness, of dissatisfaction, with only the rare fleeting peak of joy, of interest, of excitement, of—abandon."

" 'Abandon.' " She repeated the word like an echo, yet oddly, fascinated by it, by the word—by the idea. "It is such a false thing. It is nothing but a pep talk to oneself. And I think it is shallow, with nothing beneath it to stand on. It evaporates like a cloud. Abandon, I think, is the opposite of peace, and its mortal enemy. For one thing, you would always be only chasing it. And it is gone even as you think you hold it in your hands, cage it. It is false, really, and to seek it is false, chasing a bird, faster than any of us."

"Still it's the one thing most people spend their lives chasing, or live for. The imaginings of men dwell largely upon it. Most of the time they either are seeking it physically or imagining it and planning to seek it."

"But never really obtain it. For is anything really obtained that is held only in terms of seconds, minutes, or hours? I don't think so. It can't sustain."

Gaskin sighed. "No, it can't. I'll have to admit it. But what else is there? What is one to do with one's life if not to chase after that? At least chasing is better than mere vegetable non-chasing."

"That is not the only choice, those two."

"No, perhaps not," he said slowly. "Do you know about this hobby of mine of sailing paper airplanes out the window?"

"I believe I've heard of that," Charity Cabot said, not with an excess of admiration.

"Well, sometimes," Gaskin said genially, "I put a message on them. Just a little thought, don't you know. Are you acquainted with Samuel Daniel?"

"No, I don't believe I am. Does he work at the office?"

"Not any more. He died in 1619. He was an English poet, not the most famous one actually but I like him. Well, anyhow, I flew out one of my airplanes bearing one of Samuel's messages. That must have been a couple months ago. Well, today, I got a letter from Tompkins Armbruster! From Africa!"

"Who?"

"Oh, I guess you don't know Tompkins, do you. He's a 'management consultant' the magazine brought in some time back for some reason that was never made clear, at least to me and I don't think to Tompkins himself. Roomed with me for two or three weeks while trying to tone things up at the big magazine. *Was* a management consultant, I should say. An English professor before that. Very bright type. His own man, don't you know. Well, it seems that that little airplane, bearing Samuel's message and descending gallantly some thirty-four floors, made a very fine landing on the nose of none other than old Tompkins, walking by on Fifth Avenue." Gaskin took a deep breath. "Well, sir! Since our rooming days, old Tompkins, it seems, has gone and made himself a perfectly enormous pot of money on the stock market. You know what he's doing with it?"

"No, I really don't," Charity said.

"Hang on just a minute. I think I've got it with me."

Gaskin dug in his jacket pocket and pulled out a rather battered envelope. Removing the letter he started to read:

" 'The combination of Samuel Daniel and a paper airplane made it hardly necessary to read the signature for me to guess this was a production of Henry Gaskin's . . .' So on and so on. Now! Old Tompkins goes on to say here that he is taking all that money and—get this now—trying to get going a school in Africa to train African students. Yes, sir, a school. It's to be called the Africa-American School. A kind of University of Africa eventually, I gather . . ."

Gaskin read some more, then stuck the letter away. "I thought I'd just like to read that to you. Tompkins Armbruster!" he exclaimed in fond nostalgia, and abruptly he seemed very thoughtful. "By gad! Tompkins Armbruster out there doing something like that!"

"He sounds like a man who's very alive," Charity Cabot said quietly.

"He is," Gaskin said soberly. "I'm just beginning to realize how much."

III. And again, another night:

"Have you tried it?"

"In my mind," she said honestly, for she was an honest girl, honest with others and above all honest with herself.

"Only in your mind?"

She waited a moment, then said, with a little smile at him: "Yes. Only in my mind, Henry."

"Is that a denial?"

"No," she said, drawing the word out, slowly. "It's not a denial really, not in the real sense of that word."

"Then what else is it?"

"It's a choice. One chooses, doesn't one? One has to choose."

He sighed again, but tightly now, suddenly imagining her in everything one could imagine toward such a girl, a really remarkable girl, and a really almost outrageously, scornfully endowed one.

"It may be a choice," he said then. And then he looked at her and added: "It may also be a waste. A terrible, terrible waste. That is the great sin, the only sin: to waste what one has. That, and nothing else, is original sin."

She waited yet once more and then said: "But has it ever occurred to you, Henry, that the best choice in life may be to *choose* to waste that thing which, well, perhaps glitters but is really not very valuable if unwasted, if exploited; if achieved?"

And so it went.

They had been dating each other in this fashion for some six weeks —rather intellectual dates they were, and what with the ballet, the opera, plays and the like, affording Henry Gaskin incidentally his first look in some time at this side of New York, which he, like so many other adopted sons and daughters of the city, had come in time to by-pass almost entirely—before he even so much as invited her by his apartment one night.

It was quite a place, that apartment. Indeed there was no room in Manhattan—or perhaps, for that matter, east of Oklahoma—quite like it.

Henry Gaskin's apartment was a basement and consisted of one perfectly enormous room. Almost no natural light came into it, so that when one was in it the usual element of time-appearance and discipline by which man lives—is it day or is it night?—vanished. Being

in Henry Gaskin's apartment was like being in Thule, Greenland, during the winter months of the twenty-four-hour darkness. Take the
consciousness of time as signified by light and dark away from man and
see what happens. Nothing shapes man more than the fact of rhythmic
light and darkness. The very world began by the making of this distinction. "And the earth was without form, and void; and darkness was
upon the face of the deep. And God said, Let there be light: and there
was light. And God saw the light that it was good: and God divided
the light from the darkness." Time and light are very disciplining elements to man, perhaps the most disciplining of all, and being without
them, without this division, can have strange and unpredictable effects on him.

That was quite an apartment even aside from the way it obliterated
time and light. With the prevailing dark in it people could be on one
side of the room and not even see people on the other, even if it was
high noon and a blinding sunshine outside, and scarcely hear them unless the shout was employed. The room looked—when the two dim
lamps, which were all Gaskin had, were turned on so that you could see
at least the vague outlines of it, like the ghostly shape of a ship on the
far horizon on a murky day—like the common room of the cowhands'
bunkhouse on some ranch in Arizona or Texas. Or at least what Hank
Gaskin conceived such a room to look like. Henry Gaskin was a Massachusetts boy and had never seen a live cowboy, had seen no more
than a few horses and cows in his life and these in the distance out
some train window. But he really had the Western bug.

When Gaskin brought Charity Cabot by that night the first thing
that confronted her was a full-grown taxidermy horse, his glassy pop-
eyes looking right at you the moment you opened the door and a little
sadly as if asking for a lump of sugar. Charity Cabot looked back quite
as pop-eyed, startled slightly as she was, before recovering herself.

"It's a Tennessee walking horse," Gaskin explained easily. "Must
have been quite a noble animal, don't you think, to look at him now?
Notice that proud look."

"Quite noble."

"Would you like to try a tequila martini?" her host asked, taking
her coat.

"Not just now, thank you, Henry."

"The usual then?"

"Yes, the usual, Henry."

After hanging up the coat Gaskin disappeared into the kitchen to fix
his guest a Coca-Cola and himself a tequila martini. When he came
back in with them she was frankly inspecting his apartment. He joined
her in the tour, to serve as guide if needed. She was planted before the
main wall of the room—a long thing adequate for a small museum and

interrupted only by a tremendous almost seagoing fireplace (the room at one time had been the kitchen in an old brownstone mansion of Henry James' day, and, later on, rumor had it, Masefield had actually inhabited it—in his pre-Laureate days). Hanging there were a pair of spurs, a gigantic Western sombrero, a Larro cowfeed calendar, a bridle-and-bit, and two other items which she now specifically asked about.

"What is that?" she said, pointing.

"Why, that's a branding iron." Gaskin took a sip of his tequila martini. "Notice the 'G.' "

"Why, yes. And that—what is that?"

"Why, that's a Smith and Wesson .38. Handsome piece, isn't it?"

"Why, yes, it is."

She turned to the opposite wall.

Along this wall was a long, earth-colored, sawhorse Western table with backless benches on the two length sides capable of seating a total of twenty people. It was at this table that his guests ate the Western-Mexican dinners which Gaskin served at his Sunday soirees—roundups they had better be called. The wall above this table was given over to the illustrative arts.

"Who's that? That girl."

"Oh, that's Lucille Mulhall. She was the first cowgirl." Gaskin gazed at her with admiration and affection. "Yes, Lucille Mulhall," he said nostalgically, as if he had known her personally and perhaps dated her. "She flashed like an American Valkyrie across the Eastern firmament," he said rhapsodically, "dazzling New York in Madison Square Garden, oh, a half-century ago. Quite pretty, isn't she?"

"Yes, indeed."

Her eyes moved to two woodcuts of some ghostly-looking horses, lithe-flanked and heads held proud and high, striding the distant mesa.

"O'Hara. One of our finest woodcut men of the Southwest," Gaskin said proprietarily.

Moving a step she stood before a pair of copies of paintings.

"That first one," Gaskin explained, "is Biernstadt's 'Last of the Buffalo.' That other one's by Seth Eastman and is called 'Lacrosse Playing Among the Sioux Indians.' "

"Isn't that interesting. I never realized the Sioux played lacrosse."

"Oh, yes. The Sioux were a very versatile people. Very adaptable—very versatile."

"Apparently."

"Another thing we stole from the Indians: lacrosse."

The remainder of the wall was obliterated by some twoscore eleven by fourteen blowup prints of photographs *Vital* photographers had shot over the years on stories dealing with cowboys or rodeos. It was a most virile-looking collection. There were cowboys calf-roping, cowboys bulldogging, cowboys riding bucking steers—Gaskin, between sips of his martini, now explained the technicalities of each of these operations to his absorbed guest—cowboys eating, herds of white-faced cattle driven onward and the wake of white dust rising up behind their hoofs on the Western plains. Very strange, almost spectral, haunting, to see all this in an apartment in Manhattan and hear a subway hurtling by in the not-faraway underground, in fact almost immediately beneath, so that if Gaskin's apartment had ever collapsed while he was asleep he and his bed would have come to rest approximately on top of the D train, a fact he had often reflected on with due fascination, especially when he had an overnight guest.

Gaskin's eyes proudly swept the wall, and his hand raised and arced to indicate the sawhorse table beneath. "I give parties here Sunday afternoons. We start out with tequila martinis and then the twenty of us—I always have twenty people, including myself—sit down right here to a Western-Mexican dinner I prepare—sometimes with a little help. *Guacamole, tostados, enchiladas, frijoles refritos, sopa de arroz, tacos,* with of course plenty of *jalapeños*—naturally all washed down with more tequila martinis . . . Ah!" Gaskin kissed his cupped fingers like a French chef. "It is quite a repast. Quite a repast. Have you ever cooked any of these dishes?"

"I've never *eaten* any of them."

"Well, you don't know what you've missed. Would you like to come sometime to one of my Sunday parties?"

"I'd be delighted to."

That took care of the two main walls, and she turned back into the room. And now she noticed, for the first time, so much had her attention been otherwise absorbed, the floor, which resembled a taxidermy shop before a sale to get rid of a serious surplus stock.

"And all these, Henry," she said, indicating the floor. "What are these?"

"Well, that's a buffalo skin," Gaskin said, starting to tick them off with the toe of his shoe. "This one," he said, moving a little, "is a bear. This—coyote. This—a steer. This—this—this—this . . ." he was almost dancing, soft-shoe, as he ticked them off. "And *this*—I've never been able to figure out and the man himself wasn't sure. I'm planning to take it up to the Museum of Natural History some day to see if *they* know. But I liked the looks of it and the bare space needed something. They fill it rather neatly, don't you think?"

"Yes, they just about fit, Henry. And the colors are nice."

"What's more they're soft to sit on—sooner or later at my Sunday parties everyone ends up sitting on the floor. And in the event dancing is decreed they kick back swiftly to make a floor for dancing larger considerably, you'll notice, than the average floor of the average overcharging New York night club. And now shall I show you the *pièce de résistance?*"

"What could that be, Henry?" she said, wondering what possible further Western wonders, short of a live cow stabled in the bathroom, could be in store.

"Just close your eyes," Gaskin said.

She did so and Gaskin stole in silent stealth across the bridge of animal pelts. He made a few deft movements. And suddenly Charity Cabot jumped, startled clean out of her wits, as if she had been stimulated by a red-hot branding iron—perhaps bearing the initial "G"—thrust on her smart little rump.

> *Come a ki yi yippee yippee yi yippee yay,*
> *Come a ki yi yippee yippee yay!*

"You can open your eyes now!" Gaskin roared over the din.

It was a scarcely necessary command. Charity Cabot's eyes had not only opened but were now staring bug-eyed at Henry Gaskin in his element. He was standing by a proud possession, a magnificent ultra-high-fidelity sound-reproduction system—"set" would be far too modest a word for it—consisting of a fifteen-inch Tannoy speaker, Garrard changer, Shure diamond needle, Bell amplifier and Bogen tuner, fit to bring forth at their finest the moving sounds of the New York Philharmonic.

> *Come along, boys, and listen to my tale,*
> *Tell you of my troubles on the Old Chisholm Trail!*

The song burst like siege guns from the speaker, setting the draperies flapping, the walls trembling slightly and the pelt-covered floor quivering nervously.

> *Come a ki yi yippee yippee yi yippee yay,*
> *Come a ki yi yippee yippee yay!*

Gaskin, perhaps fearing that with the present limited sound—after all they both apparently still had their eardrums intact—the maximum effect was not being obtained, gave one of the several dials a twist and now a sound like nothing she had ever heard erupted, leapt forth, from the Tannoy.

> *Ten-dollar horse and a forty-dollar saddle*
> *I'se gonna punch them longhorn cattle . . .*

And crescendoed in one final and prodigious twangy, mounting shout . . .

> *Come a ki yi yippee yippee yi yippee yay,*
> *Come a ki yi yippee yippee yay!*

The record dropped mercifully down.

"Shall I put on some more of my collection of cowboy records? It's really quite extensive."

"Later, Henry," Charity said.

"May I freshen your Coca-Cola?"

"Yes, please."

"You're sure you won't have a tequila martini?"

"I believe not just now, Henry."

"Just have a seat and I'll have them up quicker than you can bull-dog a Brahman, I'm told."

He disappeared into the kitchen to prepare her another Coca-Cola and himself another martini. Returning with these two beverages he was headed automatically in the direction of the sitting area when he heard a voice off to the side.

"Why, Henry, what are these?"

He stopped, his two hands still armed with the Coca-Cola and the martini, and squinted off into the relative gloom. Then the gloom was dispersed. A light came on and he saw her peering upward.

"You haven't explained this wall to me, Henry. What are those arti-facts?"

The wall at which she was gazing stood above the mammoth French couch which by day was covered with a prodigal number of pillows of every conceivable shape, triangles, quadrangles, hexagons, heptagons, octagons, and every color, and which at night transferred itself, with a little help and heaving, there being some twenty-five pillows and Gaskin adding new ones from time to time, into Gaskin's bed.

"What are these?" she repeated, gazing with the curiosity of a cat —or of a woman—up at the wall above it. "More cowgirls?"

The contrast of this wall, and the items it displayed, to the rest of the room could not have been greater. For ranged and hanging there was about as non-Western a gallery as one could hope to find. It was a gallery of photographs of women and there was nothing whatsoever Western about them. Without exception, in fact, they were all in de-cidedly non-Western dress, and what was more, and also without ex-ception, all were quite smartly dressed, even chicly so. Furthermore, without exception, they were very pretty and attractive girls and one or two of them would have qualified under the adjective "glamorous." Studying them for a moment or two each—as Charity Cabot was now doing with a rather casual keenness, as only a cat—or a woman—can —one would have guessed that some of the photographs could have been out of the society pages of the New York *Times,* some of those girls could have been secretaries in some of the more acceptable New York offices, a couple could have been *Vital* cover girls, a couple or so of arresting foreign flavors. These guesses would have been most accurate. From time to time there would be an addition to the gallery.

The pictures were a mild source of humor to Gaskin's friends. Nevertheless, aside from the humor, the impression was left, given the positioning of the photographs, that the women had one and all, at one time or another, been different varieties of clover in lavish growth upon that bed just below their likenesses. Though Gaskin certainly never said so. He only laughed when this possibility was mentioned. He even laughed when someone at one of his parties remarked: "My God, Gaskin, how juvenile can one get? Hanging up there like that. What are you trying to do, prove your virility?" "You guessed it," Gaskin said, not irritated at all. "You see, I can't do it, so I have to hang those pictures as a substitute for virility-proof." That was a jealous man who made that remark, I think, for there was an astonishing amount of feminine beauty on that wall. At least he made it in a quite irritated way. And Gaskin's answer far from turning away wrath irritated him the more. It was very hard to get at a man like Henry Gaskin.

"What a handsome lot of women, Henry," Charity Cabot exclaimed mildly.

"Here's your Coca-Cola," Gaskin said.

However, Charity Cabot did not move from her post of fascination. Indeed she became more fascinated. Moving slightly closer she turned the light—it was one of those gooseneck, spotlight affairs—over the bed upward.

Her eyes moved. And then she made a slow count. "One, two, three . . . five, six . . . seven, eight, nine. Nine!"

She turned back to the room.

"Here's your Coca-Cola," Henry Gaskin said.

She looked at the drink rather oddly for a moment, as if it were something strange . . . esoteric . . . repulsive.

"Henry," she said. "I believe I'll have that other drink. That . . . what do you call it?"

"A tequila martini."

"Hank," she said. "I believe I'll have a tequila martini."

Deep in the earth beneath them a subway train roared by, carrying the citizens to their various rendezvous, destinies and encounters with the great god chance.

That knowing Englishman, Sir Thomas Beecham, who knows much more than just music, once said:

"It is a melancholy truth that in most works of fiction produced during the last two millennia, the unobtrusive nobility of the saint has generally failed to compete with the uninhibited roistering of the sinner. I trust that I shall not be accused of discourtesy if I attribute much of this seemingly unaccountable preference to the ladies, but for this there is a completely reasonable explanation. At no time have they manifested genuine esteem for excessive virtue in the male animal; undoubtedly for the reason that there is a superfluity of it in themselves. I am tolerably sure that at the court of King Arthur they unaffectedly preferred the company of Sir Lancelot and Sir Gawain to that of Sir Galahad."

A few days later Henry Gaskin went over to the Guaranty Trust Company and got a fresh, crisp and crackling new hundred-dollar bill and delivered it to Montgomery Shanks, who on its receipt beamed happily.
"I told you so, Henry. If Montgomery Shanks can't make it with a woman, nobody can."
People did notice two things.
It was noticed that after that Henry Gaskin had only one girl help him with his Western-Mexican dinners and that the dinners under her guidance actually improved—could she have Mexican blood in her, people wondered, they were that good, had that really certain touch, don't you know. But the name Charity Cabot didn't sound very Mexican.
And people noticed something else strange. All the pictures of women that Henry Gaskin used to have on his wall had, like the walls of Jericho, come tumbling down.

18

Eric the Red

Goddesses are not supposed to exist on this earth any longer. They all left sometime in the seventeenth century. But one day one came down.
She was a young goddess. She was like a thoroughbred colt. Her flanks lean and lithe. Her hindquarters taut and trim. Her breasts as though fashioned by the fondest sculptor. Her little belly flat as a sand dollar. Her eyes the blue one might see only alongside a coral reef. Her hair that rarest of colors, red as a cardinal's wing, and soft-looking as sea foam. Her complexion faultless but for a delightful decoration of three little freckles on her nose and four on each cheek. She seemed to have not a gram's-weight of fat on her. She had an alert yet easy quickness of movement, and a curiosity and awareness in her face, eyes, and even the posture of her body. She caught the breath, transfixed the eyes, and made the heart stand still and the hair on the back of the head on end. It was this goddess out of Norway via America whom,

looking up one day from his desk, Jason Hightower saw standing there like a young Viking princess amid the grimy prospect of strewings from the AP ticker, old dirty carbon paper, old newspapers, smiling down upon him and saying in tones sweet as the bell of the Angelus:

"Good morning, Mr. Hightower. Well! Here I am. Graduated from Potawatami Presbyterian Normal College and all ready to go to work."

That had been a week ago. Jason, at this apparition, had had two reactions: He was overwhelmed by her loveliness, as one would be. He was appalled at the prospect—indeed almost the moral obligation, considering that campaign train promise so remote and so careless and so reckless—of having to get her a job.

Jobs weren't handed out at *Vital* just like that. Not even to goddesses. And what was more, he had had to face up to the exposure of himself as not quite the figure in the office that he had cut on the campaign train. In journalism distance makes the job seem ever so bigger, and here on the home shoals, inundated in clippings and picture blow-ups, it could be readily seen that he was not quite the wheel he might have appeared to be when covering the President of the United States.

Lilleba Ericsson, though a goddess, was not exactly loaded down with money, so first Jason attended to the basic needs. He made arrangements for her to stay with Charity Cabot while he and Henry Gaskin were working on a job for her. He and Gaskin had several strategy sessions on this matter, reminding Jason a little of the one when Gaskin had got *him* a job on the magazine. The same basic rationale held: She must on no account apply for a job at the magazine. The problem was that in some way the magazine must be made to come to *her*. Finally one day Jason told Crystal Bidwell he wanted to talk with her sometime soon when she had a fair amount of free time—and she said why not now? He went into her office.

"Crystal," he came right to the point. "Do you realize we don't have a single red-headed researcher on the entire staff?"

It was, curiously enough, precisely the sort of approach that would get her a job, if anything would.

"No, Jason, I hadn't been particularly aware of that unpardonable shortcoming. But now that you mention it"—Crystal paused, whizzing down the long list of researchers in her mind—"now that you mention it, we don't." She turned to him gaily, for Crystal really liked this sort of challenging, wit-sharpening kind of thing. "What do you think we should do about this situation?"

"Correct it."

"I see. What do you have in mind?"

"Well, I happen to know a girl. Probably the brightest red-haired girl in the Eastern United States."

"Oh?"

"We may have to move very fast before *Life, Look, Time, News-week,* the *U. S. News and World Report,* or one of those outfits, gets her. If we move pretty fast we may have an outside chance at her."

"She does sound terribly hard to get, as well as rather a paragon of talents."

Jason realized he may have gone too far and he slowed down. "Well, it's just that someone else *may* get her first," he said vaguely. "But I really think we can get her. I know she would really *prefer* very much to work here."

"Who wouldn't?"

"That's interesting your saying that, because that's precisely what I told her. What I said to her exactly was, 'Why work anywhere but the best?' "

"And what did she say to that illuminating question, Jason?"

"Well, I think it went home all right. I think she prefers us over anyone else."

"We certainly don't want anyone who doesn't, do we, Jason?"

"I was wondering if you should give her a call."

"What do you think?"

"I really think you should. I've gone so far as to tell her all about you."

"*All,* Jason?" Crystal laughed gaily.

"I've told her—well, really she knew it anyhow—what a privilege it is to work here."

"Oh? Is she interested in pictures?"

"Very. She thinks they're here to stay."

Crystal laughed appreciatively. "Boy! *Quel* wit. You know what I like to see in a person?"

"No, what is that, Crystal?"

"Wit!" Crystal Bidwell exploded the word. "Not much more important around here than wit, is there?"

"Very few things."

"Of course zest is important. How is her zest?"

"Zest? She's full of it."

"And initiative. That's terribly important. Has she got initiative—with a capital I?"

"You know, I believe she really has," Jason said thoughtfully.

"Could you give me an example of her initiative?"

"Well . . ." Jason stalled for time. Then he told a little story about meeting her on the campaign train and how all the correspondents were greatly taken with her.

"And you know what a cynical, hard-boiled, bastardly crew *they* are," he concluded gravely. "If they were taken with her: well, that speaks volumes, doesn't it?"

"I'll bear that opinion in mind. Has she had any experience?"

"None whatsoever."

"Well, that's good. I hate to have to mold people with preconceived experience. That's the really tough thing."

"I imagine."

"I doubt it. However. Do you think she would make a good *Vital* type?" Crystal asked.

"The material is there, Crystal. And I've seen what you can do when the material is there."

"What a flatterer you are, Jason."

"Well, if you're going to do it," Jason said, "you might as well shovel it on with a trowel, as Disraeli recommended that the master of ceremonies always do with royalty."

Crystal exploded into laughter. "You know, Jason, you do have a way with you. Have you ever realized that you have a way with you?"

"Why, thank you, Crystal. That's very kind of you," he said with mock solemnity. "It's a real pleasure to hear that from you."

"Jason, tell me one thing."

"Yes, Crystal?"

"As the man says, I don't want jes' no sexy deadhead around here. Is this redhead sexy?"

"Not to me, Crystal. But maybe I can't see it for her brains. Brains in a woman blocks out her sexiness to men, I believe. I think that's probably true. Anyhow: I'd like your opinion on that when you see her."

"Who said I was going to see her?" Crystal said, playing hard to get.

"Well, nobody. It was just a suggestion." Jason put on the soft approach himself. "I've made her promise not to do a thing until she hears from you. Not to offer herself, that is, to *Life, Look, Time, Newsweek, U. S. News and World Report,* or one of those outfits. She's promised me she'd hold off."

"How sweet of her. All right," Crystal said with one of those bursts of decision that were so characteristic of her. "How do I get in touch with the little bitch?"

The next step of the Hightower-Gaskin strategy consisted of two things. One of these was a general prepping of Lilleba Ericsson on the deportment she should maintain when interviewed by Crystal Bidwell. This part of the strategy Lilleba mastered very quickly. She learned that she should show an attitude of initiative, but not overaggressiveness. To demonstrate zest but not overenthusiasm, on which *Vital* frowned. To exhibit a willingness to learn, but not to appear namby-pamby. Finally Jason and Gaskin conducted a number of skull sessions testing the effect of their workmanship, with Gaskin playing the part of Crystal. Lilleba had all this down very quickly, both he and Gaskin noted.

All of this called for Jason to spend a good deal of time with the
young creature, and the learning went both ways. He was learning a
good deal about her. And nothing so far was calculated to repel him.
He should have known. For true goddesses are never haughty. The
true goddess is warm and likes people. The reason is simple. She has
no need of hauteur as a counterfeit for the absence of quality or for the
presence of imperfections, of envy, of greed, of cutting remarks—in a
word, of the small, calculating mind. Only self-supposing goddesses
have call for such coin. Never the real article. So that her essence as a
person in all ways matched her physical aspect. She was warm. She
was interested, and truly so, not trying to ingratiate herself. She was
natural as a bird. She did not throw her personality around any room
she happened to be in. It didn't need it. It was its own spokesman, natural and flowing on its own, requiring no automatic fuel-injection system every five minutes. She was self-assured but not vain. She had too
much cultivation, true cultivation, to be vain, and a liking for people
and a curiosity about the world in all its manifestations that kept vanity out of where vanity might justifiably have found habitation. People who have a healthy curiosity about the earth are never vain. She
made her own values: but not beating her chest about it as a conform-
ing nonconformist. Goddesses, like writers, are born, not made. They
are sent down by God above—on loan, doubtless—to show poor, sod-
den, small-minded, nose-to-the-golden-grindstone, mire-stuck man just
what true beauty, true womanhood, a truly beautiful, humorous, warm
woman could be: which was, when it happened, absolutely the greatest creature on earth.

It was in the prepping for the second part, however, that Hightower
and Gaskin ran into serious trouble. The second part consisted of
teaching Lilleba how to drink martinis.

Unless you could stand up to Crystal martini for martini in that first
luncheon interview, well, the chances were that you had had it. It was
not that *Vital* was looking for alcoholics for its staff. Quite the contrary. It was looking for *temperate* people, if anything. And surely the
fullest proof—almost one-hundred-proof, in fact—of temperance is
that alcohol should have none or little effect on you. What greater test
of this, of temperance, could there be than the ability to put away a
half-dozen martinis at lunch? And in any event it was an unshakable
conviction of Crystal's, like a woman's intuition. Nothing could change
it. If a researcher couldn't handle the stuff, she felt that somehow he
or she just would not, for some mysterious reason, make a good "*Vital*
type," as the gory phrase went, in the long run.

Gaskin and Jason discovered to their horror that not only was Lilleba Ericsson not a good martini drinker. They found, and it was a
chink in the sweet armor-plate large enough to drive a locomotive

through, that two martinis and sometimes even one pretty much finished her off. They were shocked and horrified. But there it was. Gaskin and Jason tested her together, time after time, in the apartment of one or the other of them, usually Gaskin's, and, the plain fact was, she just couldn't take them. It wasn't that they intoxicated her. It wasn't even that they made her sick. It was far more serious than that, and it happened long before she could possibly get enough of the mixture in her to become either intoxicated or ill. What happened was that she just ceased to operate. Folded up. After two martinis or even one all she wanted to do was lie down and go to sleep. Preferably on the floor. She practically couldn't keep her eyes open after a couple of martinis, much less carry on the conversation that Crystal would jolly well expect her to be able to carry on. Even a goddess has her chink— and, alas, Jason and Gaskin had stumbled upon Lilleba's. And a very critical one it was. And there was no accustoming her to them. They tried for two weeks on end, every night, having her put away martinis. No tolerance was built up. At the end of two weeks she was, if anything, more affected by them than ever.

"But I just don't *like* martinis," she complained rather peevishly. "What's more, if you have to go through this to work at that damn magazine"—she had just had a full martini when she used that word, otherwise unheard of from her—"I'm not sure I want to work at that damn magazine."

"Now, Lilleba," Jason said soothingly. "You don't know what you're saying. Of course you want to work at that magazine. At that damn magazine."

"Of course you want to work at that damn magazine," Gaskin seconded this.

Indeed by now, far from being bothered at her having turned up after a brief chance acquaintance a year ago expecting him to get her a job, Jason had now progressed to being absolutely determined that she get one at *Vital*. He didn't ask himself why.

"Now, Lilleba, try again," he said, offering her a martini in a coaxing, cozening voice, much like a mother offering a spoon of castor oil to her child of four. "Just try it now."

"No."

"Here now, watch me and old Hank take some and see how good it is," he said, sipping some of it, much like a mother taking a sip of castor oil to deceive the child as to the desirability of the loathsome stuff.

"No. No! I don't want it, you hear!"

"All right, all right. Don't shout, Lilleba."

"I think I'll lie down," the young goddess said.

Nothing worked, and the time drew near. The time, that is, when Crystal would phone Lilleba and ask her to drop by for an interview.

Crystal always deliberately and on principle waited two or three weeks before doing such a thing—no use to let someone think you want them too much, you know. And their time was running out.

Occasionally Charity would be present when Gaskin and Jason were making a supreme effort and she seemed to look upon the education as cruel and unusual punishment.

"The poor dear," she said one night after witnessing some of it. She put a comforting arm around Lilleba's shoulder. "Can't you see you're torturing her!" Charity exclaimed in a rare moment of wrath. "The poor dear. Why can't you let the poor dear alone?"

"The poor dear! Let her alone!" Jason barked in righteous outrage. "Why, Christ Almighty on a bicycle, Charity, we're doing it for *her* good. It's to get *her* a job."

"We can understand your point quite well without the vivid expletives, Jason," Charity said frostily.

"Well, I just want to get it straight we aren't doing this for pleasure, Charity," Jason said grouchily. "It's for *her* we're doing it. Why, she understands that herself better than anyone—don't you," he said, turning abruptly to her, "Lilleba?"

But by that time the beneficiary of all this outlay of work, energy, and feeling, and of argument, had fallen sound asleep on a buffalo skin.

It was Gaskin who made the desperate suggestion to Jason one day, as Lilleba slept like a baby on the floor on one of his animal-skin rugs. A coyote that time.

"Hightower," he said. "I think there's only one thing to do."

"We'll do it," Jason said, on blind faith, and in desperation, sight unseen.

"Yes, my boy," Gaskin said avuncularly. "The only thing left is for us to go seek out Raoul."

"Raoul?"

And then Jason remembered. "Oh, Raoul."

Next day they had lunch at Crystal's favorite restaurant, the one where she always took a new researcher, or someone trying to be one. They took Lilleba with them, and Raoul, a man professionally accustomed to the sight of smart and lovely women, was almost overcome by the loveliness of this being. Then the following day Gaskin and Jason had lunch alone at the same place. Jason turned on the full flow of his good French, and when they left they almost had Raoul in their pocket. He was so beatified that he accompanied them clear out to the sidewalk.

"Leave it to me, Messieurs," he said, clutching hard on something Jason had slipped into his left hand. "It is a situation I will take great personal delight in handling—especially for two such lovers of all things French as you gentlemen obviously are, not to mention for that angelic creature who was here yesterday. Ah, gentlemen, it takes a Frenchman truly to appreciate such a one, don't you agree? Messieurs! It is a situation made to order for a Frenchman," he added, clutching a little harder.

It was three days later that Crystal had her interview with Lilleba Ericsson at the restaurant. And it was the very next day that Jason dropped casually by Crystal's office. Jason made some small talk and then came to it: "Well, how'd it go?"

Crystal looked carefully at Jason over a pencil she was fingering like a drum majorette's baton. "Well, Jason," she began, "I finally met my match. With a capital M."

"Match?" Jason echoed. "Why, what in the world are you talking about, Crystal?"

"Jason?"

"Yes, Crystal?"

"I don't know if I've ever told you but I have a secret personnel formula—I mean as to whether to hire somebody. Do you know what it is, Jason?"

"Why, no, Crystal. I can't say that I do."

"It's this: He—or she—must be able to hold his—her—own in the martini department."

"A very reasonable qualification," Jason agreed. "Certainly almost a minimal requirement."

"It's not that *martinis* are important," Crystal expanded. "It's what that talent—or lack of it—*tells* about a person. You follow me?"

"Every step of the way, Crystal," Jason said. "At least I'm getting there. It's very astute. Though I'm frank to say I'd never thought of it that way particularly—but of course I've never been on the hiring side of the desk. But it washes. It washes, Crystal."

"For some reason it does. God knows why. I don't. The important thing is that it *works*. With a capital W. And ain't that what counts in this world, as Lord Byron said," Crystal said jocularly.

"Yes, that's what counts all right," Jason said. "By the way. Did it work?"

"Don't rush me, Jason. Here's what happened. Well, sir, I took her in there and we started ordering dry martinis from Raoul. I mean dry. Nine-to-one, don't you know. We ordered one and then another. Then we ordered another and then we ordered a fourth one. Surely she'd wilt, I said. We ordered another and then we ordered a sixth one! She was still on her feet, in her chair, I should say. *Well*. Talk about a *challenge*. But you know what I did, Jason?"

"I can't imagine, Crystal," Jason said breathlessly. "But I'm dying to know."

"Well!" Crystal took a deep breath and leaned forward a little. "I ordered a *seventh* martini for us. That, I thought surely—*that* would fix her little wagon."

"A *seventh!*" Jason exclaimed. "A cute little wagon too."

"You heard me, boy! Well, sir, I could hardly believe it, but listen to this: *Even under a seventh martini she didn't fade."*

"Incredible," Jason said.

"Wasn't it just? Even *I* had never gone beyond seven at lunch. That was when I began to know I had something unusual on our hands here."

"Well, of course as I told you, Crystal . . ." Jason started in modestly.

"Yes," Crystal cut him off. "That is when *I* knew. But I just *wouldn't* give up that easily." She leaned forward across the desk. "You know what I did then, Jason?"

"I could make an educated guess," Jason said.

"Don't bother. I ordered us an *eighth* martini!"

"Eight martinis!" Jason exclaimed. "I wonder what the lethal dose really is," he said reflectively.

"Often wondered that myself. Especially yesterday." Crystal laughed at her own expense. "Yessiree bob, boy! I ordered an *eighth* martini. Well, sir, halfway through it I got up and went to the little girlies room, don't you know, and came back, certain that she wouldn't be visible above the table. And you know what?"

"What, Crystal?" Jason said excitedly.

"Jamais de ma vie! Never in my life! Why, just this. This little red-headed creature had finished her drink and *herself* had ordered a ninth from Raoul." Crystal burst out laughing until the tears came. "Isn't that rich, Jason?"

"The most since Rockefeller," Jason said, and joined heartily in on the laughter.

"You know," Crystal said with a confiding air, "it must be the little creature's Norwegian blood, that's what I decided. I think they use aquavit for mother's milk in that country, don't they?"

"I wouldn't be surprised," Jason said, "considering what a hardy people the Norwegians are. Now go on! Don't stop there!"

"Well, that's about it. *I* was the one beginning to feel those martinis, and I tell you frankly I shall never know how I got through that lunch. I haven't the faintest idea what we ate—ham, venison, shrimp rémoulade, or sheep's eyes. She'd fixed my wagon," Crystal Bidwell said in good sportsmanship. "With a capital F. What a laugh, what a laugh. Well, *c'est la guerre.* And you know, Jason," Crystal said in afterthought, reflective. "There's one curious little sidelight I haven't mentioned to you."

"Don't leave out *anything*," Jason said. "This is too rich."

"Well, sir, it was this. When I had signed the check and handed it up to Raoul he was looking at me with the oddest expression I've ever seen. You know that little man Raoul, don't you? Well, he was positively *leering*. What do you make of that, Jason?"

"Not the foggiest," Jason said. "Crystal," he said immediately, changing the subject. He swallowed and burst out his question. "Crystal, you haven't told me. Did you hire her?"

Crystal Bidwell looked at Jason in stupefaction.

"Why, of course, boy! *Aussitôt dit, aussitôt fait.* French for no sooner said than done. We couldn't possibly let *Life, Look, Time, Newsweek, U. S. News and World Report* or one of those outfits get away with someone who could drink nine martinis at a sitting." And Crystal shook her head in fresh assaults of wonderment. "You know I have always claimed—to myself, I hope I don't go around broadcasting it three times a day—that no one—*no one*—could outmartini me. Least of all a young graduate of Potawatami Presbyterian Normal College."

"Well, you're certainly a good sport about it, Crystal."

"Bullsugar," Crystal Bidwell said modestly. She looked very keenly at Jason. "You know something, boy. I'm sure this girl will go far. Don't you agree?"

"Yes, Crystal," Jason Hightower said, casting a faraway gaze out the window in the direction of the midtown skyscrapers behind her back. "I really think she'll go just about as far as there is to go in this world. With a capital G."

That night Jason took *Vital*'s newest researcher out to celebrate at a really good restaurant, by the name of San Marino. He absently started to order them a martini beforehand, then caught himself.

"No," he said, "I guess you've had enough martinis lately. Just a bottle of Verdicchio, please," he said to the waiter.

"What's that?" Lilleba Ericsson said.

"Oh, don't worry," Jason said hastily. "It's nothing like martinis. Just a similar color. Unless you wish you never have to drink another martini."

But then she said something in that spontaneous burst-of-interest fashion that was so a part of her charm. "You know what I'd like, Jason?"

"Name it."

"I would like," she said, "a very dry martini." Across the table she looked mischievously at Jason. "A real one."

"No, I'm afraid that's out of the question," Jason said thoughtfully. "I've got some rather unusual theater tickets and I don't want you to sleep through this one."

There was something strange happening to Jason Hightower. He had shoveled out thirty-two dollars of his own money for the tickets. This was something he had never done before in the spirit of disinterested benevolence.

19

The Greatest Office Party

Vital magazine, as we have recorded, had office parties on the flimsiest pretexts. This time, however, there was an event of authentic substance as a reason for the party. Crystal Bidwell was getting married. Yes, let us repeat that. Crystal Bidwell was getting married. As if that momentous event were not enough, the party had a second barrel to shoot from. She was marrying one of *Vital*'s truly great photographers, Wolfgang Breuber von und zu Strassburg.

It was an interesting match, and for more reasons than one. In the first place its announcement burst upon the office with complete surprise, which itself was no mean achievement in an office where to preserve secrecy in any private matter, such as a liaison, even for a short time was a near impossibility. Somehow everybody at *Vital* quickly knew who was going with whom, and there was virtually no secrecy to be had in these things if it were a matter of incest—that is to say, someone from the office going with someone else from the office. The reasons secrecy was almost impossible to achieve were many and obvious but fell into two main categories: Any two people seen leaving the office together at the close of work were immediately suspect of the nefarious relation. And the second being, one of the favorite topics of pastime discussion at *Vital* was this very subject—who was lashing up with whom—so that any intelligence in the field got exchanged very quickly.

How Crystal and Wolfgang were able to demolish these two Everestian obstacles to privacy and secrecy was a mystery. At all events they seemed a highly overjoyed couple at the prospect of their impending union for better or for worse. They acted very much as if it were only for the better, and were happy as two young calves.

Everyone felt unusually warm about the upcoming nuptials, a trace of the boy researchers' emotions in the matter deriving from the relief-giving fact that Crystal now being fixed up permanently with hers, it would no longer have to come from them. The feeling was even a little wistful in some cases, for Crystal Bidwell was really not bad. She was really not bad at all.

No one asked Gaskin to take charge of the party. When Henry Gaskin felt something really strongly he didn't need to be asked. He acted. His devoted groundwork paid off in a manner not far shy of the spectacular.

The party began after work one afternoon at four-thirty. In fact, it began a little before after work, and Gaskin's intense and careful planning and preparations, as well as various non-plannings and non-preparations, began to unfold.

The announcement of the commencement of the party was heralded by a marching band Gaskin had formed consisting solely of researchers and photographers, the one standing up, as it were, for the bride and the other for the groom. It was certainly a very mixed band, too, for its sixteen members played everything from toy-store trumpets to a guitar to drums to a glockenspiel to a waist-high Trinidad steel-drum someone had brought back from his winter week and which had to be pushed by two people. Their rapture of noise crashed through the corridors of the magazine like a tall building being torn down. Preceded by the traditional martini flag used to announce parties, the band opened with the equally traditional Wedding March and continued to repeat it in its march around the corridors, interspersed with various other good old songs such as "Jubilo," "Waltzing Matilda," "Roll Me Over," "St. James Infirmary," and "The Bastard King of England." The band, as it pounded down the long corridors, immediately electrified the whole office; pencils were laid down, typewriters ceased their chattering, and the copy editor suspended in mid-air the virulent slashing of a piece of someone's copy. All came to the doors of their respective offices and burst into loud huzzahs for the band, which was led by the photographer Montgomery Shanks, who now began to pierce the atmosphere with the wild yell, "Lay to for the great photographer Wolfgang Breuber von und zu Strassburg!"

And then an even more moving scene and tribute erupted. Pouring from their offices and bullpens, the writers and editors, the researchers and artists, the copy editor, the vice managing editor and the managing editor formed a conga chain behind the martini flag and the band, which then encircled the corridors once more until at last it climaxed in the great and battered National Affairs bullpen, bringing its cheering host of followers to a halt there with one final caterwauling flourish of the instruments followed by a mighty shout and the singing, by the female staff, of "He's a jolly good fellow," and, by the male, to the same tune, of "She's a wonderful wench." Then immediately, amid a cacophony of chattering and purring, everyone fell to upon the immeasurable cases, provided by the company, of Scotch, bourbon, gin, vodka and extra-dry vermouth.

At the outset the party was confined pretty much to the large Na-

tional Affairs bullpen, which, with its battered desks, its newspapers
and blowups of photographs scattered around, and that pervading,
haunting newsprint-photograph aroma of a newspaper or magazine
office, made such an engaging setting for a party, with the city and its
eternal, tantalizing humming outside, and the lights in the midtown
skyscrapers on where charwomen went about their nocturnal chores.
The engagingness was increased by the work the Art Department had
performed at Gaskin's behest. Gigantic thirty-six by twenty-four-inch
blowups of a couple of dozen blooming, exotic and appetizing cover
girls of the past twenty years had been amputated of their original
heads, for which there had been substituted the chubby-cheeked face
of the female intended, Crystal Bidwell. Another couple of dozen
widely varying Continental personalities, such as King Gustav of
Sweden at the Nobel awards ceremony, Aly Khan at St. Leger, Maurice
Chevalier at his first postwar performance, the King of Nepal atop
his elephant at the coronation durbar and Nijinsky in "The Afternoon
of a Faun," had been similarly beheaded and for their heads that of
the male intended, Wolfgang Breuber von und zu Strassburg, inserted.
Due to the genius of the artists no one could have told without close
inspection that they were composite photographs.

A great many people were packed in the National Affairs bullpen
and they spent their time alternately refilling their drinks—the massive file labeled "Story Suggestions" made an excellent bar—and felici-
tating one or the other of the fortunate couple. They both looked
radiant. Crystal with an attractive just-a-touch-of plumpness, her
cheeks glowing and her smile blinkering like the signal light of a flag-
ship giving disperse orders to the fleet; Wolfgang—who looked like a
three-way breed of a Polish general, an Austrian violinist and an Italian
nobleman (Wolfgang had a wonderful waxed-end mustache and a
shaved head)—beaming fond affection upon his colleagues and every
once in a while casting a lecherous grin upon his betrothed.

"Henry, this is such a warming party," the betrothed commented
once euphorically to Gaskin in the rush. "It is truly a party *comme il
faut.*"

"Isn't it just," Gaskin said, pretty happy himself.

And a little later, across the jammed bullpen, Wolfgang said approximately the same thing to the man who was master-minding the
party.

"Eet eez a gut pahrty," Wolfgang Breuber von und zu Strassburg
said. "Eye-uh dahn't cahr eef eet goes on da fooking night long."

"Probably will, Wolfgang, old man," Gaskin said happily. "It just
looks like it just might do that, Wolfgang, old chop. You're a lucky
man you know," he said, looking at Crystal across the sea of bobbing
heads.

"You dahn't have to tell me!" Wolfgang chimed in enthusiastically.

"Eye-uh ahm gedding myself one fooking gut vife. Look aht 'er! Deed you ever see anything so fooking *veerginal*-looking."

"No," Gaskin said soberly. "Never, Wolfgang. She looks fooking good enough to eat."

"Dat eez da fooking troot," Wolfgang said beatifically, with a feeling of love for everything and all God's creatures.

There are so many means of communication between human beings. On many a level that was a most communicative evening . . .

6:03 P.M. "Hello, Lilleba."

Lilleba Ericsson's face lighted up at once. Charity Cabot had been a friend to her from the first, and from the first they had had a fondness for each other, and something like an understanding toward each other.

"Hello, Charity," she said, smiling.

"How are you liking life at the magazine by now?"

Lilleba gave her small, quick low laugh, a soft gurgle. "Well, I like it. I really like it. Things are . . . well, alive around here, aren't they?"

Charity smiled and looked fondly at the other girl. "Yes, no one can accuse matters around here of not being alive."

"It's not what I expected and I like it."

Charity laughed.

"And the parties!" Lilleba exclaimed, with an innocence that had something beyond innocence in it. "Don't they ever run out of parties here?"

"No, I don't think they'll ever run out of parties here," Charity Cabot said.

And both girls, looking at each other, abruptly laughed: that laugh, the most understanding and secret laugh, over absolutely nothing, that two girls can have, and which is really one of the most enchanting and wonderful of all laughs.

6:11 P.M. Strolling down the corridor en route to filling two empty glasses he was holding, Henry Gaskin paused at an object clattering in a closet off to the side, an object which in all his years of newspapering and on the magazine had never ceased to fascinate him.

It was a machine which had legs and keys like a typewriter. But though no hands were pounding them the keys were working of their own accord, as if some invisible spirit were tapping them. This machine, which was an AP ticker, had always seemed to Gaskin to be the Book of Life incarnate. Now his eyes wandered just slightly upward to observe what the keys were punching out on the endless roll of yellow paper:

BUENOS AIRES—A survey completed today disclosed that Communist penetration of Latin America has stepped up spectacularly in the last year. The survey noted a pattern of sharp increases of activity by the Soviet

Union and other Communist-bloc countries in areas ranging from the economic to cultural, with particular emphasis on exploiting the low standard of living of the masses of Latin America . . .

He turned and went on down to replenish the drinks.

6:13 P.M. "I guess it has been done," Jason Hightower said slowly. They were deep in the middle of a conversation.

"The Greeks did it, of course," James Bernstein said quietly. "They did it in drama or poetry since they had no fiction."

"No one seems to be doing it in the United States right now," Jason Hightower said. He turned to his colleague with much interest. "Tell me this, Jim. Do you know of any American writer who is . . ."

6:19 P.M. "Charity, I want to tell you a secret," Montgomery Shanks said with a certain swagger in his voice. "Or at least the part of it that's not confidential."

"I certainly wouldn't want you to tell me anything that was told you in confidence," Charity Cabot said, meaning it, truly sweetly and not snide.

"No, naturally I wouldn't do that. Only the part that's not confidential."

Shanks waited for a rising to the bait and when none came, went on anyhow. "Charity," he said, "did you know that Hank Gaskin had a terrific bite on you at one time."

"Oh? What's a 'bite,' Monty?"

"Just a word I just made up. He really had it for you."

"Oh, did he?" Abruptly Charity was enjoying herself a little more.

"Yes," Shanks said. "Doesn't it sound kind of funny?"

"Funny? How do you mean funny, Monty?"

"Well, just this. You and I can now talk of it in a detached way, I'm sure."

"Talk of what, Monty?"

"Why, that trip to Florida."

Now Charity Cabot did something that really irritated Montgomery Shanks. She burst out laughing.

"Oh, that," she said finally. "I do remember that now. It was an amusing little game, wasn't it?"

"Game?" Shanks said, a shade huffily.

"Why, of course that's all it was for both of us," Charity said definitively.

"But about Gaskin," Shanks returned stiffly to that subject. Now he managed a careless laugh. "I thought it would amuse you to know that Henry Gaskin was once very serious about you." And now Montgomery Shanks turned on the full voltage of his charm and suavity. "I knew of course that he never stood a chance. You and Hank Gaskin!" Shanks really burst out. "Now what would someone like you ever see in Hank Gaskin, not that I don't like him, you understand. But what I mean is, well, what would someone like you ever see in Hank Gaskin. I mean you with your looks and . . . what should I say, *air,* and all," Shanks said insinuatingly.

Charity Cabot, without rising either to that quite honest bait, looked for a moment at Montgomery Shanks parked there so nonchalantly on Gaskin's couch. Then she looked over his shoulder.

"Oh, I don't know," Charity Cabot said. "I see what you mean, I suppose. However, one might see one thing. One rather important thing."

"What in the world could that be?" Montgomery Shanks asked.

And now Charity Cabot looked right at Shanks and whether that touch of an expression around her mouth was a smile, well . . . who could say?

"Henry Gaskin is, I believe," said Charity Cabot, "a man. Yes, I just believe he is." She stood up. "Now I just believe," she said, quite happily it seemed to the baffled Shanks, "I'll fix myself another drink."

6:33 P.M. "Haven't I seen you somewhere before?" Ward Weed asked the astonishingly fetching girl in the red hair.

Lilleba Ericsson's head turned slowly and her sea-blue eyes looked into his—at a level, for he was on the short side.

"My name is Ward Weed," he announced.

"Oh, certainly, Mr. Weed! Yes, naturally I've heard a great deal about you. Those pictures of yours on the juvenile gang—I thought they were wonderful."

"Why, thank you, thank you." Ward Weed smiled earnestly. "But as to my question: Haven't I seen you somewhere before?"

"Well, maybe up and down the corridors here," the creature with that remarkable red hair said. "I seem to spend a lot of time traveling up and down these corridors." She laughed girlishly. "But I suppose it's good for the health."

"Apparently," said Ward Weed, with an appraising sizing-up by the peripheral vision. "But no. Somewhere else I mean. Out of the office."

"I can't imagine where," Lilleba Ericsson said. "I've only been in New York two months."

"No, I guess not then," Weed said. "Unless of course it was outside New York. Where were you before New York?"

"Well, I was at the Potawatami Presbyterian Normal College."

"What was that?" Ward Weed said.

She repeated it.

"Well, no," he said, smiling. "I haven't been around the . . . that college in the last few years, I don't think."

"Or the years before that?" Lilleba Ericsson said brightly.

Ward Weed smiled. "No, I guess I've never been . . ." Then his

smile froze into the look of sudden discovery. "Did you say Potawatami?"

"Yes, sir."

"Is that in New York State?"

"Yes, sir."

"Did a Presidential campaign train ever happen to come through
Potawatami—say, last year's Presidential campaign train?"

"Why, yes," Lilleba Ericsson said. "As a matter of fact that's how I
happen to be standing here talking to you. You see, aboard that campaign train was a *Vital* man, by the name of Jason Hightower. Do you
know Jason Hightower?"

"Oh, yes, I know Jason," Ward Weed said, all sorts of light breaking
slowly but in a highly revealing dawn upon him. "I know Jason all
right."

"Well, you see, Jason . . ."

And then it happened. Lilleba Ericsson told a little story about how
Jason Hightower had rescued her from leaping off the train, promised
to get her a job when she should at last graduate from the Potawatami
institution, and climaxed the story appropriately with the amusing little
incident, at which she gave a fond laugh of recollection, of their ditching
some *Vital* photographer.

"Isn't that an amusing little story, Mr. Weed?" she finished.

"Terribly amusing," Ward Weed said.

"You know," the young goddess—my God in heaven, how he would
like to have at her!—said thoughtfully. "That reminds me of something.
I've often meant to look up who that photographer was. Would you
know who it was, Mr. Weed?"

"Yes," Ward Weed said, and he looked extremely thoughtful. "His
name was Ward Weed."

7:35 P.M. Sometimes Charity Cabot thought Jim Bernstein knew more
about more things than any human being she had ever met. Unless
someone else brought a subject up, however, Jim Bernstein would
simply talk about the ordinary things most people talked about, be it
the weather or the whimsicalities of commuter trains. But if the other
person projected some loftier theme of converse, it was astounding how
he could always talk intelligently about it. She found him highly delightful, quiet and comfortable.

"Go on, Jim," she said simply now.

"Well, I suppose there have always been people who had this urge to
better the world or do something for people," Jim Bernstein said. "What
fascinates me is that it was presumably the same urge that propelled
the good ladies of the New England mission societies to make Mother
Hubbards for the Hawaiians as propelled Albert Schweitzer to start his
hospital."

"Do you think maybe it was the difference in era?"

"Well, that could have something to do with it," Jim Bernstein said quietly. "But I think there's another element in it too. Brains, maybe. Or sense. A sense of humor would help too. For do-gooding to do any good, I think you have to have more elements than just the urge."

"But the time is different. Surely the time is different now."

"Yes," James Bernstein said. "The time is different now." He paused. "Different, I think, than it has ever been. That's the one big fact, isn't it?" Then he laughed quietly and a little ruefully. "And there is one great and oddly curious difference. To do good now: Well, it is almost a necessity for survival . . . And yet today of all days it needs the doing of good without calculation. And between the opposite poles of the necessity and the absence of calculation: there in that gulf, I believe, lies our problem . . ."

7:39 P.M. "Well, young lady! Do you like the party?"

"It's a good party. It's a better party than what we had at the Potawatami Presbyterian Normal College. Though we had some pretty good parties there, you'd be surprised."

"Not too much. You look like you had some pretty good parties at the Potawatami Presbyterian Normal College."

"However, they had to end early. They were pretty firm up there about the curfew hour. A pretty tight ship where curfew hours were concerned."

"Well, a tight ship is a happy ship, you know. You'll let me know if anyone molests you?"

"Oh, immediately."

"You're my ward, you know. In a manner of speaking."

"Oh? I didn't know, as a matter of fact."

"Yes, that's the rule," Jason said—rather protectively, really.

7:56 P.M. "You know, Henry," Crystal said as she looked over the crowded bullpen, "I really believe that Wolfgang is one of those truly rare beings of the earth."

"I've often thought so myself," Gaskin said appropriately.

"He's such a complete and wonderful *polisson*," Crystal said affectionately.

"That he is," Gaskin agreed, not having the faintest idea what she was talking about.

"Vagabond child," Crystal translated. "Yes," she continued reflectively. "He has—what shall I call it? He has absolute genius of course."

"One of our very best photographers," Gaskin said agreeably. "A true artist of the Rolleiflex. A Rembrandt of the 35-millimeter."

"Oh, he's much more than that," Crystal said, as if, in present lights and knowledge, this was small and almost irrelevant praise indeed for such a one. "For, Henry . . . ?"

"Yes, Crystal?"

"He's far more than that. That isn't all, you know. It doesn't even begin it."

"I'm sure it isn't and I'm sure it doesn't," Gaskin said. "I'm sure you wouldn't be marrying him simply because he's a genius of photography."

"I should hope not," Crystal said with a certain acerbity. Then, in a volatile and astonishing change of mood that was much unlike her— this alone made Gaskin feel the thing, whatever it was, was valid—she burst into a virtual whinny of laughter. It was downright ribald laughter. "After all, Henry," she said, leaning slightly toward him, lowering her voice, and giving him a pinch on the inner arm that almost made him cry out. "After all, Henry," she said slyly and ribaldly, "you can't go to bed with a Rolleiflex."

"Not very satisfactorily anyhow," Gaskin, rubbing his arm, said, rather ribaldly himself.

8:14 P.M. "Actually," Ward Weed said in his modest way, "it's been a hardship more than anything else." How he would like to have at this arousing creature! "It's no bed of roses having an IQ of one fifty-five."

"One . . . fifty . . . five!" Lilleba Ericsson exclaimed in authentic admiration.

"The fact itself creates problems for me," Ward Weed said. "You see, it makes your level of sensitivity so much higher."

"Yes, I can see how that might be the case."

"It isn't a question of 'might,' " Ward Weed corrected her. "It's a matter of *fact*. I'm terribly sensitive. It's one of the crosses I have to bear. However, it's what makes me the photographer I am. Talent always has to pay its price, doesn't it?"

"Yes, but it has its rewards too," Lilleba Ericsson said soothingly. "I should imagine."

"People really resent it though," Ward Weed said doggedly. "But here I am talking about myself." Ward Weed, abandoning that fascinating subject in mid-air, suddenly let out an explosive laugh. "If there's anything that gets me where . . . that gets me, it's for someone to talk about himself all the time. That's why they almost never send me any more to cover anything in Hollywood. I won't take that guff, that's all. Have you ever noticed how Hollywood actors do *nothing* but talk about themselves?"

"I'm afraid I haven't known any," Lilleba Ericsson said. "But it would be interesting to."

"No, it wouldn't," Ward Weed corrected her. He laughed again, in memory of something obviously touching and pleasurable. "Oh, well. I guess you can put up with anything for a fitting reward."

"What reward is that?" Lilleba Ericsson said innocently.

Ward Weed looked at her suspiciously. Ward Weed, besides or because of all that IQ, was suspicious of just about anything and everybody and of anything anybody said or did anywhere. But no, nothing.

"Well . . ." For a moment, with this amazing creature—how he would like to bundle her up proper! it was becoming very nearly a necessity—Ward Weed was almost shy. Nothing could have been more uncharacteristic. Then he recovered in part. "Well, you see," he said, dropping his voice conspiratorially. "I have had one or two . . . maybe even three or four . . . possibly just five or six . . . well, I suppose someone like yourself would use an expression like *crushes* with certain figures in Hollywood."

"No," Lilleba Ericsson said brightly. "That isn't at all the expression someone like me would use."

8:19 P.M. Sidling down the corridor with a beatific smile, a reflection of his own pleasant state at the joy around him unconfined and growing more so, Henry Gaskin stopped idly by the AP ticker:

MOSCOW—The Premier of the Soviet Union claimed today that Russian rockets could "bury alive" the United States within twenty-four hours . . .
. . .

WASHINGTON—Americans possess more television sets per capita than any other nation in the world, a Federal Communications Commission official said today . . .

8:33 P.M. "Well, now, I'm sure I've seen you somewhere," Harrison Duckworth said in that genial *noblesse* manner employed by people of position when talking with people of non-position whom they are absolutely positive they have seen only in passing and should know their name but don't. "I'm sure I've seen you somewhere," he said to the surprisingly handsome girl.

"Yes, I'm sure you're sure you're sure," she said drily.

A little haughty, eh, Harrison Duckworth thought. Well, actually that wasn't a bad sign.

"Let me see now. You're the new girl in Religion."

"Religion!" she exclaimed. "New girl!" she exclaimed again. "My good man," she said with a condescension that actually, for some reason, tantalized Harrison Duckworth, "I'm not in Religion and I've been employed here eight years."

"Eight years!" Harrison Duckworth exclaimed. "One of our older employees. Only in point of service," he added with quick gallantry. And true gallantry. She couldn't have been an hour over twenty-five.

"We must have violated the Child Labor Act to get you," he added facetiously.

"Very funny," the girl said drily.

Didn't laugh easily at men's jokes. A very good sign actually, Harrison Duckworth thought.

"Heh, heh," he laughed. "Laughter in the wings. Now give me ten minutes and promise absolutely that you won't tell me who you are."

"You like to play games don't you, Buster," this quite handsome but forthright girl said. And then added, "I've no intention of it."

A very good sign, Harrison Duckworth thought, actually.

8:41 P.M. "Honk," Wolfgang said. "Ven I dink dat deez . . . deez"— Wolfgang cupped his fingers searching for the precise word, like Henry James—"deez *voman* has been right 'ere all da time unter my verr-y nahz . . . Vell! Honk, I dink Volfgang Breuber von und zu Strassburg —a man oo," he said, as if speaking of a famous colleague, "ohfter all has votographed some of da most beyootivul fooking vomen in da fooking vorld . . . Vell, I am a joodge of deez mahtters," Wolfgang said. "I gez I am a joodge all right of mahtters like deez."

"I've always felt that very strongly, Wolfgang," Gaskin said. "Von und zu Strassburg," Gaskin said as if they were discussing a famous photographer not present, "has probably photographed more beautiful women than any other photographer alive—or dead."

"Eezn't eet da troot!" Wolfgang agreed enthusiastically. "Dat is vell known, eez eet not, Honk?"

"Practically everybody knows it," Gaskin said.

"So-o-o!" Wolfgang exclaimed. "Da verr-y fahct von und zu Strassburg peecks out any certain voman to may-ry. I sayed *may-ry,*" Wolfgang repeated for effect. "Doesn't dat say everytink about a voman?"

"It says all I need to know," Gaskin said.

"She's an expeereeunced voman. Dat eez vat I like best. Expeeree-unce. Deez notion ve Ahmericans have dat yoot is everytink may be our most reedeeculous notion of all. Yoot is naading in a voman really. Ahny reel man knows dat. Yah-sss," Wolfgang said, gazing off dreamily, "Creestal has expeereeunce."

"She's got it all right," Gaskin said offhandedly. "Experience."

"How do you mean dat?" Wolfgang barked with a sudden threat in his voice that both startled and surprised Gaskin, who had not meant too much by the remark and after all was only trying to concur—a good practice in these situations. It suddenly occurred to him that as a man of the Continental code Wolfgang might be terribly jealous, where his own betrothed was concerned.

"Just experienced," Gaskin said hastily. "Just general all-round experienced."

And then suddenly—and this really startled Gaskin—Wolfgang laughed slyly . . . ribaldly . . . then actually reached over and rapped Gaskin's knuckles with the cane he always carried. "Vell, Volfgang dahsn't mind," he said. "Volfgang vants a voman who has been ahround. Yah-sss," Wolfgang said, looking off musingly into space, "Creestal has eet."

"She has what you say, Wolfgang?" Gaskin, rubbing his knuckles, said cautiously.

"Creestal has *eet!*" Wolfgang exploded so loudly people on the other side of the room looked up.

9:39 P.M. "So you say you were on the campaign train with Hightower. You know, I find that particularly interesting."

"And why is that, Mr. Weed?"

"Call me Ward. Oh, for various reasons. Various reasons. Did you enjoy the trip on the campaign train?"

"Well, of course I was only on it for about eight hours. Only the time it took to go from Potawatami to New York."

"Of course, of course. Well, did you enjoy *that* time on the train?"

"Yes, very much."

Ward Weed looked at the young thing suspiciously. "I suppose Hightower showed you all through the train. He's good at that sort of thing."

"Isn't he!" Lilleba said with genuine enthusiasm. "Yes, he showed me quite a bit. We went down and saw the Secret Service man. Then we walked back to the correspondents' car and saw that. Very interesting. There they were, batting their typewriters away as the train tailed it for New York."

Ward Weed looked startled for a moment but then realized it was only the poetry of youth. "I see," he said. "Well, now. Seeing the Secret Service man—whatever that was for—and seeing the correspondents' car . . . even both of those time-consuming enterprises together would hardly eat up the better part of eight hours, would they?"

"Oh, no. They only took about twenty minutes."

"So that leaves seven hours and forty minutes." And now Ward Weed, looking at her very cannily, bore in. "And what, may I ask, did you do with the other seven hours and forty minutes?"

"Do, Mr. Weed? I mean Ward."

"Yes, *do!*" Ward Weed shouted as if he were a father fetching up his thirteen-year-old daughter for extreme malfeasance of some kind or another. "What did you and Jason Hightower *do* with those seven hours and forty minutes?"

"Do, Mr. Weed?" Lilleba Ericsson said. "Why," she said, looking into his face with authentic innocence, "we communicated."

9:47 P.M. "I know who you are!" Harrison Duckworth exclaimed like Columbus discovering America. "You're Clarabeth of the Morgue!"

"Well, don't make it sound like E. Allan Poe," drily said Clarabeth, who like all the Morgue girls was intellectual and egghead to the core.

"Just imagine," Duckworth went on excitedly. "Clarabeth. I must have talked to you a thousand times on the phone."

"Isn't that a fascinating statistic? They'll doubtless put it in the next edition of the World Almanac."

"Heh, heh, hee, hee, hee, haw, heh," laughed Harrison Duckworth. "Clarabeth of the Morgue! Well! They grow them pretty sharp down there, don't they?"

"Who did you think manned the Morgue," Clarabeth said. "Apes?"

"Hee haw haw heh hee haw," laughed the vice managing editor. "We've had this prize package stuffed down there and locked away."

"Well, I rather like it in the enlisted men's foc'sle," said Clarabeth.

"You do, eh?" Harrison Duckworth leaned over in a confidential air. "How would you like to come up here in officers' country?"

"Make me an offer," Clarabeth of the Morgue said, not drily at all this time. Hard, bright, and bargaining.

9:54 P.M. "Well, Cy," Hank Gaskin said, "they make a pretty pair, Wolfgang and Crystal, don't they?"

"Amp zoop," Cy Tadlock, the managing editor, said. "Zinfrow roup."

Gaskin was just able to translate this as, "They'll have discovery times ahead, I'm sure." He laughed appropriately.

"Yes, I imagine so," Gaskin said pleasantly. "Tell me, Cy, did you ever suspect it?"

"Ramp noup anfrom zor."

Gaskin just managed to translate this as, "I'm sure they fooled even themselves."

He laughed appreciatively. "Yes," he said, gazing at them across the room, "they make a healthy, virile-looking pair."

"Arp noup zon amix zampa."

Translated: "They better get a reinforced-concrete bed."

10:05 P.M. "Well, old Gaskin really rounded up a good one this time, didn't he, Charity?"

"The party? Yes, he's very good at rounding up parties."

She is a fine and delightful woman, Jason thought. He thought theoretically of asking her what else Gaskin was good at, but of course didn't. "Yes, sir," he said instead. "There is quite a man. Quite a man."

She said nothing, and he repeated: "Quite a man, don't you agree?"

"Oh, yes, he is," Charity Cabot said, rather absently. And then she said something—almost blurted out, and she was not a blurting-out girl —that really surprised and perplexed Jason.

"Quite a man," she repeated. "And he ought not to be here."

10:14 P.M. "Well, Georgia! What a fetching dress that is you're wearing."

"Oh, hello, Monty," Georgia Dewey said unenthusiastically. "I'm terribly glad you like it."

"You look very well in black, if I may say so."

"You may, and almost any woman does."

"But not so much as you, Georgia. However, it is a fact that black is my favorite color for a woman."

"How terribly interesting to know that," the woman photographer said.

"Yes," said the man photographer, "I do like black on a woman. And you really stand out wonderfully in it," Montgomery Shanks said, giving those magnificent ramparts a glancing blow with his eyes.

"You make very pretty compliments, Monty. Yes, you do."

"Yes, I like black on a woman. I like black outside and then I like black below that. Do you, Georgia?" Montgomery Shanks said suavely.

Georgia Dewey, with a fine little smile, looked him straight in the eye. "Do you know something, Monty? You'll never know. You'll never, never know," she said, holding herself projected out toward him to where he was but inches away from them. "Isn't that a terribly interesting fact? Excuse me, my drink needs fixing," she said, withdrawing them.

10:24 P.M. Henry Gaskin crouched over the AP ticker:

ATLANTIC CITY—The American Medical Association convention was told today by a Harvard Medical School dietetics expert that thousands of Americans annually "eat their way prematurely to the grave" by excessive food intake . . .

. . .

NEW DELHI—A report by a special commission of the Government of India disclosed today that a majority of Indians live on a diet considered below the level of bare subsistence. Untold thousands of Indians, the commission said, die annually of malnutrition . . .

. . .

WASHINGTON—The Department of Agriculture today announced that the United States Government spent nearly one billion dollars last year merely to store farm surplus food the nation could not consume. Furthermore, the Department said, the bill for storing the farm surplus is growing at the rate of a million and a half dollars a year.

"How to dispose of this tremendous food surplus," said a Department spokesman, "is perhaps our most pressing problem."

10:39 P.M. "Have you ever thought about rising out of the Morgue, Clarabeth? Like Lazarus, I mean, heh, heh."

"Very funny. A perfect scream." Not a flicker of a smile creased her set mouth. "Oh, yes, I've thought about it. What do you have in mind?" she said directly.

Harrison Duckworth laughed. "My, you don't beat about the bush, do you?"

"You asked me a question," she said crisply, "and I gave you an answer. It's a free country."

"So you did. So it is. Well, why don't we think about it?"

"Just what do *we* have in mind?" Clarabeth of the Morgue said, as direct as one could get, especially at *Vital* magazine.

"Well, I was thinking," Harrison Duckworth said.

"Do you find that an intolerable strain?"

For a moment Harrison Duckworth didn't know whether to be peeved and mount his high horse, or to laugh. He looked at her—she was really a very fetching thing—and did the latter.

"You know," he said, "I think we might just have been wasting you."

"I'm glad you think so," Clarabeth said forthrightly. "When do we start not wasting me?"

"This night," said Harrison Duckworth, "may change your life around. Doesn't that impress you?"

"Not until it happens," Clarabeth said crisply. "There's only one thing will impress a buried Lazarus. Heh, heh."

Not a flicker of a smile creased that very set mouth. A very nice mouth, Harrison Duckworth thought.

11:02 P.M. "I love you," said one of the lovebirds.

"You dahm vell bedder," said the other.

The first lovebird laughed. "Wolfie, we're going to have so much *fun*. With a capital F."

"And 'at ain't all," said the second lovebird.

The first lovebird burst into a whinnying scream of delighted laughter. "Harrison," she said to the man talking to Clarabeth a few feet away. "Harrison! Come right over here and protect me. This man is getting positively rye-bald."

"Vit a cahpidal Arr," said the second lovebird.

11:24 P.M. Lilleba Ericsson's eyes watched Bernstein's face. It was a good face.

"Besides the high incidence of parties," he said, and smiled, "it's a pretty good observation tower."

"I understand about the parties," she said. "But what's this about an observation tower?"

"Well, now, I mean when you come out of school," he said quietly, "the magazine's a pretty good observation tower from which to take your first look at the world. Or haven't you found it so?"

Lilleba Ericsson looked thoughtful. "Yes, I have. You do get quite a large view of things from here, is that what you mean?"

"Yes, you do," Jim Bernstein said, "and yes, it is, more or less. And

I'm not talking entirely about world events. Although it is possible to see how things are heading there maybe a little quicker here. That is" —and she felt she saw a flicker of a twinkle in his eyes—"if you want to see such a thing."

"You mean some people don't want to?"

He smiled down at the bright young face. How young, he thought, how full of the desire to search and know. "It seems," he said, "to be the last thing in the world a lot of people want to see, to know."

11:38 P.M. Hank Gaskin and Charity Cabot wandered into the Special Projects office. Splayed out on a huge table there was a set of eleven by fourteen blowups of color photographs for a story in the magazine's "The Five Continents and the Seven Seas" series, this one on Africa . . . on Togo and Ruanda-Urundi, on Entebbe and Zanzibar, on Ruwenzori, Lake Chad and Fernando Po. The couple stood over them.

"My good Lord," Gaskin said, caught up by their mystery and beauty. "It makes the mouth drool, doesn't it?"

"Don't they look exciting!" Charity Cabot exclaimed, so caught up herself that she didn't even notice the rather coarse expression of Gaskin's haunting reactions. "Do you think they're really that way?"

"Well, you know what they say about the non-prevaricating camera," Henry Gaskin said sententiously.

They looked in awe and fascination at the strange-blue mountains, the great stretches of plains. Then Charity Cabot spoke, still looking at them, spoke very slowly.

"I was just thinking," she said, "wouldn't it be a crime to die without seeing them?"

"A felony," Henry Gaskin said. "It would be felony in the first degree never to see them."

They both looked at them one moment more. Then Henry Gaskin walked over and shut the door. He walked back, and taking her face ever so gently in his hands, kissed her, lightly, almost a brush, on the lips. Then he walked back and opened the door.

"Let's go back to the party," he said. "For now."

11:42 P.M. "Ah, Jason," Crystal said, "I am truly *éperdu d'amour* with that man. French for madly in love."

"I can surely tell that," Jason murmured. "Of course *he* is enormously fortunate . . ."

"*Quel charmant,* Jason," Crystal said coyly, "of you to say so."

". . . but also you, my dear, are almost too fortunate for me to express it. Wolfgang Breuber von und zu Strassburg is no ordinary man. In fact, if there's anything Wolfgang doesn't have I don't know what it is."

"*Quel savoir-vivre* in him!" Crystal exclaimed, and now her eyes fondly sought her future husband out across the room. *"Quel distingué! Quel éclat! Quel élan! Quel sang-froid! Quel dégagé! Quel haut ton! Quel insouciance! Quel joie de vivre! Quel intransigeance! Quel chevalier sans peur et sans reproche!"*

And now Crystal leaned over more closely to Jason. "But, Jason, there's something else. Will you think it bold of me to say it?"

"If you can stand the boldness so can I."

"Oh, Jason!" Crystal bubbled, pinching his arm quite crisply. *"Allez-vous-en. Quel douceur!"*

Now she leaned over until her lips were almost against his ear and Jason waited for a truly great revelation.

"Jason," Crystal said. "Wolfgang gives those *petits soins*—French for little attentions—that a woman so likes. However. He does not neglect *les grands soins,* if you know what I mean. Such *empressement.* French for ardor," Crystal said delicately. "If you know what I mean."

"I believe I do—in general," Jason said soberly.

"And, Jason, in that respect, one other thing: We are *comme deux gouttes d'eau.* French for like two drops of water."

"Yes," Jason said, "and *il a la mer à boire.* French for he has the sea to drink up, in you."

"Why, Jason, *quel blagueur.* French for flatterer. But *quel quel charmant!"*

Crystal looked once more across the room at her husband-to-be. Suddenly she pirouetted in astonishment.

"Why, Jason! I never realized you spoke French."

"Only sparingly, my dear," Jason said, feeling actually fond toward Crystal of a sudden. And she smiled fondly back—knowingly, so that he said, meaning it:

"Crystal, you are *pas si bête.* French for . . ."

"Not so bad. *Merci mille fois,* Jason."

11:53 P.M. Ward Weed's hand, very weaving now, weaved in glancing blow toward the ramparts we watch. Even with such a target he missed easily. Georgia Dewey simply turned, quite contemptuously.

"What ridiculous dreams of glory you do have," she said, and swiveled away. For all the ramparts she was very lithe on her feet.

12:08 A.M. "Ray ark mah," Cy Tadlock said.

Harrison Duckworth immediately knew this meant, "This is a truly great party."

"Zamp arp mast rap?"

Meant: "We mustn't let it stop, must we?"

"No, we mustn't, Cy. We surely mustn't."

"Ramp ack spoopow. Zamp ap wamp. Tay ampow. Wantow marpee."

"Righto, Cy!"

Harrison Duckworth went into his office, picked up the phone and passed along the boss's order: "Three cases of Old Grand-Dad, three cases of J and B, three cases of Gordon's, two bottles of Noilly Prat."

12:20 A.M. Gaskin edged his way through the crowd to where Lilleba Ericsson was sipping her drink and watching and soaking up everything with wide-eyed interest.

"How you doing, Eric the Red?"

She looked up and smiled. "Just fine, Hank."

"Not drinking those nasty martinis, I see," he said, gesturing to her glass.

She laughed, that low gurgle. "Not yet." She looked down at her weak Scotch and water thoughtfully. "You know, sometime I think I might try them again."

Gaskin looked slightly alarmed at the idea.

12:46 A.M. "One might ask the question, Duckworth," said Clarabeth, who was nothing if not frank, "exactly what are your motives?"

"Motives?" the vice managing editor said, a shade startled but smiling at least outwardly. "Motives, motives? Who said anything about motives, Clarabeth. I don't see any motives running around loose here."

"I do," Clarabeth of the Morgue said.

"Hellsfire, Clarabeth, the world itself is one big motive," said Harrison Duckworth, and pretty profoundly too.

"Don't tell me what I already know," Clarabeth said with a bite. "I'm asking: What's *yours?*"

"Clarabeth, if you don't mind my saying so, you aren't the most subtle girl I've ever known."

"Never tried to be. Don't want to be. Lay it on the line, Duckworth."

"Clarabeth! Clarabeth! Do try to be a little subtle."

"All right," she said in a change sudden as a hurricane's shifting course, "I'll try. I'll out-subtle the hell out of you." She made a movement. "How do you like that, Duckworth?"

"My God," Harrison Duckworth said. "My God, my God!"

1:03 A.M. No one was ever quite sure exactly what specific movement or word led to it. But the rumor that Wolfgang Breuber von und zu Strassburg had once been a high-competition fencer was dramatically verified. Wolfgang had been getting tighter and tighter throughout the evening. And the agility with which he reacted, considering his consumption of ninety-proof, was even fuller testament to his prowess with the épée.

Leaping back, Wolfgang pulled his sword out of his cane—until then no one even knew that was a sword cane he carried—and boomed out the classic and completely unaccented, since Wolfgang spoke perfect French: *"En garde!"*

The challenged was none other than Ward Weed, who, whatever he had done—and no one but the ladies, who had a pretty good idea, was ever sure precisely what—didn't mean anything at all personal by it. He did it—whatever it was he did—as naturally as some men replenish their drinks at a party. But Wolfgang, in these matters, was a man of the Continental Code.

"En garde, Veed!" he cried, leaping back.

In fact, even as they cleared a circle for the pair, people hardly knew whether it was a planned part of the entertainment or for real. If one had looked, one would have seen a thrilled expression on the face of Crystal Bidwell—thrilled by the virility and masculinity of her fiancé's reaction to the stimulus of whatever it was Weed had done. She was the most fascinated spectator, among many quite fascinated ones.

"En garde!" cried Wolfgang, going into that position in the middle of the National Affairs bullpen.

"Run him through!" a voice was heard to scream ecstatically.

And suddenly, as people thrilled and gaped, Wolfgang was leaping on and off tables, desks and chairs with an amazing agility reminiscent of Benvenuto Cellini and Cyrano de Bergerac in their combined prime. Weed, joining in, for sport, or for protection, grabbed up a straight-back Do-More chair and held it out like Clyde Beatty facing the lions. Wolfgang easily lunged through this guard, and with a cry and a yelp Weed dropped the chair. He had been pinked lightly on the inner arm, becoming possibly the first man wounded in a duel in the New York area since Burr and Hamilton in 1804 on the Hudson Palisades.

Immediately Wolfgang laid down his sword across a researcher's desk and with a broad beaming smile and a victor's magnanimity went over to succor his fellow photographer. Still smiling he said to him, "Joost ree-member ohfter deez, Veed: keep your fooking hands off my bee-troothed." And he looked around at the gathered company. "And dat goes vor *ohl* of you," he said in such a genial though forceful way that all could not but appreciate it.

Thrilled to the core by such masculine, un-American protection, Crystal Bidwell rushed over and threw her arms ecstatically around her fiancé, whilst a round of cheers went up—chiefly from the ladies, whom Ward Weed left quite unmolested for the remainder of the evening.

1:29 A.M. "Jason! How have things been with you?"

"Pretty well, Georgia. I'm not clear all the way up there yet, but I'm still looking up there."

Georgia laughed. The two liked each other.

"You'll get it," Georgia Dewey said.

"What'll I get, Georgia?"

"Well, I think you'll get whatever you want."

"Well, I appreciate that confidence."

"You're the kind that does. But I mean what you *really* want."

"Tell me what it is, Georgia."

She laughed again. "I think you know."

"I'm not so sure. But I do hope to find out. That's very truthful what I just said."

She laughed again. "Jason, *I* know."

"Don't tell me. I want to find out myself."

"You will, Jason. You're the kind who will."

1:38 A.M. "Henry," Charity Cabot said. "I think I may be starting home pretty soon."

"No, no!" Henry Gaskin exclaimed, startled at the idea. "You mustn't think thoughts like that."

"But it's nearly two—A.M., Henry."

"That's the whole point. It's very dangerous to be out on the streets of New York at this hour."

"Nonsense. It's the safest city in the world."

"There were four muggings on one day . . . night . . . last week."

"Not in this section, Henry," Charity Cabot said drily.

"Still there can always be a first time where sections in New York are concerned. You recall the Brink's armored-car robbery in Boston?"

"What in the world does the Brink's robbery in Boston have to do with it, Henry?" Charity Cabot said, a little irritatedly.

"Just that it happened in the most traveled part of the city, that's all."

"Well, this isn't Boston. And I'm not Brink's."

"I question the second part of that statement," Gaskin said gallantly, but most truly. "Please stay, Charity. For my sake. For my peace of mind."

"All right then," she said and smiled a little. "I'll stay—but just a little longer, you understand?"

"Don't give it another thought," Henry Gaskin said airily. "Here, let's go down to my office and put on some records. If Gaskin can't keep you here," he said self-deprecatingly, "maybe Bach can."

"All right," Charity Cabot said sleepily. "But only a little longer now, you understand? No later than two-thirty at the latest."

"Roger," Gaskin said. "At half past two o'clock we'll reopen the entire subject."

1:41 A.M. Harrison Duckworth went into his office and closed the door.

Then he went into his closet and closed that door.

In the closet he mounted his Exercycle and pedaled it furiously for fifteen minutes.

Much refreshed and re-invigorated, he went back to the party, with an air of manly self-approval. He looked around eagerly for Clarabeth of the Morgue.

"Clarabeth," he said immediately when he found her, "how's your metabolism?"

2:03 A.M. "So I am now *hors de combat!* Well, I've enjoyed things wouldn't you know it," Crystal Bidwell said, "but things just aren't set up for a woman to go it single forever, isn't that the truth now, Henry? It's so *pis-aller*. French for makeshift. To think," she said in fond reminiscence, looking somewhat coyly at him, "that you were one of mine."

Something in Gaskin froze. However he managed a warm if somewhat waxen smile. He hoped Wolfgang was well out of earshot.

"I'll never forget it, Crystal," he said in a whisper-croak. "It's our own little secret, isn't it? Secret," he repeated in a sibilant whisper.

2:05 A.M. "I want to say something," Montgomery Shanks said.

"Say away," Georgia Dewey said icily. "You often do."

Montgomery Shanks swallowed. "I just want to say this: The fact is, you're a better photographer than just about any of us—including the great Shanks himself."

Georgia Dewey looked at him strangely. It was the one thing Montgomery Shanks would not say unless he meant it. "It's good of you to admit that—finally," she said—but just the barest bit less icily.

2:08 A.M. "Well, Lilleba!" Crystal Bidwell said. "You don't mean to tell me you've been drinking martinis all this time."

The young creature sipped and smiled across the pool of the oily liquid. "Nope," she said truthfully. "This is my first martini. Don't they taste good though?" And somehow they did tonight.

Crystal Bidwell laughed. "No more than ten martinis now, remember, girl!" and waggled a gay and happy finger at her.

"I want to see if maybe I can hold them," Lilleba said, like a student at a problem.

"*Quel* wit!" Crystal exploded. "With a capital W."

2:17 A.M. "Well, it's a problem all right, Hank," Jim Bernstein said. "They'll write the age up on the basis of it."

"Not my problem, Jimmie boy," Gaskin said, "but it interests me."

"Participation or non-participation," Jim Bernstein said, stirring the ice cube in his drink with a finger. "That's the real thing everyone has to decide."

"I wonder," Hank Gaskin said rather abruptly, "if anyone has ever combined withdrawal and participation . . ."

2:31 A.M. Looking across the crowded National Affairs bullpen, Jason Hightower could see a number of colleagues clustered around Lilleba Ericsson like flies around fruit. A number of male colleagues. He was surprised at the quick sliver of jealousy that splintered through him. However, it was understandable, he told himself readily. After all, she was his ward in a manner of speaking—was it not true that but for him she would not even be here?—and he had almost a duty to see to it that she didn't get taken down the wrong track, don't you know, and that sort of thing. Yes, it was clearly his duty, nothing less. Slowly, holding his drink high, he began to make his way through the flies toward the fruit.

3:02 A.M. Ward Weed, having returned from getting his duel-nicked arm bandaged at the dispensary on the twenty-third floor—which, as a part of the magazine's Benevolence and Paternalism, was remaining open the party long, with a young doctor and nurse in attendance—collapsed almost fully inebriated into the arms of the most beloved member of the *Vital* staff: the great leather couch with the office of its own.

3:17 A.M. As he waited for Charity to get her coat, Henry Gaskin leaned on the AP ticker. It was marvelous to wonder what the keys would clatter out next, what city—Berlin, Paris, Moscow, New Delhi, Djakarta, Tokyo, Cleveland, Ohio, or Houston, Texas—would appear, and to try to guess in that second between the spelling out of the city's name and the beginning of the story, what the story would be about, what frightful or otherwise fascinating news the keys would commence pecking out.

The keys now clacked:

MOSCOW—The Soviet Government claimed today that it was at least a year ahead of the United States in the missile race and was gaining . . .
. . .

WASHINGTON—A House of Representatives sub-committee today voted to cut the appropriations for foreign aid requested by the President. Another sub-committee passed overwhelmingly the Rivers and Harbors "pork barrel" bill . . .
. . .

LONDON—The U.N. Secretary-General in a stopover here enroute to the crisis in . . .

With a rather abrupt movement he pushed himself erect and wandered, idly but rather thoughtfully, down the corridor. His peripheral vision drew his attention into a room where sat a battery of machines. Impulsively he went over and sat down at one of them. His hands rested a moment uncertainly on the keys. Then his fingers began to tap out some words . . .

3:18 A.M. In the Chicago printing plant, where the magazine was just going to press, an ink-grimed man looked up from a machine similar to the one in New York and yelled something very loudly to the printing-room foreman.

"Hey, Ernie. Something funny's . . . going on . . . here. Come over here . . . and look . . . at this!" he said more urgently. The teletype operator, from years of operating one, talked like a teletype himself, staccato-fashion.

The printing-room foreman came over and looked over the teletype operator's shoulder. "That's odd. It doesn't make sense, but it looks like New York is trying to tell us something. What do you think, Oscar?"

"Well, of course . . . I'm not paid . . . to think," Oscar said with a small thrust of acerbity, "but it . . . does look . . . as if . . . they're trying . . . to tell . . . us *something*."

Then the machine began to tap out again, and Oscar and Ernie both looked in bewilderment at the sort of thing that was coming over it. It was set as poetry, of all things, and they looked on in utter confusion as the keys rapped out:

Samuel Daniel reporting:

> *Knowing the heart of man is set to be*
> *The centre of his world, about the which*
> *These revolutions of disturbances*
> *Still roule; where all th'aspects of miserie*
> *Predominate; whose strong effects are such*
> *As he must beare, being pow'rlesse to redresse;*
> *And that unlesse above himselfe he can*
> *Erect himselfe, how poore a thing is man!*

"What the hell they mean putting something like that on the machine?" the foreman exploded.

"And who . . . the hell . . . is . . . Samuel Daniel?" the teletype operator shouted, quite angry himself now at this sort of thing coming over his machine. "Don't know . . . anyone on . . . the staff . . . by that . . . name."

"Christ, those editorial buggers never know their ass from upstairs," the foreman neatly summed up the situation and his assessment in general of the entire editorial staff in New York. "Christ up the creek!"

Then, becoming more sober—after all it did appear they were trying to tell him something urgent—he yelled in a bull-moose voice down the line to the men at the printing presses.

"Stop the presses! Yes, you heard me! Stop the presses!"

"Now, Oscar," he said urgently as the great presses ground to a stop, "get those buggers on the horn. Ask them what the hell is going on, tell them we're in mid-edition—if the buggers know what that means . . ."

"I'll tell . . . 'em . . . all right," Oscar said, grabbing up a telephone and beginning to bang it. "I'll tell . . . the buggers."

3:29 A.M. In New York a telephone operator, unable to raise a soul on any of a dozen lines she had tried, all of them in the National Affairs bullpen, where she knew another Babylonian exercise was going on tonight, scurried up the corridor toward the booming party. She spoke something urgently to one of the staff members. She had to tell him three times. Then this worthy started running up the corridor, his voice raised in imperative shout:

"Where's Duckworth! Duckworth's needed urgently here! The magazine has stopped! Is Duckworth around anywhere? Duckworth, I say! Does anyone know where the able Harrison Duckworth is! There'll be no magazine this week unless we get the able and potent Harrison Duckworth almost immediately . . ."

3:31 A.M. "Mr. and Mrs. Harrison Duckworth, Stamford, Conn.," the man registered with a determined air. "Caught unexpectedly in the city overnight," he explained, perhaps a mistake, to the desk clerk.

3:58 A.M. "You know, Charity," Henry Gaskin said to her in his kitchen, "I have a strange feeling. I believe this may have been my last office party."

Charity Cabot looked up at him, startled, from where she was rustling the scrambled eggs with Mexican *jalapeños,* the way Gaskin liked them, insofar as possible trying to keep the *jalapeños* on one side of the pan, since they burned her tongue. His face was bland and smiling.

"Why, Hank, what a strange thing to say."

"Well, I'm glad it was such a good party, if it *is* to be my last one." He looked down at her. "Would you like it if it were your last one," he said carelessly.

Something caught at her, something which warmed and thrilled her. "I might at that," she said, trying to match his careless tone. She reflected, and then repeated it. "I just might."

She felt his hand on her shoulder and a strange, unexperienced thrill leapt through her.

"Well, old girl, it might. Yes, it just might."

Thoughtfully she went back to stirring the scrambled eggs, trying to keep the *jalapeños* to one side . . . Then: *

"Wait a minute," he said abruptly. "I want to show you something."

He disappeared into his rodeo-like living room and was back in a moment carrying an envelope. She felt a strange excitement, not at all characteristic, in him, almost surrounding him.

"I just want you to hear this," he said. "You remember my telling you about Tompkins Armbruster?"

"The one who's starting a school in Africa?" she said immediately.

"Right," Gaskin said, quite excitedly. "Well, I just got another letter from him. Listen to this," he said, flapping out the letter like a spaniel flushing quail.

Charity Cabot's eyes widened and she stopped stirring the eggs, feeling perhaps instinctively that some memorable moment in Henry Gaskin's life—and, who could say, perhaps hers as well—was at hand.

"Listen to this," Gaskin repeated. "Listen to this, which is written from very Africa itself: 'I hope, old man, that this will be the first of a complex of such schools around the world. What I'm saying is, I would like eventually to have a Southeast Asia-American School in Bangkok or Malaya, or somewhere around there; and so on. All for one purpose, to give an education to the young of these countries. Well, it sounds like a big order, even though I've made a really embarrassing sum of money to put into it—incidentally, you'd be surprised what a man concentrating on it a little can come off with in the stock market these days. Fantastic, my boy, perfectly fantastic. It made me feel like a Brink's truck on two legs, just walking around. But that's not all in the kitty. Would you believe it, since I last wrote you, the Rockefeller Foundation people, the Ford Foundation people, and a couple other such sources of the big coin, have indicated a really banging interest in the idea and that they might just unlock some of their more choice coffers to flow into it. The schools would just be, well: first and foremost and lastmost, very good schools, teaching liberal arts first, then adding engineering, medicine, and so on, all the knowledges and skills these people need. They wouldn't have a shred of propaganda about them, though I confess I am gnawed at by the exciting idea that a truly educated man rarely buys *any* form of tyranny, that to such a man such an ideology is as ridiculous as a pig in a bikini and as horrifying as a bathtub full of cobras. And would you listen to this please: My preliminary forays on the home soil suggest that there are any number of Americans—teachers, doctors, practitioners of all the skills and arts—who are ready, yea, eager, to become a part of this and make their lives add up to something more than two TV sets in every room. What I mean, old boy, they would venture forth to new countries as did the colonists of old, but in a very different sort of colonization, to wit: *Bringing* something to these peoples instead of trying to *get* something from them. A very different kind of colonization, now isn't it? Sometimes, old sot, I think the whole trouble of this world can be summed up in the fact, to paraphrase the great Sir Winston, that so few have tried to get so much from so many.

" 'Now. Here it is. During my sojourn in your quarters I came to feel, perhaps wrongly, that you had a large and idle reservoir of energy which just might be tapped and used. There's no question about the idle part—God knows you managed more idleness at the great magazine than any adult man I saw in my entire rather spectacular career on the management-consultant scene—and I'll trust my instincts on the large part. So: I would like for you to be my sort of chief of staff, for want of a better title, for this operation. It begins small and it's going to be a rough tough hard-work job but it can grow. It can grow! And it will give these people the one thing we need to give them . . .' "

Gaskin, putting the letter back, breathed a deep sigh. And he looked at Charity Cabot. "Well, my dear. Shall we sign on?"

Charity Cabot felt very close to transfigured, and the scrambled eggs and the *jalapeños* burned on the stove.

"Yes," she said, mesmerized. "Let's go."

In no more than half an hour they had left the apartment, with its aroma of slightly scorched eggs and *jalapeños,* and were walking toward Charity's apartment. And in twenty minutes more they were seated in a Checker cab.

"Idlewild Airport," the Gypsy Writer said to the cab driver. "Please, sir."

He put their combined luggage, consisting of two green passports and two air travel cards, in his pocket. Then as the taxi started up Sixth Avenue he spoke almost in afterthought.

"We really should tell our friends, shouldn't we?"

"Yes," she said at once. "And we really should say good-bye, shouldn't we? They're good people."

"Yes. Driver. Instead of Idlewild will you please make that The Fun House . . ." Gaskin quickly caught his lapse as the driver's head cocked suspiciously a half-turn around. "I mean the Vital Building. And when you get there, will you just wait."

"You still going to Idlewild?" the driver said, wanting to get the facts straight, wanting to know what *he* was going to be doing.

"Oh, yes, indeed," Gaskin said. "We're certainly still going to Idlewild. Aren't we, dear?"

"Oh, yes," Charity Cabot said. "Yes, indeed. We are certainly going to go to Idlewild."

The party was still going strong when they debarked from the elevator onto the thirty-fourth floor. It was true that some had fallen by the way-side, and, as they passed down the corridor, they could see a body sprawled out here and there in an office, across a couch, sunk in heavy, even audible sleep in a Do-More chair, and, in the Education office, curled up neatly on a desk, stockinged feet anchored in an Outgoing basket. But as they debouched from the corridor into the bulging National Affairs bullpen, they could tell at once that a happy pandemonium still reigned unchecked and, if anything, seemed to swell and increase as the night pushed on. The noise was admirable. In one corner Gaskin could make out, to his astonishment, what appeared, from pictures he had seen of them, to be an Exercycle, and mounted on it, peddling furiously away and yelling like a Sioux going into battle on his favorite steed, Razorback Creech. In another, the photographer Montgomery Shanks seemed to be in a posture of supplication, indeed almost of genuflection, to his fellow photographer Georgia Dewey, almost as if entreating the original she-God or Earth Mother, Which seemed to be listening in an attitude of seeing if the obeisance and the abasement were sufficient to grant forgiveness and even measured reward. The enjoyment had reached such a pitch of decibels that Gaskin was perplexed as to how he could do it. The plane schedule certainly did not leave them time to say individual good-byes and the chances of contravening that noise by a single human voice, even long enough for an announcement, seemed slim indeed. Then his eye lighted on a lone trumpet, lying in a disordered pile of clippings and blowup prints on a desk. He stepped over and appropriated it. Then, with an agile leap, he was atop the desk itself. Gaskin had good lungs. Hoisting the instrument and giving it all, he got some blasts through it that would have pierced the Bessemer process. Even so he had to give another volley of blasts. This one brought enough eyes upon him that with the added, visible flapping of his arms he was at last able to get quiet. Quite a pond of eager eyes looked up at him from generally ecstatic, if arrested, faces.

"*Viva* Gaskin!" someone shouted. There was a general rustling and laughter. Gaskin smiled, and raising his hand once more, got a really Quaker-meeting silence.

"Good friends," he said. "I will not detain this spirited assemblage for long . . ."

"Hear, hear!"

". . . However, I have a short announcement to make."

Gaskin paused and then got the whole blessed blooming thing out at once.

"Charity Cabot here and I are getting married and are emplaning in about an hour to go to Africa and work."

"Good God!" Two enormously distinct words burst like crisp rifle shots into the silence. Startled by these words almost as much as by the announcement itself, everyone including Gaskin himself turned eyes to its source—for it was none other than Cy Tadlock, the managing editor, from whom the surprise of the announcement brought the first articulate speech anyone present had ever heard that genius utter. Then the eyes swept back in astonishment to Gaskin, who was climbing down. Immediately, as one man and woman, the great horde in the National Affairs bullpen bore down on their departing colleagues with outpourings of genuine love and affection.

There was an enormous tumult then, but here and there some unmistakable words were able to pierce their way through it.

"Honk, deez eez da best nooz seence Creestal and me decided da same. Vat a gut example ve have set!"

"Hank. So this is your *chant du cygne*. French for swan song."

"Bonheur ne vient jamais seul. Dat means, Hoppiness never cahms alone," Wolfgang said.

"Hank, you sweet man"—this from his betrothed—"I must kiss you good-bye. Just a *coup de bec*. Peck."

"Dat's enuf," said the other betrothed after perhaps half a minute.

"Hank! *Au revoir!* You will be *brillé par votre absence*. French for conspicuous for your absence."

"Yes, Crystal. But *homo vitae commodatus non donatus est*—Publius Syrus. 'A man is lent not given life.' And as Horace said, *In medias res*. 'Into the midst of things.' Also, *Dum vivimus vivamus*. 'While we live let us live.' "

"Yes. *C'est la guerre*."

"Dat means, Dat's var," said Wolfgang, a little drunkenly.

"Yes, we must *bouter en avant*—push forward," Crystal said, looking at Gaskin. She was not drunk, not drunk at all. And what she said next made Gaskin sure that Crystal Bidwell—a very bright woman really and in so many ways a good one—knew quite precisely what he was up to. "*Comme il faut*. I know you're leaving to live. With a capital L."

And now the photographer Montgomery Shanks made his way through the crowd. He was opening a billfold. Sidling up to Gaskin on the flank away from Charity he slipped him two hundred-dollar bills.

"Here's your hundred dollars and the hundred I owe you," he hissed.

As Gaskin stuffed the bills hurriedly in his pocket, Jason and Lilleba got through. Lilleba embraced Charity, and Jason—also knowing what Gaskin and Charity were up to in taking off—shook long his friend's hand and smiled up at him.

"As you are fond of saying, old man, Monogamy is our leading evil—and variety life's spice . . ."

"Yes, but you see," came a crisp and saucy voice, "I'm the original variety pack. *Multum in parvo*."

The heads of both Gaskin and Jason snapped around in startlement and the mouths of both fell open. Neither had realized she was in hearing range.

"Charity!" Gaskin said, shocked.

And Jason, shaken a little himself, suddenly realized, in some awe, a little more of just what his friend Gaskin was getting—in addition to that new life in Africa.

Gaskin raised his hand once more. "Good-bye, all!" he said. "It's been wonderful!"

And it had, truly. It was, as we said at the outset of this monograph, a truly wonderful magazine. There was nothing like it. Nothing.

Suddenly all heads turned to a deafening noise. The band which Gaskin himself had assembled for the party in honor of Crystal and Wolfgang had regrouped from somewhere down the corridor, and now

with arms flashing and knees pounding high, was entering the room to
the thrilling sound of trumpets and the other instruments and playing,
perhaps in honor of Gaskin's love for Western and cowboy music, "The
Yellow Rose of Texas." In its vanguard came the great martini flag.
Never had it seemed to fly so nobly. Arms reached down to hoist
Gaskin and Charity high on massed shoulders and escort them, preceded
by band and flag, to the elevator. There they waited as the band finished
in flourish. Then the managing editor leaned over to say something
urgent to Gaskin.

"Tamp roup suzaow mapp wymakck zeefrow!"

"He means for someone to order up three more cases each of Old
Grand-Dad, Gordon's and J and B," Gaskin translated. "So that a
second party—in honor of Charity and myself—can commence immediately."

Fresh shattering cheers greeted the translation. Then, as the elevator
doors opened, and Gaskin and Charity stepped inside, there went up in
their honor as mighty a shout as those halls had ever heard:

> "Hip Hip—Hooray!
> Hip Hip—Hooray!
> Hip Hip—Hooray-y-y-y-y-y-y-y-y!"

before the door closed on the massed faces, and Henry Gaskin and Charity Cabot started their descent. He reached over and held her hand.

"Stop on the next floor," he said suddenly to the operator. "And will
you wait—we'll be but a minute."

The floor was one of the business floors, all deserted, and he led her
into the nearest office, stuck a piece of paper in a typewriter, and as she
looked over his shoulder typed out

> To the barricades—and to love.

made it into a very fine airplane and sailed it out the window.

And as, downstairs, the taxi roared off up Fifth Avenue into the
silence of early morning, and into a new and unknown life, he heard,
it seemed to him, the voices of the great and the defiant of his land, of
Jefferson and of Lincoln, of Wilson and of the two Roosevelts, sounding
down the years and calling to a new yet ageless fray all the best that
this Republic of the United States was, that it had to offer this em-
battled world, that it *must* offer this world. For it was as one of those
said, and he heard the cadenced words even now ringing in his ears like
the sound of bugles: *We, here in America, hold in our hands the hope
of the world, the fate of the coming years; and shame and disgrace will
be ours if in our eyes the light of high resolve is dimmed, if we trail in
the dust the golden hopes of men.* There isn't much time, he thought.
The clock is running out. There isn't much time left, so we had better

start moving fast, fast. And as the taxi fled around a corner, jostling them back against the seat, Hank Gaskin reached over and laid his hand in that of Charity Cabot's two, cupped like a nest in her lap.

"Oh. We can get married, if that meets with your approval," he said, "in Casablanca, en route. Or would you prefer Zanzibar?"

"It meets with my approval," she said, feeling as though she were flying into the future on wings of glory, "anywhere."

6:05 A.M. Lilleba lay asleep on the couch, out cold from the two martinis she had had. Jason sat by her, playing Gaskin's hi-fi set at a low pitch and looking in rhythmic arc fondly at her and out the window at dawn assaulting the great city. He thought about the thing Gaskin had done. A great thing, really. It was a step . . . a step! It was throwing oneself up against the forces, to shatter upon them or to prevail. And, whichever, one's life was a victory. The only life that wasn't was that life which stood mute and uncommitted, uncounted, throwing itself against—nothing. He sat thinking, and his eyes looked up and rested on Gaskin's artist's drawing of the city as it would look a quarter hour after an H-bomb had hit it.

And suddenly as he sat there an awesome fact bore in upon him with the clarity of the light that hit Saul of Tarsus on the road to Damascus. He seemed to look down the years and he knew, knew as clearly as the fact he was sitting where he was sitting, atop New York, that the mighty conflict would be resolved sometime within the next few years. By 1970 at the latest, he thought, and perhaps earlier. And he felt two things: He felt fear, a wind of fear sweep through him and chill him, from the realization of the fact. And he felt the most total compulsion to do something with his life. For if one really felt such an awesome fact, felt the fact that he was moving into history's one decisive decade, into the great Gethsemane of mankind, one felt at the least the obligation to live, and at the most to do something about it, whatever one man could do. Honorable man had but two choices in this kind of world: to commit himself completely to fight the horror; or, to get out, really to get the hell out and enjoy oneself, live one's life, of the senses and of personal excitement, to the full, discover oneself. Anything in between was some form or other of vegetation; of defeat. It certainly was not to live. And yes, Gaskin had made a choice! A thousand years from now, Jason thought, history will ask of each man alive today one question and one alone, and nothing else will have mattered: Did he commit himself in the struggle? And their names would include that of Henry Gaskin.

His eyes moved and held the artist's drawing on the wall. Then, swiftly, he was looking out the window again. He saw, there in the soaring steel and rock flesh, the great city with its mighty towers leaping toward the heavens, and beneath them he saw in mind's eye the millions going about their work, their snarling, their hating and their loving, their doing bad and their doing good—yes, man does both, and so hope lives —and then a horrible vision came to him and he saw the great towers fallen and three millions lying dead amongst the red, dissolving, smoking masonry and another three millions struggling in the ruins, and he heard their terrible cries for succor to attend their severed bleeding limbs, their exploded bellies oozing from them, their smashed and bleeding horrors of what had been faces. And he felt a cry like nothing he had ever known within him. And then another, counterpointing cry: I believe in man. Against all the evidence I believe in him. Somehow man would, must triumph. Man will prevail. Somehow, somehow . . .

He walked over to the window and stood looking far down upon the city. It stood below him in appalling magnificence, the great shafts bathed in the ghostly white-red light of oncoming dawn. It seemed transcendental, as if it would live forever, built upon the very heartstone of the earth itself and immortal and indestructible through all the ages that man might be. And yet it seemed impossibly unreal, a crackerjax fairyland, as if the slightest push would send it all crumbling tumbling down. Not a soul was in sight. The city lay stripped and silent. He might have come upon the greatest ghost city of history, all mankind vanished, evaporated, destroyed, taken away to somewhere, to unknown worlds, to eternity or to the absence of eternity—which was it that was there? Jason wondered—and but these two mortals left waiting to measure themselves against the final assault. Then his eyes found the form of the great statue.

From here it did not look gold and tawdry, as it did close up, but somehow, caught in the whitened redness between the dark and the dawn, and as upon a field of valor standing off against the great, menacing regiments of darkling buildings, magnificent and deathless as the man it configured. *Go and persuade the sea wave not to break,* that defiant answer to the messenger of the gods who came offering freedom in return for surrender welled up in his mind like the summons of trumpets. *You will persuade me no more easily.* And he thought: *What can one man do?* And the answer seemed to come back to him, mounting slowly as though up corridors of ancient time until it became as a mighty shout rising from the pit of the great city and flooding the last recesses of his spirit: *Prometheus was but one man.*

What a great age it was to have been born into, to have been born into this most fateful of all man's ages, this age when it would all be decided! What legions of men great and near-great over the long aeons of man past would have given their all to have been born into this age! To see how it all came out, and perhaps not only to see . . . And suddenly, seized in exaltation, he felt some great and eternal hand laying hold upon him and summoning him as it were to the immortal battle. And he knew, knew in the great breakthrough of his life, that he had a lot to do in this world.

He looked back at the sleeping girl, and a fondness and tenderness welled up in him and moved him as he watched her, and an awe no human tongue could tell. She seemed to shiver a little, cuddling her arms against herself, so he got off the floor one of the animal skins Gaskin had recently brought there—a coyote, he thought—and spread it over her. Taken in wonder, given glimpse into a world he had never known and stranger than a dream, he stood above her for a moment counting her freckles: four on each cheek, three on her nose. Leaning down, he touched with one finger a strand of her red hair. A sudden gust of wind rustled the H-bomb picture, startling him momentarily. Then he returned to his chair and sat looking out the window, thinking, thinking, and thinking.

ABOUT THE AUTHOR

WILLIAM BRINKLEY was born in Custer City, Oklahoma, a minister's son and the youngest of five children. He was a reporter on the *Daily Oklahoman* and the Washington *Post* before going into the Navy in World War II. He spent approximately four years on active Navy duty, most of it in the Mediterranean and the Pacific. After being attached to a naval unit which set up advance bases in Sicily, Brinkley was assigned as naval correspondent for the *Stars and Stripes, Mediterranean.* In this capacity he did duty on many types of naval vessels, including destroyers, cruisers, PT boats, PC's, aircraft carriers and landing craft, and participated in the Anzio, Elba and Southern France operations. Sent to the Pacific, Mr. Brinkley took part in the Okinawa operation and the early stages of the Japanese occupation.

After the war Brinkley worked again on the Washington *Post* before going with *Life* magazine, where he remained for six years before giving up journalism in favor of full-time writing. On *Life* he worked first as a corrrespondent in the Washington bureau, then as an assistant editor and finally as a staff writer, covering subjects that varied from the guided missile down range in the Bahamas to the Air Force base at Thule, Greenland, and from Capitol Hill and a campaign train to a round-the-world assignment on American women overseas.

Mr. Brinkley's first novel, *Quicksand,* was published in 1948. His second, *Don't Go Near the Water,* was published by Random House in 1956.